Praise for the novels of Patricia Davids

"*The Inn at Harts Haven* is filled with delightful and complex characters that readers will adore. Hope, romance, and suspense combine perfectly in this heartfelt story from one of my favorite Amish fiction authors."
—Jennifer Beckstrand, *USA TODAY* bestselling author
of *First Christmas on Huckleberry Hill*

"Patricia Davids has done it again. *The Inn at Harts Haven* might just be my favorite of her books, and I've loved all of them. But a bit of suspense mixed with a romance full of conflict and torment had me reading long after I needed to get to bed! If you love Amish fiction, this one will go on your keeper shelf."
—Lenora Worth, *New York Times* bestselling author

"Patricia Davids is one of the best writers in the Amish fiction genre. She's now on my must-read list!"
—Shelley Shepard Gray, *New York Times* bestselling author

"Patricia writes with heart, integrity, and hope. Her stories both entertain and edify—the perfect combination."
—Kim Vogel Sawyer, award-winning, bestselling author

PATRICIA DAVIDS

A MATCH MADE AT
Christmas

Recycling programs for this product may not exist in your area.

ISBN-13: 978-1-335-45347-1

A Match Made at Christmas

For questions and comments about the quality of this book, please contact us at CustomerService@Harlequin.com.

HQN
22 Adelaide St. West, 41st Floor
Toronto, Ontario M5H 4E3, Canada
www.Harlequin.com

Printed in U.S.A.

This book is lovingly dedicated to the memory of my mother, Joan Stroda.

A MATCH MADE AT

Christmas

One

"**O**h, Karl. Yoo-hoo!"

Karl Graber cringed at the sound of Rose Yoder calling his name. He was in no mood to deal with her this morning.

After burning the oatmeal at breakfast, he discovered his renter had moved out in the night without giving notice or paying his back rent. Now Karl was going to be late getting to the store because his buggy horse was limping.

He pretended he hadn't heard Rose. Maybe the elderly Amish woman who claimed to be the most successful matchmaker in Harts Haven would go pester some other poor fellow.

Bent over Checker's front foot, Karl noticed that a stone lodged between the horse's steel shoe and his hoof was the gelding's problem.

"Hallo, Karl! I must speak with you."

The tenacity of the eighty-four-year-old romance peddler was another difficulty Karl had to face this morning.

"I'm not interested in meeting your latest hopeful," he muttered under his breath.

If the stubborn stone would come out, he could be on his way before the elderly woman reached the end of the block and crossed the wide street.

"*Daed*, Granny Rose is calling you." His six-year-old daughter, Rachel, stood up and waved. Rose wasn't related to Karl, but due to her advanced age most of the children in Harts Haven called her Granny.

"She's coming this way," Clara informed him from the front seat of the open buggy. His ten-year-old daughter wasn't any more excited to see Rose than Karl was. She suspected the same thing he did. Rose was on a matchmaking mission.

"Hallo, Granny Rose," Rachel shouted happily. "We're taking our puppies to the store so someone can buy them. Would you like to see them?"

The offending stone popped loose. Karl dropped Checker's hoof. "Got to get the store open, Rose. Can't take time to visit."

When he spun around, it was already too late. She had reached the buggy ahead of him. How did someone her age move so fast? She didn't even look winded.

"*Guder mariye*, Karl. I'm so glad I caught you. There is a chill in the air this morning, isn't there?"

It was the second week of November. Of course the air was cool. Rose hadn't intercepted him for idle chitchat. He moved to step around her since she was blocking the buggy door. "Customers will be waiting for me."

Rose didn't budge. Other than picking her up and setting her aside, he had no hope of leaving until she finished having her say. He resigned himself to hearing who she thought would be perfect for him this time. As if any woman could take the place of his Nora.

"Did you find us a new mother?" Rachel's hopeful tone stabbed his heart. Rachel was too young to remember much about the mother who died when she was three. She only knew other children had both mothers and fathers, and she wanted the same thing.

Clara scowled at her sister. "We don't need a new mother. Ours is in Heaven. No one can replace her."

Clara understood. She was old enough to remember what Nora had been like. A sweet, gentle, bright and loving woman. The world was a darker place without her.

Rose's cheerful expression softened with sympathy. "I'm still looking for someone special to join your family. Clara is right. She won't be your mother. Instead, she will be your stepmother, but she will love you and take care of you as if you were her own."

Rachel sighed. "I hope you find her soon."

"That's enough, Rachel," Karl said. "What do you want, Rose?"

"I'm here to tell you about the new teacher. She arrived yesterday. She and her sister are staying at the inn for the time being. They are Grace Sutter's nieces from the Amish side of her family."

Grace was another elderly widow, Old Order Mennonite, and co-owner of the Harts Haven Inn along with Rose and Rose's widowed daughter, Susanna King. The trio were all fond of meddling. A single man stood little chance of remaining unattached in this Amish community unless he avoided the widows. Rose's knowing smile put Karl on his guard.

Rachel clapped her hands. "Yay, the new teacher is here. Now I can go back to school and be in the Christmas program.

I hope I get to be an angel like Thea and Miriam Bachman last year. Their mother made the most beautiful wings for them."

Rose grinned. "Your teacher's name is Sophie Eicher. Her sister is Joanna. They are lovely young women."

"Also single and hoping to find husbands in Harts Haven. I know what you're doing, Rose. Not interested!" If his cutting tone didn't drive his point home, maybe his scowl would.

Rose puffed up like an angry little hen. "Don't take that tone with me, Karl Graber. For shame."

He was thirty-two years old, but she made him feel like an errant toddler. "I'm sorry."

She inclined her head. "You are forgiven. I stopped to tell you we are hosting a welcome party at the inn on Saturday so folks can meet Sophie and her sister. Would you kindly spread the word?"

He eyed her suspiciously. Where was the catch? "Sure. What time?"

"We'll start at noon, but folks can come and go as they please." She turned to his daughters. "I know you girls must be excited to go back to school."

"Teacher Becky had to leave to take care of her mother because she got sick," Rachel said. "I only went to school for one week. I don't think I learned much."

"I taught you letters and numbers," Karl said.

Rachel's lower lip jutted out. "Only so I could help at the store. Not to read a book."

There weren't enough hours in the day to run the hardware store, manage the farm work, cook, keep house and still find time to instruct his daughters. Most days, he struggled just to get out of bed. He was doing the best he could.

"How soon will school resume?" he asked Rose.

"The bishop and the school board haven't decided." She leveled her gaze at him. "I know you'll be at the welcome party."

That was the catch. Grimacing, he shook his head. "Social gatherings aren't something I enjoy."

Her eyes narrowed. "It is common courtesy to introduce yourself and your *kinder* to the new teacher. You remember what courtesy is, don't you, Karl?" Rose turned on her heels and strode away.

His conscience smote him. It wasn't right to be rude to anyone, yet alone an elder. He caught up with her in a few steps. "Rose, wait. I'm sorry."

Glancing over his shoulder to make sure the girls couldn't overhear; he lowered his voice. "It hasn't been easy for me. Nora was the one who loved company. It doesn't feel right to do things without her. It just makes me miss her more."

Instantly, he was sorry he had shared that much.

Rose's expression softened. "You have your daughters to consider. Nora wouldn't want them shut up in the store all day. Nor would she approve of you taking them home straight after church services instead of letting them play with their friends so you can avoid talking to people. I understand grief, Karl. I buried my husband and a son-in-law who was dear to me. We all cope with loss differently, but don't let your grief rob your *kinder* of their childhood."

He focused on his feet. Maybe Rose was right. In his struggle to get through each day, he hadn't always put his children's welfare first. "I reckon I could close early for once. I'll bring the girls to meet their new teacher."

He looked up with a hard stare. "But don't get the idea that I'll go along with any of your matchmaking schemes."

She shook her head. "Sophie needs someone special. You are completely wrong for her. I'm afraid the two of you would be at each other's throats within a week."

He drew back. "If she's hard to get along with, should she be teaching?"

Rose poked her finger into his chest. "You are the problem, not Sophie."

"Me? What's wrong with me?"

"Plenty. You figure it out. Relax. You aren't on my list of potential suitors."

That made him smile. "You have a list already? I thought she only arrived yesterday."

Rose grinned and winked. "There aren't that many single Amish fellows in this area."

Karl watched her walk away with a sense of relief that was quickly followed by an unsettling question. What did Rose think was wrong with him?

He kept to himself, but who could blame him? Losing his wife, his childhood sweetheart, had nearly broken him. Standing by helplessly as cancer sucked the life from her despite everything the doctors tried had devastated him.

His beautiful Nora had endured terrible pain. In her last days, he had stopped praying for her to be healed and only asked that God end her suffering and take her home. The guilt from those anguished thoughts never left him. He couldn't love another woman. He was better off alone. He had his daughters. That was enough.

"*Daed*, we're going to be late," Clara called out.

Clara was trying hard to be his helper at home and in the business the way her mother had been. She worked hard. Perhaps too hard for a child her age. He returned to the buggy and got in. At least he didn't have to worry about Rose trying to set him up with the new teacher. He wasn't on her list.

Her sister, Joanna, barged into Sophie Eicher's room and threw open the curtains. Bright sunlight streamed in. Sophie closed her eyes against the sudden glare. Sometimes Joanna's eagerness to embrace life was annoying. "Will you shut those?"

"In a minute. I'm ready to see this new town of ours, aren't you?"

Was she? What if coming to Harts Haven had been a mistake? She would meet all new people while keeping her secret. Could she pretend she was fine, and that everything was normal? "I think I'd rather rest for another day."

Joanna spun around with her hands on her hips. "Honestly, Sophie, if you're just going to sit in a dark room and contemplate your own death, why did we move a thousand miles to the middle of nowhere?"

"You didn't have to come, and I'm not contemplating my death."

Maybe she thought about dying more than most people, but she had good reason. She had survived breast cancer for now, but it would be back. How many weeks or months would she have? She took her *kapp* from the nightstand, put it on and pinned it in place as she prayed.

Please, Gott, *let my sister return to Ohio before then and if she won't, let me live long enough to see her settled.*

Joanna left the window to kneel in front of Sophie. "I came with you because I wasn't about to let you have an adventure without me. I'm sorry if I upset you."

"You didn't." Sophie couldn't stay annoyed with her sister for long. They weren't related by blood, but they were sisters of the heart. Joanna had been adopted as an infant when Sophie was nine. They looked nothing alike. Sophie was slender, blond, with sky blue eyes and an ordinary face. Joanna was full-figured with abundant dark curly hair that she hated, coffee-colored eyes and adorable dimples. Sophie always felt plain beside her, but she wasn't jealous of her sister's beauty. It was a gift from God.

Joanna grasped the ribbons of Sophie's *kapp* and tugged gently. "You need to start enjoying your new life."

"Please don't pull on my *kapp*." Sophie's hair had finally grown long enough to part in the middle and tuck behind her ears allowing her to look like a normal Amish woman. Losing her hip-length hair during her chemotherapy had been devastating. She checked to make sure her bobby pins were secure.

"You look fine. Let's get out there and discover the best place to have coffee and shoofly pie. And a post office. I want to mail a letter to *Daed*. I need stamps."

Their father had recently married a widow with three young children. It was another reason Sophie had taken the job in Harts Haven. She didn't want to be a burden to the new family when her illness returned. Joanna had refused to stay behind. Perhaps because she knew in her heart that Sophie would need her at the end, even if she would never admit that. Joanna believed Sophie was cured.

"We should go house hunting soon," Joanna announced. "It's wonderful that *Aenti* Grace is letting us stay at her inn, but don't you want your own home?"

Sophie rolled her eyes. "You can't know how eagerly I look forward to picking up after you, cooking for you and doing all the chores, including your laundry again."

Joanna's infectious grin widened. "*Goot*. That's the spirit. We are going to love living here. Just to show you I have matured, I will do my own laundry in our new home. Can we go now? I want to see what Harts Haven has to offer."

Her sister's unflagging optimism had supported Sophie through the devastation of her diagnosis and the worst of her treatments. She couldn't love her more. "Unless I miss my guess, you are more interested in checking out the local bachelors rather than real estate."

Joanna giggled. It was a sweet sound that always made Sophie smile. "We girls never know when the right fellow will come along. It could happen today."

"For you maybe." Sophie looked away. Marriage was out of the question for her. How could she burden any man with what she knew waited for her?

Joanna gripped Sophie's hand. "You can't give up on love because Nate turned out to be a coward."

Sophie flinched at the painful reminder. "Nate was simply being practical when he broke our engagement. He didn't want to be tied to a dying wife." She had hoped for his support, but she couldn't blame him for his decision.

Everyone in their small Ohio community knew Sophie Eicher was a walking dead woman. Breast cancer had killed her mother and her grandmother. The pitying looks, the way people chose their words so carefully around her, had been stifling. It had been like living in a coffin waiting for the funeral to begin, but it had been even harder on Joanna, who didn't share the community's outlook. She railed against it until the bishop reprimanded her for not accepting God's will.

Joanna grabbed Sophie's shoulders and shook her. "You didn't die. Your last scan was negative. You beat your cancer."

Her little sister was still railing against the inevitable.

"You can't say that with any confidence," Sophie said gently.

"Bah! Only *Gott* knows our fate. Until then, live life to the fullest. Have faith in *Gott*'s goodness and mercy. I believe my stodgy older sister will scold me and love me for a hundred years."

"That is unlikely."

Joanna sighed and sat beside Sophie. "You don't want anyone here to know about your illness. I understand that. We came to Harts Haven so you could start over. Here people will see a kind, generous, intelligent woman, not someone who is sick, but only if you go out and meet them. Now, get rid of that anxious frown and let's go."

Sophie might not have years to live, but dwelling on the

fact wouldn't change the outcome. Joanna pulled her to her feet. Once she was upright, Sophie pushed aside her reservations about their move. She had made her decision and would stick to it. This was the right thing for her, but more importantly for Joanna. If Joanna refused to return home, then before Sophie left this earth, she would do everything in her power to see her sister happily married and settled. She would need someone to lean on when the time came.

"All right. We'll explore the town, but I want to see the school as soon as possible. There's no telling what shape the last teacher left things in. I sincerely hope she was a good record keeper. I need to know exactly what I have to work with before I meet with the school board."

Work was exactly what Sophie needed. Setting things to right, solving problems, creating order, opening children's minds to the value of learning, those were the things she loved.

"You need to dress warm. It's chilly out. Take your heavy bonnet, a scarf, your winter coat and gloves."

Sophie arched one eyebrow. "Is there a blizzard blowing?"

"I know you still get cold easily."

It was true. The cold affected her more than it used to. She had lost weight during her cancer treatments. And strength.

Sophie pulled Joanna close and hugged her. "You are the best sister ever."

Joanna hugged her back. "I'll remind you of that the next time I do something that drives you up the wall."

"Which will be shortly, I'm sure."

Joanna laughed as she drew away. "O ye of little faith. Let's go."

The two women went downstairs, where they found their aunt in the large kitchen rolling out dough. Grace Sutter was Sophie's father's sister. She had been raised in an Amish home but chose not to be baptized into the Amish faith. Instead, she married a Mennonite farmer. Now a widow, she had come to Kansas and settled in the Amish and Old Order Mennonite community of Harts Haven a few years earlier. The family kept in touch by writing numerous letters. It was Grace who first suggested Sophie apply for the teaching position in Harts Haven. It had been Joanna who had nagged Sophie into doing so. It was still hard to believe she'd gotten the job.

Teachers were either in short supply or Grace's recommendation carried a lot of weight with the local Amish bishop. Grace knew about Sophie's past illness, but like Joanna, her aunt believed Sophie was cured and had agreed not to mention it to anyone.

Grace looked up from her work. "Are you off to do some exploring?"

"We are," Sophie said. "Joanna wants to find the best place for coffee and shoofly pie."

"You don't have to go far. Just through those doors to our dining room. You won't find better baked goods anywhere within a hundred miles."

"There," Sophie said. "Now we don't have to go out in the cold."

"We still need to find the post office and the school."

The outside door opened. Rose Yoder came in. Sophie had taken an instant liking to the spry elderly woman with twinkling eyes behind her wire-rimmed glasses when they met the previous evening.

Rose smiled widely at the sight of her guests. "Good morning to you both. I hope you slept well."

"We did, but now we are off to see Harts Haven," Joanna announced.

"Would it be too much trouble to ask you to stop by the hardware store and get a roll of lamp wick for me?" Rose asked.

Grace laid her rolling pin aside. "I thought you got some a few days ago."

Rose waved a hand. "We need more. I was going to get it this morning, but I was sidetracked when I saw—someone."

Grace propped her hands on her hips. "And did you announce your intentions in your usual absurd fashion?"

Rose chuckled. "Of course not. Quite the opposite. On rare occasions, being subtle is better."

Sophie exchanged a puzzled look with Joanna. What were they talking about?

"I'm sorry I neglected to get the wicks," Rose said. "You know how forgetful I can be."

"Uh-huh." Grace picked up her rolling pin again. "I imagine it will get worse before it gets better."

Rose chuckled. "I shouldn't wonder if it will."

Sophie didn't understand the pointed looks that passed between the two older women. "We'll be happy to pick up lamp wicks for you, Rose," she offered. "How wide?"

"One inch. Grace, can you think of anything else we need at the hardware store?"

Grace grinned, but quickly sobered and began vigorously flattening her dough. "Not right now, but I'm sure something will occur to me later."

"I'm sure it will, too," Rose said, with a distinct twinkle in her eyes.

Sophie met her sister's gaze. Joanna appeared puzzled by the odd conversation, too. "We don't mind running errands for Rose and you, Aenti Grace. It's the least we can do."

"Absolutely," Sophie echoed her sister's sentiment.

Rose smiled and patted Sophie's cheek. "That's sweet of you to say. Oh, Grace, we're having a party on Saturday."

Grace tipped her head to the side. "When did we decide this?"

"When I saw you-know-who."

"Who?"

"Honestly, Grace, you astound me." Rose shook her head and left the kitchen.

Sophie nodded toward the door. "We should get going."

Grace went back to rolling her dough. "The road out front will take you straight to Main Street. The post office is on the corner. You can't miss it. The hardware store is two doors down. A party on Saturday. As if I didn't have enough to do. Oh, now I know who Rose meant. How silly of me."

Sophie and Joanna slipped outside. On the covered porch, Joanna grabbed Sophie's arm. "What was that all about?"

"I have no idea."

"I'm not sure we were part of the same conversation as those two. Pray we don't sound like that when we get to be their age." Joanna took off toward the street.

"I don't expect to see that age," Sophie muttered and followed her sister.

The town of Harts Haven was smaller than the village where Sophie was from. Everyone they met smiled and called out a cheerful greeting. The houses were modest and well-kept, but they were connected to electric lines, so the inhabitants weren't Amish. That wasn't unusual. The Amish preferred country living to town life. Sophie's father ran a dry goods grocery but lived on ten acres outside of town to allow grazing for the buggy horses and a large garden.

Joanna had been right to insist Sophie wear her gloves and heavy coat. The sun was shining in the bright blue sky, but the wind stole any warmth from the air. She was used to cold winters, but not to the blustery gusts that seemed determined to pull her bonnet from her head and burrow under her coat.

The walk to the business district didn't take long. The town was only four blocks wide.

Joanna pointed to a small building with a flag fluttering out front. A horse and buggy stood at the hitching rail. "I see the post office."

"And I see the hardware store," Sophie said when she spotted the sign.

"You go on. I won't be a minute." Joanna rushed up the wooden steps and went inside.

Sophie looked up the street and saw a young Amish girl come out of Graber's Hardware carrying a small stool, followed by an Amish fellow with a large cardboard box. He put it down, wrote something on the front and went back inside.

The child sat beside the box and looked in. A moment later, the front paws and head of a puppy appeared. The child lifted the black-and-white dog out and held it, earning a face licking in return. A second and a third pup appeared and began trying to climb out. One red-and-white puppy succeeded and tumbled to the sidewalk.

"Clara, come help me!" the girl called out as she tried to grab the second puppy while a third, this one black and brown with white markings, tumbled out of the box and headed for the curb.

A pickup roared past, alerting Sophie to the potential danger. If the puppy made it into the street, the results could be horrible. She dashed toward the child.

Two

Sophie grabbed the red-and-white pup at the edge of the curb as another car flew past. She held on to the squirming puppy and picked up the black-and-brown one heading for the street, too.

"Oh, *danki*," the child said in relief, putting her black-and-white puppy back in the box marked Aussies for Sale. "I reckon I need something taller."

Sophie nodded in agreement. "You certainly do. Can you find something that will work better?"

"Yup. We have more boxes around the back, but I can't leave my puppies."

As her racing heart slowed, Sophie smiled at the child. "A problem easily solved. Why don't I watch them for you?"

"*Danki*. I'll just be a minute." The child darted into the alley beside the store.

Sophie placed all the puppies back in the box, then perched

awkwardly on the small stool and spoke softly to soothe them. It didn't work. Having discovered they could escape once, they all set about climbing over each other to get out. As soon as she pushed one back in, the next one hopped over the edge. She didn't have enough hands. In desperation, she unbuttoned the top buttons of her coat and tucked two of the puppies inside while she cradled the other one.

The coat worked so well that she was trying to get the third one in when Red wiggled his head free and began licking Sophie's chin, making her laugh. Black-and-White got her head out and added her tongue to the assault, going for Sophie's ear. "Stop that. I already washed my face this morning."

"What are you doing?" A man's deep, annoyed voice came from behind her.

Sophie looked over her shoulder to see the same fellow who had brought the box out earlier. He had dark hair and amazing stone-gray eyes rimmed by thick black eyelashes. A fierce, daunting scowl marred his face. Full lips above his neat beard were pressed into a tight line that matched his furrowed brow.

"I'm getting licked by puppies. What does it look like?"

"I see a woman trying to stuff my dogs into her coat. Where's my daughter?"

The black-and-brown pup in her arms joined the kissing session. Sophie tilted her face back to get out of their reach, lost her precarious seat on the stool and fell backward.

The man caught her before she hit the sidewalk. After righting her, he took one pup from her arms.

Flustered by his nearness and grim expression, Sophie forced a smile. "Your daughter has gone to get a taller container. If I wanted to steal your puppies, I would have picked up the box and walked away with them."

His scowl deepened. "It looked odd, that's all I'm saying."

It was hard to maintain a commanding pose while seated with her coat full of wiggling fur balls, but the old Sophie would not have allowed herself to be intimidated on her first day in a town. She drew on her years of teaching experience and the advice of the teacher who had trained her.

Never let them see they've rattled you.

Meeting the man's gaze, Sophie looked him up and down, then arched one eyebrow. "Looks can deceive, and baseless assumptions are usually wrong. You owe me an apology."

The rude dog owner looked taken aback. A flush climbed up his neck and stained his cheeks a dull red. He inhaled sharply and then cleared his throat. "I reckon that's so."

It wasn't much of an apology.

When he wasn't glaring at her, he was a good-looking man. There was something compelling about his gray eyes. Their gazes locked. A strange connection passed between them, surprising her and him by the way his eyes widened. She blinked hard and looked away. His beard proclaimed he was a married man. And rude.

"Puppies!" Joanna's delighted squeal alerted Sophie to her sister's presence. "Oh, how adorable."

She took the red-and-white one from Sophie and cuddled him. "Isn't he sweet? Sister, we need a dog. Can we keep one? Please say yes," Joanna beseeched her.

Sophie shook her head. "*Nee*. We can't repay *Aenti* Grace's generosity by returning with a puppy."

"How can you bear to be so sensible? I love this one." Joanna kissed her pup's nose.

The little girl returned with a box almost as tall as she was. "That one is Mick," she said, putting her burden down beside Joanna and stroked Mick's head. "He is my favorite."

Joanna smiled at the child. "Mine, too. I'm Joanna Eicher."

"I'm Rachel Graber. This is our store."

"We were just on our way in. This is my sister, Sophie."

"That's my *daed*," Rachel said, pointing.

His expression softened as he gazed at his child. He was definitely good-looking when he wasn't scowling. He turned his stunning eyes back to Sophie. "I'm Karl Graber. You must be the new teacher."

"I am." She nodded slightly. His gaze remained on her face until she grew uncomfortable with his scrutiny. What was he staring at?

"Can I be an angel in the Christmas program, teacher? Please?" Rachel asked in a pleading voice.

Sophie smile at the adorable child. "I haven't decided on a program yet."

"But Christmas is almost here, and everyone will want to see an angel," Rachel insisted.

"That's enough," her father said. "Don't pester the woman."

Sophie placed her black-and-white pup in the box. The pup immediately started crying.

"Biscuit is crying because she misses her *mamm*. We had to leave her shut up at home so she wouldn't follow us. My *mamm* is in heaven," Rachel said with a catch in her voice. "She died from being sick."

Tenderhearted Joanna hugged the child. "I'm sorry. Our mother passed away, too. Sometimes I feel sad when I think about her, but I know she is smiling when she sees I'm happy. That's why I always try to be cheerful."

"Granny Rose is looking for a stepmother for us," Rachel added. "I pray she finds one soon. Are you married? *Daed* says you must be here to find husbands."

Joanna blushed and giggled. "If *Gott* has someone in mind for me, I will consider it."

This was something Sophie could nip in the bud. She gazed

at the child. "I'm not looking for a husband. Married women can't be teachers, and I love teaching. It makes me happy."

Rachel looked up at her father. "It would make *Mamm* smile if you could be happy again, *Daed*. Don't you think so?"

When he didn't answer, Sophie glanced at his face and saw his eyes fill with pain. The muscles in his jaw clenched.

Overcome with sympathy for him, Sophie stepped between him and his child to take the puppy from his arms. She gazed into his sorrow-filled eyes as he struggled to gain control of his emotions. "I'm sorry," she whispered. "It is difficult to lose someone dear."

His gray eyes turned stormy and locked with Sophie's. His fierce scowl returned. She wanted to help, but his expression said he didn't appreciate her interference.

Karl pushed his pain deep inside the way he always did. He didn't need Sophie Eicher's sympathy. That this stranger thought she understood what he was going through infuriated him. His grief was his own. He didn't want to share it.

"That pup's name is Buck," Rachel said.

"Like the dog in *The Call of the Wild*?" Sophie asked a bit too cheerfully as she turned away from him. "That was one of my favorite books as a child."

She lifted the pup to look him in the face. "You'll have to grow into a mighty fine *hund* to live up to that name. Rachel, do you know the story?"

Rachel shook her head.

Sophie smiled. "It's a wonderful tale about a brave sled dog in the Yukon. When school starts, I will make a point of reading the book to everyone."

"Oh, I can't wait." Rachel grinned and clapped her hands.

Hearing the excitement in his daughter's voice eased the tightness in Karl's throat. It had been one of his favorite books, too. He was a little surprised that the new teacher made the connection. The story was the reason he had named the pup Buck.

But right now, he had a business to run. He needed to know how soon he would lose Clara's help in the store. "When will school start?"

Sophie cuddled the pup. "A week if everything goes well. I want to get the students back in class before Thanksgiving."

"What has to go well?" A week wasn't much time for him to find a clerk to take Clara's place. How he would pay someone without the rent from the *daadi haus* was another problem he had to solve.

"I'll have to do an inventory at the school. Make sure I have adequate school supplies and books for the students. Then I need to review all the students' records and make sure they are current because I understand the last teacher left abruptly. Lastly, I want to meet with the parents and families to get an idea of what they expect and let them know my expectations. In other words, a lot, but first on my list is finding the school."

"That's easy," Rachel said. "It's across the road from our house."

"That's *goot* to know," Joanna said. "But where do you live?"

Buck started barking furiously and struggled to get free. Karl saw what had the pup's attention as Sophie tightened her grip. Three half-grown lambs were trotting toward them up the sidewalk.

"Not again." Karl clenched his hands into fists. "Rachel!"

"I locked the gate, *Daed*, I did." Her lower lip quivered as the young sheep surrounded her, butting her for attention and bleating. "I don't know how they got out."

"If I've told you once, I've told you a hundred times to make sure it's latched tight." He didn't have time for this. Now he'd have to close the store and lose a morning's worth of business to take Rachel's pets back to the farm.

Sophie laughed as one lamb nibbled at her apron hem. "Mary had one little lamb, but Rachel has three as white as snow."

"And everywhere that Rachel is, the lambs all try to go," Karl finished dryly. "One problem with letting your child raise bottle babies."

Rachel hung her head. "I can take them home, but who will watch my puppies?"

"I will," Joanna offered quickly.

"Is that okay, *Daed*?" Rachel asked.

"That's fine. I'll close the store and take you to the farm as soon as I finish with these customers."

Rachel could easily walk that far. She did it all the time, but it was too far to send her by herself with the sheep. There wasn't much traffic on their rural road, but having the lambs along might distract her when she should be paying attention.

Sophie handed her puppy to Joanna. "I can walk Rachel home, make sure the miscreants are safely locked up again and visit the school since it's nearby."

Rachel tilted her head. "They aren't miscreants. I don't know that breed. These are Rambouillet sheep," she informed her teacher solemnly.

Sophie hid a smile behind her hand, but quickly recovered her composure. "My mistake. I'm not familiar with sheep."

Rachel smiled at her. "That's okay. They're about the most popular breed in the world because they have really soft wool."

"I see." Sophie's grin returned. "May I walk your daughter and her Rambouillet flock home for you, Mr. Graber?"

Two *Englisch* customers entered the store, tourists by the look of them. He didn't like the idea of being beholden to Sophie, but she was going to be his child's teacher, and it was turning out to be a busy morning. "Fine. If you have the time to spare."

"I do. Joanna, will you get the item Rose needs?"

"In a minute." Joanna held the puppy close and rubbed her face in the dog's fluffy fur.

Sophie rolled her eyes. That was always Joanna's answer when she didn't want to do something. "Never mind."

She turned to Karl. "Rose Yoder asked us to get a roll of one-inch lamp wick for her. Do you know what kind she prefers?"

"Sure." He walked into the store, then stopped and turned to stare at her. "Rose sent you?"

"That's right."

"Rose bought a roll of wick two days ago. Why does she need more?"

Sophie shrugged. "I don't know. She asked if we would pick some up since Joanna and I were going to the post office. I distinctly remember her saying that she had intended to pick some up herself this morning but forgot about it when she ran into someone she knew."

"Hmm." Why send the teacher to his store today on such a questionable errand? Was Rose up to something? She could be crafty. Some folks thought she was addled. He knew better.

Sophie tilted her head to the side. "Is something wrong?"

Rose said he wasn't on her list of prospective husbands for this woman, so he didn't need to worry that she was matchmaking, but something felt off. Perhaps Rose had simply mislaid her wick roll. She was getting older.

He eyed the new teacher closely. Rose said Sophie needed someone special, but why? He saw nothing out of the ordinary about her. She was a pleasant-looking slender woman. A shade on the skinny side but she had an attractive smile when she wasn't chiding him.

She brushed her cheek with one hand. "Do I have something on my face?"

"*Nee.* Why?"

"You keep staring at me."

"Sorry." He turned away, determined not to look at her again. He quickly found the brand of lamp wicks that Rose preferred and handed them to Clara at the counter. "This is your new teacher, Sophie Eicher."

Clara barely glanced at Sophie. "Rachel's silly sheep are outside."

He nodded. "Don't worry about it. Teacher is going to take Rachel and the lambs back to the farm."

Despite Clara's dour expression, Sophie smiled at his child. "I'm delighted to meet another of my scholars. Are you excited about returning to school?"

"I'm not going back. *Daed* needs me here."

That surprised him. He did need her, but they hadn't discussed keeping her out of school.

Sophie glanced from Clara to him. "Finishing your education is important. I'm sure your father will agree."

"He'll homeschool me. That will be four dollars." Clara held out her hand.

"We'll talk about it later." He didn't want to have the conversation in front of her teacher. His *Englisch* customers left without buying anything.

Sophie pulled a five out of her purse and handed it to Clara. "I hope you'll decide to come to school. Learning with your friends is always more enjoyable."

Clara ignored Sophie. "We're getting low on sheet metal screws. Shall I add it to the order form for next week?"

"I'll take care of it." He had meant to order those last week.

Sophie took her purchase. "It was nice meeting you, Clara. And you also, Mr. Graber. I'm sure I'll see you around."

He walked her to the shop door. "The girls and I will be at your party on Saturday, but not until late."

She gave him a puzzled look. "What party?"

"Rose is giving a welcome frolic for you and your sister. She asked me to spread the word."

Sophie chuckled. "I heard her tell Grace that they were having a party Saturday, but she failed to mention it was for us. Grace was none too pleased at the short notice."

"Rose travels a zigzag path of her own. The rest of us don't even try to keep up. I should warn you that Rose thinks of herself as a matchmaker. Don't be surprised if she introduces you to single fellows left and right."

Sophie's smiled faded. She looked away, but not before he caught a glimpse of pain in her sky blue eyes. "Rose won't have any success with me. I'm not looking for a husband."

He heard a deep sadness under her words. Why? "Well, I have warned you."

When she looked at him, her expression was serene once again. "*Danki.* I intend to devote my life to teaching. If Rose wants to find a husband for Joanna, that would be *wunderbar.*"

He rocked back on his heels. Okay, now it was making sense. Rose had him in mind for the younger one, not the teacher. He knew something was up with Rose needing another roll of lamp wicks. Well, she was going to be disappointed in her matchmaking. "Thanks for seeing Rachel and her sheep home. Make sure the gate gets latched this time."

"I will. Please give careful consideration to Clara's schooling. I know you'll do what's best for her."

She walked out the door. He watched as she followed Rachel and her mini-flock around the street corner and disappeared.

She was a nice woman. Helpful. Maybe a bit outspoken, but that was to be expected from someone who had to keep students in line. He glanced at Joanna, holding a puppy in her arms while she talked to a young boy who seemed interested in the dog. Rose was slipping if she thought he'd fall for that one. She was prettier than Sophie, but she was far too young for him. He found her mature sister more appealing.

That Sophie wasn't husband hunting was the most attractive thing about her. Only why wasn't she? She had claimed she wanted to devote her life to teaching. If that were the case, what had caused the sadness he'd glimpsed? Had she recently lost someone she loved?

He surveyed the store. Clara had started restocking the shelves. There weren't any customers. He wasn't needed now. He really should make sure Rachel got her sheep home safely.

"Clara, I've changed my mind. I'm going to go with Rachel. Your teacher has things to do to get ready for school. She doesn't need to be looking after your sister."

"I can manage here."

She could, but he hated leaving her alone.

"Mr. Wilson is next door if I need anything," she added, giving him a look that said she didn't require anyone's assistance.

"Okay." He walked outside and told Joanna where he was going. She quickly offered to keep an eye on Clara and the dogs. Relieved, he headed down the block at a quick pace.

Sophie followed Rachel as she skipped along with her sheep following. The child was adorable, bright and talkative. "This lamb is April. That's May, and that one is June."

Sophie couldn't tell them apart. "Does your father raise sheep?"

"*Nee.* These belonged to our neighbor, but their mama rejected them. He didn't want to have to bottle feed them. He asked if I would take care of them. He said I could keep any that lived, and they all did."

"You must have taken very good care of them."

"Clara helped. *Daed* says we will sell them in the spring. Clara and I get to keep some of the money. He says that is only fair 'cause we did a lot of the work."

Karl Graber sounded like a generous father. One lamb stopped to nibble at a patch of alfalfa. Rachel kept walking. Sophie looked at the lagging lamb and waved her hands at it. "Go on. Shoo. The others are leaving you."

Rachel was a dozen yards ahead. Sophie called to her. "Rachel, this one isn't following you."

The child stopped. "That's April. She'll come. Give her a push."

Rachel resumed waking as Sophie stared at the straggler. She had no experience with sheep. What part did she push on?

She shoved against the animal's side. It stepped over but kept eating. "Rachel, I think you should come back. She doesn't want to go."

Sophie was startled when Karl jogged up to her. "I decided you might need a hand in case the sheep had other ideas about going home."

She grinned with relief. "This one certainly does. I can't get it to move."

He grabbed a handful of wool near the shoulders, lifted her slightly, and then shoved her in the right direction with a knee to her rump. April decided she wanted her friends more than her next nibble and ran to catch them.

Sophie chuckled. "I guess I need to be more persistent. *Danki.*"

"You're welcome."

She fell into step beside him as they followed Rachel. He shortened his stride to match hers.

"The school is across from my lane. You can see it from here. It's the white building set back from the road."

"Did you go to school there?" she asked.

"I did. My grandfather donated the land for it. I remember the summer the community raised the building. I must have been five. I wasn't eager to go to school."

"Like Clara?"

He nodded. "She wants to continue helping me at the store, but I haven't made up my mind."

One of the lambs stopped to eat at the side of the road. Sophie nudged it firmly in the rump with her knee. It trotted ahead.

"You catch on quick." There was a hint of laughter in his voice.

"I've dealt with a few reluctant scholars in my time. I can be persistent." She wanted to see him smile, but he didn't oblige. Was he normally a somber man?

"Have you been a teacher long?" His tone was serious again.

"I taught for four years back home." Happy years that had ended abruptly with her diagnosis instead of with her marriage.

"You enjoyed it?"

She smiled. "I did. Very much so." It had been a wonderful and fulfilling career.

"Then why move here?"

Grim memories replaced Sophie's happy ones. "Things change."

Unwilling to share more, she quickened her pace to catch up with Rachel.

The school turned out to be just over a mile outside of town. It was a single-story building with white clapboard siding and four large windows along each side. Sophie nodded in satisfaction at the sight. They would provide plenty of light inside for her and her students. A school bell hung from the porch ceiling just outside the front door. Her fingers itched to ring it for the start of class. She had missed teaching during her treatments. When she was surrounded by eager young children again perhaps she could forget her own troubles.

A red storage shed with white trim stood behind the school. The wide lawn appeared neatly kept. A playground consisting of several swing sets of various heights, a teeter-totter, a tetherball pole and a ball diamond with a wire backstop completed the school grounds. The community obviously took excellent care of the property. It was an encouraging sign.

Sophie looked at Karl. "Is the school building locked?"

"It is, but I know where the spare key is kept. Rachel, wait here."

"Can I swing?"

"You may but keep an eye on your lambs."

As they walked toward the shed, Sophie looked back toward the town. "I'm surprised April, May and June went all that way to find her."

"When they were too little to be left home alone all day, I took Rachel and the lambs to the store with me. So, they know the way."

"How funny."

"Not to my way of thinking. Three sheep wandering along the road are just asking for trouble. Rachel needs to be more responsible when she feeds them." He opened the shed door. Inside were two stalls for horses and a room for coal storage. He took a key off a hook just inside. "Look around all you want."

He took her hand and placed the key in her palm. "Keep this one until you get your own set from the school board."

When his fingers touched hers, a startling sensation raced

across Sophie's nerve endings like a wave of warm water sweeping over her skin. Glancing at his face, she saw his eyes widen with shock. Did he feel it, too?

Sophie took a quick step back as Karl did the same. She couldn't stop staring at him. He looked away first and cleared his throat. "I need to get these sheep home and get back to the store."

"I need to—" What did she need to do? Her mind was a blank as her heart hammered in her chest. She'd never experienced such a startling reaction to any man's touch. Not even with Nate, and she had been ready to marry him. It made no sense. She barely knew Karl Graber.

He spun on his heels and walked away. "Rachel, let's go."

Sophie watched them cross the road and walk down the quarter-mile-long lane. Just before Karl disappeared behind the cedar trees surrounding his farmstead, he looked back, and her heart started racing again. Rachel waved. Sophie raised her hand and waved, too. Karl didn't. He turned around and kept walking.

When they were out of sight, Sophie crossed the brown grass to the steps of the school and sat down abruptly. What had just happened?

In the past, her chemotherapy had left her with what the nurses called "brain fog," but this was different. Maybe it was a delayed reaction to all the medications she had taken, but she had finished those drugs six months ago.

Had her cancer moved to her brain? That might explain her unexpected reaction. Or maybe it was because Karl was a handsome and compelling man.

This would never do. She was here to be a teacher, not to get involved with Rachel's father.

She drew a deep breath and blew it out slowly. There would not be a repeat of this. She would make sure of it. Avoiding

Karl in such a small community would not be possible, but she wouldn't be alone with him again.

Sophie looked at the key in her hand where a sense of warmth still lingered. What she needed to do was stop thinking about Karl Graber and get to work on the job she had been hired to do.

Three

Karl was grateful for the rush of work that kept him occupied at the hardware store until past noon on Saturday. When he was busy, he didn't think about Sophie Eicher. Much. It bothered him that he couldn't put her out of his mind altogether. She was disturbing.

Rose had said they weren't compatible. She was right. He'd do his best to avoid future dealings with her. That included skipping the party today. It was being held so people could meet the new teacher. Well, he had met her. They had talked about his daughters' education. She held the opinion that Clara needed to return to school. He wasn't so sure.

He *was* sure he needed to keep ample distance between himself and Sophie Eicher. Touching her hand had brought to life feelings that should have stayed dead. He didn't like it. He was used to his grief. It fit like a well-worn coat.

He missed his wife, her touch and her laugh. He missed everything about Nora.

"Have you met the new teacher?"

Karl looked around to see Dr. Bertha Rock smiling at him. The energetic, white-haired *Englisch* doctor claimed to be semiretired, but she still maintained a busy practice in the town where she had been raised. She was a close friend of the widows at the inn.

He began putting out cans of spray paint. "*Ja*, I've met her."

"What do you think of her?"

He kept his eyes on his task. "Pleasant enough."

"I'm on my way to the welcoming party. I wanted to pick up a small, practical gift for her and her sister. A good pair of pliers can be useful in so many situations. Which color do you think she'd like? Blue-jay cerulean or cardinal red?" She held up two pairs. Bertha was an avid birder. She and her group spent hours out at the nearby wetlands with binoculars in hand.

"I don't think it matters," he said.

"Cardinal it is. Grace mentioned you were closing the shop so you and the girls could come by the party. I'm so glad."

"I did tell Rose that, but since we've already met the woman, I don't see a reason to lose a half day of business."

"But we have to go," Rachel said from near his feet where she was dusting the lower shelf.

"That's right." Bertha grinned at the child. "You can't miss a welcoming party. Grace has made her famous chocolate cake, and the major is bringing homemade ice cream."

The major was Herbert Young, a retired army lawyer and another devoted birder.

"Please say we'll go, *Daed*," Rachel begged. "I want to tell Joanna about the people who bought the puppies."

They had sold two, but Buck was currently sleeping behind the counter with his head on Clara's shoe. Karl had been determined to avoid getting attached to any of the pups and had encouraged his girls to do the same, but Buck made that tough. He was a lovable goofball.

Bertha returned the blue pliers to the rack and added the red ones to her basket. "Do say you'll bring the girls out to the inn. Everyone will be there. I'm sure they'll have loads of fun with the other children."

"Please?" Rachel's dark eyes, so much like Nora's, pleaded with him.

He remembered Rose telling him that Nora wouldn't want the girls shut up in the store all day. She was right. Nora would have already been at the party with the girls and loving every minute.

It shouldn't be hard to avoid Sophie in the crowd that was sure to be there. He hesitated, but then nodded. "Okay, we'll go for a little while."

"Yay!" She ran toward the front of the store. "Clara, we're going to the party."

Now that he couldn't call the words back, he carried the half-empty case of paint to the front.

Clara scowled at him. "Is that a good idea? We could lose customers."

When had she become so gloomy? "I thought you'd be happy to get out of here for a few hours."

She looked down. "What are you going to do with worthless Buck?"

The pup was still sleeping with his chin on her shoe. She hadn't moved from her spot in over an hour. She might pretend she didn't like the dog, but he knew better. Clara didn't want to get attached to things, either. He understood, but it was sad to see in a child her age.

Rachel grabbed the puppy and lifted him in her arms. "He's going to come to the party with us."

"He's not," Clara stated firmly.

"Daed?" Rachel turned her heartrending gaze on him.

"I don't see the harm in it. Fix him a leash from a length of rope at the back of the store."

She grinned and hugged the dog. "Come on, Buck. We're going to a party."

Bertha stood at his elbow and leaned closer. "Wrapped around her little finger, aren't you?"

"That is so true." Clara rolled her eyes. "We can't afford to close. I'll stay here."

Glancing at Bertha, he saw her give a tiny shake of her head. Why was he letting the widows of Harts Haven manage his life?

Because it was easier than making his own decisions. "We're going as a family, Clara. I'll write up a sign so people know where to find me if they need something that can't wait."

"Fine, but we aren't staying long." She rang up Bertha's purchase and then locked the cash drawer.

The French doors of the dining room at the inn were open to the patio so people could visit inside or out as the day was unseasonably warm. Sophie noticed the men stayed mostly outside, standing in small groups, sitting on the benches or enjoying a game at the horseshoe pit. A band of youngsters had set up a volleyball net and were engaged in a heated game. Smaller children were racing about playing a game of tag under the watchful eyes of two teenage girls. The women gathered inside near the food tables where Joanna was serving plates of cake. Sophie circulated among the attendees.

She met the Weaver family and their four rambunctious children first. Energetic Ben was a second grader who had trouble standing still. Janet was a year older. Zack was in the sixth grade, and Edna would graduate from the eighth grade in the spring. Mrs. Weaver sent the children to fill their plates and turned to Sophie. "Do you have a Christmas program planned? The children always look forward to it, and this will be Edna's last year."

Sophie was jolted by the woman's words. She'd given little thought to a Christmas program, but what if this was the only year she'd be able to direct one here? What memories did she want to leave with the parents and students of Harts Haven?

She pasted a smile on her face. "I have so many things to do that I haven't given Christmas much consideration."

Mrs. Weaver's brows drew together. "Oh? My parents and sisters come from Cedar Grove in northeast Kansas every year to watch the children preform. I don't want to sound immodest, but our school is known for having fine programs."

"I'm sure I can come up with something adequate, but the children's education must come first."

Mrs. Weaver's scowl deepened. "Of course." She walked away with a frown on her face.

Sophie saw her a little later in conversation with several women. They all cast covert glances her way. None of them looked happy.

One of the women left the group and introduced herself to Sophie as Mrs. Bachman. Her girls were Miriam and Thea. Sophie suspected the pair might be a discipline problem by their brusque answers to her questions and shared sidelong glances behind their mother's back. Mrs. Bachman beamed at them. "Miriam and Thea were angels in last year's Christmas play. I still have their costumes if you'd like them to be angels again this year. They were so natural in the parts."

"I'll keep that in mind."

"You may not know it, but many outsiders come to enjoy the true spirit of Christmas our children display."

Sophie tried to change the subject. "What strengths and weakness do you feel your daughters have in school?"

"You must have arranged some wonderful programs in the past."

Sophie kept her smile in place but didn't reply. What was this fixation on a Christmas program the mothers seemed to share? The children in her former school had performed by singing hymns and reciting poems, not a play with costumes and wings.

The Kemp family arrived next with their six children. Only four were old enough to be in school. Laura and Lamar were adorable blond-haired, blue-eyed, first-grade twins. Phoebe was in the fourth grade and Bartholomew, the oldest, was in the sixth grade.

Their mother sent them outside to play after meeting Sophie. "Laura and Lamar are so excited to be in the Christmas program this year. They worried there wouldn't be one without a teacher, but now that you're here, I've assured them they will get to take part. They couldn't be happier. Last year the play was amazing and so was the singing."

"I'm sorry I wasn't here to see it," Sophie said brightly. Was her face permanently frozen into a smile yet?

By two o'clock Sophie had met the Kauffman, Lehman, Imhoff and Stoltzfus families and their school-age children, along with most of the grandparents, aunts, uncles and cousins of her students. She didn't see Karl and his daughters.

None of the parents wanted to know about her lesson plans or if she expected the students to do homework. They all asked about her plans for Christmas Eve. It was clear the program had to become a priority. What type of presentation could she put together in such a short time? It would have to be simple this year. She and the children wouldn't have much time to prepare anything as elaborate as the community seemed to expect.

"The amount of food at an Amish gathering is always astounding," a man said beside her. Sophie turned to see a short *Englisch* fellow with a wild mop of curly red hair and a heaping plate in his hand.

"Gatherings in every rural community call for mountains of food, Amish or *Englisch*. I'm the new teacher."

He smiled brightly. "Sophie Eicher. I met your sister when she filled out a change-of-address card the other day. I'm Lance Switzer. My wife, Crystal, and I run the post office. She'll be here soon. The post office closes at one on Saturdays, just so you know," he added in an official tone.

"I'll remember that."

"What do you think of our little town? It was founded by Sheriff Harts's family after the Civil War. The Amish first arrived in 1907. It was said that Custer camped near here on his way to the Little Bighorn, but I haven't been able to confirm that."

"Is Lance bending your ear about Harts Haven history?" Grace asked, coming out from the kitchen.

Lance chuckled. "I like history as much as you like birds."

"Then that's a lot. I'm going to steal Sophie. Benjamin—I mean Bishop Wyse—would like a word with her. He's on the back porch. Go through the kitchen, dear. I'll be there as soon as I speak to Rose. Oh, and take another piece of cake for him, please."

Sophie nodded and stopped at the dessert table.

"Aunt Grace has an unusual gleam in her eye today," Joanna said with a wink.

Sophie rearranged the plates to fill the empty spaces evenly, ignored her sister's irritated huff, then picked up a plate with a large piece of cake. "I know she enjoys hosting people."

"I think she enjoys hosting Benjamin-I-mean-Bishop-Wyse, but is he wise enough to see what a good catch she would be?"

Sophie shook her head. "Don't be silly. She isn't Amish."

"Old Order Mennonite is close to Amish, and she was raised in an Amish home. She could jump back over the fence."

"You should join Rose's matchmaking group."

Joanna looked intrigued. "Interesting idea. I wonder who she'll find for me and you?"

"She won't have trouble finding a husband for you. If she's looking for someone to pair me with, she'll be disappointed."

"What about the widower Karl Graber? He's handsome."

"I hadn't noticed."

"Liar. I saw the sparks between the two of you when you met the other day."

"All you had eyes for were the puppies, so I don't know what you imagined you saw. I've barely given the man a second thought." It wasn't an outright lie. She tried desperately not to think about him.

"If you don't want him, I'll take him."

"Then he's yours." Annoyed with Joanna for the first time in ages, Sophie took a second piece of cake, went through the swinging kitchen door and ran smack into the man she couldn't stop thinking about. Both plates of cake went flying.

He grabbed her shoulders to steady her. She flinched and hunched forward hoping he wouldn't notice her uneven chest. She was naturally small busted and wore a bra padded on that side, but she always felt her disfigurement was glaringly obvious.

He dropped his hands and stepped back. "Sorry."

She knelt to gather the spilled cake pieces into her apron.

"It was my fault. I should know better than to charge through a swinging door."

He joined her in picking up the mess. "Rose said the bishop wanted another slice of cake. I was coming to get it for him."

Sophie sank back on her heels. "Grace asked me to take him a piece on the back porch."

"He and the school board members are out there." Karl stood and reached to help her up but rubbed his hand on his pants instead.

She surged to her feet. "Joanna will get you a piece while I sweep this up."

"Okay."

Sophie raised her chin. If she had to speak to him, she might as well find out his decision about his daughter's education. "Is Clara going to return to school?"

"I haven't given it much thought."

Sophie's mouth dropped open. "Your daughter's education is important. It will affect her entire life. You need to give it a lot of thought."

"It's just that we've been busy."

"Too busy to see to your child's future?"

A faint scowl appeared on his face. "I'm seeing to her present, which is just as important as her future."

"Ha! That is a short-sighted attitude."

He folded his arms. "I don't need a spinster telling me how to raise my children."

She planted her hands on her hips. "I might be a spinster, but I have had years of experience dealing with *kinder* and their parents."

"Four years hardly makes you an expert."

The door hit Sophie's backside, silencing her next comment. Rose looked around the edge. "Oh, I'm sorry."

Feeling foolish for arguing with him in public, Sophie managed a smile for Rose. "No harm done."

Rose stepped into the room. "Karl, I just heard your *daadi haus* renter has flown the coop. That's terrible. I know you depend on that rent. I happen to know someone who is looking for a place right away."

His scowl disappeared. "You do?"

"*Ja*. Suitably employed. Amish. Neat and quiet. I can vouch for both of them."

"That sounds great. Who are they?" he asked eagerly.

Rose's smile spread from ear to ear. "Why, Sophie and Joanna. It will be perfect for them and so close to the school. I'm surprised you didn't think of it."

"That won't work," Sophie and Karl said at the same time and exchanged embarrassed glances.

Rose folded her hand together. "Why ever not?"

"Because," he muttered and fell silent.

"That's right." Sophie stepped into the pointed silence.

"I see. I worried the two of you wouldn't get along. I reckon I was right. I hope this isn't how you will treat all the parents of your scholars, Sophie. Arguing like a pair of schoolchildren. Disgraceful, the pair of you. Grace went out on a limb to assure the bishop you were right for this position."

Sophie carried her apron load of crumbs to the trash can. "Karl and I were having a discussion, nothing more. It's not that we can't get along. I mean, I don't know him that well. What kind of landlord would he be?"

"And I have the girls to think about," he said. "They might not like having their teacher live next door."

Rose scoffed. "That's the most ridiculous excuse I've ever heard, Karl. I'll just go ask Rachel and Clara what they think of the idea. I know Rachel will love it."

He held out both hands. "Wait. I can handle this myself, Rose. Sophie?"

Was he looking to her for help? She racked her brain. "I need—some time to think it over and discuss it with Joanna."

"Right!" he said quickly. "You don't want to make a hasty decision without consulting your sister."

"Oh, I don't. Absolutely not."

He shot her a grateful look.

"Hmm." Rose glanced between them. "I don't see why it won't work. It's a wonderful solution if you ask me. Go see the house tomorrow, Sophie. I think you'll like it." Rose spun around and went into the dining room.

They both relaxed when she was gone. Sophie shook her head and glanced at Karl. "Does she boss everyone around that way?"

"I've found if Rose has her mind set on something, she is like a train. It's safer to get out of her way than to argue."

Sophie eyed him closely. "Is this one of her matchmaking schemes?"

"I don't think so. She said I wasn't on the list for you."

Sophie's mouth fell open. "She has a list of men for me? I haven't even been here a week."

A wry smile lifted the corner of his dour mouth, making him look much more approachable. "There aren't that many single Amish fellows between our two church districts."

"You and Rose have been discussing my marriage potential? How humiliating. Is there a way to convince her I'm not the marrying type?"

"Nothing I've said has worked. She's more stubborn than a hardheaded mule."

"I heard that," Rose said from the other side of the door.

"People who eavesdrop never hear *goot* about themselves, Rose," he said in a loud voice.

Silence followed his words. When he met Sophie's gaze, a hint of a smile curved his full lips. "Maybe I'm making progress."

She chuckled, and he grinned. A genuine smile that softened his features, crinkled the corner of his eyes and made him amazingly attractive.

What was he doing? Karl sobered when he realized he was grinning like a fool. Something about this woman turned him upside down. He hadn't felt this kind of interest in a very long time. It was more than the fact that he found Sophie's pretty smile and bright eyes appealing. He felt a connection to her on some level that he didn't understand.

Was he being disloyal to Nora? He didn't care to examine his feelings toward Sophie, but he did need the rent. Muscling his features into stern lines once more, he took a step back. "Talk to your sister. Sleep on the idea of renting my place. If you are still interested, I'll meet you there after work on Monday. If you aren't there, I'll know you decided against it. No hard feelings. Agreed?"

"Agreed." She nodded once.

They didn't shake on it. Karl wasn't about to touch her again.

She rubbed her hands on her apron and looked toward the swinging door. He sensed her sudden unease. "I should— I need to get another piece of cake for the bishop."

Since she had taken over his errand, he had the perfect excuse to leave. He had attended the frolic as Rose had insisted and now it was time to go back to work. Only he didn't move. "Guess I'll get one for myself."

He held open the swinging door. She ducked under his arm to scurry through. The room was filled to overflowing with members of his church group and Amish from the nearby community of Castleton. He saw two young men he recognized standing shoulder to shoulder in front of the dessert table where Sophie's sister was blushing a pretty shade of pink as she loaded their plates with two pieces of cake each.

He waited behind Sophie. Joanna peeked around her admirers. "Would you kindly step aside so someone else can get dessert?"

The men, boys really, stammered an apology and let Sophie up to the table. She took a plate. Joanna smiled at her. "It's nice to see your appetite is improving."

"There's nothing wrong with my appetite," Sophie said, quickly casting a fugitive glance behind her. "This is for the bishop. Karl made me drop the last piece. I mean, it was an accident," she muttered quickly.

A speculative look entered Joanna's eyes as her gaze darted from Sophie to Karl. "So Karl made you butterfingered?"

"I bumped into her," Karl said, hoping to end Joanna's scrutiny. It didn't work. If anything, her interest increased.

"On purpose?" she asked, a smile twitching at the corner of her mouth.

"Of course not," Sophie snapped before he could answer. "I said it was an accident."

"All right. Don't bite my head off, sister. She's not usually this cranky, Karl. She's had a trying afternoon."

"Has she? What happened?" He couldn't believe he was interested but he was.

"Nothing," Sophie said. "I met a lot of people is all. It's difficult trying to remember so many names."

"My sister likes an orderly existence. The move has been stressful for her, but she is adapting," Joanna said brightly.

"And what about you?" he asked.

"Me? I'm happy to be having an adventure that doesn't involve a hospital."

Sophie sucked in a quick breath. Joanna's grin vanished. Regret filled her eyes. She looked at Karl. "Forget I said that."

"Have you been sick?" he asked.

"Someone else in the family was, but they are fine now. Help yourself to more cake. I need to speak with my aunt."

"The bishop is waiting. Excuse me." Sophie snatched up a fork and went through the swinging door.

Karl got his slice of cake and followed her.

A group of elders sat in semicircle on the back porch.

"Ah, my cake. *Danki*." A tall man with bright blue eyes in a deeply tanned face and a white beard that reached to the middle of his chest rose to his feet from a lawn chair. He was an imposing figure. "I am Bishop Wyse. Sophie, these are the members of our school board, and we have a few questions for you. First, what kind of Christmas program do you have in mind?"

Four

Joanna lay on her bed in their room later that evening. "What did you tell the bishop when he asked about the Christmas program?"

Sophie was lying on her own bed. "I said I would keep it a surprise until I'd had a chance to meet all the children."

"That was clever. Was he satisfied?"

"Not really but what else could he say? I did learn from Rose that Karl Graber has a *daadi haus* he rents out. It's currently empty."

Joanna sat up. "Do you mean we could live near Rachel and Clara? Wouldn't that be fun. I like those girls. I hope he will rent it to us. He seems nice."

Sophie carefully studied her sister's face. Was living near Karl part of the draw for her sister? Sophie shuffled the idea around in her mind.

He was older than Joanna, but that wasn't a bad thing. He

was settled but somber. Could her buoyant sister lighten his grim attitude? Maybe. Sophie nibbled on her bottom lip. The trouble was that she would be living next to Karl, too.

Her attraction to him simply had to be put aside. Ignored. For Joanna's sake she could do that. It would ease her mind if she knew Joanna would have someone to look after her in the future. When worse came to worst, Joanna wouldn't be alone.

"I'll see if we can view the place first," Sophie said. "We might not like it."

"Adorable children, a puppy and three lambs, Sophie. What's not to like?"

After spending a quiet off-Sunday with the widows and a few guests at the inn, Sophie was eager to get to work Monday morning. She spent the day at the school going over the student records. There were a pair of problem boys according to the previous teacher's notes, Zack Weaver and Bartholomew Kemp, but one thing that caught Sophie's eye was Becky Schrock's notes about Clara from the year her mother passed away.

Clara has become increasingly sullen and withdrawn following the death of her mother last year. I worry her father doesn't see how much she is struggling. Her grades are still passing, but much lower. She has missed nearly a quarter of the school days because she claims her father needs her help at the store. I will have a conference with him next week.

Sophie checked, but it didn't look as if the conference had taken place. If it had, there weren't any notes about it. She found another comment from the opening week of the current school year before teacher Becky left.

Clara doesn't want to be here. I will try to motivate her, but I feel she is shutting me out.

There was only one notation about Rachel.

What a joy she is.

Sophie couldn't agree more.

When five o'clock rolled around, she locked up the school and walked down the steps. Rachel's sheep were grazing on the lawn, but their little shepherdess wasn't far away. She sat on the swings, holding on to a rope around Buck's neck. He never took his eyes off the sheep.

Rachel hopped up. "*Daed* said I could wait for you."

"Why did you bring the sheep?"

Rachel sighed. "They were already here. They got out again but at least they didn't go into town. *Daed* shut Buck's *mamm*, Misty, in the barn again this morning. Otherwise she would have kept them home."

"Well, let's take them back."

Rachel came over and handed Buck's rope to Sophie. "He'll nip their heels to get them moving. His mother taught him."

Rachel walked on. Sophie followed the little flock following their shepherdess. Buck knew exactly how to keep them headed in the right direction.

The state of the farm was disappointing when Sophie arrived. Although the flower beds, lawn and vegetable garden were spent and winter brown, it was easy to see the weeds had taken over during the summer and the grass hadn't been mowed. At least the large red barn and corrals were in decent repair.

Adjacent to the two-story white farmhouse stood a modest single-story *daadi haus*. At the back corner of the small front porch sat a pair of blue wooden rocking chairs flanking a small table of the same color. It was an inviting spot. Sophie could imagine herself and Joanna sipping coffee there on nice mornings.

The main house was overdue for a coat of paint, but it seemed in good order except the curtain in the picture window overlooking the farmyard was hanging askew. What was the rest of the inside like?

Sophie's curiosity got the better of her. "What happened to the curtains?"

Rachel looked at her feet. "*Daed*'s been going to fix it."

Something in the child's tone struck Sophie as odd.

Rachel pointed to the side of the barn. "See. The gate to the sheep's pen is still closed. I did latch it."

She was right. The gate was securely fastened. Sophie could hear a dog barking inside the barn. Buck ran to scratch at the door, but Sophie didn't want to let his mother out until she understood how the lambs were escaping. She opened the gate and Rachel led the lambs inside. Sophie examined the white board fence. "How do you suppose they got out?"

"I don't know, but it wasn't my fault. You'll tell *Daed* that, won't you?"

"I certainly will." On closer examination, Sophie noticed clumps of fleece along the lower edge of the middle board. "Maybe if you go around the corner of the barn and call them while I'm watching from over there, we can discover how they did it."

"That's a smart idea." Rachel ran to the other side of the barn and began calling.

The lambs milled about for a minute and then one of them put his head between the fence boards and pushed the middle one up. He crawled out over the bottom board and the middle one dropped back into place. A moment later, the next sheep did the same thing. The last one quickly followed the others.

Sophie walked up to examine the fence. The nails holding the middle board on one end were missing. The reason it didn't fall down completely was because it was resting on top of a single remaining nail. The other end of the board had a single nail in the center that was acting as a pivot. From a distance, it looked like a perfectly sound fence, but she raised and lowered the board easily.

"Did you see how they got out?" Rachel asked as she walked back with her babies crowded around her.

Sophie showed her how the escapees managed it. "All we need to fix this is a hammer and a few nails. Then I think your problem will be solved. Do you know where we can find some?"

"*Daed* has a workshop over there." Rachel led the way to a small building behind the house.

Inside the shed, everything was neatly organized and clean, in stark contrast to the overgrown garden around it. Sophie lifted a hammer from a hook on the wall. "This should do it."

"*Daed* doesn't like us to take his tools."

"He also doesn't like your sheep following you into town. I'll put the hammer back as soon as I'm finished, and he won't mind. Where can I find some nails?"

She began opening various drawers. She discovered what she wanted and took several. "This should do the trick."

In less than five minutes she had adequately fastened the plank and only hit her thumb once. "Let's put them inside and you try calling them again."

Rachel ran to the other side of the barn. The sheep tried getting under the board almost immediately, but it didn't budge. They ended up milling around for a few minutes and then lay down by their hay feeder. Rachel came back to join Sophie. "Did it work?"

"It did. They will stay put as long as you keep the gate latched."

"I almost always remember, but sometimes I forget. I'm hungry. Can I have a snack?"

"I don't see why not. Let's go find something for you in the kitchen." Sophie was eager to see the inside of the house. She was oddly curious about Karl Graber. It occurred to her that she was snooping but going inside had been Rachel's suggestion.

The kitchen was clean, other than a few dishes piled in the sink. She saw there was food in the propane-powered refrigerator when Rachel opened it.

"Do you want something?" the child asked, looking back.

"I'm fine." Sophie walked over to the sink. Karl wasn't home yet. It would only take a few minutes to wash what was here. "Do you think your father would mind if I did these dishes?" She had a thing about keeping the sink empty and scrubbed.

"Clara does all the dishes. I'm sure she won't mind."

"Does your *daed* do all the cooking?"

"Sometimes Clara does that." Rachel wrinkled her nose. "She's not a good cook. Neither is *Daed*."

Rachel sat at the table with an apple and spread peanut butter on slices Sophie cut for her.

Sophie finished the dishes and dried her hands. Her eyes caught the curtain hanging crookedly in the other room. She had the hammer and a nail. It would just take her a minute to fix it. There was already a kitchen chair in front of the window. She pulled it closer and stood on it. Raising her arm over her head was still painful, but she managed to hammer the curtain rod in place. Then she smoothed the fabric closed.

"What do you think you're doing?" Karl demanded behind her.

Startled, Sophie spun around and wobbled on the chair seat. "I saw the curtain rod had come down, and I thought I would fix it while I waited for you. I'm sorry if I was intrusive." She shrugged nervously. "I never put off until tomorrow what I can do today."

"You need to leave." Karl yanked the curtain open. The rod stayed up, but the material ripped away from it.

Karl's hand shook as he curled his fingers into the torn fabric of the blue curtain. How dare this woman come into his house and change Nora's place. Grief sharp as the tines of a pitchfork pierced his chest, making it hard to breathe.

Sophie's pale face showed her confusion. "I'm sorry. Truly I am. I thought I was helping."

"You didn't help. Just leave."

"I don't understand."

"And you never will." Why wouldn't she go? He turned to gaze out the window reliving the worst day of his life.

"I'm sorry."

He didn't reply. After a long moment, the sound of her footsteps leaving the room told him she'd gone.

She shouldn't have been in here. This was where he and Nora had greeted each new day together knowing it would soon be their last and praying for one more. It was where he sought peace now. Only he never truly found it.

His arms ached to hold his wife. Try as he might to keep his memories of her alive, they were fading. What he wouldn't give to hear her voice. If only he could touch her face once more, see her smile.

"*Daed?* I'm really sorry." Rachel's trembling words drew him out of his anguished longing.

He kept his gaze focused out the window so she wouldn't see the tears in his eyes. "It's okay, Rachel. I'm not angry with you."

"I told teacher you wouldn't like her taking your tools."

"What?" He wiped his face on his sleeve and glanced at his daughter.

"She took your hammer to fix the place where my lambs were getting out. She was going to put it back."

Karl realized he had the hammer in his hand. He must have snatched it from Sophie's grip but didn't remember doing so. He held it toward Rachel. "Put it back for me, will you, honey?"

She took it from him. "I'm sure Sophie is sorry."

"I'm sure she is, too."

"She washed the dishes. That was nice of her, wasn't it?"

He pressed his lips into a tight line. "We don't need her help."

When Rachel left the room, he pulled the chair Sophie had been standing on back to its place and sat down. The rod she had reattached had stayed in place, but he had ripped the curtain material across the top. He tried to leave it hanging as before, but it wasn't the same now.

This was the place where he'd held his wife every morning during the last month of her life. Nora had loved watching the sunrise. She used to say that she could almost glimpse heaven in *Gott*'s gift of a new day. Near the end she had been too weak to get out of bed on her own.

Karl would put on a pot of coffee and go out to do his chores in the dark of the early morning. When he returned to the house, he would pour a cup and leave it on the little wooden table beside the chair. Then he would draw back the curtain and go into the bedroom.

Sometimes Nora was asleep but usually she was waiting for

him with smile of gratitude. He would bundle her in a quilt and carry her to this chair. With her snuggled in his arms, they shared sips of coffee from the same cup, the way they had shared so much in their lives, and watched the sun come up together. Sometimes they talked but often they simply sat in silence. He had treasured every moment with her as the end crept closer. It didn't matter if it had been cloudy or raining; Nora wanted to watch the light growing stronger.

If only she could have grown strong with it.

That last morning he'd had trouble with one of his horses. It took him longer than usual to finish his chores. The sun was already halfway above the horizon when he hurried toward the house. He saw her at the window. Somehow, she'd made it on her own. He watched her fall and pull down the curtain with her. When he reached her, she was gone.

Gathering her in his arms, he sat and held her lifeless body with the light of a new dawn and his tears bathing her face for the last time. He couldn't bring himself to fix the curtain. Every morning since that day he sat here looking out at the sunrise so he wouldn't forget that he should have been with her.

"I can mend the curtain," Clara said softly.

He glanced to where she and Rachel stood together looking worried in the kitchen doorway. They didn't know what to make of his outburst.

He wasn't an angry man by nature, but it had been a shock to see Sophie closing the curtain. It felt like she had come to shut out that part of his life. She hadn't, of course. She didn't know about anything Nora. He had been wrong to order her out of his house, but there was something about her that got under his skin.

Keeping control of his emotions was vital to his sanity. Sophie Eicher managed to stir them up without trying. She left him off balance and he didn't like it. The less he saw of her the better.

He wouldn't be able to avoid her indefinitely. It was a small community. Somehow, he would have to find a way to apologize without revealing the pain that prompted his rude behavior.

What could he say to explain himself? Not the truth. His wife died opening this curtain, and he couldn't bear to see it closed.

Was that the reasoning of a sane man? He thought it was until he saw Sophie's shocked expression, her complete confusion over his anger because she had fixed a broken drapery rod.

He fingered the dusty material. A fellow in his right mind would have repaired it long ago. Nora was gone. No matter how many days he sat in the same place, he would never hold her again.

"Are you okay, *Daed*?" Clara asked.

He glanced at his girls huddled together. The truth slowly dawned on him. Nora would not have wanted his shrine to her memory. She had only asked him for one thing. That he love and care for their daughters as she would have done. He had failed her but maybe it wasn't too late.

He blinked back tears and swallowed the lump in his throat. "I think it's time for some new curtains in here, don't you?"

"*Mamm* bought those," Clara said cautiously. Both girls knew not to intrude into this corner of the room.

It wasn't right. This was their home. They should be comfortable in every inch of it. He smiled to reassure them. "Do you remember we had to go all the way to Wichita to find this material? She wanted this color and wouldn't stop looking until she found it." It was a soft sky blue with a hint of shimmer in the fabric. Perhaps a shade too fancy for an Amish home, but he never could refuse her.

"I remember that day." Clara walked to his side. He put his arm around her shoulders and drew her close.

"I don't." Rachel's voice cracked with sorrow. He held out his other arm. She darted over and hugged him.

The warmth of their small bodies thawed a part of his heart he hadn't realized he'd shut away. Sophie had made him angry, but he owed her a debt of gratitude for this.

"You were too little, Rachel. I'm surprised Clara remembers. It was a long time ago."

Clara buried her face against his chest. "We got ice cream afterward in that store with lots and lots of flavors. I had butter brickle."

"That's right. It took your *mamm* forever to pick one."

Clara leaned back and smiled. "Then she chose vanilla 'cause that was her favorite."

Karl chuckled at the memory. "She did."

"What kind did I have?" Rachel asked.

He cast his mind back to that happy day. "Let me think. You had strawberry. I remember now because your face broke out in a rash."

"It still does if I eat them."

He looked at the other two windows in the room. There would be more than enough material to make something useful out of the curtains. "Why don't I have Granny Rose's daughter, Susanna, make a new dress for each of you from this fabric? I think your *mamm* would have liked that."

"And one for my doll?" Rachel asked.

He smiled at her. "If Susanna has enough left over. What do you think of the idea, Clara?"

"Do you really think *Mamm* wouldn't mind us taking them down?"

"I'm sure of it. She loved you both so much. All she ever wanted was to see you happy."

"If we're happy, she will be smiling, Clara. That's what Joanna said."

"I loved her smile," Clara said softly.

"I wish I could remember it," Rachel said sadly.

"I see it when I look at both of you." Karl wiped his eyes, got up and went around the room taking down the curtain rods and pulling the material off. Small clouds of dust filled the air as he did. He wasn't going to win a prize for housekeeping.

The women of the church had offered to come in and clean, but he had refused them every time. Eventually they stopped offering. Keeping things unchanged hadn't lessened his grief; it only allowed dust to gather in what had been Nora's clean and tidy, happy home. He missed her. He would always miss her.

He turned to his daughters. "I think the first thing we should do is wash them."

Then he needed to apologize to Sophie Eicher.

"He actually yelled at you?" Joanna asked aghast.

Sophie sat on her bed in their room at the inn facing her sister, who was sprawled on her bed with an open book beside her.

"It wasn't so much that he raised his voice, but his tone was cold as ice. All I was trying to do is put up a curtain rod that had fallen down, but for some reason it upset him terribly."

The look of pain and anger on Karl's face was something she'd never seen before. Thinking back, she realized it was anguish more than anger. She had made a terrible mistake, but she didn't know what she had done. It must have had something to do with his deceased wife.

There was more to Karl's story than she knew. Learning what that was might give her some insight into his reaction. Strangely, she wanted to understand him.

Joanna sat up and snapped her book closed. "He has upset you, and that upsets me. We are not renting his house."

Sophie dismissed the notion with a derisive huff. "I'm certain that option is out of the question now. I just hope he decides to keep Clara in school. If my actions have given him a disgust of me, that's fine, but if it keeps Clara from completing her schooling, I will feel terrible."

"I think I should go give him a piece of my mind."

Sophie smothered a smile. "You're going to have to stop doing that."

Joanna scowled. "I can speak up for myself. I can speak up for you, too. I've done it before. Remember that horrible nurse at the cancer center?"

"I don't. They were all wonderful."

"One of them couldn't bring your pain meds on time so I said something. I can't remember her name."

"See? That's why you have to stop giving people a piece of your mind."

"Why?"

"Because it's almost gone."

Joanna's chuckle lightened Sophie's battered spirit. "Okay, I'll hang on to what little I have left. Unless I see him or anyone else being mean to you."

Sophie raised her chin. "If Mr. Graber continues to be disagreeable, I will handle it myself." Next time she wouldn't scurry away like a frightened mouse. If there was a next time. It would be difficult to avoid him when his children were going to be her students.

Joanna tilted her head to the side. "You look better today."

Sophie pressed a hand to her face. "What does that mean?"

"You have more color in your cheeks. I would say there's even a sparkle in your eyes. Perhaps I've been too hard on Karl Graber."

"And I still have no idea what you're talking about."

"I think your little confrontation has done you good. It's taking your mind off your own worries and given you something to focus on."

"I'm not focused on Karl Graber. The man can be infuriating but I'm not going to let him push me around," Sophie insisted vehemently. Maybe he had a strange effect on her, but she would get over it or learn to ignore it altogether.

"I was thinking of Clara."

Sophie knew she was blushing. She looked away from her sister's sharp gaze and cleared her throat. "You're right. Clara has been on my mind. And Rachel."

"That little child is so cute, and those sheep are endearing the way they followed her to town."

"I don't think they'll be doing that again. I fixed the fence where they were getting out."

"Wait. You fixed Karl's fence and you tried to fix his curtains? Are you sure you weren't intent on impressing the man?"

"Of course not. Why do you insist on making this about an attraction between Karl and myself?"

Joanna arched one eyebrow. "I didn't know I was. Is there an attraction between the two of you?"

"How could I possibly be drawn to a man who is rude to me?"

"Only you can answer that one." Joanna smiled knowingly. "Given your penchant for order, I'm surprised you didn't sweep and mop the floors for good measure while you were there."

Sophie chewed the corner of her bottom lip. "I like things neat and tidy. There is nothing wrong with that."

Joanna leaned forward with a knowing grin. "You did sweep his floor, didn't you?"

"I washed a few dishes that were left in the sink. That's all."

"You are priceless, sister. I hope he appreciated all you did."

"Ordering me out of the house is hardly the way a person expresses appreciation."

"True." Joanna leaned back. "I'm not in a big hurry to move again. Grace said we can stay here as long as we like."

"But it was Rose who suggested Karl rent his house to me. Maybe she would rather have paying guests in this room instead of nonpaying family, but she is too polite to say so."

"I'm sure that's not true."

"We'll keep looking for a place," Sophie declared. Living next door to Karl Graber had been a bad idea from the start. "I'll find something and when I do you can return to Ohio."

"What? Not a chance. You're stuck with me, sister. What are your plans for tomorrow?" Joanna asked.

"I'm going back to the school. I need to finish setting up my lesson plans and I absolutely must decide what kind of program we will have Christmas Eve."

"That's right. You don't have much time to come up with one."

"I'll only have four weeks once school resumes. I wanted it to be something simple, but that's not what the town wants."

"I'm sure the parents won't be expecting an elaborate program."

"Oh, but they are. I heard all about last year's program, the wonderful play and how people come from miles around to see the children here perform. It was almost the only thing folks talked about on Saturday. Any suggestions?"

"Me? Not a one. I'm your frivolous kid sister, remember? You do all the heavy lifting and thinking."

"I have never called you frivolous."

"I'm aware of my deficiencies even if I don't try hard to

correct them. Maybe Rose or Grace will have some ideas. They must have seen dozens of school programs in their time."

Sophie pointed at her sister. "That is not a frivolous idea. It's an excellent one. Let's find them and see what they suggest."

Five

Sophie and her sister found all three of the widows in the sitting room at the front of the inn where a sofa and chairs were arranged to take advantage of the light coming in the bay window. Two elderly *Englisch* folks, a man and a woman, and the widows were gathered around a young Amish couple. The woman was holding a tiny baby. All the women were cooing over the child while the father and the elderly gentleman looked on proudly.

Grace glanced up. "Come and meet the newest member of our bird-watching group."

Sophie and Joanna advanced into the room. "Who do we have here?" Sophie asked, gazing at the beautiful infant.

The young mother turned the baby so the sisters could see his face. "This is Henry Joseph Troyer. A future pupil of yours. He's three weeks old."

"He's gorgeous. You are so blessed." Sophie pressed a hand

to her heart as tears pricked the back of her eyes. She loved teaching, but she always thought she would marry and have children of her own. The loss of those dreams still stabbed like a knife when she allowed herself to think about them.

Rose grinned as she straightened. "This is Abby Troyer and her husband, Joseph. They are newcomers to our community. I take the credit for getting them together except for the parts where the Lord intervened." She folded her hands primly. "It was His plan. I was a simple tool He used to bring two people together."

"Your modesty has slipped sideways again, *Mamm*." Susanna's long-suffering tone made everyone chuckle.

Rose patted her *kapp* to make sure it was in place. "*Nee*, it hasn't."

Susanna merely shook her head.

Abby smiled at Sophie. "Would you like to hold him?"

Sophie stepped forward eagerly. "I'd love to."

Sitting beside the young mother, she took the infant tenderly into her arms. The weight of his tiny body, the feel of him stretching inside his blanket warmed her heart.

Grace indicated the other visitors. "This is Herb and Dr. Bertha. My nieces from Ohio, Sophie and Joanna Eicher."

The elderly man with snow-white hair and bushy white eyebrows drew himself up ramrod straight. "Major Herbert Young, US Army JAG Corps, retired, ma'am," he said proudly. "Pleased to make your acquaintance."

Dr. Bertha pulled on his sleeve. "Herbert, you know the Amish aren't impressed with titles, especially military ones." She smiled at Sophie and Joanna. "Herb is a fine fellow even if he is a bit pompous at times."

Some of the starch went out of his bearing. "Old habits die hard."

"What is a JAG Corps?" Joanna asked.

"It means he was a military attorney, and he's still a wonderful lawyer. If you ever need one, I highly recommend him," Abby said. "The best part is that he doesn't charge his Amish clients."

"I've been repaid many times over by the lasting friendships I have made in Harts Haven," he said, leaning over the baby to grasp Henry's tiny fist. "The people here are the closest thing to a family that I have."

"Did you girls need something?" Grace asked.

"I do." Sophie tore her gaze away from the baby's face. "I hope to have all *kinder* back in school before Thanksgiving. It will be an adjustment for everyone—I understand that. What I need help with is planning a Christmas program. I'm not sure what will be suitable here."

"Becky Schrock came up with the most amazing plays for the *kinder*," Susanna said. "It's the only time Amish children are encouraged to perform in front of others. Our programs are well attended by our Amish families, friends and *Englisch* neighbors. My children prepared for months learning songs and plays and poems, often ones they wrote themselves. And the clothing I had to make. Angels, shepherds, clouds, stars. Once I made a sheep costume. That was hard."

"My daughter is right," Rose said. "The Christmas Eve program is something the entire community looks forward to every year. This year will be no different."

"Did the previous teacher have a program in mind?" Sophie asked hopefully. Perhaps she could build on that.

The Amish women glanced at each other and shook their heads. "Not that we are aware," Susanna said.

Hiding her disappointment, Sophie glanced around the room. "I am open to suggestions. Those of you that have been in the community a long time know the children. Who can

I ask to sing a solo? Who has a good speaking voice? Who is afraid to stand up and speak in public?"

"Perhaps you should meet with the mothers after the church service next Sunday and ask these questions of the people who know the children best," Bertha suggested.

"I will certainly do that. Other than Karl Graber, are there any other single fathers in the community that I should speak with?"

"Charlie Schrock, teacher Becky's brother, is a widower," Rose said. "He's in the market for a wife if you or Joanna are interested. Of course, Karl Graber should be looking for a mother for those adorable girls."

"Charlie's boys have both graduated from school," Susanna said. "They are the same age as my grandsons. I didn't know Charlie was looking to remarry. Mary Sue Bieler was asking about him the other day. Perhaps I will mention that to her."

"Mary Sue Bieler isn't his type," Rose said. "You're wasting your time if you try to fix those two up."

Susanna's brow darkened. "We shall see. You're not the only matchmaker in Harts Haven."

"We are digressing from the subject at hand," Bertha said. "You must have experience at putting on a Christmas program, Sophie. Perhaps one of your previous programs or elements from them could be combined."

"I'm afraid my school favored a scaled-down version with the children singing Christmas carols and reading a few poems. Would the children and the parents here be happy with that?" She glanced among the older women. They didn't look too sure.

"Take it up with the mothers after church. That will give you a better idea. I'm sure the children will work hard to make it a fine Christmas program."

"I just don't want to disappoint anyone. Being the new

teacher, it will reflect badly on the bishop's decision to give the job to an outsider if things don't go well. I would like to keep the job next year."

"Benjamin—I mean Bishop Wyse." Grace paused as her cheeks turned pink. "He based his decision to hire you on what is best for the community. You don't need to worry about having a job next year."

Abby reached for her son. "We should be going. We have several other stops to make on Henry's first outing."

Sophie reluctantly handed him over and got to her feet. "You've all been helpful." She started to walk out of the room.

"What did you think of the Graber *daadi haus*?" Rose asked.

Sophie glanced back as her cheeks grew warm. "I didn't get a chance to see it."

A slight frown creased Rose's brow. "Oh. I thought Karl was meeting you there today."

"Something came up," Sophie said, not wanting to elaborate.

Joanna leaned forward. "He was rude to her."

Sophie grabbed her arm before her sister could give them her angry-sister version of the story.

Rose's frown deepened as her sharp eyes remained fixed on Sophie's face. "Should I speak to him?"

Sophie shook her head. "It was nothing. We need to get going. It was nice meeting you, Abby and Joseph. Thank you for letting me hold Henry. He's so sweet. Come on, Joanna." Sophie pulled her sister out the door before Rose could come up with more questions.

In the hall, Joanna stopped. "What was that?"

"I told you about Karl's outburst in private and you were about to repeat my story."

"Okay, but next time tell me when we're having a conversation I shouldn't share."

Sophie's mouth dropped open. She snapped it shut. "It would be best to assume they are all private."

Joanna rolled her eyes. "Sure. Okay. The widows weren't exactly helpful about the Christmas program. Advice but no concrete ideas. However, I must say I am really pleased with you."

"With me? Why?"

"Because you said you wanted to have this job next year. That's the first time I've heard you talk about your future since your diagnosis."

Stunned, Sophie knew Joanna was right. She had come to Harts Haven expecting to fill a temporary teaching vacancy for this year. She hadn't been thinking ahead to teaching here after that. Was it fair to the children and the community to allow them to pin their hopes on having her for another year? She thought of teaching Rachel and Clara as they grew up. She wanted to do that. And there was the mystery of Karl Graber to be solved.

There was something about this town that made her want to look further ahead. "Well, I didn't come all this way to sit in the dark and contemplate my own death. Isn't that what you told me?"

"I did. Another first. You never listen to me."

"Because you usually say something foolish like 'Let's bring a new puppy into a place where we are guests.'"

"I did want a puppy, but what I *really* want is for my sister to start believing she's well."

Sophie managed a smile, but she couldn't give Joanna the reassurance she sought.

Rose closed the outside door after waving goodbye to Abby and Joseph. She turned to the others in the room. "Karl didn't show her the house. Why not? He needs that rent to keep his business going. What could've happened?"

"Something must've come up at his work," Herbert suggested, helping himself to a cookie from the plate on the side table.

Grace shook her head. "I saw the look on Sophie's face when Rose asked about the house. Whatever happened, she didn't want to tell us about it. Joanna said he was rude."

Susanna looked pensive. "Normally I would say the two of you are making a mountain out of a molehill, but this time I think you're right. Joanna definitely seemed like she wanted to say more, but Sophie stopped her."

"What are we going to do?" Bertha asked.

"You could try leaving the fellow alone." Herbert earned a glare from all the women with his comment. He picked up another cookie.

"We can't leave it be," Rose said. "If anyone in this town needs our help, it's Karl Graber and his girls."

"Are you sure my niece is right for him?" Grace asked. "Sophie has had such a difficult time with her illness and her broken engagement. It may be too soon for her." They all knew Sophie's history but would never mention it to her.

Rose nodded emphatically. "She's the right one. I just know it."

Susanna scoffed. "You may be certain, but how are you going to convince them?"

Rose sat down on the sofa. "I'm not sure. I hate to admit it, but I may need outside help this time."

"Karl Graber, I want a word with you!"

Karl glanced toward the front door of his store where Rose stood glaring at him with her shopping basket hooked over one arm and her free hand propped on her hip. A scowl darkened her face. He closed the cash register drawer and handed the change to Levi Martin. "Tell Barbara I said hello."

Levi took the money and slipped it in his wallet. "I will. Rose seems upset with you."

"So I gather." Karl suspected he knew the reason. He hadn't considered that Sophie would share their exchange with the widow. What had she said? Who else had she told?

Clara and Rachel were sweeping the aisles near the front of the store. He knew they were listening.

Levi chuckled. "I'm glad it's you and not me. Have a good day. Or as good as it can be with Granny Rose in one of her moods."

"I heard that, Levi," Granny snapped. "I do not have moods. I have problems to solve, and there is nothing wrong with my hearing."

Levi fought back a smile. "My mistake."

"How is little Micah?" she asked in a mollified tone.

"Growing like a weed. Barbara said you should come out for a visit one day soon."

"I'll do that. Now run along. I wish to speak to Karl."

"Yes, Granny." Levi tipped his hat, cast Karl a sympathetic look and went out the door.

"What can I help you with, Rose?" Karl asked.

"Exactly what did you do or say to upset Sophie?" she demanded.

He tried to bluff. "Nothing that I recall."

"He yelled at her," Rachel said, emptying her dustpan in the trash. "She took his hammer."

He pressed his lips together. Scolding his daughter for telling the truth wasn't an option, but he didn't need her reciting the details. "Rachel, take Buck across the street to the park and let him run around for a bit. Clara, go along and keep an eye on your sister."

He hadn't found a buyer for the last pup, who seemed content to stay by the girls. Maybe he should consider letting them keep the dog.

When the children were out the door, he crossed his arms and leaned back against the counter. "Exactly what did Sophie tell you?"

"All she said was that you didn't show her the house. When I asked why, she said something came up. It was the way she said it that led me to suspect the two of you were at odds."

"And you assume it was my fault?"

She set her shopping basket on the counter next to him. "Am I wrong?"

"You're the one who said we would be at each other's throats within a week."

She gave a slight nod. "I was hoping the two of you could make it past five days. What did you disagree about?"

Knowing Rose, she wasn't going to let it go. He had to tell her something. "I walked in to find her fixing things in my house."

Rose's eyebrows shot up. She tipped her head to peer at him over the top of her spectacles. "Fixing things? What do you mean?"

"She washed the dishes that I'd left in the sink." It sounded stupid and he knew it. Better to sound foolish than to admit the painful truth. He couldn't share his grief even with Rose.

"How terribly inconsiderate of Sophie. Did she use a hammer on the dishes?"

Rose really had a way of getting under his skin. "She used the hammer to fix the fence where Rachel's sheep were getting out, and then she put up the curtain rod had come down in my living room. I don't like people using my tools," he added in a rush, knowing it was a flimsy excuse.

Rose rocked back on her heels. "Well, I can see you were provoked. My husband was the same way with his tools. Still, you can't yell at our new teacher. You're going to have to apologize. Poor Sophie is wondering if she will have a job here next year."

Would she be returning to Ohio? That might be for the best. He hadn't been able to stop thinking about her last night. He kept remembering her laughter when she had her coat full of puppies and then the shocked expression in her wide blue eyes when he ordered her out of his house.

"I'll get around to apologizing soon."

"Not soon. Right now."

She couldn't be serious. "Rose, I have a business to run."

"I will mind the store while you go speak to Sophie. She's working in the school today."

"I don't even know what to say." That was the truth. Where did he start without explaining about Nora?

Rose dusted her hands together. "Try saying you're sorry and see where it goes from there. She won't bite."

"Rose, this is ridiculous. I'll see her after work."

"I never took you for a coward, Karl."

"Now see here, Rose. That's uncalled-for. What business is it of yours, anyway?"

Rose clasped both hands over her chest as her eyes filled with unshed tears. "Sophie is a guest in my home, the niece of my best friend. You are a dear friend, too. It troubles my heart to think two people I care about have had a falling-out. I'm an old woman. I might not live to see you make amends. Humor me, Karl." She sniffled.

He knew when he was beaten. "You're going to outlive me, Rose."

"I pray that isn't true."

He pulled off the long canvas apron he wore at work and laid it on the counter. She was right. An apology needed to be made. The longer he put it off the harder it would be. "I'll be back as quick as I can. Clara knows where everything is. I'll send her in."

Rose smiled, all traces of her distress gone in an instant. "And Rachel, too. She is such a dear child and so eager to please. We'll have a lovely visit while you're gone."

Sophie looked up from the paperwork on her desk to see Karl Graber standing in the open doorway of the school. Her heart lunged in her chest. Even if he was still upset with her, she wasn't going to let him gain the upper hand. Gathering her courage and taking a deep breath, she tried to appear calm.

"May I help you?" she asked, pleased that her voice sounded normal.

He stood there with his hat in his hand for a long moment, then crossed the schoolroom to stand in front of her desk. He picked up one of the student folders and laid it down. "Are you finding everything you need?"

That wasn't what she expected to hear. He looked ill at ease. "I seem to be. The previous teacher kept excellent records."

"That's *goot*." He turned aside and walked to the blackboard, where he picked up one of the erasers and patted it against the board, leaving dusty chalk rectangles on the surface. "When I was in school here the teacher had me stay after school and clean the erasers every week."

"As a punishment? Or as a reward?"

He turned to look at her. "Which do you consider it?"

The tenseness left her shoulders. She relaxed since he didn't seem angry anymore. "That depends on the child. Some children are eager to please. I will let them take on the chore to make them feel useful. Other children find it tedious, so it isn't a pleasant exercise for them."

"I found it tedious."

"What earned you a weekly session?" She was uncommonly eager to know more about him.

"Inattentiveness mostly. School was boring. I wasn't a good student."

"Perhaps you just had the wrong teacher."

He glanced at her. "Maybe."

It wasn't a social call. There was a reason he was here. She waited for him to tell her.

Putting the eraser back in the tray, he picked up a piece of chalk and started writing.

I'm sorry I was rude to the new teacher.
I'm sorry I was rude to the new teacher.
I'm sorry

He paused and looked at her over his shoulder. "Shall I write it one hundred times or will fifty be adequate?"

She looked down to hide her amusement. He could certainly be disarming when he made the effort. "If you write it a hundred times, you will have to stay to clean the eraser and wash the blackboard. Three times will be enough."

He finished writing the sentence and put the chalk down. "I think the new teacher is letting me off lightly."

An apology but no explanation. Studying his tense demeanor she decided that was enough for now. She walked to his side, picked up the chalk and began to write below his sentences.

I'm sorry I upset you. Please forgive me.

He stopped her before she could write it again and pulled the chalk from her fingers. She quickly clasped her hands together to stifle the tingle brought on by his touch. She took a step away.

Laying the chalk down, he kept his gaze lowered. "There's nothing to forgive. I overreacted. I don't get much company. I was shocked to see someone in my house."

"As you no doubt realize, I can be intrusive and pushy. Those are two of my many faults."

"How many is many?" A faint grin appeared, softening his harsh features when he looked up. He needed to smile more often.

Her determination to keep him at arm's length softened. She couldn't help smiling in return. "More than a few."

His grin faded and he looked away. "Have you found a place to live?"

"We are still looking. Have you made a decision about Clara returning to school?"

"I have. I want her to attend."

Sophie smiled with relief. "I'm so glad."

"I can't guarantee you that she'll learn anything. She won't be happy about my decision."

"You get her in the building. I will find a way to keep her here."

"You sound confident." He finally cracked a real smile. It was small and brief, but Sophie felt like she'd won a prize.

"It's my don't-mess-with-the-teacher tone. I practice it for thirty minutes every night."

"I almost believe that."

"There is something you may be able to help me with." Was it foolish to think he would be interested in her Christmas program dilemma? Maybe not. His daughters would be involved.

He frowned slightly. "I'm listening."

No, this was something she needed to solve on her own. She shook her head. "Never mind."

"Let me guess. Is a reluctance to ask for help another one of your faults?"

It was her turn to smile. "I am working to overcome it."

"What's troubling you?"

His caring tone caught her off guard and smothered her reluctance. "I'm struggling to plan a Christmas program for this year. I don't know the students. I don't know the community's likes and dislikes. Any insight you have will be deeply appreciated."

Sophie bit her lower lip. Why had she confided in him? He couldn't possibly understand what an awkward position she found herself in.

Instead of dismissing her concern, he rubbed his beard between his thumb and his forefinger for a few moments. "Our former teacher was fond of elaborate pageants. You won't have much time to help the *kinder* prepare something."

Maybe he could understand. The thought lifted her spirits. "That is my dilemma. I don't know the children or what they can do."

"Phillip Kauffman has the best singing voice. He's one of your seventh-grade students. Lydia Stoltzfus wrote a Christmas play two years ago that folks enjoyed. She'll know the aptitudes of your students."

Sophie was surprised by his insight. "That's very helpful. Thank you for coming here today. I hope this means that we can be cordial to one another in the future."

Suddenly, his expression hardened. She felt his withdrawal and it hurt.

"Sure. Look, I need to get back. Rose insisted I leave her in charge of the store, but I'm sure it was a bad idea."

His mouth snapped shut and his eyes darted away from hers as if he regretted his words.

Something was very odd. "Rose works for you?"

He cleared his throat. "She doesn't."

"But she is today?"

"She stopped in and offered to watch the store while I came here."

It occurred to Sophie what he was trying not to say. "Wait. Rose made you come see me, didn't she?" Why was that thought so painful?

He looked into her eyes with an unwavering gaze. "Rose did suggest I come, but I'm here because it is the right thing to do. I was rude to you. That never should have happened."

Slightly mollified, Sophie accepted his explanation. "I appreciate that, but Rose shouldn't have interfered," Sophie said primly.

He shook his head. "Try telling that to Rose. She's a law unto herself."

He walked to the door but stopped with his hand on the knob and looked back. "If you are still interested in the house I have for rent, you can stop by any evening. I close the shop at five. I'm usually home by five thirty."

He left, and Sophie plopped onto the nearest chair.

So Karl was willing to see more of her. Her spirits rose despite her attempt to keep them in check. The seesaw of emotions she experienced when he was near was exhausting.

There was no way she was going to rent his house. Living next door to a man she found as attractive as Karl was not a good idea. It would only serve as a painful reminder that she didn't have a future that included love and a family.

Six

Karl walked away from the school as rapidly as he could. What had possessed him to tell Sophie she could still rent his place? She disturbed his peace of mind. He didn't need her living next door.

At least she hadn't jumped at the chance. Maybe she wouldn't take him up on his offer. Should he tell her he had changed his mind? What excuse could he give for that?

When would he see her again if she didn't come to look at the place?

He stopped walking and shook his head to clear it. That was the point. He didn't want to see her again. She turned him inside out with her chin-up determination and her cute lopsided grin. He wasn't trying to forget Nora. He couldn't imagine that was possible, but Sophie had a way of making him put aside his sorrow for little while.

That felt like he was being unfaithful to Nora.

He didn't hear the buggy coming up behind him until it stopped beside him. Joseph Troyer grinned at him from the driver's seat. "Just the man I was coming to see. Is the hardware store open today?"

"It is. I'm on my way back now."

"Would you care for a lift since we're going in the same direction?"

Karl nodded. If he was conversing with Joseph, he wouldn't be thinking about Sophie.

"I met the Eicher sisters at Rose's place yesterday," Joseph said, spoiling Karl's chance to forget about the new teacher. "Abby and I were making the rounds with Henry. A lot of folks want to see him. I can't blame them. He's cute as a button."

"I take it he and Abby are doing well?"

"Right as rain, both of them. It's a little frightening how happy we are. I never thought I would have a family again after losing mine. *Gott* certainly works in mysterious ways. Well, *Gott* and Rose Yoder. I must give her some credit. She told me I was an answer to Abby's prayers the day we met." He chuckled softly. "Abby didn't agree."

Like everyone in their small town, Karl knew Abby's and Joseph's stories. Pregnant and destitute, Abby had come to Harts Haven pretending to be Amish to hide from her criminal father and her abusive boyfriend. Summers spent with her Amish grandparents had given her an understanding of the language and customs. She nearly succeeded, but her powerful father discovered her whereabouts. With the help of Joseph, the widows, Herbert Young and Bertha Rock, Abby was able to escape and claim the farm her grandparents left her. She and Joseph were married a month ago.

"I reckon Rose has to be right once in a while," Karl admitted. "I wish she would quit trying to find someone for me."

"Has she told you she matched you with a new teacher?" Joseph asked with a grin. "Rose is blunt if nothing else."

"Surprisingly, she told me I was all wrong for Sophie. She has that right."

Joseph looked puzzled. "I've met her. She seems nice enough. A little reserved, but she took to Henry so she's all right in my book. Why would Rose think you're wrong for each other?"

"Because we are."

Joseph mulled that over for a second. "I wonder who she has picked out for Sophie then?"

"She mentioned she had a list."

Joseph laughed. "Of course she does. Charlie Schrock maybe."

Karl dismissed the idea. "He's too old for Sophie."

"Eli Hostetter or his brother Jeff maybe?"

"Jeff is too young, and Eli is too set in his ways."

"You seem to know her pretty well. Who do you think Rose has in mind for her?"

Karl reviewed the single men in the community and couldn't come up with one he thought Sophie belonged with. There was nothing wrong with any of them; he just couldn't see Sophie holding hands or kissing any of them. The idea of her with anyone made him oddly uncomfortable.

Fortunately, Joseph pulled up in front of the hardware store just then. Karl got out. "I'll leave the matchmaking to Granny Rose. What did you need?"

"Weather stripping for around the doors and windows. Winter is on its way, and I promised Abby I'd have it done before Thanksgiving."

"I've got some. Come on in." Karl entered the store. Two customers were waiting beside the empty counter. He looked around for Rose. She was seated on a crate near the window with Rachel on her lap. They had their heads together whispering about something.

He turned to his customers. "Sorry for the wait." He quickly rang up their purchases. Rose noticed his return and came over.

"Well, I must be off. Rachel and I had a lovely visit. She is growing up so quickly."

"Where is Clara?"

"I had her run an errand for me since I needed to stay here. She should be back any minute."

The door opened and Clara came in. She handed Rose a small paper sack. "This is the only kind of cinnamon they had."

"*Danki*, Clara. Karl, how did your task go?"

"Fine."

Rose smiled. "*Goot*. Rachel, remember what we talked about."

"I will. *Danki*, Granny Rose."

"I will see you all at church if not before. Goodbye."

When she went out the door, Karl turned to Rachel. "What did you and Rose talk about?"

"Woman stuff." Rachel propped her hands on her hips and frowned at him. "There's a lot to know about growing up and you haven't told me any of it. How am I going to learn everything I need to know without a mother?"

Karl opened his mouth and closed it again. He didn't have a clue how to answer her.

"Rose, I would like a word with you. In private." Sophie nodded toward the patio door. She wasn't eager for this conversation, but the elderly woman needed to be set straight. Rose had to stop interfering. Sophie suspected she knew the reason behind Rose's behavior. Whatever plans Rose had hatched for matchmaking had to end now.

Seated at one of the tables with Bertha and Grace, Rose looked surprised by Sophie's request, but she got up and followed Sophie out into the garden.

"What can I help you with?"

Sophie drew a deep breath. "Karl mentioned that you went to see him today."

Rose looked around. "Well, I went to the hardware store. He was there."

"Did you go with the intention of sending him to apologize to me?"

"I went with the intention of buying more clothespins."

Sophie had seen numerous children attempting to look just as innocent when she questioned them about their naughty behavior or missing homework. She immediately recognized the signs in Rose's wide eyes and bland expression.

"I would rather you didn't interfere, Rose. Karl and I are both adults. Any differences we may have should be resolved between the two of us."

"And did you resolve your differences?" Rose asked hopefully.

"Did you get your clothespins?"

Rose laughed. "You are quite surprising, Sophie. People rarely see through me. You're a sharp woman."

Sophie wasn't mollified by Rose's flattery. "I hope you aren't matchmaking. Karl warned me that you would be introducing me to the local single men on your list. Please discard that list, Rose. I'm not interested in marrying Karl or anyone else." She was attracted to the man but that didn't change her situation.

"Oh, Karl is totally wrong for you," Rose said quickly.

Sophie frowned. "Why do you say that?"

Rose tipped her head slightly. "Isn't he? Was I mistaken?"

Sophie held up her hand to stop Rose's probing. "I can manage my own life, Rose. I'm sure Karl feels the same."

"We all need a little help sometimes. Karl certainly does. He's been struggling since his wife's passing. It breaks my heart to see his unhappiness. Those little girls need a woman's influence. You may not want to marry, but does Joanna feel the same? Because Karl is wrong for you doesn't mean he isn't right for someone else."

"Karl and Joanna?" Sophie chewed her bottom lip. The idea didn't sit well, but it wasn't outrageous. Hadn't she thought the same thing? Sophie clasped her arms over her chest as she contemplated the idea. Only God knew how long she had left. She wanted to see Joanna happily settled before then.

Rose peered over her glasses at Sophie. "Your sister would never consider someone you didn't get along with."

Rose was right about that. "*Nee*, she wouldn't."

"It may be that they aren't meant for one another, but I didn't want a stumbling block in their way before they had known each other a week. That's why I suggested Karl apologize to you. I'm glad he did. I knew he would even if I hadn't said anything—it just may have taken him a few days. He's a fine man. I hope that you and he can be friends, for your sister's sake."

"You think they would make a good match?"

"Don't tell me you can't see them together. Karl is an attractive man with an established business. He owns a farm and a rental house. His girls are precious, and he's a devout member of our faith."

It was all true. Perhaps Joanna's cheerful nature could ease the sadness Sophie sensed in him. She could put aside her attraction to Karl if he was the one her sister wanted. Joanna was the one who had a future, not Sophie.

"Unless there is some reason you think Joanna and Karl wouldn't suit," Rose said, watching Sophie intently.

Sophie straightened. "None that I'm aware of, but I want her to marry for love."

"As do I. Love is one of *Gott*'s greatest blessings to his children. I simply help people discover that." Rose turned around and walked back into the inn.

Joanna came out the door as Rose went in. She looked from Rose back to Sophie. "What were you and Rose discussing that was so serious?"

Sophie pushed her feelings for Karl to the back of her mind. She liked him a lot, but a relationship was out of the question even if he was interested in her. Which she was sure he wasn't. Joanna deserved to be happy.

Pasting a smile on her face, Sophie said, "I told Rose I didn't appreciate her attempt at peacemaking between Karl and myself."

"I don't understand."

"Rose went to the hardware store and sent Karl out to the school to apologize to me."

Joanna mouth dropped open. "No one should have had to send him."

Sophie realized her mistake at once. She needed to present Karl in a good light if her sister was to view him as a romantic possibility.

"You misunderstand. He didn't apologize because of Rose. Karl had already intended to speak to me. Rose simply gave him an opportunity to leave the store and do it sooner. He came to see me because he knew it was the right thing to do. He apologized and very nicely, too" She smiled at the memory of him writing on her chalkboard like one of her errant scholars.

"I'm happy to hear he can admit when he's wrong." Joanna didn't sound impressed.

"It certainly shows strength of character and that's important."

Joanna gave Sophie a discerning look. "I agree. I'm glad to hear you speaking more highly of him."

Sophie smiled. Now she was on the right track. She would have to praise him more often. "He's still willing to rent his house to us. What you think? It's close to the school."

"I reckon there's no harm in going to look at it. It might not be to our liking even if the location is *goot*."

Sophie nodded. "My thoughts exactly. You won't mind living near him, will you?" She watched Joanna's face carefully.

Joanna shrugged with indifference. "I doubt we'll see him much if we do rent the place. He spends all day at the hardware store. Grace wanted me to tell you supper is ready. Come on. I'm starved."

It wasn't exactly the reaction she expected if Joanna was interested in getting to know Karl better, but at least her sister didn't object outright to being his neighbor. It was a start.

The next day was overcast. A chill wind out of the north brought with it a cold promise of the winter to come. Sophie pulled her coat tight under her chin as she left the inn to walk to school. Joanna had decided to help Grace with the baking this morning. She would meet Sophie at the school at five thirty that evening. They would go to see Karl's rental house together.

Eager to gauge her sister's reaction to Karl, Sophie hoped the house was what they wanted and needed. If Joanna was interested in Karl, it would be an ideal situation for them to get to know each other better.

When she arrived at the school, she found the building unlocked and the coal-burning potbellied stove glowing brightly. The inside of the one-room school was almost toasty. She wondered which of the school board members had been kind enough to start the fire for her. It wasn't until she glanced at the blackboard that she realized she had Karl to thank. She recognized his handwriting in the note scrawled across the board telling her to order more coal.

She smiled as she erased his message. He had taken time out of his morning to make sure she would be comfortable today. Was he still trying to make up for his outburst, or was this a normal part of his routine since he lived near the school? It was nice to think he cared for the people in his community, but a small part of her wanted to believe he had gone out of his way for her.

She had been tempted to ask Grace about him last night after supper but decided against it. She didn't want to fuel unwanted speculation about the two of them.

She slipped off her coat, stuffed her gloves in the pockets and went to hang up her things. They wouldn't be needed inside thanks to Karl's thoughtfulness. Mentioning it to her sister would be sure to raise Joanna's estimation of him.

In the coatroom she found a cardboard box filled with assorted books. Unsure if they were something to be given away or to be kept, she left them alone until she had a chance to ask the school board about them. A meeting with the board had been planned for the end of the week so they could review and approve her lesson plans. Once that was done, school could start on Monday. The bishop would announce the opening at the church service on Sunday.

Drawing up lesson plans and making sure she had the correct number of workbooks and textbooks for her students took up most of the morning. She stoked the fire a little after twelve o'clock and put her thermos of soup on the stove to heat. A niggling sense of excitement was building in her midsection. She tried to convince herself it was only because she would be glad to find a place to live, but she couldn't avoid the truth. She was looking forward to seeing Karl again.

Knowing that only work would make the hours pass quickly, she wrote out the last of the lower grades lesson plans. After that, she made sure the pump outside worked. It did and she was able to wipe down the student desks, the library shelves and mop the floor.

By five o'clock she was worn-out. Her energy levels hadn't yet recovered following her cancer treatment. She was better, but she had to pace herself when fatigue pulled her down. She didn't want a scolding from Joanna about doing too much.

Karl wouldn't be available to show her his rental until after five thirty. She banked the fire and put on her coat before stepping outside. She was surprised to see Karl sitting on the bottom step of the school.

"I thought you wouldn't be home until five thirty?"

He shrugged. "It was a slow day. I closed a few minutes early."

She looked around for his daughters. "Where are the girls?"

"I sent them home with orders to pick up the house. My previous renter didn't leave it in the best shape. Is your sister coming?"

Was he eager to see Joanna again? Sophie couldn't tell by his expression or tone. "I told her to meet me at five thirty, so we have a few minutes before she gets here."

Sophie sat on the top step making sure she wasn't close enough to accidentally touch him. Even without physical contact she was acutely aware of him. He was a big man with broad shoulders. She felt tiny beside him. The sun was low in the sky but still bright enough to give off welcome heat. She closed her eyes and tipped her head back slightly to enjoy the warmth on her face. "This feels wonderful."

"My wife enjoyed basking in the sunshine, too," he said softly.

Sophie heard the sorrow in his voice overlaid with fondness. That he chose to share his memory touched her deeply. "My sister has accused me of being part cat. I can find a pool of sunlight streaming through a window and just stay there until it gets too hot to bear. When I was in the hospital, she made the staff move my bed in front of the window." Sophie snapped her mouth shut wishing she hadn't told him that.

"You were sick?"

"Minor surgery." She tried to make it sound insignificant instead of the heartbreaking ordeal that it had been.

Thankfully, he didn't ask what kind of surgery. She wasn't prepared to lie but she didn't want anyone here to know about her illness. She would have to be more careful. Karl was an easy man to talk to. "I wanted to thank you for lighting the stove this morning. It made my day much more pleasant. Who should I talk to about getting coal?"

"I took care of it."

She smiled at him. "Karl, you don't have to keep going out of your way to make things easier for me."

He rubbed his palms on his pant legs. "I didn't. Dwight McDonald happened to come in the store today. He runs the Prairie Farm and Ranch supply store and handles local coal deliveries. He'll bring it next week and bill the school board."

It had been silly to think he'd done it for her. She quickly squelched her feeling of disappointment. After all, he couldn't deny he'd had her comfort in mind when he fired up the stove that morning. "*Danki*. I did appreciate finding a warm school this morning."

"You're welcome. Are you almost ready for students?"

"I'm making headway. I've reviewed all the student records and finished the lesson plans for grades one through six. I should be able to finish the rest tomorrow. I need to do an inventory of the books in the library so I know what extra reading I can assign. I noticed a large box of books in the cloakroom. Any idea why the previous teacher boxed them up?"

"I remember Clara saying someone stopped by with a donation the first week of school. I think it was from some church group in Wichita. Maybe those are the books, and Becky didn't finish going through them before she had to leave."

"That makes sense. I'll divide them up and have the school board and some of the parents read them to make sure they are suitable. Would you like to take some?"

"I don't have much free time for reading. Not enough hours in the day."

It must be hard being both mother and father as well as a farmer and a businessman. "That's okay. I'm sure Joanna can help. She hasn't found a job yet. Frankly, I don't think she's looking. She's enjoys being able to do as she likes."

Sophie realized she had made her sister sound frivolous and sought to cover her mistake.

"What I mean is she wants to be free to help me if I need it until school starts. She's thoughtful that way. I appreciate her consideration. She's a very caring person."

"You two are close?"

Sophie nodded and gazed into the distance remembering the way Joanna had supported her when she was diagnosed with cancer. Their mother had lived three years after her diagnosis. It would soon be a year since Sophie received the devastating news. If two more years was all she had, she would spend it making sure Joanna knew she was loved and appreciated.

"We have always been close. Joanna is my rock. I don't know how I would have managed without her."

She glanced at Karl and found him gazing at her intently. She felt a blush heating her neck and cheeks. "You're staring again."

Karl looked down. "Sorry. I was lost in thought."

Sophie had an expressive face and a ready smile, but there was something sad about her. Karl couldn't put his finger on what it was, but he knew sorrow when he saw it. He was drawn to her, wanted to understand her. Should he ask what was troubling her? It wasn't any of his business, but his curiosity was hard to contain.

"Sorry I'm late," Joanna said as she rushed toward them slightly out of breath after her trek from the inn.

"*Goot*, you're here." Sophie scrambled to her feet, cast him a sidelong glance and folded her arms across her chest.

Karl stood up. "Let me show you the house. It's pretty basic."

Joanna grinned. "Sophie likes basic."

Perhaps he could discover more about Sophie from her outgoing younger sister.

Joanna gave him a stern look. "If your house doesn't have a decent bathroom, there's no point in showing it to me."

"My *daed* had all modern plumbing fixtures installed when he built it for his mother. *Grossmammi* had arthritis and had trouble getting around. Our church allows indoor plumbing and propane heat. You won't run out of hot water."

"I'm sure it will be fine." Sophie gave her sister a pointed look.

He didn't miss the way she moved away from him and took Joanna's arm so that her sister was sandwiched between them. Had he somehow offended her again? They walked together down his lane. Joanna chatted happily about her day. Sophie didn't say anything.

His *daadi haus* was a single-story white clapboard structure with a smaller front porch attached to the side of the main house. Otherwise, they were completely separated homes.

"This is nice," Sophie said. "Don't you think so, Joanna?"

"Very nice."

"Do these furnishings stay?" Sophie asked.

He nodded. "If you'd like."

She glanced around. "It would be a wonderful spot to relax in the shade during the summer months or enjoy coffee in the mornings."

Karl smiled. "My *grossmammi* loved to have her coffee out here. She always had fresh-baked streusel cake, too. I'd grab a slice on my way to school."

"Joanna makes wonderful streusel cake," Sophie said brightly.

"When I don't burn it," Joanna added with a laugh.

The door opened and his daughters came out. Rachel grinned. "Hallo, teacher Sophie. I hope you like our house and want to live here, but please don't use *Daed*'s hammer again."

Karl closed his eyes, took a deep breath and didn't say anything.

"I won't. I promise," Sophie said.

He suspected her kind tone was meant for him more than Rachel. He didn't dare look at her.

"I'm going to start supper." Clara walked away without greeting or acknowledging the two women.

"It was nice to see you again," Joanna called out. Clara kept walking.

Embarrassed by his daughter's rudeness, Karl opened the front door of the *daadi haus*. "Come in."

"How are your lambs?" Joanna asked Rachel.

"They haven't gotten out once since teacher Sophie fixed their fence."

Joanna chuckled. "My sister is good at fixing thing. She likes order and neatness."

"Do you want to see them?" Rachel asked hopefully.

"Of course I do." Joanna held out her hand, and Rachel took it.

"Don't you think we should see the house first?" Sophie asked. "It's going to be dark soon."

"You check it out. If it meets your approval, then it's fine with me." Joanna walked away with Rachel skipping along at her side.

"Joanna is *goot* with children," Sophie said in a rush. "She'll make a wonderful mother someday." She clasped her hands together and looked at the floor as a dull flush crept up her cheeks.

"I'm sure she will if that is *Gott*'s plan for her. Come in."

The outside door opened into a small mudroom. A second door led directly into the kitchen. Inside Karl realized the twilight didn't give enough light to see the place by. "I'll light a lamp if I can find one."

"There's one right here."

She lifted a kerosene lamp up off the counter and held it toward him. His fingers brushed hers as he took it. The darkness lent an intimate feeling to the quiet house as he stood next to a woman who inexplicably made his heart beat faster. He swallowed against the sudden tightness in his throat.

The wide plank floors creaked as Sophie stepped away from Karl. She rubbed her hands together to erase the tingle his touch caused but there was nothing she could do about her pounding pulse.

He set the lamp on the table, lifted the glass chimney and

lit the wick. His hand wasn't quite steady. A warm glow filled the room, but the light didn't decrease her awareness of him. She concentrated on the house and avoided looking at him.

Through the kitchen she could see a sitting room. Two large windows let in enough light to show her several chairs and a small camelback sofa. She walked over to examine them more closely. The furniture was plain and sturdy although it showed some signs of wear on the arms and needed a good cleaning.

"You don't have to keep these things if you don't want. I can store any of this in the barn. There are two bedrooms and a bath down the hall." He led the way.

She took a deep breath and followed. The bath had modern fixtures and a generous-sized bathtub. At the end of the hall Karl opened the door to a sparsely furnished bedroom. A narrow bed, covered with a blue striped mattress, stood against a bare wall along with a small dresser.

"The other bedroom is bigger," he said.

He turned to face her. She became acutely aware of him, of his size and the intense look in his eyes. The lamplight highlighted the hard planes of his face. The tension in the narrow hall thickened making it hard to breathe normally. His gaze roved over her face. Her pulse quickened and her palms grew sweaty.

It would be a mistake to rent his home if she couldn't control her reaction to his nearness any better than this. "I don't think this is for us."

"There you are," Joanna announced in a cheerful voice as she joined them with Rachel at her side.

Joanna's dress was dirty at the knees, there was straw clinging to her apron, her *kapp* was crooked and she held two fluffy yellow kittens in her hands. "Look at the cats I found in the barn. Aren't they adorable? Rachel's lambs are so friendly and cute. It's this a *wunderbar* place? We'll take it, Karl. Oh, and I bought the puppy from Clara. We have a dog."

Sophie clenched her hands together tightly. She would regret her decision, but how could she spoil Joanna's happiness? She couldn't.

"*Ja*, we'll take it."

Joanna handed the kittens to Rachel. "Where is the phone booth located? I want to call *Daed* and have our things shipped right away."

Seven

On Friday Sophie spent three hours with the school board and Bishop Wyse going over her lesson plans, her grading system and her discipline strategy. After what seemed like endless questions, the bishop announced that he was satisfied. The community would be informed at the service on Sunday that school would resume Monday. She was truly going to start teaching again. It was hard to contain her joy.

Saturday dawned chilly but clear. By midafternoon the temperature had warmed up enough to make it pleasant outside. With some of the windows open in the *daadi haus*, she got busy cleaning in preparation for the arrival of their belongings that day.

"Where are you?" Joanna's voice reverberated through the empty house above Sophie. "The moving van is here."

The truck was right on time. Bless her father for finding a reliable driver. Now the work of getting settled could start.

Sophie came out of the cellar and closed the door to the stairs. "I was checking the basement. Something we should have done before you agreed to rent this house."

"It will take more than a damp cellar to make me move away. How is it?"

"Dry. There's some trash that needs to be hauled out, but I see plenty of shelves for storing garden produce next summer. There's a good garden plot out back if Karl will let us use a portion of it. It needs weeding and clearing."

"You're looking ahead again, sister. I like that. See, this place is good for you. And you tried to talk me out of renting it even after I told Karl we wanted it."

She had tried to dissuade Joanna, but having no real objection other than her disturbing attraction to Karl, which she didn't share with her sister, Sophie gave in.

"This is so exciting. It feels wonderful to finally have a place of our own." Joanna enveloped Sophie in one of her bear hugs.

It was a fine place as long as Joanna was happy, and the owner wasn't around to disturb Sophie's peace of mind.

Joanna spun around with her hands clasped over her heart. "Now, we have to decide where the furniture is going to go."

"I suggest the beds go in the bedroom. The table and chairs should be in the kitchen. Unless you want them in your bedroom."

"You are not as funny as you think you are, sister, but I forgive you."

The front door opened. Karl came in carrying a large box followed by Rachel holding a smaller one. "Where do you want these?" he asked.

Sophie stared at him in shock. So much for her peace of mind. "What are you doing here?"

"Lance Switzer came by the store after he closed the post office. He said Grace mentioned your moving van would be here today and she asked if he could give you a hand unloading. He couldn't because of his back, but he came over and offered to watch the shop if I was able to help. So here I am."

"We would have managed." That sounded ungrateful. Sophie bit down on her lip and then offered a smile. "But *danki*."

He nodded once. "Where should I put this?"

Joanna rushed forward with a bright smile. "Just put them anywhere."

Her sister was happy, and that was what mattered. Once school started, Sophie would rarely have to see Karl. It was a small consolation at the moment.

She stepped over to read the writing on the side of the box he held. "Pots, pans and utensils. I'll take it to the kitchen. All the boxes are marked. If they aren't, they belong in Joanna's room."

Joanna rolled her eyes. "As you can see, my sister likes to be organized."

"Organization makes things easier," Sophie said primly as she grasped the box to take it from Karl.

Joanna waved one hand in the air. "She forgets there are things in life we can't control."

Things like having cancer and being dumped by a fiancé when she needed him most?

Sophie gripped the box hard enough to turn her fingers white. "*Nee*, I don't."

Joanna was instantly contrite. "Oh, sister, I'm sorry. I didn't mean that."

Sophie looked at Karl and saw his puzzled expression. She managed to smile and turned to Joanna. "Don't worry. I'm used to your teasing."

Joanna glanced at Karl and composed her stricken expression. "She should be because she knows I'm the one who would forget her head if it wasn't attached."

He nodded but his expression didn't change. "I'll start bringing in the rest."

As soon as he was out the door, Joanna threw her arms around Sophie. "I'm sorry. That was thoughtless of me."

Sophie endured another hug. "No harm done. Let me put this box down. It's heavy."

"Can I help you open the boxes?" Rachel asked.

Joanna released Sophie and sat down on the floor beside the child. "Of course you can. This one isn't marked. I wonder what's in it. Oh, what fun. Open it, Rachel. Hurry."

The child eagerly ripped away the packing tape. She looked disappointed as she stared at the assortment of cooking spices. "Did you pack any toys?"

"I packed our games and puzzles, but I don't remember which box I put them in," Joanna said. "We'll just have to look in every one."

Clara came in with two boxes stacked on each other. Her cool expression displayed her displeasure at the chore. "Where?"

Sophie looked them over. No writing. "They're Joanna's."

"Oh, goody." Rachel jumped up to take them from her sister. She then sat on the floor and began opening the first one.

"Joanna, we have a lot more boxes waiting outside," Sophie suggested, hoping her sister would take the hint to go out and help.

"In a minute." She leaned in to help Rachel rip away the packing tape. Sometimes Joanna seemed like a child herself.

"Rachel, come help me," Clara said.

"In a minute. Oh, here are the games!"

Clara heaved an exasperated sigh. Sophie knew exactly how she felt.

Sophie walked to the door, where she paused and looked

back. She exchanged a long-suffering glance with Clara. "Little sisters can be such a pain."

Clara's wary expression softened. She rolled her eyes and nodded. "That is for sure and certain."

Sophie smiled as they headed out the door. She and Clara each accepted a box from the men before Karl and the van driver emerged carrying a large box between them. Sophie read the writing. "My bedroom."

"Which one is that?" Karl asked.

"The one with the east window."

The two men juggled the box to get a better hold. Sophie added two more boxes to the top of hers and hurried to open the door for them. Clara grabbed another box, too.

Karl scowled at Sophie's loaded arms. "Aren't Joanna and Rachel meant to be helping?"

"In a minute," Sophie and Clara said at the same time. They glanced at each other and grinned.

It was the first break in Clara's cool manner toward her. Sophie couldn't have been more delighted.

Clara's smile was the first one Karl had seen from her in ages. It transformed her grim little face into that of a child once more. A child who should have more to smile about. Regret stabbed his heart. Had his grief kept his daughter from recovering her happiness? Had he been too wrapped up in his own sorrow to console his children? What kind of father did that make him?

He drew a deep breath. One who could do better.

Karl helped the van driver maneuver the box through the door. Joanna and Rachel were on the living room floor unpacking games they had spread all around themselves. He and the driver put the box in the smaller of the two bedrooms and came out.

"Rachel," he said softly.

She looked up and her smile faded. "Yes, *Daed*."

"Let's let the games wait until after supper. Maybe Clara or Joanna will play with you tonight."

Joanna grinned at him. "That would be great fun. Let's pick these up, Rachel, and we'll decide which one to play later. What do you need me to do now, sister?"

Sophie set her three boxes on the kitchen counter. "I think we should get all the boxes out of the van so our driver can head home. He has had a long trip."

"Thanks, ma'am. I would like to get on the road again."

Sophie smiled at him. "But you will stay for supper first, won't you? I'm sorry. I don't know your name."

"It's Chester Grover. I don't want to put you out seeing as how you haven't even unpacked."

"I suspected this might be the case, Chester, so I asked my aunt Grace to prepare supper for us. She should be here soon and there will be plenty for everyone."

Rachel rubbed her tummy. "Yum. Your aunt Grace is the best cook in Harts Haven. Do you think she'll bring us cinnamon rolls?"

"I'm sure of it. I specifically requested some. There are still boxes waiting to be unloaded." Sophie held the door open to let the girls go out in front of her.

"And your minute is up." Clara nudged Rachel and exchanged another grin with Sophie as they all went out.

"I told you she likes to be organized," Joanna said as she walked past Karl. "What to do for supper never crossed my mind."

It hadn't crossed his either. Sophie wasn't just organized. She was kind to include Chester, a man she'd just met, and Karl's family in her plans for the evening meal. There was a lot to like about Sophie Eicher.

Nora had been the same way, always including others, making them feel welcome. She'd had a warmth about her that people noticed right away. Something in her smile. Nora had smiled more than Sophie did. He wondered again about the sadness that seemed to surround her.

"I reckon we can't let the women do all the work," Chester said.

Karl arched one eyebrow. "Are you sure we can't?"

Chester laughed. "Something tells me Miss Sophie could manage."

"I think you're right, but we'd better help just the same." Outside, they found Sophie directing the unloading.

"Clara, why don't you take this one? It has my grandmother's pie plates and her serving dishes. They mean a lot to me." She glanced at Karl. "I don't want to trust them to the men. Just put it on the kitchen counter."

"I'll be careful with them." Clara walked away with cautious steps.

"Rachel, this one has mittens and winter scarves. It should go in Joanna's room."

His daughter left with her burdens, and she smiled at Karl. "These five go in the living room." She picked up one and headed down the truck ramp.

Karl picked up the next ones. It was heavy. Chester grunted when he lifted his box. "I wish she had given me the one with mittens in it."

It took several dozen more trips but eventually the truck was emptied while every room in the rental house now had stacks of boxes waiting to be unpacked. Karl and Chester carried in the kitchen table last while Joanna and the girls each brought in a chair.

Sophie carried in two and placed them at the table. "That is the end of it. Clara and Rachel, I don't think we could have done this without you. You both worked very hard and I'm grateful." She smiled at his girls, who beamed at her praise.

Rachel flexed her arm to show her muscle. "I'm stronger than I look."

"But still annoying," Clara said, good-naturedly nudging her sister with her elbow.

"You both did well," Karl said, earning a shy smile from Clara.

"Reckon I'll get the truck closed up." Chester went back outside.

Joanna sat down in the chair she had carried in, leaned back and hung her arms limply to the sides "I am *soo* glad that's done."

"Only half done I'm afraid." Sophie stood massaging her left arm. Her face was pale. She looked worn-out.

Karl had noticed her favoring her arm earlier. "Did you hurt yourself?"

She straightened with a startled look. "*Nee*, I'm fine."

Joanna jumped to her feet. "I hope you didn't overdo it. You should rest."

Sophie turned away to look out the window. "Don't be silly. I haven't worked any harder than anyone else. I see that Grace has arrived. I'll help her bring supper in."

"I can do it," Joanna said. "Sit down for a minute."

If it was possible, Sophie's back grew even straighter. "I said I'm fine."

"I know that. Girls, let's go see what Aunt Grace has brought for us." Joanna went out with his daughters. Sophie's ramrod straight posture relaxed slightly.

"I hope you don't mind if I sit." Karl watched her closely. There was nothing wrong with admitting that she was tired. Why was she trying so hard not to show it?

She looked over her shoulder at him. "Of course I don't mind."

Pulling out a chair, he took a seat and waved a hand toward another. "You may as well sit until they bring in the meal. I don't mind admitting I'm bushed. It's been a long day. Did you pack rocks from home? Some of those boxes weighed a ton."

She turned around. "Books, not rocks, and only the ones I dearly cherish."

He glanced at the boxes spread across the living room floor. "Did you leave any in Ohio?"

"Twice as many as I brought with me, I'm sorry to say."

"You must like to read."

She tilted her head. "I do. Don't you?"

He thought about it for a moment then nodded. "Yeah, I do though I haven't done much lately."

The last time he'd opened a book had been to read to Nora during her illness. He thought the joy he'd once known in discovering a good story had perished with his wife, but he realized a flicker of that enjoyment remained. Maybe it could be rekindled.

"You may borrow any of my books and so may your daughters."

"Danki."

"I should be thanking you for your help today. You made this so much easier than it would have been." Sitting down she grimaced as she moved her arms to rest them on the table.

He frowned. "You did hurt yourself."

"It's nothing. A pulled muscle." She didn't meet his gaze.

"You should stop trying to do it all by yourself."

"I wasn't trying to do it all. You helped. Joanna helped. Even your daughters and Chester helped."

"I saw how you worked. You made twice as many trips as

your sister, and you lifted boxes that you should have left for us men."

Her chin came up. She looked ready to argue but then seemed to think better of it. "Perhaps I did work too hard."

"Perhaps?" He arched one eyebrow.

She tipped her head in acknowledgment "Okay, I did. You can stop scolding me now. You're as bad as Joanna."

"Me? Scold the teacher? Not when she has an empty blackboard just down the lane waiting for my written apology."

She chuckled. "I have a small one in a box here somewhere. You won't have to walk all the way to the school."

"Do you have chalk and an eraser for me to clean, too?" It pleased him that the memory made her smile. He liked the twinkle in her blue eyes when she was amused.

She inclined her head slightly. "In fact, I do. However, I will give you a pass on your punishment until after I unpack."

He laughed. "It isn't fair to punish me for telling the truth."

"True, but don't expect a gold star for good behavior by your name this week."

"I don't think I ever got one when I was in school."

"Your poor teacher."

"I was a trial. The work is done, so take a well-earned rest. Finish unboxing after supper."

A wry smile lifted one corner of her mouth. "I haven't unpacked the plates. We won't have anything to eat on. I know they are in one of the boxes in the kitchen."

"Not to worry," Rose said from the doorway. "Grace and I thought of that and brought paper plates. Hello, Sophie. Good evening, Karl. What are you doing sitting in the dark?"

He'd barely noticed the fading light. It had been pleasant to sit and talk with Sophie. Something about her soothed him. The realization unsettled him.

"Karl, Joanna tells me you and the girls have been a great help today."

"I didn't do anything special. Helping a neighbor is expected," he said.

"Indeed it is." Rose grinned. "I'm sure Sophie will be able to return the favor before long. Joanna and Clara decided it was best that we eat in your kitchen, Karl. I hope that's okay."

He didn't like people in his house. Rose didn't give him a chance to object.

"I knew you wouldn't mind. Sophie, I spoke to Eli Hostetter this morning. He and his brother Jeff will pass by here on their way to church tomorrow since it will be at the home of Levi and Barbara Martin. They will take you and Joanna to church."

"I don't wish to put anyone out." Sophie's eyes narrowed as she gazed at Rose. Karl shared her suspicion of Rose's motive.

Rose waved one hand. "It's no trouble for them, I'm sure. Jeff and Eli are both single fellows. Eli has a solar panel business. He and his *Englisch* partner sells all over the state. He makes a good living. He's hardworking and an upstanding member of the church."

Karl clenched his jaw. Was Eli the one Rose had picked out for Sophie? Karl couldn't see it. Eli was too set in his ways to make a good husband for Sophie. The man didn't even like to read. Jeff was younger but wasn't he going out with a girl from Castleton? Karl decided it would give him a little satisfaction to disrupt Rose's plan. "Sophie and Joanna can ride with us. It only makes sense."

A tiny frown creased Rose's brow. "I did think of you first, but I know you don't stay and visit after the service anymore. I'm sure Sophie wants to get to know the community members, especially the ones with *kinder* who will be her students."

"We'll be staying after this Sunday," he said. "The girls

have been missing their friends. There's no need to have Eli stop by."

"Joanna and I can walk," Sophie said. "I don't want to put anyone out."

"You aren't. We're going to the same place," he stated firmly.

Rose shrugged. "If you're sure, Karl. I guess that will be fine. I don't know how I will let Eli know."

Karl smiled. "I'll have the moving van driver deliver the message on his way out of town."

"Very well. I'll go finish helping Grace. Come over when you're ready."

"Don't you think you should have asked me to use my kitchen first?"

"*Nee.*" Rose turned around quickly. He glimpsed a smile on her face before she went out the door.

Was he willing to share his home again? Every inch of it reminded him of his life with Nora. He could hardly throw everyone out, and Rose knew it. Glancing at Sophie, he realized she had already changed his home by her one uninvited visit. It wasn't the snug cocoon of grief it had been before she set foot inside. He'd spent the next morning in Nora's chair in front of the window watching the sunrise, but it hadn't felt the same. The chair had stood empty since then. He'd taken down the curtains and put shades in their place. Now Rose and Grace had invaded his kitchen. Why did it feel like he was leaving Nora's memory behind?

"I guess it was nice of Rose to think about Joanna and I getting to church." Doubt clouded Sophie's eyes.

"Rose always has another motive for the things she does. I warned you that she would be trotting out eligible bachelors for you."

"Is that what she is doing?" Sophie looked appalled.

"You didn't catch the hints she gave about how suitable Eli would be? Single, prosperous business, devout."

Sophie's jaw dropped. Then she snapped it shut. "I expressly told her I am not interested in marriage."

"I can pass that message on to Eli tomorrow. There's no telling what Rose said to him."

"Please do. And tell anyone who asks the same thing. Joanna is a different story. I want to see her settled before—" She stopped speaking abruptly.

"Before what?"

She looked away. "Before she gets too old."

"Then she has a few years to look around. What is she, nineteen?"

"She's twenty. That's old enough to start seeking a husband."

"At twenty? What's your rush? She has plenty of time before folks start labeling her an old maid."

Sophie stared at her clasped hands. "I just want her to be happy."

Marriage might bring happiness for a while, but it didn't always last. Sometimes it brought unimaginable pain. He stood and braced himself to see Nora's kitchen full of other women.

"Let's get some supper." He walked out the door without looking back.

Sophie sighed as she watched him leave. His sadness was like a heavy cloak about his shoulders. For a few minutes he had thrown it aside, but at the mention of marriage he'd pulled it tight around himself once more. If only there was something she could do to help. No, Joanna was the one who could help him. Somehow, she had to get her sister to focus her attention on Karl, not just Rachel.

Sophie rubbed her aching arm and shoulder where the surgeon had removed lymph nodes when they took her breast. She had been told the weakness could linger for months, even years, despite the physical therapy she'd been given, and that was proving to be true. Her arm was much weaker. She needed to schedule a checkup with a new doctor before Christmas anyway. Perhaps Dr. Bertha could offer a more effective suggestion.

She flexed her fingers and arm to quell the stiffness and went to join the others. She paused outside the kitchen door remembering Karl's outburst the last time she'd entered his house. She prayed she wouldn't trigger another one although she still didn't know what she had done the first time. Why had she upset him so?

The answer she wanted wouldn't be found out here. She reached for the doorknob. Inside, the kitchen was a hive of activity. Clara and Rachel were setting the table as Rachel chatted happily. "It's so nice to have company. No one ever comes to visit us."

"We are just next door so you will see us all the time," Joanna said, putting out bowls of potato salad and corn.

Rose was slicing fresh bread onto a platter. Karl was already in his place at the head of the table with a grim expression on his face. Grace carried a pitcher of tea over and set it in the middle. "We need another chair, Clara."

"We don't have another kitchen chair." Clara cast a covert glance at her father.

"There's one in the living room," he said softly.

The girl's eyes widened. "But that's *Mamm's* chair."

Sophie cringed. The chair she had stood on to fix the curtain rod had some special importance to Clara and Karl, too. "I'll fetch one from our place."

"It's okay if our guests use it," Karl said gently.

"Are you sure?" Clara looked from her father to Sophie and frowned.

"It's fine." Karl stood up, went into the living room and returned with a chair. He set it beside Clara for Sophie.

Sophie hesitated.

"It's fine," he said again, giving her a pointed look.

Rose carried a platter of fried chicken to the table and took her seat. Karl returned to his place. Everyone sat down. Sophie eased onto the chair under Clara's angry gaze. The child's eyes suddenly filled with tears.

"I'm sorry," Sophie said quietly, hoping to mend the tentative friendship that had developed between them.

Karl bowed his head for the silent prayer. When he finished, he took a slice of bread and handed the plate to Clara. "Pass the bread to your teacher."

"She's not going to be my teacher. I'm not going back to school!" Clara jumped up and dashed out the door.

Karl saw the stricken look on Sophie's face as Clara rushed out of the room. She pushed back from the table. "This is my fault. I should go after her."

"*Nee*. She is my daughter, and you are a guest in my home. I will take care of this. Finish your meal." Karl got up and went out the door.

He glanced around wondering where Clara might've gone. Buck whined and strained at his rope. Karl reached down and untied him. "Go find her."

The dog made a beeline for the barn. Karl followed him. Just inside the door, Karl lifted down the lantern he kept there and lit it. The soft glow showed him his daughter huddled on a pile of hay with Buck in her lap licking her face.

"Stupid dog." She pushed him away, but he crawled back beside her and rested his head on her thigh. She fondled his ear.

"Not so stupid. He knows you're upset. Is it something we can talk about?" Karl hung the lantern from a hook on a post.

"I wish she had never come here."

"Who?" He suspected he knew the answer.

"The new teacher."

"Sophie is a nice woman. We need the rent she will pay us."

"She's changing everything. Why did you let her have *Mamm*'s chair?"

Karl sat down in the hay beside his daughter and slipped an arm around her shoulder. "Because it's only a chair. Letting someone use it doesn't mean I have forgotten about your mother or the fact that she liked to sit and watch the sun come up every day. The love I have for her I hold in my heart. It is not tied to the chair."

"Sometimes I can't remember her face. I don't want my memories of her to fade."

He ached for the pain he heard in her voice. "I feel the same."

Clara looked up at him. "You do?"

He nodded. "The bishop says it is wrong to dwell on the ones *Gott* has called home. We can't understand His reasoning, but he needed your mother with Him. If we don't accept that, then we are saying that *Gott* made a mistake."

"I think He did."

He struggled to find the right words. "*Liebchen*, *Gott* is the infallible creator of the universe, and all life belongs to Him. He created your mother so that I might love her and be gifted with two beautiful daughters. There is no mistake in that. I have been wrong to grieve so long. If my example has caused you to doubt your faith, then I have committed two grave sins. Your mother is in paradise. It is selfish of us to wish her back in this world." Karl searched his heart for the faith to believe the words he was telling his child.

"I know you're right, but it's hard."

"Faith in what we cannot understand is hard. But without our faith in *Gott*, we are lost sheep without purpose or direction. Like Rachel's sheep when they get out."

"Their purpose is to find Rachel."

"Exactly. They need their shepherdess, just as we need ours. Now do you want to tell me why you don't want to go to school?"

"Because I'm old enough to take care of things at home and work in the shop so you don't have to do so much. Only I can't do that if I'm in school."

"Sophie will be upset if you don't keep up with your studies."

"I don't care if she is."

"I had the feeling earlier today that you were starting to like her."

"She's okay, I guess, but she wants to change things. I don't like that. Please don't make me go back to school. I can learn everything at home just the way I have been doing."

"We both know I'm not a very good teacher."

"We will do better. Together. I will study harder, and you can spend a little more time checking my work."

Guilt over his neglect sat like a stone in his midsection. He could feel his resistance crumbling. He wanted her to be happy. "Will you truly be content to work in the store all day instead of going to school with your friends?"

"I will."

There was so much hope in her eyes that he couldn't deny her. "Very well."

"Truly?" She threw her arms around his neck. "*Danki, Daed*. You won't regret it."

He wouldn't regret having her with him all day, but he didn't look forward to telling teacher Sophie his decision.

Eight

Sophie helped Rose and Grace clean up in the kitchen as she waited anxiously for Karl and Clara to return. Joanna and Rachel were in the other room playing a game of Sorry! She could hear their giggles and cries of fake outrage.

"Don't fret," Rose said. "The child will be fine." She covered the two uneaten plates with foil and placed them in the oven to keep warm.

Sophie stacked the dirty dishes in the sink and began to fill it with water, remembering the last time she had cleaned up in this spot. If she had left her compulsive personality at the door, none of this would be happening. "I seem to upset this family at every turn."

"Sometimes letting go is painful, but it isn't healthy to cling to the past. A chair is just a chair. We remember the person, not their possessions," Grace said as she brought over the flatware.

Sophie glanced at the other women. "Clara misses her

mother. We all know that feeling." They all nodded in agreement. "No matter what age you are when that happens it's painful, but Clara is so young to have endured such a loss."

Grace picked up a towel and began drying the dishes Sophie handed her. "*Gott* allowed it. Clara may be young, but there was no call for her to be rude to you. She owes you an apology. You are her teacher. Her elder. She must respect you. If she does not, that attitude may spread to other students. As a new teacher you have enough on your plate without facing a rebellious student. Karl must take care of this."

"I'm sure he will." Sophie handed Grace the last plate. "I've had a long day and I'm tired. I'm going back to the house. Thank you for bringing our supper. It was delicious."

"Aren't you going to wait for the child to apologize?" Rose asked.

"She can come see me privately." Sophie had caused the child enough distress. She didn't want to compound it by having her beg forgiveness in front of everyone.

There had to be a way to mend the rift between them. Sophie wasn't sure how, but she knew it wouldn't happen with an audience. She would just have to wait and watch for the right opportunity and trust the Lord would show her when it arrived. She glanced at the grim faces in the room. "Let's talk about something else."

Grace sighed and nodded. "Have I told you that you and Joanna are invited to Thanksgiving dinner at the inn?"

"You haven't mentioned it. *Danki*, that will be nice. What shall I bring?"

"Can you make a frog-eye salad?" Rose asked.

Sophie looked at her in shock. "You don't mean you actually eat frog eyes?"

Rose laughed. "It's a fruit salad made with *acini di pepe*, those little balls of pasta—hence the name. It has whipped cream, coconut, pineapple, mandarin oranges, little marshmallows and sometimes pecans. It's closer to a dessert. I'll write out the recipe for you."

Appeased, Sophie nodded. "I'll make it if I can call it something else."

Rose smiled. "Call it Rose's favorite whipped-topping fruit salad."

"I will." Sophie finished the dishes and helped the two women pack up the leftovers in their baskets.

After telling Joanna about the Thanksgiving invitation, Sophie went back to the house. In her box-filled kitchen, she sighed heavily. There was so much work left to be done, but it would have to wait. She rubbed her aching arm, annoyed that she still didn't have the energy she'd had before her surgery. Shouldn't she be recovered by now? Was it a sign that the cancer was lurking inside her? Her mother had grown weaker by the day during the last part of her illness. Was that to be her fate, too?

If this was the path *Gott* had set her feet upon, she would endure it. She envied her sister's faith that all would be well, but she didn't share it. The coming pain would be endured but she was going to cherish every good day until then.

At least she wouldn't pass this grim disease on to her own daughters. For that she should be grateful instead of weighed down with sadness.

Marriage and a big family had always been part of her dreams. She loved books and learning but she longed to be a mother. Working as a teacher until the right man came along had seemed like a perfect plan. Then the right man came and went. Sophie's dreams of a family vanished the moment she heard her diagnosis. Having watched her beloved grandmother and then her mother succumb, she knew she could never put someone she loved through the agony of watching her die.

When Nate broke their engagement, she was hurt but some part of her was relieved. She truly cared for him and didn't want him to suffer the way her father had when her mother was dying.

Sophie drew a deep breath. At least she still had teaching for however long God willed. It was her solace. She dearly loved her job. There was nothing to compare to seeing the light in a child's eyes when they discovered they could solve the problem or read the word. She loved watching their minds open to what was possible. While the Amish did not pursue education beyond the eighth grade, they valued it, as much or more than the people who took it for granted.

She hoped Karl valued it, too.

After making up her bed, Sophie was debating whether she should unpack at least one box or wait until morning when she heard the kitchen door open.

She left her bedroom and saw Karl and Clara waiting for her. She walked into the kitchen and stopped in front of them. "I'm sorry I upset you, Clara."

"I apologize for my rude behavior," Clara said, keeping her eyes glued to the floor.

"Apology accepted. *Danki.* I hope you have changed your mind about attending school."

Clara looked up at her father. He cleared his throat and hooked his thumbs in his suspenders. "Clara will not be returning to the classroom. She's going to continue helping me in the store."

Sophie had difficulty hiding her surprise. "For how long?"

"That's hard to say. We bid you good night."

He turned around but Sophie grabbed his arm. "You can't be serious?"

"Go on into the house, Clara."

"Don't let her talk you into changing your mind, *Daed.*"

He glanced down at her hand. Sophie pulled it away. He opened the door. "I've given you my word, Clara. I won't go back on it. You will return go to school when you are ready and not before."

Clara nodded and left.

Sophie folded her arms across her chest. "The child pitches a fit and you give in just like that?"

"I don't expect you to understand."

"I'd certainly like to."

"I've neglected my daughter. She's unhappy. I see a way to remedy that. She wants to work with me, and I can use the help. I know you disapprove but she is my child."

"All right. Educational choices are up to the parent. You do plan to continue homeschooling her, don't you?"

"Sure."

"That means her studies must be comparable to what public schools teach. Six hours a day, one hundred and eighty-six days each year? That is a serious commitment."

"I'll make it work."

"Kansas has no laws about what should be taught in a private nonaccredited school, which is how homeschooling is viewed by the state. But a child should still learn reading, writing, math, science, geography, American history, plus health and hygiene. Do you feel comfortable teaching those?"

"Like I said, I'll make it work. Tomorrow morning I'll take you and Joanna to church. *Guten nacht.*"

He went out the door and she didn't try to stop him. It was clear he wasn't going to listen to her. Drained by her failure, Sophie left her boxes unpacked and went to bed.

This was a mistake. Karl sat stiffly beside Sophie on the front seat of his buggy. Clara had chosen to ride in the back with her sister and Joanna, leaving Sophie the choice of enduring Clara's cold looks on the ride or sitting beside him. Was she regretting her decision? He was because he was painfully aware of the woman sitting beside him.

She happened to glance his way as he looked at her. She quickly turned her face away, but not before he saw her cheeks were rosy from the cold north wind. Wisps of her wheat-blond hair fluttered about her face from beneath her black traveling bonnet. The posture of her slender frame was straight as a board. If she sat any farther away from him, she would topple out the side of the buggy. He couldn't see her face well enough to gauge what she was thinking, but he knew she was still upset with him.

He had no trouble reading the surprise looks of his neighbors as he drove into Levi's yard with her at his side. He could feel the heat rising up the back of his neck. There would be speculation aplenty about his connection to the single woman seated beside him this morning.

Karl stopped the horse at the front of the house. Levi came forward and took hold of the bridle.

"Sophie, Joanna, this is Levi Martin," Karl said.

"I'll take care of your horse. Do you need help with the baskets?" Levi asked.

Sophie shook her head and stepped out of the buggy. "My sister and I can manage the food, *danki*, Levi."

"Welcome to our community. You'll find my wife, Barbara, inside. She'll show you where to put your things."

As the women and his daughters walked up to the house, Karl got out and began leading Checker toward a long row of buggies parked beside Levi's barn. Levi fell into step beside Karl.

"So that's the new teacher. What do you think of her?"

"She's a nice woman. I think she'll do well with the children. My Rachel is taken with her."

"But not Clara?"

Karl sighed and shook his head. "Clara is going through a difficult time. She doesn't want to return to school."

"Why not?"

They reached the row of buggies. Karl unhooked Checker, and Levi led him into his corral, where he secured him beside a dozen other horses all still in harness and munching on the hay Levi had spread out for them.

"Clara feels it is her duty to take care of the house and help me in the store."

"Are you going to let her stay out of school?"

Karl shrugged. "I do need her help until I can find another clerk. She knows every part of the business, but I also want her to feel useful."

"What does the new teacher have to say about this?"

Karl looked toward the house. "Not much but I can tell she isn't happy with me."

Sophie paused beside Joanna on the front porch as she tried to quell the butterflies in her stomach. The welcome party at the inn had been stressful enough, but this was their first venture into their new church group. This wasn't about being the new teacher.

"Relax," Joanna whispered. "It's going to be fine."

These were the people who would support and comfort Joanna when Sophie's relapse came. "If we decide to join this church, every baptized member of the congregation will have to vote to accept us."

"You are going to tell me to behave and be modest in all things. I will. I promise. It might be weeks or months before the bishop puts it to a vote."

"Let's hope not." Sophie didn't want to wait that long. The sooner she got things settled for Joanna the better prepared she would be to face her own future. There would likely be doctor's fees and medical bills to settle. The church would help cover those for their members.

"You worry too much," Joanna said.

Sophie bit back a reply and followed her sister inside.

They stepped into a spacious, airy kitchen with a black-and-white linoleum floor and finely crafted oak cabinetry. A petite woman with dark hair stood at the table already laden with food. She smiled at Sophie and walked toward her, wiping her hands on her apron.

Rachel ran up to her. "Can I go see Micah?"

"He's in the bedroom in his crib. Please don't wake him if he's sleeping." She smiled at Sophie and Joanna. "I'm Barbara Martin. Welcome. The service will be held in our basement. Can I help you with your things?"

"I'll be out back with my friends." Clara put the basket she carried on the table and walked away.

"Come see Micah, Joanna. He's a sweet *bobbli*." Rachel bounced with eagerness.

"In a minute, Rachel. Where should we put the food we brought?" Joanna asked.

"Here on the table or the counter will be fine. You can put your empty baskets in our spare bedroom down the hall. I'll show you where."

Rachel waited until Joanna set out her dishes of food and then grabbed her hand and pulled her away. Sophie gathered the empty baskets and followed Barbara.

"Are you finding your way around town?" Barbara asked as she opened a door halfway down the small hallway.

"Around town but I'm not familiar with the countryside yet."

"I'll be happy to go with you if you want to explore."

Sophie added her containers to the boxes and baskets stacked around the room. "I appreciate that. I do need to find where my students live and plan visits with each of their parents."

"I've lived in Harts Haven all my life so I'm familiar with everyone in our church."

"I may take you up on that offer."

"I noticed you came in with Karl," Barbara said casually. Too casually.

Sophie sensed her interest. "It only made sense to ride with Karl since we are living on his property."

"You've rented his *daadi haus*?"

"We did."

"I always thought it was a lovely little house. Levi and I looked at it when we first decided to marry. It just wasn't big enough. We wanted to start a family right away and his mother was going to live with us."

"It's perfect for my sister and me. I'm glad Rose suggested it."

Barbara tipped her head slightly. "Do I detect a hint of Rose's matchmaking in that arrangement?"

"Just the opposite. Rose had arranged for Eli and Jeff Hostetter to pick us up this morning, but Karl volunteered to bring us instead."

"Did he?" She seemed genuinely surprised.

"I think Karl enjoyed putting a crimp in Rose's plan. According to him, she has plagued him with suggestions for a suitable new wife."

"I'd have thought Rose would point out how suitable you are for him and his girls."

"*Nee*, she made a point of telling him we wouldn't suit and I'm glad. We wouldn't." She wasn't about to admit how attractive she found him. It didn't matter. She wasn't the woman Karl needed.

A baby began crying in the next room. "That's Micah," Barbara said. "I was hoping he'd sleep a little longer."

"I'm sorry if Rachel woke him."

"I don't have his bottle ready. Would you see to him while I fix it?"

"Of course."

Sophie went into the room next door. A chubby dark-haired little boy about seven months old was standing in his crib looking over the top rail. There were tears on his dark eyelashes. He rubbed one eye with his fist and gave another sob. Rachel and Joanna weren't in the room. Sophie crossed to the crib. "Hello, Micah. What seems to be the trouble?"

He eyed her suspiciously for a long moment then reached out his hand, opening and closing his fingers.

"Do you want me to pick you up? I can do that." She reached down and lifted him over the rail. He was an armful with chubby legs and a round belly peeking out between his T-shirt and diaper.

The wonderful, sweet baby smell of him made her heart contract with happiness. There was something amazingly comforting about holding a baby even if it wasn't her own. He babbled happily as he stared at her face and patted her cheek with one hand.

"Aren't you just the most precious fellow." She took his hand in hers and brought it to her lips.

"Has he made a new friend already?" Barbara asked as she came in with his bottle.

"He's trying to get on the teacher's good side early." Sophie chuckled as she swung him gently back and forth. "Rachel said he is the sweetest baby, and she is absolutely right. You are so blessed."

"I know it and I give thanks to *Gott* every day. Would you like to feed him? I'm needed in the other room."

"I would be delighted." Barbara left and Sophie settled him against her chest in the crook of her arm. She thought about the part of herself that was missing. It was a painful reminder that she would never have children of her own. He was heavy in her weak arm. She looked around for a place to sit and saw a rocker in the corner.

Settling herself in the chair, she held the bottle to his mouth. He grabbed it with both hands, gave her a milky smile around the nipple and began drinking.

"That's what you wanted," she said, smiling at him. Just for a moment she could pretend he was her child. She relished the feeling of completeness that settled in her heart. But the illusion couldn't last. His mother came in to check on them a few minutes later.

She turned to speak to Barbara. As she did, Micah grabbed the ribbon of her *kapp* and pulled it off her head, sending her bobby pins plinking to the floor and revealing her short hair.

Barbara stunned expression proved Sophie's plan to keep her illness a secret was doomed. She tucked her hair behind her ears as best she could.

"What happened to your hair? Never mind," Barbara said quickly. "It is none of my business. Let me help you." She picked up the scattered bobby pins from around Sophie's feet and poured them into her outstretched hand.

Barbara lifted Micah from Sophie's arms. "I have a hairbrush that you can use."

"I would be grateful." Sophie smoothed her short, fine hair with her hands.

Barbara nodded and left the room. She returned a minute later and handed the brush to Sophie. She took it and tried to make an even part in the middle. "How does that look?"

"It looks fine."

"I'm fortunate that the style of *kapp* in our church is stiff.

Otherwise I would have to use padding to fill out the back." She settled her prayer covering on her head and pinned it in place.

Barbara tipped her head slightly as she scrutinized Sophie's face. "You can't tell. It looks quite normal."

A normal appearance was what she hoped to achieve but maybe that had been foolish. She could see the curiosity in Barbara's gaze, but the young mother was polite enough not to ask anything.

Amish women never cut their hair. It was considered their crowning glory, to be seen only by God and their husbands. She could imagine the questions running though Barbara's head. Wasn't the truth better than speculation? Sophie took a deep breath. "I didn't cut my hair."

"You don't have to explain."

But Sophie found that she wanted Barbara to know the truth. "It fell out during my chemotherapy treatments."

"How awful that must've been for you. I can't imagine."

Sudden tears gathered in Sophie's eyes as she relived that horrible day. "It was devastating. I woke up one morning and most of it was lying on my pillow in long strands. I gathered it up and held it the way you are holding your son and I cried and cried…" Her voice broke. She had tied it all together, braided it and placed it in her dresser drawer where she could look at it daily and mourn.

"But it's growing back," Barbara said gently. "*Gott* is *goot.*"

Sophie couldn't speak past the lump lodged in her throat.

Barbara dropped to her knees beside the chair and laid a hand on Sophie's knee. "Are you well now?"

Managing a thin smile, Sophie nodded. She swallowed hard. "They tell me I am."

"Then I praise *Gott* for His mercy, and I will finish feeding this boy so your *kapp* stays safe."

Sophie dried her eyes with her fingers. "I should find my sister. *Danki* for letting me hold him." She got up from the chair. "Barbara, I would rather that others didn't know about this. I don't want to be treated differently."

"I understand completely. I won't say anything. I'm cooking Thanksgiving dinner for Levi's parents. You and your sister are welcome to join us."

"*Danki*, but we are eating at the inn with Aunt Grace, Rose and Susanna."

"I should have guessed." Barbara sat down in the rocker and Sophie left the room. She found Joanna with Grace.

"We were getting ready to look for you," Grace said. "The service is about to start." She led the way to the basement, where backless wooden benches had been lined up on either side of a center aisle. Men sat on one side while the women sat on the other. The preachers would stand in the middle. Only married women sat up front, so Sophie and Joanna found a place several rows back with the other unmarried women and girls. Rachel sat beside Joanna. Clara chose a place well away from them. Once she was seated, Sophie realized she had an unobstructed view of Karl sitting across the way among the married men. Their eyes met, and he quickly looked down. She dismissed the tiny stab of disappointment she felt and opened her hymnal.

Karl did his best to listen to the sermons. Their community had two preachers who assisted the bishop. Each man took turns speaking from the heart on a subject the men had decided on shortly before coming in to preach.

He could've stopped going to church after Nora's death. His bitterness toward God had been soul deep, but that would have resulted in his shunning. It would've only brought more heartache to Nora's family and to his children. So he sat through the services and then escaped back to his empty house when the preaching was done. That way he avoided the well-meaning condolences, sad glances and even the speculative looks from a few of the unmarried women. Today would be different. He would be staying for the meal and the visiting that went on during the afternoon. Because of her.

He glanced over at Sophie. She had her eyes closed. There was a look of peace on her face. Beside her Joanna fidgeted. They were as different as two sisters could possibly be. One so serious and one so energetic. He caught Rose looking his way and he quickly transferred his gaze to his prayer book. He didn't want her thinking that Joanna had caught his interest.

It was the one Rose had said he was all wrong for who intrigued him. Not that he was interested in courting her, but he found she was on his mind a lot. The few minutes that they had spent alone in the house last evening before Rose interrupted them had given him a sense of closeness that had been missing in his life for a long time. It had been a simple conversation that had nothing to do with his work or his loss. Their easy comradery had surprised and delighted him.

But Clara had changed that. Was there a way to recover the friendship he sensed he could have with Sophie without upsetting his daughter?

Nine

The kitchen was crowded with women setting out food and preparing for the meal when Sophie came upstairs after the service. There seemed to be enough hands, but she offered to help anyway. Her offer was declined by everyone with kind smiles all around. No one looked at her with sadness or pity. It seemed that Barbara had kept her word and hadn't mentioned Sophie's illness. Her secret was still safe, but how long before word got out?

It had been foolish to think it wouldn't. Grace or Joanna was sure to let something slip sooner or later. Sophie's *kapp* might be pulled off by another child or the restless Kansas wind since her hair wasn't thick enough to hold it securely. She had to prepare for the eventuality that others would find out she was living on borrowed time.

Clatter in the basement told her the men were rearranging and stacking some of the benches to make tables. That meant only a limited number of people could eat at one time. The bishop, ministers and married men would be served first. As a single woman, Sophie would be in the last group to dine. Once the married women were done eating, Sophie planned to quiz the mothers of her students to see what talents their children possessed and maybe get an idea of what kind of Christmas program she could have. It might be her first and last, and she wanted to do a good job.

Since her help wasn't needed in the kitchen, she left the house by the back door to wait her turn to eat. The sun was shining brightly in a cloudless azure blue sky, but the breeze was cool. Fallen leaves coated the lawn and the smells of fall permeated the air.

Joanna sat on a quilt several feet away with six youngsters gathered around her as she entertained them with a dramatic story. Rachel sat beside her gazing up with rapt attention. The two of them were growing close. That was good if Joanna was going to be her stepmother.

Sophie wrestled down a stab of envy. Joanna deserved happiness. She had a warm heart, a generous nature and her whole life ahead of her. She would be a fine mother if that was God's plan for her. If Sophie could aid her to that end, it didn't matter if she suffered a few pangs of regret. She would hide her feelings for Karl if he was the one Joanna wanted.

She looked around for Clara and saw her sitting alone on the bench beneath a maple tree dropping a flurry of leaves with each gust of breeze. Several girls her age were clustered in a group nearby. The hurt looks they cast at Clara told Sophie there had been some sort of disagreement. Clara didn't appear happy either.

Sophie crossed to the tree and leaned against the trunk. "What a beautiful day."

Clara didn't comment but she didn't get up and leave. Encouraged by that, Sophie continued, "I enjoyed the sermons today, particularly the one Bishop Wyse gave. What did you think of it?"

"It was okay, I guess."

The grudgingly given reply was encouraging. "I liked the part where he talked about the ways our pride can keep us from the happiness *Gott* wants us to know. Do you think that's true?" Sophie asked.

Clara glanced up at her with narrowed eyes. "I'm not going back to school."

"Did I say anything about school?"

"I'm not stupid. You're going to tell me that I take pride in working at my father's store and that's wrong."

"Amazing. I've never had a conversation with someone who is so sure what I will say next. Or so wrong. I don't believe it is prideful to want to help your father. In fact, I think it is admirable. Not every girl your age could manage the store and provide him the help you do."

"That's right."

Sophie nodded toward the group watching Clara. "What did you say to those girls that upset them?"

"What makes you think I said something?"

"Judging from the expressions on their faces when they look in this direction, they are either upset with this beautiful tree or the young woman who is sitting under it."

Clara huffed in disgust. "They wanted to play some silly game. I'm too old for that, and I said so."

"Well, of course you are. Silly games are for children. No one your age wants to have fun." She hoped Clara caught her sarcasm.

Clara rolled her eyes but didn't respond.

"I think you are forgetting one very important thing about being mature."

"What?"

"A mature person considers other people's feelings. Did you think you might be ruining their fun?"

Clara scowled at her. "What do you mean?"

"I don't know your friends, but if they asked you to join them it has to be because they want your company, right?"

"I guess so," Clara answered cautiously.

"Then it stands to reason that by refusing them you have taken some of the fun out of their game. I mean, they don't look like they are enjoying themselves, do they? I would go so far as to say they look like their feelings have been hurt. I know that I hurt your feelings last night. I'm sorry for that. I hope you can forgive me."

Clara shrugged one shoulder. "I guess I can."

Sophie smiled at her. "I'm glad. *Danki*. I know you are too old for silly games, but are you too old to make your friends happy? How would you feel if someone deliberately upset Rachel?"

Clara gazed in their direction. "Do you really think I hurt their feelings?"

"The grown-up thing to do would be to apologize and let them enjoy spending time with you even if you don't join the game. It's possible they have missed you."

"I guess I could go talk to them for a bit."

"That's a very mature attitude," Sophie said, holding back a smile.

What was Sophie saying to Clara? Karl watched the exchange from across the way with trepidation. He didn't want his daughter to create a scene in front of the church members the way she had last night.

Clara got up suddenly and went to her group of friends. She hugged each one. Even from this distance he could see the self-satisfied smile on Sophie's face. A few moments later, the group with Clara got up a game of tag. They were soon laughing and shrieking, including his daughter, as they dodged the outstretched arms of the boy who was it.

"I like to see Clara having fun. I'm glad you stayed after the service today." Bishop Wyse sat on the back of Levi's farm wagon beside Karl.

Karl nodded. It felt good to see his daughter laughing and playing like a child her age should. He glanced at the bishop. "Rose made a point of telling me I have been robbing my *kinder* of their childhood by leaving early after the services and not allowing them to play with their friends."

"Rose isn't always the most tactful person, but she has a good heart, and she means well. I'm glad you took her advice. Clara is growing up. She looks more like her mother all the time."

"I wish Nora could see her." He cleared his throat to overcome the grief that squeezed his throat.

"It's hard to watch our lives moving on without them, isn't it?"

Karl knew the bishop's quiet question was referring to the loss of his own wife as well as Nora. Both women had passed away in the same year.

"How do you manage so well?" Karl asked.

"What makes you think that I'm managing any better than you?"

Startled, Karl looked at him. "You preach. You counsel. You comfort the people who need you. I couldn't do any of that."

"I lean on the Lord so that I may continue to do what He asks of me. Without His strength I would fall to my knees sobbing. I do occasionally when I'm alone."

"When I buried Nora all I wanted to do was to lie down on her grave and let the grass grow over me, too."

The bishop stared off into the distance. "I know that feeling."

The two men sat without speaking for a long while. In the silence, Karl discovered a kinship with the man that he had never felt before. Rose had been right about something else. He wasn't the only one who knew grief intimately.

Karl pushed his hat back on his head. "They said it would get better, but it doesn't."

Bishop Wyse nodded. "A man can lose an arm and live. He can adjust. He can thrive, but he will always remember what it was to have two arms. It hasn't gotten better for me. I think I've just gotten used to living with the pain."

"And if I can't get used to it?"

The bishop gave him a sad smile. "Then you will never thrive and that would be a shame to waste every other gift that *Gott* has lavished on you. It's hard to keep living, but He is with you always. He will carry your burden when you falter."

Karl wanted to believe that, but he wasn't sure God was ready to help someone who was still angry with Him. "I will keep your words in mind."

"You have your daughters. I have my sons and my grandchildren to make life bearable. I have my friends, too. Including Rose despite her matchmaking efforts on my behalf."

That surprised Karl. "You, too?"

"That woman won't be happy until every last single man in Harts Haven has met his match."

Karl chuckled. "I've thought the same thing."

"What do you think of our new teacher?" the bishop asked, changing the subject abruptly.

Taken off guard, Karl frowned. He wasn't ready to discuss his feeling about Sophie. "She seems nice."

"I'd call that lukewarm praise. Do you have concerns about her?"

His concern was that he couldn't stop thinking about her. "I'm sure she'll do well as our teacher. She seems eager to get started."

"But?"

Karl looked away. "No buts. She's serious and determined to do a good job."

"And the sister?"

"A bit flighty but a sweet young woman."

"Do you think Sophie will set a good example for our children?"

"I do. Speaking of children, Clara wants to continue working in the store instead of returning to school."

"I see. Are you going to consent to that?"

"I am. Do you object?"

"I will leave that decision up to you as her father." The bishop leaned back, grinned and slapped both hands against his thighs. "Now, what do you know about Sophie's plans for our Christmas program?"

Sophie passed on her chance to go to the basement and eat. She wasn't hungry anyway. She was in a hurry to speak with her pupils' mothers. Before she could decide how to approach any of the women, Rose came out of the house with all the mothers Sophie had hoped to visit with behind her.

Rose smiled brightly. "I remember you mentioning you wanted to talk to these mothers about a Christmas program."

Leave it up to Rose to put her on the spot. Sophie forced a bright smile. "I did. As I'm sure you know, the *kinder* won't have much time to prepare a program this year. I was thinking of having them sing a few songs and perhaps do a few readings. What are your feelings?"

The women exchanged confused looks. "We were expecting something more elaborate." Mrs. Bachman seemed to be the leader of the group.

"The children are eager to show their skills," Mrs. Weaver said.

Sophie's hopes for an easy program faded. "Of course. You must realize I don't know the children at all. I'll have to spend time getting to know their strengths and talents, but you can help me. Which children have pleasant singing voices?"

"They all do," Rose said.

"I'm sure that's true, but in every group, there are one or two who stand out."

Several of the women nudged Mrs. Kauffman. A burst of red colored her cheeks. Rose patted her shoulder. "It isn't prideful to acknowledge a God-given gift."

"I think everyone will agree that *Gott* has gifted my son Phillip with a lovely singing voice," Mrs. Kauffman said softly. The women around her murmured their agreement.

"That's helpful." Sophie smiled at her. "And there are always some children who are uncomfortable speaking in front of a crowd. They might not tell me, so I certainly don't want to put undue pressure on any of them."

"My Betty is painfully shy," Mrs. Lehman admitted. "She would be terrified to have to speak in front of so many people."

"Ben is the same way," Mrs. Weaver admitted. "He has a stutter."

"Thank you for telling me. Do any of the other children have talents or problems I should be aware of?"

"Tamara is hard of hearing," Mrs. Stoltzfus said. "She wears a hearing aid but if the battery goes dead, she is nearly deaf."

"Noted. I'll make it a point to keep extras in my desk if that should happen."

Mrs. Stoltzfus smiled. "That would be *wunderbar*. She's been known to forget hers."

"Clara Graber used to write adorable little stories for the younger children," Mrs. Kemp said. "Phoebe would bring them home and read them to our little ones. They loved them."

"I wasn't aware of that." Sophie wondered if she could somehow use the information to encourage Clara to return to the classroom.

"My girls still have the angel wings they wore last year," Mrs. Bachman said brightly.

Several of the mother turned stern looks in her direction. Mrs. Bachman quickly regrouped. "I'd be happy to loan them out in the event that other children are chosen to be angels."

There were murmurs of approval this time leaving Mrs. Bachman smiling once more.

Sophie glance at the faces around her. "You've been a great help. It is a privilege to teach your children. I thank *Gott* every day for leading me down this path, and I will endeavor to be worthy of the honor. In the coming weeks I will be visiting each of you in your homes to give you a progress report on your children and listen to any concerns you may have."

"You'll need someone to show you the way. Perhaps one of the young men in the community can drive you. Or even Karl," Rose suggested, looking pointedly innocent.

"Barbara Martin has already offered, Rose. You don't have to hunt up an unmarried fellow for the job."

All the women chuckled. Rose looked miffed for a moment but then she laughed, too. "Old habits die hard. Many of these women owe their happy marriages to my interventions."

"True," Mrs. Kemp said. "I never would have walked out with Herman if you hadn't brought him out to my *daed*'s farm to look at a plow he didn't really want to buy."

Rose nodded. "I remember. Sometimes it's simply clear to me when two people should end up together."

"And who have you picked out for Sophie?" Mrs. Stoltzfus asked.

"No one," Sophie said quickly. "I'm not interested in getting married. Teaching is the path the Lord has set before me."

She saw the odd looks the women gave her. It was clear they didn't understand that kind of thinking. An Amish woman's only ambition should be to marry and have children. Those who didn't find a husband were pitied. Teaching was a job young Amish women took until they wed. The community didn't expect a woman to have the job for long.

"Her sister doesn't feel the same." Rose gave the women a knowing look. "I have someone in mind for her."

"Who? Who?" A rapid chorus rose from the curious women, making them sound like a flock of owls, but at least Rose had turned their attention away from Sophie. She was grateful.

Mrs. Imhoff clapped her hands. "I know. It's Karl Graber, isn't it? He brought them to church today."

Rose held up one hand. "I'm not ready to say, but Sophie is helping me."

"As a *goot shveshtah* should," Mrs. Imhoff declared, making everyone grin.

Sophie nodded and smiled. She was determined to be a good sister even if it caused her heartache.

It was midafternoon when Karl and Levi lost their second game of horseshoes to Eli and Jeff Hostetter. The brothers were excellent players and Karl was out of practice.

"Another?" Jeff asked.

Karl shook his head. "I think I'll call it a day."

He had noticed Sophie heading toward his buggy. He hoped

she was ready to go home. He had done all the visiting he could stand while answering questions about Sophie and Joanna. Two new single women in the community elicited a lot of interest.

"Before you go, can I ask you something?" Jeff hooked his thumbs in his suspenders and shifted nervously from one foot to the other.

"Sure."

"Do you know if Joanna intends to stay for the singing this evening?"

"I have no idea. She didn't mention it."

"I was thinking about asking to drive her home. If that's okay with you. I don't want to step on your toes."

Karl almost laughed out loud. "My toes aren't in any danger. I thought you were seeing a girl over in Castleton."

"I was but we decided we didn't suit. I'm sort of glad because otherwise I would have had to ignore Joanna. I'm not sure I could. She's something, isn't she?"

Karl remembered the thrill of excitement that flooded a young man's veins when he first met an attractive girl. "Feel free to ask Joanna with my blessings."

"*Danki.*" Jeff grinned and hurried away.

Karl had been watching, but he hadn't seen Sophie return from the buggy. He walked over to see why. He almost missed her in the back seat. She was stretched out on the seat with her head resting on her arm. She looked pale and frail.

"Are you okay?" he asked.

"I'm fine." She sat up so quickly he wished he hadn't disturbed her.

"You don't look fine."

"I reckon I shouldn't expect flattery from you." She brushed the front of her dress and checked her *kapp.*

"I prefer plain speaking."

"Actually, so do I. I'm tired and I have a headache. I thought I would close my eyes for a few minutes."

"Then I came along and bothered you. Sorry."

"That's all right. I should go back to the house." She reached for the door handle.

"Rest a little longer. You look like you could use it."

She gave him a wry smile. "Okay, maybe I don't prefer such plain speaking."

"Too bad. I was about ready to head home. You can stay here while I get the girls and check on Joanna. She might be staying for the singing."

Sophie frowned. "Did she tell you that?"

"Someone else mentioned it. It's okay if she does, right? She's young and single. I'm sure she would like to spend time with other young people."

She leaned toward him, with an earnest expression in her eyes. "My sister comes across as young sometimes, but she can be very mature when others are depending on her."

She sounded almost desperate to change his opinion of Joanna. "I'm sure you know her best. I'll go speak with her."

"*Goot.* She'll probably want to come home with you. I mean us."

"Okay. Grab a few more minutes of rest before Rachel descends on you with her constant chatter."

Sophie smiled and leaned back. "I don't mind her chatter. I find both of your daughters charming."

It made a father feel good to know his children were appreciated. Karl left Sophie and found Rachel and Clara easily. "Girls, I'm ready to go."

"Already?" Clara asked.

Rachel opened her mouth to argue but thought better of it when he gave her a stern look. "Okay."

It was amazing how much disappointment she could pack into one word. "Where is Joanna?"

Clara and Rachel both shrugged. It didn't take him long to locate Joanna sitting on the sidelines watching a volleyball match some of the youngsters had gotten up. Jeff was seated on the other side of her.

Joanna looked up at Karl. "Is it time to go?"

"I'm sure someone will take you home if you want to stay longer. There will be a singing here this evening."

"I'll see that she gets home," Jeff said quickly.

Joanna started to get to her feet. "I should go home with Sophie."

"I told her you might be staying," Karl said.

"Oh? And what did she say?"

"That it's fine. She's tired and has a headache. I thought I should take her home."

"I can see that the girls get home if they aren't ready to leave yet," Rose said.

He turned around to find her watching him with a decided glint in her eyes.

"I don't want to put you to any trouble," he said.

"It won't be any trouble. I enjoy their company."

Rachel pressed her hands together and gave him a pleading look. "Please, *Daed*, can we stay longer?"

It would ensure that Sophie had a quiet ride home. He sighed. "Okay, just this once. You are not to annoy Granny Rose, do you understand? Jeff will see that Joanna gets home if that's okay with Joanna."

She glanced at the young man beside and nodded shyly. "That's fine with me."

Jeff smiled at her. "I'm right glad to hear that."

Both Karl's girls went back to their friends. He started toward the buggy, but Rose followed him looking rather pleased with herself.

"Jeff is on my list for Sophie. It will be good to see if he gets along with her little sister."

"Honestly, he seems very interested in Joanna."

Rose waved that aside. "Nothing will come of this evening but friendship between the two of them. You don't have a thing to worry about."

Karl kept the smile off his face with difficulty. He could see right through Rose's scheme to fix him up with Joanna and it didn't bother him a bit.

It was amusing to watch Rose's plans falling short. Jeff might be on her list for Sophie, but the young man had ideas of his own.

Sophie was still sitting in the corner of the back seat with her eyes closed when she heard footsteps approaching. She hoped seeing her this way would convince Joanna to sit up front with Karl. She felt the buggy shift under his weight when he stepped in, but she didn't hear the girls. She opened one eye. He was alone in the front seat.

She sat up quickly. "Where are the children?"

He glanced back. "Sorry to wake you."

"I wasn't asleep. I was just resting my eyes. Where's Joanna?"

"Rose offered to bring the girls home later so that they could play with their friends a while longer. Joanna is staying for the singing. You will be happy to know that Jeff Hostetter will bring her home."

"Why would I be happy to hear that?"

He turned around in the seat. There was a huge grin on his face. "Because Jeff is one of the men on Rose's list for you."

Sophie couldn't contain her annoyance. "I have repeatedly told that woman I am not interested in marrying."

"You don't have to worry. Jeff has his eye on Joanna. Two birds have been killed with one stone today." He turned around and lifted the reins to get his horse moving.

"What is that supposed to mean?"

"Rose's plans for you and me have been upset by Jeff's eye for a pretty girl."

Sophie gritted her teeth. Joanna was going to end up losing Karl if she didn't start showing some better sense. "I doubt it's anything serious. Joanna probably agreed so that she could meet new friends here."

"Probably."

He didn't sound concerned. She decided to probe a little bit into his feelings for Joanna. They had reached the highway at the end of the Martin's Lane. There would be fewer prying eyes to see them sitting together. "Would you mind very much if I came up front with you?"

"Not at all. I never liked riding in the back myself."

She got out and quickly climbed in the front. "I reckon it's the closed-in feeling you don't care for."

"You're right. I like to be able to see what's coming at me and what's coming up behind me."

She stayed just far enough away so that she wouldn't accidentally come into contact with him. "I understand why you think Rose's matchmaking scheme for me was foiled by Jeff's choice, but what did you mean when you said her plans for you were upset as well?"

"Rose is trying to match me with Joanna."

If he had figured out that much, no wonder he was resisting the idea. Very few people liked to be told what was good for them, even if it was. "I'm sure you're mistaken about that."

"She's barely older than Clara. You don't think I could be interested in someone her age, do you?"

Sophie laced her cold fingers together. "My sister is at least ten years older than Clara. Joanna isn't a child."

He turned to give her a hard look. "Did you and Rose hatch the idea together?"

"Of course not." She looked away from his piercing gaze. "I came here to teach school not to play matchmaker for my sister. Rose comes up with her own schemes. You know that."

She stared at her tightly clenched fingers. It wasn't quite the whole truth, but she hadn't arrived in Harts Haven with the idea of becoming Joanna's matchmaker. She simply wanted her sister to be settled before…

"What aren't you telling me, Sophie?"

Her gaze shot to his face and the concern in his eyes. Swallowing hard, she kept her expression blank. "Nothing."

"I'm not sure I believe that."

Thankfully, he didn't say anything else. He dropped her at the gate to her small front yard and went to put the horse away. She stared at him for several long moments as he unhitched the horse. If only she could share the truth with him…

But she couldn't. She turned away. It didn't matter. This was her battle to face alone.

Ten

Karl had been watching for Sophie to leave the house on her first day at school. He told himself he only wanted to offer her encouragement, but it was really an excuse to talk to her again. After pouring a cup of coffee, he went out to the porch that overlooked hers and almost missed her. She was halfway up the lane. Leaving his coffee on the porch railing, he ran up behind her while she was waiting to cross the road.

"Are you ready for this?" He was out of breath from the dash but hoped she didn't notice.

She took take a deep breath and gave him a nervous smile over her shoulder. "You would think so, but I find I'm a bit light on courage."

"Never knew teachers were as worried about the first day of school as the pupils. Rachel has packed and repacked her lunch box three times already. Twice I had to remind her to finish her chores."

Sophie turned and gave him a sympathetic look. "Poor baby. I promise she'll enjoy the day."

"I'm not worried. I know you'll take good care of her. And all your scholars," he added quickly, not wanting her to think he expected her to favor his daughter.

"*Danki*. I reckon I should go. I see two of my students walking this way." A boy and a girl were still a short distance down the road.

"Looks like the Imhoff *kinder*."

She closed her eyes. "That would be Debra, who is in the fifth grade, and Jason, who is in the seventh grade. Jason loves baseball and Debra enjoys quilting with her grandmother." She opened her eyes and looked at Karl. "Am I right?"

She had been memorizing their names. It showed she wanted to relate to each of her students. "You are correct."

"Now if I can just keep the rest of them straight."

He wanted to ease the worry he saw in her pretty blue eyes. "You'll do fine. How is your headache? You look better this morning."

Her concern vanished to be replaced by a flash of humor. "I believe that might have almost been a compliment."

A surge of heat climbed his neck. He cleared his throat. "Slip of the tongue, nothing more. Don't let it go to your head."

She chuckled. "I won't. My headache is gone, and I feel ready to face the day. Almost."

"I hope you're ready to face Isaac Kemp. I see his buggy coming this way. I recognize his horse."

Sophie clasped her arms across her chest. "Oh, no. He's one of the school board members, isn't he? I met him last Friday. I don't think he was impressed with my discipline plan."

"Don't let old Isaac bluff you. He's a pushover especially where his grandchildren are concerned. Just remember that you are the teacher. You are in charge of the children while they are at school."

Sophie raised her chin. "You're right. I'm in charge."

"Until the school board tells you differently anyway."

"That is a worrisome thought. You're not helping now. Don't you have to open the store or something?" She looked around. "Where are the girls?"

"Finishing their chores. Rachel won't be late, but I will be if I don't get a move on."

"I meant to ask if you found someone to help in the store."

"Not yet. I still need Clara, and she is determined to do the job."

"I understand. I really do. My father runs a dry goods store. My sister and I both worked there along with our mother until she passed away. My *daed* recently remarried. His wife and his stepchildren work with him now. The entire family has to pitch in to make it a profitable business."

Karl was relieved that she understood. He hated that Clara was a sore point between them. "I appreciate that. It wasn't an easy decision."

Isaac Kemp nodded as he drove past and turned his horse and buggy into the schoolyard, where he stopped by the hitching rail.

Sophie looked at Karl. "I should get going."

"I should, too."

Neither of them moved. Sophie appeared as reluctant as he was to end their brief time together this morning. It was better than yesterday when he'd gotten the impression that she'd been relieved to get out of his buggy and away from him. Had it been because he had asked if she was hiding something? Or was it simply that she didn't enjoy his company as much as he enjoyed hers? He couldn't exactly ask her which as much as he wanted to know the answer.

Either way, he had a store to run. He tipped his hat. "Have a *goot* day."

"You do the same." She turned away and crossed the road toward the school.

It was amazing how much he was starting to like her and worrisome. He still loved his wife. So why was he thinking about spending more time with the new teacher?

Sophie resisted the desire to look back and see if Karl was watching her. Instead, she went inside the schoolhouse and hung her coat in the cloakroom beside the large overcoat belonging to Isaac Kemp. He had taken a seat in a folding chair at the back of the room. She had made sure to have half a dozen seats available as she expected a few mothers to visit. Mothers would often come to support and reassure the youngest students, especially if they didn't have older siblings in school. Sophie knew Rachel and Tamara Stoltzfus were the only ones without a support person there that day. Tamara because she was an only child and Rachel since Clara had chosen not to attend school.

Sophie walked to her desk at the front of the building. She wasn't going to think about Karl today. She was going to concentrate on getting to know her students and restarting the disrupted school year.

Knowing that her first-grade students understood a limited amount of English, she chose a place where they could sit in little chairs in a semicircle near her desk when it was their turn for attention. Otherwise, they would sit at the normal student desks in the front row.

The Amish spoke Pennsylvania Dutch at home, or Deitsh as it was referred to by them. English was the language spoken by their non-Amish neighbors and businesses, so children needed to become proficient in it. For that reason, only English was spoken in an Amish school except when instructing the first-grade students.

Rachel would be the rare exception. She worked in her father's store and had been exposed to English from a young age. Sophie was hopeful she could depend upon Rachel to help the other children adjust.

She set up an easel near the chair for the beginners and put out four small jars of paint in the primary colors on a side table. Children learned by doing and today they would learn the English words for the colors while they enjoyed painting a picture for their parents of their first day in her class.

Next, she opened her desk drawer and took out the workbooks that would be used for each grade and placed them on the appropriate desks. While some Amish schools believed in separating boys and girls, she had been pleased to learn that Harts Haven didn't. It was her opinion that a group of boys sitting together got up to more mischief than when there were girls placed in among them. Girls were less likely to engage in whispered conversations if the boys could overhear them.

Isaac Kemp made himself useful by stoking the stove. Before long the hot top would be covered with foil-wrapped potatoes and other dishes the children brought for lunches. Sophie took a large black teakettle off the stove and filled it from the small sink tucked into the corner of the room. The kettle would add humidity to the room and supply her with hot water for tea at lunchtime.

She started hearing children's voices outside. Even on the coldest days, many of the children would prefer to play outside until the last minute. Joanna had been one of those children. Sophie hadn't been.

The door opened and several students came inside. One took his seat at a desk, and the other two went to the bookshelves of the school's library and took down a book each.

Sophie smiled at them. She had always preferred to be inside reading until it was time to put her book aside.

She kept one eye on the clock at the back of the room. A few minutes before eight, she slipped on her coat and stepped out to the front door. A bell hung from the ceiling of the porch. Grabbing the thick rope connected to the clapper, she rang the bell vigorously.

The students who were still playing outside immediately stopped what they were doing and filed quietly into the schoolhouse. They came in, put their coats and lunches away, then took their seats. Rachel dashed up to Sophie. "I'm so happy to be in school again."

"I'm glad but now you need to take your seat." Sophie didn't want the other students to think she had a favorite just because she lived next door to Rachel's family.

Sophie moved to stand in front of her desk. "Good morning, scholars."

"Good morning, teacher," they said in unison.

"I am Sophie Eicher, your new teacher. I'm delighted to be here. I know we will have a wonderful school year. Let's go around the room and I want you to tell me your name and what you like best about school. Please stand as you do. I'll start at the back with the eight-grade students."

Sophie had a seating chart on her desk to refer to later, but she wanted to get a sense of each student.

One of the girls at the back stood up. "I'm Betty Lehman. What I like best about school is helping the young ones. I hope I can be your teacher's aide this year."

"That sounds like an excellent idea, Betty. Thank you."

After that she learned that Phillip Kauffman liked singing the best, while Zack Weaver and Bartholomew Kemp prized recess above all subjects. Miriam and her sister, Thea, both said they enjoyed preforming in the Christmas program. It was another reminder that Sophie had to come up with one soon.

When the children were finished, she nodded to the class. "Very well done. As you can see, Isaac Kemp, who is a member of our school board, has decided to visit us today. I'm sure you will be on your best behavior."

Sophie then moved to the blackboard that covered the front wall of the school and wrote out the date and the arithmetic assignments for each of the classes. When she finished, she picked up her Bible. Each day she would choose a passage to read from the Old or the New Testament. This morning she chose Matthew 5:15–16.

"Neither do men light a candle, and put it under a bushel, but on a candlestick; and it giveth light unto all that are in the house. Let your light so shine before men, that they may see your good works, and glorify your Father which is in heaven."

She closed the Bible. All the students rose, clasped their hands together and repeated the Lord's Prayer in unison. When the prayer was done, Sophie withdrew her copy of *Unpartheyisches Gesang-Buch*, their German songbook, from the top drawer of her desk.

Singing was a normal part of every Amish school day. Without being told, the children filed to the front of the room and lined up in their assigned places, the oldest students making sure the youngest ones knew where to stand. Sophie smiled. Their previous teacher had done a good job with them.

She handed the book to Edna Weaver. "Why don't you choose a song this morning."

Edna announced the title and began the hymn that they all knew by heart. The other children joined in. Their voices rose together in unison as they sang without musical accompaniment as the Amish had always done.

Sophie had Phillip Kauffman pick the second song. When he began singing, she knew why people said he had the best voice. He was sure to become a *Volsinger*, or song leader, in the church one day if he remained Amish. She encouraged shy Ben Weaver to pick the third song. He happily did so and sang without stuttering. When the singing was finished, they all returned to their seats.

"After our lunch break, I have a special treat planned. I will be reading one chapter each day of the novel *The Call of the Wild*, by Jack London. I know you will enjoy it. Now, if Rachel, Sam, Laura and Lamar will come up here, we're going to do some painting."

Sophie handed Betty Lehman the readers, which Betty distributed to the three lower grades. The older students took out their arithmetic workbooks. All the children knew what was expected of them, and they did it without instructions. Sophie began to relax. The day was going better than she had expected. She carefully opened four jars of paint.

Jason Imhoff raised his hand. "Yes, Jason?"

"There's someone at the door. Should I see who it is?"

"Someone is knocking?" She hadn't heard anything.

"More like thumping."

Parents knew to simply walk in quietly. Who would be thumping at the door? "I'll see who it is, Jason. Thank you."

She walked to the back of the room and opened the door. April, May and June darted inside, knocking Sophie off her feet. Her knee twisted painfully as she fell. She didn't see everything that happened next, but she heard Rachel's cry of distress, someone screamed and then one of the boys said, "We'll get them!"

By the time she sat up, the lambs were in a panic, jumping

on top of desks and dashing under them to evade the enthusiastic wranglers. "Stop! Everyone, stop!"

No one listened to her. Mr. Kemp rushed to the front of the room and managed to get a grip on one sheep. In the struggle, he staggered backward and knocked over Sophie's easel. The paint jars went flying. The yellow ended up on his dark suit, and most of the blue landed on May before she got loose and ran into Laura Kemp. The rest splatted on the first-graders who scrambled out of their chairs to get away. Sheep and children slipped and slid in the paint as they tried to evade each other.

"Don't hurt them," Rachel wailed. One of the captured sheep was being pulled by her back legs toward the door by a pair of grinning boys.

Another sheep with a red ear headed toward Sophie and the open door behind her. She tried to scramble out of the way just as Zackary Weaver dived on top of the animal. They both slammed into Sophie. She doubled over in agony and crumpled to the floor.

Karl was cleaning the front window of the store when Rachel came running up in the middle of the morning with tears streaming down her face. "*Daed*, it was awful." She wrapped her arms around his legs and buried her face against him.

"What was awful? What happened?" He had sent a happy child to school that morning. What could've caused her tears?

"My lambs came to school. They wrecked the school and ruined everything. Teacher got hurt and Laura Kemp got a bloody nose, but that wasn't my lambs' fault. Then Mr. Kemp dismissed school and took Laura home. Now everyone is mad at me," she wailed.

Sophie had been hurt? He knelt and grasped Rachel's shoulders to hold her away so he could see her face. "Calm down and tell me what happened. How badly was your teacher hurt?"

"Mr. Kemp said she had the wind knocked out of her and she'll be fine. It was awful." Between Rachel's sobs and her explanation, Karl had a fair notion of what Sophie's first day must have looked like. Her injury didn't sound serious. He prayed it wasn't, but he needed to find out.

Rachel kept crying so he picked her up and went inside the store. Clara rushed over. "What's wrong with Rachel?"

"She had a rough first day at school. I guess the lambs decided to attend. She says they wrecked the school."

"They—did!" Rachel managed between sobs.

Karl patted her back and looked at Clara. "We're going to close up shop and take her home."

For once Clara didn't protest.

At the farm he found three multicolored lambs safely locked in their enclosure. He knocked on Sophie's door but there wasn't any answer. He left Rachel with Clara and walked back to the school. The door stood open, so he stepped inside. Sophie was righting a tipped-over desk and picking up books and sorting papers.

"I thought Rachel had to be exaggerating." He straightened the closest desk. "Are you okay?"

Sophie held her left arm close to her chest. Her face was pale. He could see she was in pain. "I'm fine. What did Rachel tell you?"

"That the lambs wrecked the place."

She gathered several pencils from the floor. "They had a lot of help. Most of this was caused by the older boys trying to wrestle the lambs into submission. April, May and June panicked when the boys tried to grab them. I had no idea they were such strong animals."

"How did you get hurt?"

"Zack Weaver made a dive for one of the sheep. He plowed into me instead. The boy has a hard head."

Karl picked up a textbook and handed it to her. "So just an ordinary day at school?"

She gave a halfhearted chuckle. "I wouldn't go that far. Having a school board member in the mist of the catastrophe added a special touch. I hope the yellow paint comes out of his pants."

"I don't imagine he asked about the Christmas program."

She smiled at him. "I was spared that inquisition today but I'm sure the board will want an update soon."

She sat on the nearest student desk with a weary sigh. "I hope I have a job tomorrow."

He sat down at a desk across from her. "They can't hold you responsible for Rachel's misbegotten sheep."

"Probably not but the pandemonium that followed was because the children paid no attention to me. I should've used your Granny Rose tactic, but it all happened so fast I never even got to my feet."

"I don't understand why you are the one cleaning up. Where is Joanna?"

"She was here for a while, but I sent her to let our aunt know what happened before she hears it from someone else and to assure her that I'm okay. Truthfully, I needed some time to myself."

"I insist you leave the rest of this until your students come in tomorrow. They should be the ones setting things to rights."

She looked around. "I guess you're right. This is their school as much as mine and they should take ownership of it."

He stood up. "Come on. I'll fix you a cup of hot tea."

Her expression brightened. "I believe that is exactly what I need." She dropped the pencils on the floor and got to her feet. She winced, rolled her shoulder and gripped her arm.

"How many times will Zack Weaver have to write 'I will not headbutt the teacher' on your blackboard?"

"I think five thousand will be enough, don't you? Plus he'll have to clean the erasers until he graduates."

Karl laughed. "I was mistaken. You're much tougher than my teacher was."

Sophie liked his laugh. She liked his smile, too. The glint of humor in his eyes did funny things to her insides and made her want to giggle. She was much too mature to actually giggle but she felt like it. Thankfully the pain in her chest and arm let her keep a straight face.

He waited by the door as she got her coat from the cloakroom. He helped her slip it on. The feel of his hands on her shoulders sent a shiver down her spine that had nothing to do with the cold wind blowing in the open door. She quickly stepped outside. "Thank you for coming to check on me. I know Rachel was upset."

"She will recover. It's highly unlikely that she will forget to latch the gate properly after this no matter how excited she is."

"The poor child. She was so eager to start school again this morning." Sophie pulled her coat tightly against the chill. Her arm and chest were aching dreadfully now, but she was determined not to show it,

"You were excited, too," Karl said softly.

She cast him a sidelong glance. He was staring at her. The intensity of his gaze sent heat rushing to her cheeks. "I certainly got more than I bargained for. If tomorrow doesn't go any better, I may have to find another profession. Are you still looking for someone to clerk at your store?"

"I was thinking of asking Joanna if she wanted the job."

Sophie looked up in surprise. "You were?"

"Do you think it's a bad idea?"

"*Nee*, it's an excellent idea."

He was sure to notice her sister's good qualities if they were working side by side every day. Sophie stared at her feet to hide her unhappiness at the prospect.

Karl wasn't surprised when Grace and the bishop showed up at his place later that afternoon. News, good or bad, travels quickly in the Amish community despite the lack of telephones.

He was standing on the front porch when the pair got out of the bishop's buggy. "How is she?" Grace asked.

"Upset, as you might imagine. This wasn't how she expected her first day of school to go."

"Isaac Kemp was upset, too," the bishop said.

"How is Laura?" Karl asked. "Rachel said she had a bloody nose."

"It's not broken but she's going to have two black eyes for a while." The bishop looked toward Sophie's house. "I'd like to speak to her."

"You can," Grace said, "but I will check on her first. Joanna told me Sophie took a hard blow when Zack Weaver plowed into her."

The woman didn't wait for the bishop to answer. She just went into Sophie's house and closed the door.

Karl turned to the bishop. "Physically I think Sophie is okay, but she's worried about her job."

"It was an unfortunate incident. Isaac Kemp is very upset. You must bear some of the responsibility, Karl. They are your sheep."

He nodded meekly. "I'm aware of that."

The front door of Sophie's home opened. Grace beckoned them in.

Sophie and Joanna were in the living room. Sophie held an

ice pack against the front of her left shoulder. She started to put it aside but both Joanna and Grace objected. Sophie reluctantly replaced it while Joanna finished fashioning a sling and knotted it behind Sophie's neck.

Sophie frowned at her sister. "I'm not wearing this to school tomorrow."

"You will wear it this evening and keep an ice pack on that shoulder for at least another hour," Grace said in a tone that brooked no argument.

Sophie grimaced as she slipped her arm in the sling. "It's not as bad as it looks, Bishop."

"It's a nasty bruise and there may be some ligament damage," Grace said. "If it isn't better by the end of school on Wednesday, you will see Bertha. I will send her a message to expect you."

Sophie nodded. "Won't you please sit down, Bishop Wyse. Everyone. Would you like some coffee or tea?"

"Coffee would be *goot*. Just a half a cup." Bishop Wyse took a seat in the wingback chair across from the sofa.

Joanna moved from her spot on the arm of the sofa beside Sophie. "I'll get it."

Sophie shifted her arm uncomfortably. "Bring some of those snickerdoodle cookies we made yesterday, too."

The bishop leaned forward in his chair. "Karl has made me aware that you are worried about your position. I must tell you that Isaac Kemp has asked for your resignation."

Eleven

Grace sprang to her feet. "That's ridiculous, Benjamin. You can't fire her."

Bishop Wyse held up one hand. "Save your indignation, Grace. Sophie has no reason to be concerned about her job. It was an unfortunate episode and nothing more."

Karl saw the relief in Sophie's eyes. "*Danki*, I wasn't sure that Isaac Kemp would feel the same way."

The bishop chuckled. "He is a fair-minded man even if he was upset about his granddaughter's injury. I reminded him that he gave me a bloody nose in the fifth grade when we quarreled over which one of us Jenny Barkman liked the best and no one asked for our teacher to be replaced. Children get bumps and bruises at school sometimes, although sheep are rarely the culprits. I only came by today to make sure you are okay, Sophie. And to remind Karl to keep his sheep penned up properly."

The front door banged open, and Rachel raced into the room followed by her three drenched lambs. The smell of wet wool was overpowering. Rachel skidded to a halt in front of the bishop, where she stood with her head bowed and her hands clasped in front of her. The sheep huddled behind her as if they knew they were in trouble. Their paint had faded but it wasn't completely washed out.

"It wasn't teacher's fault, Bishop. It was mine. I'm the one who should be punished. Please don't send her away." She dropped to her knees and threw her arms around the lamb with a pink-hued ear. "April, May and June are very sorry."

Clara came rushing. "I'm sorry, *Daed*, I couldn't stop her. Rachel, you shouldn't interrupt when grown-ups are having a discussion. It's rude."

"But I have to save teacher's job. Bartholomew Kemp said his grandpa was going to have her fired."

The bishop smiled kindly at Rachel. "I have not come to fire your teacher."

"Get those sheep out of here. When did you see Bart?" Karl asked.

"He just came by to tell her she would be getting a new teacher," Clara said.

The bishop frowned. "Bartholomew is guilty of carrying tales. I will speak with him about repeating gossip. It is good that you want to protect your teacher, Rachel, but your sister is right. It is rude to interrupt grown-ups when they're having a discussion."

"I'm sorry," Rachel said meekly.

"Take your lambs outside and finish washing the paint off them," Karl said sternly. "And make sure they are locked up."

"Okay." She left with her head bowed. The lambs followed meekly after her.

The bishop chuckled. "You have your hands full with that one, Karl."

"She needs a mother's influence as well as a father's guiding hand," Grace said.

Karl and Clara both scowled at her. "Not that again," he said.

"I'm sorry. I spoke out of turn," Grace said, but she didn't look the least contrite.

Sophie broke the tense silence. "Clara, why don't you help Joanna in the kitchen. She's fixing coffee for everyone. There's some lemonade for you and Rachel in the refrigerator. Have your sister come in when she is done with her sheep."

Clara nodded and left the room after one more unhappy glance at Grace.

Karl and the others sat in silence until Joanna came in with a tray of cups and a coffeepot. She filled the cups and handed them out. Clara set a plate loaded with cookies on the little table beside the bishop's chair and then went outside.

"How's the arm feeling now?" Grace asked.

"Better. Can I take the ice off?" Sophie asked.

Grace took the ice pack from Sophie and handed it to Joanna. "See that she uses it for twenty minutes at least twice more before bedtime."

"I will." Joanna took the pack into the kitchen and returned. She snagged a cookie from the plate and settled on the arm of the sofa beside her sister.

The bishop took a bite of his. "There are *wunderbar*. Almost as *goot* as yours, Grace."

Karl caught the look that Grace exchanged with the bishop before she blushed a pretty shade of pink. Joanna grinned and nudged Sophie. Was something going on between the older couple? Grace wasn't Amish, but the bishop was looking at her with a special tenderness. Karl and the bishop had talked about how much they missed their departed wives only the day before. If the bishop had formed a tenderness for Grace, then maybe Karl wasn't misguided in his growing feelings for Sophie.

Rachel and Clara came in without the sheep, putting an end to Karl's speculation. He'd ask Sophie about the bishop and her aunt later.

When his girls had their glasses of lemonade in one hand and a cookie in the other, the bishop smile at Rachel. "Did your teacher share her plans for the Christmas program with the school today?"

Rachel shook her head. "Nope. Are you going to do that tomorrow, teacher Sophie?"

Sophie shook her head. "The truth is I haven't finalized my plans, Bishop."

"Everyone in the community is eager to hear what you've decided on," he said.

Clara chuckled and nudged her sister. "The school already has a shepherd with you and your flock. We'll find you a donkey and a cow and they can have a living Nativity."

Sophie cocked her head to the side. "What did you say?"

"I said you already have a shepherd."

Excitement filled Sophie's eyes. "A living Nativity. Bishop, has it been done before?"

He shook his head. "Not that I recall."

"Would it be permitted?" Grace asked.

"I can't see a problem. We have often had the children portray the holy family, angels and shepherds."

"I have twenty kids. Mary, Joseph, a shepherd. What else do we need?"

"A couple of shepherds," Clara said. "Plus the innkeeper who turned Mary and Joseph away. We could have a few townspeople and the three wise men. It could be a play with everyone saying their lines."

Sophie bit the corner of her lip. "*Nee*, we don't have time for that. We can't expect all the children to learn lines and parts in four weeks. It would be better to have a narrator tell the story while the children acted out the parts."

"You wouldn't want the animals in the school," Karl said.

As quick as it had come on, her enthusiasm faded. "You're right. It wouldn't work."

Karl shook his head. "I'm not saying it wouldn't work. I'm saying it would be better to hold it outside."

"You mean move the parents and visitors outside to watch? That might be a little risky. What if snowed or rained?" Sophie asked.

Grace waved aside her objection. "Bah, who's afraid of a little weather? We're out in it every day anyway."

Joanna laughed. "You're right. I can't see Mrs. Bachman being put off by a few snowflakes if her girls were going to be angels again."

"I wanted to be an angel this year," Rachel said, a pout pushing her lower lip out.

Sophie leaned toward her. "The shepherdess is going to be a much more important character this year."

Rachel sat up straight. "Really?"

"I promise." Sophie had no idea how she would manage it, but Rachel and her sheep would have a major part.

Bishop Wyse rose to his feet. "We should get going. I have a few more stops I need to make."

Grace leaned down and pulled a pint jar from her bag. "Rose sent this along. It's one of her herbal teas. You are to make a cup and drink it before bed. It will help you sleep."

Joanna took the jar from Grace. "I'll make sure she drinks it."

Karl got up, too. He didn't have an excuse to linger in Sophie's company. Joanna led the way to the front door. He held back as the others went out. "If she needs anything, don't hesitate to come over and ask."

Joanna smiled and patted his arm. "*Danki*. I know you care about her."

It surprised him that Joanna noticed something he'd only recently realized for himself. He glanced into the sitting room. Sophie had her head back and her eyes closed but her drawn features told him she was still in pain. "I do care about her. I'll help any way I can."

By morning Sophie could barely move her arm. The muscles of her chest ached unbearably. The small mirror on her dresser showed a dark purple bruise around her scar extending into her armpit. She gently probed the area. When her fingers found a small lump in the middle of the bruise, she stopped breathing.

No.

Her fingers shook as she took note of the size and location. It was almost identical to the cancerous lump she had found a year ago. As much as she had been expecting her cancer to return, it was devastating to find proof that it had.

She sat on the end of her bed and struggled not to cry. "You knew this day would come, Sophie Eicher. Don't waste tears on it."

She believed that she was ready to face the inevitable, but it came too soon.

"I wanted more time with Joanna and with my schoolchildren. Please, Lord, I want to see Joanna marry. I hadn't dared hope I would hold her baby one day but Dear Lord, I wanted to meet him or her and to know our family is going on into the future."

And she wanted more time with Karl. They could have

been friends, close friends. She longed to instill a love of learning in Clara and Rachel and watch them grow.

The loss of those moments was the most painful to face. "I thought I was ready, but I'm not."

She wouldn't tell Joanna, of course. Her sister would be distraught. Joanna would insist on all kinds of tests that Sophie didn't want to endure again. Grace had made an appointment with Dr. Rock. Sophie would keep it although she didn't believe there was anything that could be done. This was God's will.

Getting dressed proved to be excruciating. Her arm had been weak since her surgery, but now she could barely move it. As much as she hated the idea, she realized she was going to have to wear the sling if she had any hope of getting through the day.

When she came out of her room, she was surprised to see Joanna had breakfast ready. Her sister took one look at her and rushed to her side. "Is it bad?"

Sophie forced a smile to her stiff lips. "Bad enough for me to wear the sling."

"Did you get any sleep?"

"Rose's herbal tea helped. It makes me wonder what's in it."

"It's probably best that we don't know. You look pale."

It was terribly tempting to share her discovery, but she couldn't. There would be time later. If Joanna knew, she would stop looking for a spouse. She'd devote herself to taking care of Sophie and that was the last thing Sophie wanted. If her sister could find love, Sophie could leave this world without regret.

She moved away from Joanna. "It aches. I'm sure it will get better the more I move. Just coffee for me this morning."

"Nonsense. You need to keep up your strength. You don't want the children running roughshod over you. They're like wild dogs, you know. They sense weakness."

Sophie chuckled. "That is a terrible thing to say about children."

"Maybe but I still think it's true. Your lunch is in the paper sack on the counter."

"That's very sweet of you."

A smug grin appeared on Joanna's face. "I know it is. I'll fix breakfast and a lunch for you from now on until your arm is better. I told you I was going to be more mature in our new home."

"You did. Does that mean you will be doing the laundry this week?"

"Of course," Joanna said quickly but Sophie could tell she had caught her sister off guard.

"Don't worry about it. I'll take care of the clothes."

"Nonsense. You are going to take it easy when you get home. I didn't nurse you through cancer to lose you to unruly sheep and rough boys." Joanna went back to the stove, turned the bacon frying on the back burner and stirred her scrambled eggs one more time before taking the skillet off the heat. She dumped the eggs onto a platter. "This is ready. Sit down."

Joanna was such a dear. Tears pricked the back of Sophie's eyes. "I hope you know how much I love you."

Joanna gave her a puzzled look. "You aren't usually emotional. What's wrong?"

"Nothing that a couple of aspirin won't cure. It all smells wonderful."

Sophie sat down and folded her hands to pray. When she had finished praying, she took a sip of her coffee. Joanna ladled eggs and two slices of bacon onto Sophie's plate and then added some to her own. Sophie took another sip of coffee. Was this a good time to tell Joanna Karl was interested in offering her a job or should she wait for him to say something?

No, she didn't have time to waste. "Karl wondered if you might be interested in working at his store."

"Me? Really?"

Sophie reached over and patted her sister's hand. "You would do a fine job and it wouldn't hurt to have a little extra money coming in. Christmas is coming. It would be nice to send some home to Papa and his new family."

Joanna frowned. "I don't know."

"Would you mind working with Karl?" How could Joanna not want to spend time with him? Sophie couldn't think of anything better than working beside him.

"It's not that. I just don't want to be unavailable if you need me. I should have been with you at school yesterday instead of unpacking boxes."

"I doubt it would have made a difference. Besides, if you do go to work for Karl, you would only be a mile away."

"True. You really think he would hire me?"

"You've had experience working with *Daed* in the grocery store for years. Karl would be fortunate to have you. I think he likes you, and you like him, don't you?"

Joanna smiled at Sophie. "Of course I like him. You do, too."

Sophie looked down at her coffee hoping Joanna couldn't see how much she cared for Karl. "You should speak to him."

Joanna tipped her head slightly as she considered the suggestion. "Was this your idea?"

"Not at all."

"It seems like something you'd come up with to get me out from underfoot."

"That isn't fair."

"You're right. I'll consider it. After Thanksgiving. We still have more unpacking to do."

"I'm sure you'll enjoy having a job again." Why did the idea of Joanna working with Karl hurt more than her bruised chest? That was what she wanted, wasn't it?

She knew the answer. It hurt because she cared for Karl. It was time to admit it. If things have been different, she might have considered walking out with him. Not that he would've asked her. That was a foolish thought, but he was a special man. She had been drawn to him from the first day they met.

But he needed someone like Joanna, not her. Someone cheerful and loyal who adored his kids. Joanna and Rachel already shared a special bond. If Joanna worked with Karl day in and day out, he would soon see she was the person who could heal his heart.

Tears gathered in Sophie's eyes, but she blinked them away. She would be happy for both of them. Karl would take care of Joanna. She wouldn't have to worry about her sister when the end came.

It wasn't possible to keep her fake smile in place a second longer. Joanna would be crushed when she found out Sophie's cancer had returned, but she wouldn't learn it today. "I should get going. I don't want to be tardy. Thanks for making my lunch. I'm sure I will enjoy it."

Sophie escaped out the front door without meeting her sister's eyes. She had hoped for a few minutes to compose herself as she walked to school but she found Karl, Rachel and Clara waiting for her.

"Good morning, teacher. We're going to walk to school with you," Rachel said.

Sophie squared her shoulder. "Good morning to all of you. It isn't necessary for you to escort me to school."

"It's no trouble," Karl said. "We are walking in the same direction."

"I made extra sure that my lambs can't get out. They are

locked in a stall in the barn and the barn door is closed and latched. Clara checked it, too."

"*Danki*, Clara. I wouldn't want a repeat of yesterday."

"I'm almost sorry I missed it," Clara said. "But I am sorry that you got hurt. Come on, Rachel, I'll race you to the road."

"I get a head start because I'm little." Rachel was already running by the time she finished speaking.

"Don't run into the road," Karl shouted.

"I won't," Rachel shouted back.

Karl glanced at Sophie. "How's your arm?"

"Sore." She didn't want to talk about herself. "Clara seems in a good mood this morning."

"It meant a lot to her that you considered her idea for the living Nativity even if she was jesting when she said it. I think it made her feel a little more grown-up. She appreciates it that you aren't begging her to come back to school."

"She said that?"

"Not in so many words but I can tell her attitude toward you is softening. Did you mention to your sister that I was interested in hiring her?"

Sophie stopped and turned to face him. "I did, but you should ask her anyway. She suspects it was my idea although I told her it wasn't. She thinks I try to run her life."

"Don't you?"

"Not at all. Joanna is capable of making her own decisions." As soon as she said it Sophie realized she did have trouble allowing Joanna to be in charge of her own life. She would have to stop interfering. Once Joanna was settled.

Sophie started walking. Karl caught up with her in a few steps. "Is something wrong?"

Keeping her eyes down, she avoided looking him. "Why would you ask that?"

"Sometimes I get the feeling that you are hiding something."

She glanced at him then. He was too observant for his own good. She would have to do better at hiding her illness. "That's nonsense."

It was his turn to look away. "I reckon you're right."

They had reached the road where Clara and Rachel stood waiting. "I won!" Rachel shouted.

Clara rolled her eyes. "Only because I let you."

Rachel threw her arms around her sister. "I wish you were coming to school with me, Clara."

"I have to help *Daed*."

"I know." Rachel's disappointment was clear.

"It won't be forever," Karl said.

Rachel stepped back. "But if Clara doesn't come back to school now she won't get to be in the Christmas program," Rachel said. "And it was her idea."

"Maybe there is a way Clara can be part of the program without coming to school. I'm told you have written some wonderful stories," Sophie said.

Clara shrugged. "I wouldn't call them wonderful."

"I would," Rachel said. "Especially the one about the bunny in the backyard. I liked that one the best."

"Would you be interested in writing the part our narrator will read during the play? I know you are busy helping your father, but he could consider this part of your homeschooling. Basically, you would be explaining the Christmas story while the children portrayed the characters. I will be happy to help you with it. You wouldn't have to be the one to read it unless you wanted to do that. What you think?"

It wasn't the same as having Clara in school, but it would give Sophie a chance to help her with her writing skills and with her English comprehension.

Clara looked at her father. "What do you think, *Daed*?"

"I think it's something you would be good at, and it would be a way to be a part of the program even if you're not in school."

Clara nodded. "I'll think it over and give you my decision tomorrow."

"Wonderful." Sophie tried not to think about how many months she would have to help the children of the community develop a love of learning. She had today, and she was grateful for that.

She turned to Rachel. "Are you sure the sheep are contained?"

Rachel nodded vigorously. "They won't get out today."

Sophie held out her hand and Rachel took it. "Then let's go to school and learn something new. I believe if I don't learn something new every day it's a wasted day."

Rachel dipped her head to the side. "But you're the teacher. Don't you know everything already?"

Sophie laughed and looked at Karl. "Shall I let her go on believing that?"

He grinned. "She'll find out soon enough that adults, even teachers, aren't all knowing."

As he smiled at her, Sophie was glad he wasn't the stern fellow she had met the first day with her arms full of puppies. Glancing at the schoolyard, she paused. "I thought I was going to be late but none of the children are playing outside. Has school been canceled?"

"No one told me that." Karl walked beside her as she crossed the road and went up the steps. He opened the door. All the children and their mothers were inside. The desks had been straightened, and papers and books had been picked up. At the front of the room several of the students were washing the paint off the floor. Bartholomew Kemp was writing on the blackboard with his grandfather overseeing the boy's work.

Mrs. Weaver caught sight of Sophie and rushed over. "I'm so glad you are well enough to return to school today. When Zackary told me what happened I don't know which one of us was more upset. Is your arm broken?"

Sophie shook her head. "I don't think so but it's painful when I try to move."

"I'll be here all day in case you need anything. If you find you need to go home early, Mrs. Kemp has agreed to take over your class. She was a teacher years ago."

"Bless you, Mrs. Kemp. How is Laura?"

"She's fine today. I think she more frightened than truly hurt. Her grandfather overreacted. Laura is the apple of his eye."

Sophie tried to see what Bart and his grandfather were doing. "What is Bart writing?"

Isaac Kemp turned around and came to stand in front of Sophie. "The bishop suggested he write 'I will not spread gossip' one hundred times. I'm to make sure he gets them all done, and I'd like to apologize for my hasty words that led Bart to believe I was going to have you fired. I'm sorry for any distress Bart and I caused."

"You are forgiven. It was a stressful day for all of us. Children, if you will take your seats, I have an announcement about the Christmas program."

Once the room was quiet, Sophie went up front to her desk, where she noticed three cardboard boxes. "What's this?"

"Open them," Mrs. Kemp said with a wide grin.

Sophie pulled back the flap and saw a ham surrounded by several jars. Picking up one of them, she saw it was pickled beets.

"We thought you might have difficulty fixing a Thanksgiving dinner, so we all pitched in," Isaac said.

Sophie's throat tightened with emotion. "This is very kind. Joanna and I have been invited to the inn so we will be able to share this bounty with our Aunt Grace and others. *Danki*. Rose asked me to make frog-eye salad." Sophie patted her sling. "I'm going to need help catching the frogs. Do I have any volunteers?"

Everyone laughed. Looking over the smiling faces in the room, Sophie grew determined to give this caring community the best possible Christmas Eve program.

Karl left the school with Clara and walked toward town. "I hope Sophie's second day of school goes better than her first."

"If anything else happens it won't be because of Rachel's sheep. Did you get the order for those new lamps sent?" Clara asked.

Buck came running down the road after them and began frisking at Clara's feet and nipping at her shoestrings.

Clara glared at him. "Should I take him back home?"

Karl shook his head. The pup might officially belong to Joanna, but he seemed to prefer Clara's company. "I expect Joanna will know where he has gone. I'll get the lamp parts ordered first thing in the morning."

"That's what you said yesterday."

"That was before Joseph Troyer came in with his supply list. He's doing a big remodel on Bob Taylor's auto store. It took me most of the morning to get together everything he needs. He's coming in today to pick up his order."

"Then you should finish that, and I will choose the new lamps and get that order in the mail. Buck, stop that." She scolded the dog for tugging on her skirt. He immediately settled down. He minded Clara better than anyone.

"How do you know which lamps I want?"

"You won't care what they look like as long as people buy them."

There was no arguing with that logic.

He spent the morning getting Joseph's order together and stacked on the loading dock out back. When he came inside, he saw a couple of tourists stop to peer in the front window, but they went on down the street. Which was too bad—a couple of sales would've brightened his day.

He chastised himself for being greedy. Joseph's order would bring in enough to see the business through another week. He had another three weeks before the mortgage payment was due on the building. The banker had been understanding in the past when Karl hadn't been able to make a payment.

The bell over the door jingled. He looked up to see Rose coming in with two Amish women he didn't recognize. He could feel his muscles tensing as he fought the urge to scurry away to the back room. "Morning, Rose."

"Good morning, Karl. I'd like you to meet Wilma and Fannie Youtsey. Mother and daughter. They are hoping to open a café here in town."

The older one of the pair looked to be in her forties with a few streaks of gray in her dark hair. The daughter couldn't be older than twenty-five. "Nice to meet you. Welcome to our community."

Wilma looked from him to her daughter and back again. "Rose tells me that you are a widower with two daughters. My daughter is very good with children."

Fannie blushed bright red but stared at her shoes without saying a word. He couldn't imagine Sophie being so meek in the same situation.

He glared at Rose. "I hope Rose also told you I have no desire to remarry."

Wilma didn't bat an eye. "She did mention that, but meeting the right girl can change a man's mind on such matters."

He inclined his head slightly. The girl might change his mind, but knowing who his mother-in-law would be cinched the deal for Karl. "If you need anything, my daughter Clara can help you. I have work out back I need to finish."

Wilma looked miffed. Fannie appeared relieved. Rose followed him out the back door. He turned to face her on the loading dock. "Are you ever going to give up?"

"I know what you're thinking. All I did was mention that you are a widower and you will have the shop next door to her if she buys the empty building beside you. The reason I followed you out here is to thank you for allowing the girls to stay after prayer service last Sunday. I thoroughly enjoyed having them."

Karl looked at his feet. "You were right about me taking them home early on church Sundays. Nora wouldn't have been happy with me for keeping the girls away from their friends just because I didn't want to talk to people."

"Nora was a good mother above all else."

"She was." He felt his throat tighten. It was still hard to talk about her, but he wasn't as angry as he had been before Sophie fixed the curtain rod in his living room. Funny how her simple act of kindness had infuriated him at first, but ultimately changed the way he looked at his life for the better.

"Do you and the girls have plans for Thanksgiving?" Rose asked.

He shook his head. "It will be a quiet day at home."

"Nonsense. You are all invited to the inn and don't say you can't come. We want to make Joanna and Sophie feel they are a welcome part of the community. I heard what happened to Sophie at school. Grace says she has a severe bruise and maybe some ligament damage to her arm."

"She was feeling well enough to go to school today although she is wearing a sling."

"At least she is being sensible about that, but she should go see Dr. Bertha."

"Grace said she was going to make an appointment for her."

"Be sure Sophie keeps it. She can be stubborn about medical care."

"What makes you say that?"

"Just something that Grace told me before Sophie moved here."

"She did say she was in the hospital for some minor surgery."

"It was more than minor, but I can see her explaining it away like that. I don't know the whole story, but Grace said Sophie can be pigheaded about seeing doctors. You will make sure she goes to see Bertha, won't you?"

"I don't know why she would listen to me."

"Sophie respects your opinion, but don't tell her I said that." Rose turned and walked away.

Karl smiled to himself. So, Sophie respected his opinion. It was oddly pleasing to know that.

Twelve

The following morning, Sophie's arm and chest hurt worse than the day before. The bruise had spread down her side. She dressed in a mental fog. A cup of Rose's special tea the previous night had helped her sleep but left her groggy.

In the kitchen Joanna handed Sophie a bowl of oatmeal and lifted her black traveling bonnet from the peg by the front door. "Have a nice day at school."

Sophie glanced her way. "Where are you going?"

"I promised Grace that I'd help her get ready for the Thanksgiving dinner. Bye."

"I thought you could see if Karl and his girls need help fixing a covered dish to take."

Joanna frowned. "Why?"

"A *goot* wife never goes visiting without something special in hand. The girls should be shown how to make a simple but tasty dish."

"I'm not the cook or teacher that you are, and I'm certainly not a wife."

"You could be soon."

"Not unless you know something I don't. See you tonight." Joanna hurried out.

Sophie doctored the bland, slightly scorched oatmeal with a handful of raisins and brown sugar. At the stove she found Joanna had forgotten to turn the heat on under the coffee. The pot was full of room-temperature water instead of the coffee she needed. She glanced at the clock. There wasn't time to perk some now. Nor had Joanna fixed a lunch as she had promised yesterday. Sophie settled for peanut butter on bread and an apple.

She ate her oatmeal, gathered her things together and went out the door juggling her books and her lunch in her one good arm. Karl was waiting on her porch steps cleaning a bridle. Rachel was nowhere in sight.

He stood up, tipped his hat and hung the bridle over his shoulder. "You have the sling on again. I reckon it's foolish to ask if your arm is better."

What was foolish was the way her heart broke into a gallop at his nearness. She took a deep breath to regain control of her emotions. It didn't help. She was overwhelmed with the smell of autumn leaves and saddle soap mixed with the essence that was uniquely Karl's own. Masculine and disturbing.

She could feel a blush creeping up her cheeks. She hurried down the steps without looking at him. "I'm better. Where is Rachel?"

"She went on ahead."

The aroma of fresh coffee wafted up from a cup on the steps beside him and stopped her flight. Her stomach rumbled. Should she ask? It seemed forward, but her foggy head won out over decorum. "Would you happen to have any of that coffee left?"

He looked surprised. "I do. It might not be very hot. I turned the heat off when I went out to do chores."

"Even lukewarm will be fine. Just black. I really could use a cup."

"Be right back."

He strode into his house and came out a minute later with a white mug in his hand. "It's warmer than I thought it would be."

She put her books and lunch down, took the mug from him and sipped the warm, dark brew. It was excellent coffee even if it wasn't hot. The jolt of caffeine was exactly what she needed to counteract the effects of Rose's herbal tea.

"This is *goot*. You're a lifesaver." She took another gulp.

He chuckled. "If you're out of coffee I can pick some up for you while I'm in town."

It was a kind offer. One any neighbor might make. She shouldn't read anything special into it. Only the earnest expression in his eyes suggested this was something more than a neighborly gesture. An overture of friendship? She took another sip while she decided how to respond and then stared into the mug.

"I have coffee. I simply overslept this morning. Joanna doesn't drink coffee so she forgot to turn on the heat under the pot. I didn't have time to make my own."

He reached down and picked up her books.

"I can manage those," she said quickly.

"So can I. Finish your coffee."

She gulped it down. Putting the cup beside his on the step, she held out her arm. "I'll take my things now."

He chuckled and started walking. "I never thought I'd be carrying books to school for the teacher."

Sophie glanced at him from the corner of her eye as she fell into step beside him. Her curiosity about Karl Graber couldn't be contained. "Did you carry books for a special girl?"

A sad smile curved his lips. "I carried Nora's. I was sweet on her from the day we met in the first grade."

Sophie was instantly sorry she had said anything. "You must miss her very much."

"I do, but it's getting easier to talk about her. I think I have you to thank for that."

Stunned, she stopped and looked at him. "Me? How?"

"When you fixed the curtain rod in my home you disrupted a ritual that I had held on to for far too long."

Shame at her bold and unhelpful behavior weighed her down. "I am sorry about that."

"As I am sorry for the way I reacted."

"Forgiven and forgotten," she said softly.

They walked on in silence for a dozen yards, then he spoke again. "My wife loved to watch the sun come up every morning. Normally we took our coffee out to the front porch and talked about our plans for the day. Even on rainy or cold winter days she would stand at that window to watch the sky grow lighter behind the clouds. When she became so ill that she couldn't get up herself, I would make the coffee then I would carry her to the chair by the window so she could watch the dawn. Eventually she became so weak she couldn't sit by herself, so I held her on my lap." His voice cracked.

Sophie's heart ached for his pain.

"On that last day I was late doing my chores. The sun was already coming up when I hurried toward the house. Somehow, she had managed to make it to the window without me. I saw her grip the curtain and then fall backward, pulling it down with her. She was gone when I reached her. Dr. Bertha said her heart just gave out. Anyway, I couldn't bring myself to move the chair or fix the curtain rod. It was the last place I held her in my arms. I sat there and watched the sun come up without her for many months wondering why she was gone instead of me."

Sophie fought back tears as she listened to his story of profound love and loss. "Karl, I'm so sorry."

"I know we shouldn't speak about the dead because it means we question *Gott*'s decision to take them from this life. The truth is I do question His will. I was so angry at Him for taking her from me that I couldn't see what a gift her time with me had been. Or what an immense blessing my daughters are. I made that corner of the room a shrine to keep my grief alive, not her memory. In doing so I shut out my daughters, my friends and even *Gott*."

"*Gott* understands our grief."

"I hope so. Then a busybody teacher showed up to point out the error of my ways. I'm grateful for that although I know I didn't act like it that day." They had reached the road. A few children were already playing on the swings across the schoolyard. He turned to Sophie. "What I'm trying to say is that I'm learning, teacher. Thanks to you."

Bartholomew Kemp came running up to them. "Morning, teacher Sophie. Can I do anything to help you today?"

"You can carry in her books for her." Karl handed them to the eager youth, who darted away into the school building.

Karl smiled at her and touched the brim of his hat. "Have a *goot* day and see the doctor about your arm."

"I will," Sophie managed to mutter past the lump in her throat. Why was she blessed to meet such an amazing man when her life was almost over?

The answer was suddenly and painfully clear. Because he was meant for Joanna.

★ ★ ★

The school day was uneventful except for a minor scrap she had to break up between Mark Lehman and Ben Weaver at recess. The children suggested songs for the Christmas program that they liked, and she assigned roles so that their mothers could start getting their costumes ready.

Most of the boys would wear their father's or older brother's bathrobes and simple kitchen towels for headdresses. The girls would need long dresses and hair coverings to match. She allowed Miriam and Thea Bachman to be angels again and assured Rachel that she would help make her shepherdess outfit. The boys who were to be the wise men wanted foil-covered crowns and she agreed although some might feel it was too fancy. This might very well be the only Christmas she would have with these children. She wanted it to be special for them.

After school, Sophie walked downtown to Bertha Rock's medical clinic. She was happy to see the waiting room was empty. She checked in with the receptionist and sat down in one of the blue chairs that lined the walls of the room. It wasn't long before Bertha appeared.

"Sophie, how nice to see you again. I heard about your first day of school. I'm sorry you were injured. Step into my exam room."

Sophie followed the doctor to another room and sat on the edge of a chair in the corner. "You should know a little about my history before you examine me. I have had mastectomy on my left side."

"All right. Let me check your blood pressure and listen to your heart. Then I will take down your history."

The elderly woman was brisk and thorough. She hung her stethoscope around her neck when she was finished with it and picked up a clipboard. "Your blood pressure is great and your heart and lungs sound fine. When was your mastectomy?"

"Almost a year ago."

"You're very young to have had breast cancer."

"It's hereditary. My mother and my grandmother both died of the disease."

"I'm sorry. Do you have a BRCA1 or BRCA2 gene mutation?"

"I don't know."

Dr. Bertha looked surprised. "Surely your oncologist discussed genetic testing with you before your surgery?"

"There was no point. It is *Gott*'s will."

"I understand and admire the Amish's acceptance of God's will in all things, but I am a doctor. I use both science and faith to help people. Has your cancer metastasized? How many lymph nodes were involved?"

"I don't know."

"Didn't your surgeon tell you in his follow-up visits? He should have had your biopsy results within a few days."

"I didn't want to know the details. It wouldn't change anything. He said chemotherapy was my best option. Joanna insisted I take the treatments. My mother also had a mastectomy, but her cancer came back. My cancer will return. I am grateful for the extra months that my surgery and chemotherapy gave me."

Dr. Bertha's gaze softened. "Extra months is a dim view of your surgery's success. You should be thinking years. Breast cancer is a common disease. It affects about one out of every eight women in the United States but only five to ten percent of breast cancers are related to mutations of those high-risk genes. Even if you have the mutation, it doesn't mean your cancer will return."

Sophie gripped her fingers tightly together. "It has already come back. I found another lump yesterday."

"I see. Go ahead and take off your dress. Put on one of these gowns, leave it open in the front and lie down on the exam table. I'll be back in a few minutes."

Sophie shivered as she lay down on the cool vinyl covered with crinkly paper. She tried to hold back her fear. Some part of her wanted to hear that she was fine even though she knew she wasn't. When Dr. Bertha returned, her exam was gentle as she probed the tender area. "That is a very nasty bruise. Is this the lump you felt?"

Sophie nodded, unable to speak.

"I don't believe it's a tumor, Sophie. It feels like an encapsulated hematoma to me. Basically, a blood clot under the skin, which is consistent with your injury. You can wait and see if it goes away on its own. If it gets larger or feels hot to the touch, then you should come to see me right away. Or I can do the ultrasound now and put your mind at ease."

Sophie's fingers were cold and stiff with fear as she clenched them together. "Go ahead and do it now."

It didn't take long for Dr. Bertha to bring in her machine. When she was finished, she pushed it aside. "I will have a specialist look at this, but to my eyes, it's a blood clot."

"You don't think it's my cancer?" Profound relief swept through Sophie. Did this mean she had more time? She was almost afraid to hope.

"I don't. Fear about their cancer coming back is the most common emotional challenge people face after cancer treatment. It's normal to worry about it, especially during the first months. Survivors often fear any new symptom means their cancer has returned. I suggest you keep a diary of your symptoms to discuss with me so you don't worry unnecessarily. I'm going to send for your medical records. I'll need your permission for that. If I'm going to be your primary doctor, I want to know your history in detail."

"If you think it best."

"Good. People say their fear of their cancer returning fades over time. However, things like this injury, or the anniversary of your diagnosis can make you worry unduly. That's normal. When your fear interferes with your quality of life, that is a good time to come and see me. There is also a cancer survivor group that meets monthly at the inn. I can give you that information if you are interested."

"Perhaps later."

Dr. Bertha examined Sophie's arm and chest. "You definitely have sprained ligaments, but I don't believe they are torn. I recommend you keep the arm immobile with a sling for the next three weeks. You may need physical therapy, too."

She went to the small desk in the corner and pulled out a pad of paper. "I'm going to give you a prescription for the pain. This drug can make you groggy so use it with caution until you know how it affects you. If they don't help, I want to know. Don't make me sic Rose and Grace on you to find out how you are doing."

Sophie grinned. "I won't."

"Let's see you back here in a week and again in four weeks. Now, Grace is going birding with us the Saturday after next. Would you care to join us?"

"I'm afraid I'm not a bird-watcher."

Dr. Bertha chuckled. "We'll fix that if you give us half a chance. Abby and Joseph regularly join us."

Dr. Bertha tore a page from the pad and handed it to Sophie. "I will see you tomorrow at the inn. The major and I have been invited to Thanksgiving dinner along with Joseph and Abby and Bishop Wyse. Grace tells me Karl Graber and his girls will be there, too. It's wonderful to see him coming out of the self-imposed isolation he has lived in since his wife's passing. He's too young to give up on life. He has everything to live for."

Karl would be there? Sophie wasn't sure if she was glad or dismayed by the news.

The next morning, Sophie was grateful for the pain medicine Dr. Bertha had given her as she helped her sister prepare and pack the box of food they were taking to Thanksgiving dinner at the inn.

Joanna frowned at their box. "Should I have made rolls?"

"It's too late to be asking that question. We should get going if we're to help set up before everyone arrives."

Joanna frowned. "Who is everyone? I thought it was just us."

"Dr. Bertha and the major are coming. So are Joseph and Abby."

"I'm sure Grace invited Benjamin-I-mean-Bishop Wyse," Joanna said and winked.

"She did." Sophie watched Joanna's face carefully. "Karl and the girls have been invited, too."

Joanna's expression didn't change. If she was delighted to spend the afternoon in Karl's company, she didn't show it. "I hope they like frog-eye salad. Maybe I should make more."

Sophie flinched. "Please don't call it that."

Joanna laughed. "All right. Rose's favorite fruit salad."

"*Danki*. This is enough. I'm sure there will be lots of good food. You know Aunt Grace is a mighty fine baker and the families from school supplied us with a huge ham and fixings."

"You're right. Okay, let's go."

They walked out the front door to find a chestnut pony with a flaxen mane and tail hitched to a two-wheeled cart standing at the front gate. Clara was rubbing the pony's face. "This is Buster. He's my pony, but *Daed* said you should use him today because you might want to come home early. I don't mind you taking him."

"Are you sure, Clara?" Sophie didn't want another conflict between them.

"He needs the exercise. I have chores to do." The girl started to turn away.

"Clara, would you like to come over on Saturday evening and discuss your ideas for the Christmas play?" Sophie asked quickly.

A gleam of interest appeared in the girl's eyes. "I guess I could."

"Great. I'm eager to hear them. I'd like to know what you think of the songs we've chosen, too."

"You really want my opinion?"

"I do."

"Okay. I'll be over."

Sophie wasn't positive but she thought she detected a hint of a smile before Clara walked away.

"You really want her to come back to school, don't you?" Joanna asked.

"She is a bright girl who is trying very hard to be a grown-up when she should be enjoying her childhood."

"You know she's going to work in the store until she gets married and then she's going to raise children. Does she really need an education for that?"

Sophie looked at her sister in shock. "How can you say that? Of course she needs an education. How else will she learn to make smart business decisions in the store and in her home life? How will she learn to raise children without a mother to show her what to do? Without learning to read German, how will she gain comfort from our Bible? Book learning isn't everything, but it makes our lives better. *Gott* gave us a brain. We should use it."

Joanna leaned forward and kissed Sophie's cheek. "I love it when you get passionate about something. The children of this community are blessed to have you as their teacher."

For now. For however long the Lord allowed her to stay. If Bertha was right and the new lump wasn't cancer, then she might have more time to make a difference to the children in Harts Haven. She held on to that sliver of hope and prayed the specialist reading her ultrasound would agree with Dr. Bertha.

Joanna drove the cart. When they arrived at the inn, two buggies were already in the parking lot. She recognized Bishop Wyse's, but she wasn't sure about the other one.

It turned out to belong to Jeff and Eli Hostetter. Both men were sitting in the living room conversing with Bishop Wyse. Jeff got to his feet. "Is there anything you need help with, Joanna?"

She smiled sweetly at him. "I left the pony tied up outside. Could you unhitch him and give him his feed bag? It's in the back of the wagon."

"Consider it done." He smiled brightly at her and went out.

Sophie leaned toward Joanna. "It's not right to lead the boy on."

"I'm doing no such thing." Joanna turned in a huff and went into the kitchen.

Sophie was thankful that Karl wasn't here to see her sister flirting. She would have a talk with Joanna later.

The mouthwatering aromas of baking ham, fresh hot rolls, pumpkin and apple pies filled the kitchen air. Susanna was washing lettuce for a garden salad while Grace pulled another pie from the oven. Rose sat on a stool by the counter with a cup of coffee and a slice of pie in front of her.

Sophie smiled. "Dessert first?"

"At my age, always. It would be a shame to die and miss the best part of the meal."

"Mother, that is a shameful thing to say." Susanna frowned at her. "How can you jest about dying?"

Rose chuckled. "Easily, actually. I'm not afraid of going to my rest. When *Gott* decides it's my time, He's not going to get any argument from me."

"Do you dare to assume you are going to heaven?" Susanna demanded.

"Of course not. But I'm pretty sure I can talk my way past St. Peter if need be."

Susanna dried her hands on a kitchen towel. "You are shameless and without humility. I should inform the bishop."

"Go ahead." Rose took a bite of pie. "It will come as no surprise to him."

Susanna rolled her eyes. "I am going to move the round tables out to the patio and set up a long table in the dining room. Joanna, I could use your help."

"We should get Eli and Jeff to do it," Joanna said.

"*Goot* notion." The two women left the kitchen.

Rose patted the stool next to her. "Sit down, Sophie."

"I really should help Grace." She wanted to avoid Rose's probing.

"Grace, can we do anything for you?" Rose asked loudly.

"*Nee*, I've got it under control."

Rose smiled at Sophie. "She doesn't need you. Sit and keep me company. Would you like a slice of pecan pie? It's very good. I made it myself."

Sophie shook head.

"How do you like living next to Karl?"

Sophie's pulse sped up at the mention of his name. She tried to find a noncommittal answer. "It's fine, I guess."

Rose's eyes narrowed. "You aren't getting sweet on him, are you?"

Sophie sat up straight. "Of course not. Why would you ask such a thing?"

"He's a handsome man with a sad past and two adorable little girls. Some women would find that attractive."

"He has been a kind neighbor to me and nothing more."

"*Goot*, because that man is all wrong for you."

"Since I have no plans to marry, it doesn't matter, but why do you say he is wrong for me?"

"Karl lacks the faith he needs to become a suitable spouse."

"It's true that his faith has suffered since the death of his wife, but he is repairing his relationship with *Gott* and his children."

Rose looked at Sophie intently. "How do you know that?"

"We talked about his wife's death and how he blamed *Gott*, but he has accepted her loss and is working toward being a better father and member of our community."

"Then that is truly something to be thankful for today."

"He likes Joanna, but she seems not to realize what a catch he is. I'm afraid her flirting with other men will give him a disgust of her."

"Young people don't always know what is best for them."

"How would a matchmaker help her see what a fine man lives right next door?"

"Spending time with him might help. Is there a way for her to do that?"

Sophie leaned forward eagerly. "Actually, there is. He needs help in the hardware store. He even asked if Joanna would be interested in the position."

"What did she say when he asked her?"

"He didn't ask her. He asked me to see what she thought of the idea. Now she thinks I'm the one trying to get her out from underfoot. Joanna feels she needs to be taking care of me. I don't know why. I'm fine."

"There must've been something that gives her that impression."

"I was sick before we moved here. I did need her help then, but I'm doing okay now." It wasn't an outright lie, but it was an exaggeration.

"Things will sort themselves out between Karl and Joanna if they are meant for each other."

"I hope so. She would be the perfect wife for him. He deserves someone special. Someone who can heal his heart," Sophie added softly, wishing that she could be that someone. It was impossible but the thought wouldn't leave her.

"I agree," Rose said. "*Gott* has a way of sending the right person into our life at the right time. Usually, when we least expect it."

Sophie glanced at Rose. The elderly woman had a strange knowing smile on her face as she gazed back at Sophie.

Thirteen

Karl arrived at the Harts Haven Inn with his daughters just as Susanna carried a huge ham from the kitchen and placed it in the center of a long table set with Rose's best dishes and already laden with bowls and platters of food. Amazing aromas of fresh baked ham, hot dinner rolls and apple pie filled the air.

"It smells *wunderbar*," Rachel said. "I'm starving." The girls hurried out of their coats and heavy bonnets.

Rose came into the room followed by the rest of the guests. "Karl! I'm so glad you could make it. Bishop, please take your place at the head of the table. Eli, I'll have you sit at the bishop's right. Then the major, Jeff, Karl and Joseph. I will sit at the foot of the table. Grace why don't you sit to the bishop's left. Bertha, sit across from the major. Sophie, beside Bertha, then Joanna, Abby and then Clara. Rachel, you may sit beside me. Have I forgotten anyone?"

"Baby Henry," Rachel said, pointing toward Joseph, who held the baby's carrier. He handed it to Abby. She settled the baby on the floor beside her chair.

Rose chuckled. "I'm afraid Henry's going to sleep through his first Thanksgiving. We'll leave him with his mother. All right, everyone, please sit down."

Karl found himself facing Joanna and swallowed his annoyance. Clearly Rose still harbored the idea of making a match between them. That wasn't going to happen.

Sophie was seated across from Jeff. She wore her sling again. Her eyes lacked their usual sparkle. Was she in pain? What had the doctor told her? Bertha spoke to her quietly. He couldn't hear what she said, but Sophie nodded. He wished there was something he could do to help her.

The bishop clasped his hands together and bowed his head for the silent blessing. Everyone did likewise. After a short time, the bishop straightened, indicating he had finished his prayers, and raised both his hands.

"On this day we pause to give thanks for the many blessings we have received from our Lord. The blessings of abundant food, caring neighbors and dear family members. It is an honor to share this table with all of you. Okay, Grace, pass the potatoes."

The clank of cutlery and serving spoons against the sides of dishes continued for several minutes until everyone had their plates filled. Karl checked to see that his girls were behaving. Eating at someone else's house was a treat, especially eating at the inn, where the owners had well-deserved reputations as excellent cooks. He was pleased to see they hadn't overloaded their plates.

He looked across the table at Joanna, but her eyes were glued to the young man beside him. Glancing at Jeff, Karl noticed a foolish grin on the boy's face. Sophie frowned at Joanna and gave her sister a nudge.

Joanna turned her attention to him. "Happy Thanksgiving, Karl. We're having wonderful weather. It was cloudy today but not unbearably cold. Is this typical for Kansas?"

"No such thing as typical Kansas unless changeable applies. It can be sunny and hot on Thanksgiving, or it can be blowing a blizzard. I've seen both happen on the same day."

"Do you get a lot of snow here?" Sophie asked. "I have to admit I'm surprised by the lack of it so far."

Joanna looked only mildly interested. Her gaze had drifted back to Jeff. There was definitely an attraction between the pair. It made Karl smile. Rose's matchmaking plan for him and Joanna was failing badly.

Karl looked at Sophie. "If we get snow this early it will melt in a day or two. January and February see the most snow, but March can be just as bad."

"February is the month when we go sledding and skating," Jeff said.

Joanna's eyes brightened. "Oh, I love ice-skating. We used to have skating parties all the time back home."

"We've got a swell pond on our farm," Jeff said. "We've had lots of skating parties there, especially around Valentine's Day. You'll have to come to one."

"I look forward to it."

Karl caught Sophie's eye. "Do you like to skate?"

She shook her head. "I do like the snow, though. The world is a beautiful place when it's covered in the Lord's sparkling white blanket, but I don't care for skating."

Joanna laughed. "Sophie is not graceful on skates. She's more like a moving windmill the way she flails her arms to keep her balance."

Sophie gave her sister a sour look but didn't say anything.

"I'm the same way," Karl said. "Never got the hang of it. I'd much rather go for a ride in a horse-drawn sleigh."

It was easy to imagine Sophie at his side, bundled under quilts, her cheeks red from the cold, the sound of sleigh bells ringing out in the still, cold air as the horse trotted along one of the country lanes. It was a pleasant thought.

Sophie gave him a small smile. "I enjoy that, too. Especially if it's snowing big fat flakes that drift down like goose feathers."

"I'm looking forward to my first sleigh ride," Abby said.

Joanna turned her in surprise. "You've never ridden in a sleigh?"

Abby shook her head. "I wasn't raised Amish although I spent summers with my Amish grandparents near here. Winters I lived at my father's estate in Kansas City. I wasn't allowed to go sledding or ice-skating. This will be my first winter in Harts Haven."

Joseph stretched his hand across the table to grasp hers. "You will enjoy plenty of cold-weather activities, especially when our boy gets a little older."

"I once went sledding behind a team of reindeer in Norway," the major said. "Wonderful experience. Remarkable scenery. Those huge animals simply fly across the snow."

"Can reindeer really fly?" Rachel asked from the other end of the table. "Nikki Switzer says they can. Her *daed* puts up a picture of them in the post office window at Christmastime."

The major laughed. "None of the ones I saw became airborne, but they sure run fast."

"I didn't think they could fly," Rachel said sadly. "They don't even have wings."

The rest of the meal passed with little conversation. Everyone was busy enjoying the food. Karl kept an eye on Sophie and noticed she often rubbed her upper arm as if it was paining her. After a while he could tell she was growing tired. When the meal was finished, the men moved into the living room while the women cleared the table. Karl hung back and took the plates Sophie had gathered from her hand. "Let me get this for you. I can tell your arm is hurting."

"It was feeling better, but you're right. It does hurt now."

"What did Dr. Bertha say about it?"

"It's a bad bruise. No news there, but I have sprained ligaments. They will take time to heal."

"This is not meant as an insult, but you look tired."

"I've come to appreciate your frank speaking even when it doesn't flatter me. It's the medicine Dr. Bertha gave me for pain. It makes me groggy."

Rose took the plates from Karl's hands. "I've got these. I'm going to get Jeff to drive you home, Sophie."

"I'll take her," Karl said firmly.

"Neither of them needs to take me," Sophie said. "Joanna can drive me home."

"As you wish," Rose said. "I will get her. Karl, will you fetch Sophie's coat for her. I believe it's hanging by the back door."

"I know which one it is." He smiled at Sophie. "I paid special attention when you are trying to stuff my puppies into it."

Rose glanced between the two of them. "I haven't heard this story."

Sophie's cheeks grew red. "There's nothing to tell."

Karl winked at her. "It's okay. Rose knows I can be rude. Tell her." He walked through the kitchen to the back door, found her coat and traveling bonnet and returned to the dining room.

Rose glanced at him and started laughing. "What an adorable story to tell your children someday. I'll get Joanna."

He stared at Rose in speechless shock. She patted his arm as she walked by him and left the room.

Sophie turned her back to him. "Rose didn't mean our children—yours and mine." A break in her voice made it sound as if she were fighting back tears.

He laid her coat across her shoulders. His hands lingered on her arms. "Of course she didn't. She must have meant the schoolchildren."

Even to his own ears his voice lacked conviction. Why was it so easy to imagine Sophie with a baby in her arms?

Where was Joanna? Sophie struggled to hold back her tears. She wouldn't have children of her own. Not with Karl. Not with any man. An overwhelming urge to turn around, bury her face against his chest and weep took hold of her. Fighting that desire was one of the hardest things she had ever done.

It was God's decision whether her disease was passed on to her *kinder*, but she wasn't brave enough to take that chance. How could she give birth to a child she knew she wouldn't see grow up? It was out of the question. And yet, she still mourned the loss of the unborn babes she would never hold.

Before her cancer she had dreamed of being a mother. That hope was ashes in her mouth now. The weight of Karl's hands on her shoulders gave her comfort he didn't know she needed.

He deserved more children. He believed he had failed his daughters in the past, but he was intent on righting those wrongs. In time he would succeed in being the man he wanted to become. With Joanna's help. Envy for her sister bit deep into Sophie's soul.

Rose breezed back into the room. She took Sophia's large black bonnet from Karl and tied it beneath Sophie's chin. "It seems that Jeff and Joanna have gone for a buggy ride. They didn't tell anyone when they would return. I would take you myself, Sophie, but there is so much cleanup work left to do. I'm sure you understand."

"I'll take you." Karl's voice was a bare whisper beside her ear.

She nodded mutely.

"Do you want to go in the pony cart or in my closed buggy?"

"Buggy," she whispered. If she broke down in tears, she didn't want the whole of Harts Haven to see her sobbing.

"Come on then. It's right out front."

He gently steered her toward the door and opened it for. She kept her face down so he couldn't see her distress and was grateful that the sides of the large bonnet helped conceal her from his sharp eyes.

It was only a mile and a half to his farm, but he kept the horse at a slow walk. The trip seemed to take forever.

"Are you truly okay?" he asked.

"*Nee*, I'm not." She swallowed hard against the lump in her throat.

"Do you want to talk about it?"

She shook her head. "I'd rather not."

"Was it something I did or said?"

"Of course not. All you did was mention how poorly I looked. Again."

He cleared his throat. "You look mighty pretty in that bonnet, teacher. I don't believe I've ever seen a star with as much shine as the sparkle in your eyes. Is that better?"

Sophie choked on a laugh. "Flattering the teacher will not get you better grades."

"Will it get me a smile?" He leaned forward trying to see her face.

"Not even that."

"Ah, I think the teacher is telling a fib. I hear a smile in her voice. Come now, let me see it." He leaned even closer.

She kept her head bowed but she couldn't hold back a little smile. "You can't cajole me out of my sour mood."

"All right. I give up. I won't point out something that will make you happier."

"What do you imagine would make me happier today?"

"It's snowing."

Sophie looked up quickly. It *had* started to snow. It wasn't the huge feathery flakes that she enjoyed but there was enough to cover the grass along the roadway and stick to the horse's mane. A sigh escaped her lips. "How wonderful. This isn't a sleigh ride but it's still nice."

Karl chuckled. "I guess the Lord knows how to get a smile out of the teacher."

"Do you think it will snow a lot?" She looked up at the gray sky.

"The newspaper yesterday said to expect flurries on Thanksgiving. I doubt we'll see it pile up."

"Still, it makes it feel like winter. Like Christmas is actually on the way."

"It will be here before you know it." He turned the horse onto his lane.

Now that his home was in sight, Sophie wished the ride could last a little longer. The snow was so pretty. "It seems a shame to go in."

He stopped the horse. "I thought you were tired and wanted to go home."

"I did, but I'm feeling better now." Sophie realized it was true. Her arm wasn't aching as much, and her headache was gone. "It must be the snow."

"There's a pretty drive north of here. The road winds along

the bank of the river for a short distance. Would you like to see it?"

"I believe I would. If you don't mind," she added quickly.

"Not at all."

"It isn't like we're taking a buggy ride—together." She didn't want him to think she was angling to spend more time with him for a romantic reason.

His eyes widened and he shook his head. "Oh, *nee*, not like the *youngees* do when they're courting and such."

"It's not like that at all," she assured him.

"That's right. You should see a bit more of the country-side, you being new and all. I can point out where some of your pupils live should you want to speak to their parents."

"That's a very good idea. I have been wanting to see more of the area. It's just that I've been so busy with school start-ing, and my horse and buggy haven't arrived from Ohio yet."

"Well, the holiday has given me and you a free day so we might as well make the most of it."

"That's a fine way to look at it." Sophie relaxed. Joanna couldn't object to her sister taking a tour of the area. Karl was only being kind.

He turned the buggy around, then headed north on the highway.

Sophie sat back and enjoyed watching the snow fall. It was heavier now, blocking out the distant farmsteads and trees with a gray-white curtain. She could almost forget she was sick and imagine she was taking a ride with a fella who fancied her.

"That's the McDonald farm," Karl said.

Sophie took note of the electric lines running to the house and to several new steel outbuildings. "An *Englisch* family?"

"They are. He and his wife run the Prairie Farm and Ranch Supply store. They're horse people. He raises and trains cutting horses. She gives riding lessons in that fancy indoor area they just built."

"What is a cutting horse?" She'd never heard the term.

"A cow pony, usually a quarter horse. They're used for sorting and separating individual cattle from the herd."

"Are there a lot of cattle farms around here?"

He grinned. "They're called ranches and yes, there are lots of them. We have cowboys, too."

She liked his smile, the way his gray eyes crinkled at the corners and sparkled with humor. He should smile more often.

"On your side is the Imhoff place," Karl said. "He's employed at a woodworking business in Hutchinson besides running a small dairy. Debra and Jason are two of your students."

Sophie saw a long single-story home with a large deck out front and a long low barn set back behind the house. A herd of brown-and-white cows grazed in a pasture near the road. They all lifted their heads to watch the buggy go past.

"Where is your home?" Karl asked.

"Home? In Ohio, you mean?"

"Yeah, what was it like?"

"Parker is an ordinary Amish community, I guess. Our father runs a dry goods store. Most folks are farmers, but there is a furniture-making business that employs about forty men and women."

"Do you come from a big family?"

"It's just my sister and me. Or it was. Our father recently married a widow with several children, so our family got instantly bigger."

"You don't get along with your stepmother?"

Sophie scowled at him. "What makes you say that?"

"You moved here. Why would you do that if the two of you got along?"

She pressed her lips together and looked away. "I wanted a change, that's all."

"Does Harts Haven, Kansas, fit that bill?"

"It does so far."

He pointed to a large two-story white farmhouse just off the highway on his left. There were a half-dozen buggies lined up in front of the barn. "That is the Kemp farm. They have four children in your school."

"Laura and Lamar are the twins. They're in the first grade with Rachel and Sam Lehman."

"Right. Then there is Phoebe. She's a year younger than Clara while Bartholomew is a year older. Looks like they are having company for their Thanksgiving dinner."

"I'm sure I will hear all about it tomorrow. Laura and Lamar enjoy telling me things that go on at home. Most schoolchildren do."

Karl winced. "I'll be more careful what I say in front of Rachel that shouldn't be repeated."

Chuckling, Sophie patted his arm. "I promise not to share any secrets that she tells me."

He glanced down at her hand. Embarrassed, Sophie quickly pulled away. She laced her fingers together and stared out the window. Their growing friendship made her feel overly familiar with Karl. She would have to be careful and not overstep the bounds of propriety with a man she hoped would marry her sister.

They didn't meet any traffic as the horse trotted along. After another mile the road ended at an intersection with a paved road that ran east and west. Across the highway was a dirt track that led into a grove of trees.

"The road meanders along the riverbank to a sort of picnic place that local families and fishermen like to use. It's also a place the teenagers like to hang out."

The horse hooves fell silent on the dirt track. There was only the creaking of the wheels and the jingle of the harness as they moved into the woods that pressed close to the road. A sense of peace filled Sophie.

"There is a place like this not far from my father's house where the road ends in a wooded field. The local teenagers frequent it, too."

Karl had a teasing glint in his eyes when he glanced at her. "Did your beau take you there often?"

She sat up straight and looked ahead. "I refuse to answer that question."

He laughed. "I will take that as a yes. Why isn't a smart, good-looking woman like you married?"

"Because I'm not."

"It's hard to believe the young men in your community failed to notice your charms."

"Joanna is the one with charm. I have a more practical nature. There was one man." Sophie wasn't sure why she shared that with Karl.

"What happened?" he asked softly. His kind tone told Sophie he was genuinely interested.

Explaining would ruin the peace she felt. "He decided we wouldn't suit. So, I kept on teaching."

"In my opinion he was a fool."

"He wasn't entirely to blame. I agreed with him. Better no marriage than a poor marriage, my granny used to say."

The trees opened and Sophie got her first, disappointing glimpse of the river. Instead of the wide, rapidly flowing waterways she was used to in Ohio, this wasn't much more than a slow-moving stream meandering between sandbars. Karl stopped the buggy and helped her get out. She walked to the edge of the steep bank and looked down. The water was at least six feet below her. "Which river is this?"

"It's spelled Arkansas, but in Kansas it's pronounced R-Kansas."

Puzzled, she looked at him. "How can you call the river by a different name if it's the Arkansas River?"

He shrugged. "When the river leaves our state, folks can call it anything they want. As long as it is within our state boundaries, it's pronounced R-Kansas."

"This trickle is a major American river? There's almost no water in it."

"A lot of water flows in it where it comes out of the Colorado mountains, but once it hits the dry plains it irrigates a lot of farmland. There are places where the riverbed is completely dry, or the river is underground."

He pointed to some brush caught in the tree branches five feet above her head. "During flood stage, especially in the spring and after thunderstorms, she carries a lot of water that spreads out over this area. She's no trickle then. During the fall she calms down and behaves. There is quicksand out there, so folks have to be careful when they go wading or fishing."

The sun broke through the overcast sky and the snow stopped. Sophie shaded her eyes against the brightness. "I'm beginning to understand what you mean when you say this land is changeable."

His gaze roved over the landscape, the river and the fields beyond. "It's a good place. I'm glad my great-grandparents settled here. It can be a hard place, but it can be rewarding, too."

She tipped her head slightly as she studied him. "You love it here."

He looked embarrassed. "I can't imagine living anywhere else. What about you? Tell the truth. You've been thinking about going back to the green rolling hills of Ohio, haven't you?"

"I'm not sure I belong here, but this will be my home

until…" She stopped talking as thoughts of her death weighed her down.

"Until?" he prompted.

She forced a smile to her lips. "Until the good Lord calls me home or the school board fires me."

"Maybe I'll volunteer for the school board next year. I'd like to see you stick around."

"Me and my sister."

"Of course. I meant your sister, too."

Karl's mare whinnied and was answered by another horse around the bend. A moment later Buster trotted into view with Joanna and Jeff in the open cart. The pair shared a guilty look before Jeff stopped the pony beside Karl's buggy.

Joanna smiled brightly "Sophie. What are you doing here?"

Flustered, Sophie wasn't sure how to answer. Karl stepped into the awkward silence. "I thought I would show Sophie some of the local highlights since we are both off work today."

"That's right," Sophie said quickly. "Karl's helping me become familiar with the school district. He was pointing out some of my student's homes along the highway." She frowned at her sister. "What are you doing out here?"

"Exploring," Joanna said, giving Jeff a sly smile.

Sophie couldn't hide her annoyance. "It's fortunate that we ran into each other. I can ride home with you and let Karl and Jeff return to the inn to enjoy the afternoon." She hoped her tone conveyed that she would not tolerate an argument from Joanna.

Joanna's grin disappeared. "I wasn't ready to go home."

Sophie marched over to the cart and put her hand on the dashboard. "My headache has returned, and my arm is paining me. I was hoping you would fix me some of Rose's tea. You know how much that helps."

Joanna's shoulders slumped. "Certainly." She turned and

took the reins from Jeff's hands. "Thank you for a lovely afternoon."

"I might stop by to visit on Sunday."

"I'm afraid we have other plans," Sophie said. If her sister wasn't going to be sensible, she would be sensible for her.

"Another time, then." Jeff got out of the cart with a dejected expression.

Sophie climbed in beside her sister and looked at Karl. "I appreciate the tour. I have invited Clara over Saturday evening to work on the Christmas play."

"I'll remind her." He nodded slightly and got in the buggy. Jeff climbed in beside him.

When Joanna didn't get the pony moving, Sophie spoke up. "Buster, trot on."

The pony immediately started down the road. Joanna sat in angry silence until Sophie couldn't stand it any longer. "You must be careful, Joanna. A little harmless flirting can ruin your reputation. It's time you got serious. You're old enough to marry."

"But not old enough to be treated like an adult instead of wayward child. Jeff and I were simply enjoying a ride in the country the same as you and Karl. And if you want me thinking about marriage, you're going to have to let me go out with a few young men. I like Jeff. I like him a lot."

"And Karl likes you. Surely you can see what a good match he is for you. You adore his children."

"So do you. The problem is that I don't adore Karl."

Sophie couldn't hide her frustration. "You're not giving him a chance. Are you going to take the job in his store?"

"If you stop fussing at me about getting married. What is wrong with you these days?"

Telling Joanna would only bring her pain. "I simply want to see you happily settled. I pray for that always."

"If that is the Lord's plan for me, then it will come to pass. I want the same thing for you. Karl likes you. Why push him at me?"

"Joanna, please. I'm not going to marry." Sophie fought back sudden tears.

"Sister, my prayers for you are always that you find the strength and faith to start living your life instead of waiting to die. I thought when you agreed to take this teaching job my prayers had been answered, but they haven't. Why did we move here, Sophie? Tell me the truth."

Fourteen

Sophie turned away from Joanna's penetrating gaze. "I don't know what you mean."

Joanna pulled the pony to a stop and faced Sophie. "You know exactly what I'm talking about. If you aren't intent on building a life for yourself in Harts Haven, why are we here?"

"You are here because I couldn't convince you to stay in Ohio."

"You needed me."

She had, but it would be so much easier now if she lived alone. Instead, Joanna would watch her die. "I have a headache. Please take me home."

"I thought your arm was hurting."

"It was, and now I have a headache." She wanted to bury her head in her pillow and cry until there were no more tears left.

Joanna wrapped the lines around the brake handle and

crossed her arms. "We aren't going anywhere until you answer the question, Sophie. Why did you come here?"

"Because I wanted people to stop staring at me like they could see me in my coffin!"

Joanna didn't flinch. "I believed that once, but not now. I deserve the truth."

Her sister was like a terrier after a rat. Sophie was tired of her sister's probing. She could have her truth. Just not all of it. "Do you love our *daed*?"

"Of course I do."

"Do you remember how he suffered when our mother was dying?"

"We all suffered. It was a terrible time, but we got through it together. We held on to each other and to our faith. Now he is happy with Beatrice and her children. *Gott* was good to him."

"He has found new purpose and joy in life. If I had stayed in Ohio, I would've ruined that for him."

"Sophie, you're not making any sense."

"My grandmother died of this disease. My mother died of this disease. I will die of this disease. I refuse to subject our father and his new wife to the sight of me wasting away, moaning and crying in pain while they can do nothing. I'm sorry you must see it."

Joanna took Sophie's hands between her own. "*Mamm* and *Grossmammi* accepted their illness as *Gott*'s will. *Mamm* had a mastectomy but not chemo. She didn't seek the best medical care the way you did."

"I would've been content with the same choice, but you wouldn't let me. Seeing a doctor was the only way I could get you to leave me alone."

"Can you shoe your own horse?"

Sophie frowned at her sister. "What do horseshoes have to do with this conversation?"

Joanna rolled her eyes. "Can you put a shoe on your own horse or not?"

Sophie raised her eyes in exasperation. "I do not possess that skill."

"Do we plant a garden and then simply watch the weeds take over? *Nee*, we must work to make a garden productive. Yes, *Gott* makes the sunshine. And yes, He brings the rain, but the hoe must be used by the gardener. Which is why *Gott* put your little sister, caring doctors, nurses and therapists in your life. We are the tools you needed to thrive. I refused to let the weeds take you away for want of a hoe."

"It isn't that simple."

"Isn't it? *Gott* gave me into an amazing family. He blessed me with a sister that I love beyond measure. If I could yank out your cancer with my bare hands, I would. I can't do that anymore than you can shoe a horse."

"Not every lame horse can be saved by a new pair of shoes."

"You're right. Despite all my efforts, *Gott* may take you back to Him before I'm ready. I accept that. But I'm not going to let a lame horse be put down because it has a loose shoe."

"I wish you would stop comparing me to a horse."

"Then stop being so stubborn."

"What do you want from me, Joanna?"

Leaning forward, Joanna unwrapped the driving lines. She sighed deeply and stared straight ahead. "To find the desire to live, and love and to let someone love you in return. You deserve a man who will cherish you and children of your own, not just students. I want you to want those things. That's all." She sighed and jiggled the driving lines. "Buster, walk on."

The cart jolted as the pony got going and send a stab of pain across Sophie's chest. Her sister had no idea how impossible her request was. She wasn't going to find love. She wasn't going to marry and have children. All Sophie could do was protect the one she loved from more pain.

Karl waited outside Sophie's door Friday morning with Rachel and Clara. The snow had melted away in the night, leaving the fields bare. He wished it had stayed longer because he knew Sophie enjoyed it, but he wasn't surprised it was gone. It was too early in the year for it to stick around.

Sophie came out the door and stopped when she saw him. "You don't have to wait for me all the time. I'm capable of walking by myself."

He touched his hat. "*Guder mariye*, teacher."

She tipped her head in his direction. "Good morning to you all, as well."

"We like to walk with you," Rachel said. "Right, Clara?"

"Sure. Let's go." Clara took off on her own.

"Wait for me." Rachel ran to catch her sister.

Buck tried to follow her, but Karl called him back. He pointed to the porch, where Misty was sitting. "Stay."

Buck complied with his head down and a look of disappointment in his dark brown eyes.

Karl smiled at the pup. "I reckon he thinks he needs schooling, too."

He looked at Sophie to see if she enjoyed his jest, but her eyes were following his daughters with an expression of sad longing in their depths. She noticed he was staring at her and immediately smiled. Why was she sad? He wanted to ask but thought better of it. He understood some sorrows were too painful to share. Maybe one day she could be comfortable enough with him to speak of it.

They walked together in silence. It wasn't awkward. He found it relaxing. Being near Sophie had a soothing effect on him. He noticed the leaves were dropping from the trees and drifting into piles. He saw the long grasses had changed to their winter brown as they bent over in the breeze. The sky was bright blue without a single cloud. The world was a brighter place when he was near Sophie.

Was she thinking about their time together yesterday? He was. Until its abrupt end, they had been enjoying each other's company. It had been disappointing to have her leave with her sister, but maybe the next time they could spend longer together.

Next time?

It was funny how quickly his mind went there. Would there be a next time? He hoped so. Maybe a ride over to the bird sanctuary by Joseph and Abby Troyer's place. Even if Sophie wasn't a bird-watcher, it was a pretty drive along the river. They could stop in and see baby Henry, too. Sophie would like that.

Only how did he work the invitation in?

Clearing his throat, he plunged ahead. "I enjoyed your company yesterday." He glanced her way to see her reaction.

Sophie wished Karl hadn't said anything. She wanted to continue enjoying their walks in peace, pretending that they were an old married couple and the children running ahead were their children. It was a foolish daydream but for a few brief minutes she could imagine what her life might have been like if God had chosen that path for her instead of the one she had to walk.

She wanted to tell Karl how much she had enjoyed his company, but she didn't. She was a friend of his, nothing more. That was the way it had to be.

She didn't look at him. "I appreciate you taking the time to show me the countryside and some of my students' homes."

"I'd be happy to show you more of the area." His voice held a hint of hope.

"I don't want to impose on your free time. My horse and buggy should be here next week. Joanna and I will enjoy finding our way around together. She likes an adventure."

"And you don't?"

"Adventures are all well and good when a person is young. I'm past that."

"You're not that old. You make it sound like you're fifty when you're only what, twenty-five, twenty-six?"

"Thirty." She felt much older than that today. They reached the highway. She quickly said goodbye and escaped into the school, where she hoped facing eager young minds would keep thoughts of Karl at bay.

Despite her determination not to think about him, he occupied far too much of her time. At lunch, while the children were out at recess, she sat at her desk and stared at her lunch without taking a bite. She had to find a way to keep her feelings for Karl bottled up. If she couldn't, then she would have to leave Harts Haven.

The sound of breaking glass made her jump. She was on her way to investigate when Phillip came in with his head hanging down. Zack and Bartholomew stood behind him.

"I'm sorry, teacher. It was an accident," Phillip said.

She entered the cloak room to find a shattered window and a baseball on the floor. Not only was the glass broken but the window frame was splintered on one side. "A broken window can be fixed, Phillip. Let's find something to cover it with and then pick up the glass. Be careful. Don't cut yourself. At least there weren't any coats in here to get peppered with glass. Zack, can you get the broom?"

"I'm really sorry to cause you more trouble, teacher," Zack said. He looked ready to cry.

She needed to make him feel better. "These things happen, Zack. Don't be upset. It must have been a solid hit to take a chunk out of the wood frame."

"Nah, it was a foul ball."

"Straighten the next one out and it will be a home run for sure and certain." She smiled to reassure him.

"Is your arm any better?" he asked softly.

She chuckled. "I won't be throwing any softballs this year, but I'm mending."

"We want you to like it here," Phillip said.

"Yeah, we want you to stay," Bartholomew added. "Even my *grossdaadi* says so."

She swallowed the catch in her throat. *"Danki."*

The boys cleaned up, covered the window and went back outside to finish their game. Sophie returned to her desk and her cheese sandwich. It was still unappetizing. She pushed it into the trash can, propped her elbow on the desk and dropped her chin onto her hand. It had seemed so easy when she came up with the idea to move away from home. Go where no one knew her, teach until she grew too ill to continue and pray Joanna would marry and have someone to take care of her when Sophie was gone.

Only it wasn't working out that way.

She hadn't planned on having students who cared about her. Tears threatened but she refused to cry. Running back home wasn't the answer, but she did wish she could talk to her father. He was always a good listener.

"Is something wrong, teacher?"

Sophie looked up to see Rachel standing in front of her desk. *"Nee,* nothing's wrong."

"You look sad."

Sophie managed a little smile. "Maybe a little. I miss the rest of my family, but I have lovely friends here now, don't I?"

★ ★ ★

Karl milked the cow in the barn before supper on Saturday evening while Rachel tossed feed to the chickens. Thankfully he didn't have to think of what to make for the meal. The widows had insisted he take home plenty of the leftover ham, turkey and side dishes on Thursday. There was still enough left for one more meal.

With his forehead pressed against Dolly's warm flank as he filled the pail with frothy milk, he enjoyed the last task of the evening.

"I'm worried about Sophie," Rachel said.

He stopped milking and turned his head to see Rachel slowly throwing cracked corn out to the hens. Buck went after each handful and then trotted back to Rachel's side when there was nothing for him to fetch.

"Why are you worried?" Karl asked.

"I don't know. What if she decides she doesn't like it here?"

Had Sophie said something to indicate that? "It would be sad, but there will be another teacher to take her place."

"Granny Rose says Sophie needs to stay with us. She's special."

"I'm sure that Rose likes Sophie as much as we do, but no one can make her stay if she wants to go home. Kansas is a lot different than Ohio." He resumed milking. "Has Sophie said something about leaving?"

"*Nee.*"

He let out the breath he'd been holding. "Then there's nothing to worry about. What is your sister doing?"

"She's cleaning the kitchen. The floor was pretty sticky."

"From the milk I spilled yesterday morning. I wiped it up, but I never got around to washing the floor." There were always more things to do in the day than he had time for. After working a full day in the shop, he had at least two hours of farm chores to finish before supper every day. Milking was the last of it.

He rose, lifted the brimming pail and poured a small amount into a plastic dish for the three orange barn cats keeping a wary eye on Buck from the top of the stall gate.

Perhaps Sophie and Joanna would like some fresh milk and cream this evening. He had enough in his refrigerator. It would be a shame to let it go to waste. And it would be a good excuse to see how Sophie was feeling.

He stopped on his front porch and pulled off his boots. "Take your shoes off, Rachel. We don't want to track dirt across your sister's clean floor."

Karl opened the door and stepped inside. He looked around in astonishment. Not only was the floor clean but so was the table, the countertops—even the lamp shades above the table gleamed. It was amazing how much more light the lamps put out with clean glass globes. The dishes in the sink had been washed and put away. The smell of cooking ham overlaid the scent of pine cleaner and bleach.

Rachel came in and stood at his side. "Wow. Clara got a lot done. This looks nice."

This was how his kitchen was meant to look, the way Nora had kept it. He glanced at his youngest. "You should be helping your sister with the housework more."

"She likes to do it all herself."

"That's no excuse. Set the table for supper." He went to find Clara and thank her for her hard work, but she wasn't in the house. Then he remembered Sophie had been expecting her this evening to work on the Christmas play.

He went to the sink and strained his milk, taking care to clean up the splatters afterward and place the jar in the refrigerator. Then he pulled out yesterday's batch. The cream and milk had separated nicely.

He checked the sliced ham simmering on the stove and turned down the heat. The oven was on. In it he found a green-bean casserole warming. He left the oven temp the same and went to fetch Clara, taking the jar of milk with him.

Joanna apparently saw him coming from her kitchen window because she opened the door. "Good evening, neighbor."

"Evening. Is Clara here?"

"She's in the living room with Sophie."

"How is your sister feeling?"

"As stubborn as ever. Was Jeff disappointed that Sophie whisked me away the other day?"

Karl chuckled, enjoying her forthright nature. "He was. I'm surprised he hasn't come over this evening."

"It would take a brave man to face my sister's wrath twice in one week. I understand you are considering hiring me to work in your shop."

"I am."

She looked him up and down. "Why should I work for you?"

Taken aback, he thought that over. "I'm a fair man. I don't expect anything from my employee that I can't do myself. I pay the going wage to start but if you are hardworking, I'll give you a raise."

She crossed her arms and studied him intently. "Are you open to new ideas?"

He frowned. "What sort of ideas?"

"Any kind. If I have an idea that I think will make the store more profitable, will you listen to me or assume I don't know what I'm talking about because I'm a woman?"

"You take after your sister."

She gave a nod of agreement. "I do, but that doesn't answer my question."

Crossing his arms, he tried to look stern, but reckoned the

sparkle of humor in his eyes and the smile tugging at the corner of his mouth betrayed him. "I would assume you don't know what you're talking about. Then I would decide it was my *goot* idea in the first place. When can you start?"

She burst out laughing. "Ha. I knew I liked you. Tuesday and I am bringing a list."

"I look forward to tearing it up."

"You wouldn't dare."

Smiling, he gave a quick shake of his head. "*Nee*, your sister would have me writing an apology on the blackboard for a week."

"You are getting to know her well."

"I think so." He handed over the jar of milk.

Joanna took it. "She and Clara are in the other room. I think a simple living Nativity is now out the window. Do you know anyone who owns a camel?"

He scratched the side of beard. "My neighbor has guard llama for his sheep, but I don't know of any camels outside of the zoo in Wichita."

"I wonder if they loan them out at Christmas. Go on in but be prepared to donate your skills to the project. I have to sew a robe for a little shepherdess."

"Better you than me. I would just wrap her in a tablecloth."

Joanna grinned. "That is an excellent idea. You see, I'm open to suggestions, too."

Chuckling, Karl walked into the living room where Sophie and Clara had several large sheets of paper laid down on the floor. He studied them for a moment and realized he was looking at a sketch of the town of Bethlehem, the hills at night dotted with sheep, and the inside of a stable with a manger.

Clara smiled as she looked up at him. "Sophie likes my ideas."

"And why wouldn't she? You're a smart girl." He nodded to Sophie. "How are you?"

"Better." She looked rested but kept her gaze down. If she was happy to see him, she gave no sign of it.

Disappointed, he was determined not to show it and sank to his heels beside his daughter. "Tell me your plan."

"I want to tell the Christmas story in four parts. Mary and Joseph's journey to Bethlehem. Whoever plays Joseph will lead Mary on a donkey past the hills and into town." She walked her fingers along the papers to demonstrate.

"I can see that."

"In town, they find there's no room at the inn. Mary and Joseph walk to the stable where Jesus is born. The cow, donkey, a camel and some goats will be here." She pointed.

Karl hid his smile with his hand as he stroked his beard. "The camel might be problem."

"We can do without one," Sophie said. She was struggling not to smile, too, but when her eyes met his she lost the battle. They both chuckled.

Clara glared at them and turned back to her sketches. "Then back at the hills, angels appear to the shepherds to tell them the Savior is born. Thea and Miriam are the angels of course. Rachel and her sheep, plus some of the boys from school, hurry to the stable to worship Jesus and all the angels come to sing. It's a shame we can't have a real baby to play Jesus."

Pushing his hat back, Karl studied the papers. "This seems mighty fancy. Are we sure the bishop will approve?"

Sophie wasn't. "I admit it is more than I envisioned when I suggested it, but as long as the program is meant to bring the meaning of Christmas to everyone present, I hope he will agree we can go ahead with it."

"Just having the students stand around doesn't tell the story," Clara said. Her earnest expression made Karl want to agree, but he wasn't sure it was best to encourage her in case she was disappointed.

"This is only one idea," Sophie said, giving the child a bright smile. "I will present it to the bishop after school on Monday."

"Why can't we see him tomorrow?" Clara asked.

"Because only essential work is done on Sundays," Karl said. "Tomorrow is the off-Sunday, and we are going to see your *grossmammi* in Yoder."

Sophie smiled at Clara. "Never miss a chance to visit your grandmother. I know this project is important to you, but it can wait until Monday. If Bishop Wyse doesn't feel it is appropriate, we will put our thinking caps on and come up with something better."

Clara gathered up her pieces of paper. "I don't know what would be better than this."

Sophie hugged the pouting child. "There are far too many ideas in your bright little brain to stop at one. Now I imagine your father wants to take you home for supper."

Karl stood. "That's exactly why I'm here. And just so you know, Joanna will be starting work with us on Tuesday."

Sophie's face brightened. "Oh, I'm so glad to hear that."

Clara's sour expression told a different story. She surged to her feet. "We don't need help. You and I can manage. Haven't I done a good job so far?" she demanded.

"Of course you have." At a loss for how to reassure her, he looked to Sophie for help.

Sophie recognized the panic in Karl's eyes and knew she had to render assistance. She beckoned the child closer with one finger. "This isn't about the quality of your work, Clara."

The child's mutinous expression softened slightly. "It's not?"

"You do fine work," Karl said quickly. "Better than anyone I've hired."

Sophie glanced toward the kitchen and leaned closer to Clara. "I'm going to tell you something I hope you won't repeat. This is about giving my sister something to do. She needs to become more responsible."

"She does?" Clara didn't look convinced.

"Now that I'm teaching, Joanna is by herself most of the day. She feels she isn't earning her keep the way she did when she worked with our *daed*. I'm hoping you and your father can help her. A part-time job is exactly what she needs."

Clara thought it over. "Just part-time?"

"Unless you feel you could use her more. I'm sure she'll be flexible," Sophie said.

Clara crossed her arms. "Does she have experience working in a store?"

Sophie could see she was changing Clara's mind. "She worked with our father in his dry goods store before we moved here. It's not the same but I'm sure both of you can learn from each other."

"You're not above taking a suggestion if it helps the business, are you?" Karl asked.

Clara rolled her eyes. "Of course not. It is our livelihood. I reckon we can give her a two-week trial. If she doesn't work out, you are going to have to let her go, *Daed*."

He rubbed his chin thoughtfully. "As it is my store, that's only fair."

Clara gave him a quick nod. "Thanks for listening to my ideas, Sophie. I hope Rachel didn't let the ham burn."

"*Nee*, I turned down the heat," Karl said. "You did a *wunderbar* job cleaning the kitchen. I'm proud of you for being so industrious."

Clara glanced at Sophie and blushed. Sophie gave a small shake of her head. She didn't need any of the credit.

The child left the room, but Karl lingered. He folded his arms over his chest. "What was that about?"

Sophie tried to look innocent. "Nothing."

"You came over and cleaned my kitchen while I was doing my chores, didn't you?"

She hoped he wouldn't be upset with her meddling. "I merely went to see if Clara needed help with her project."

"Then you saw my messy kitchen and decided to clean it."

"Clara didn't want to leave her work undone before she came over, so I helped her finish a few household tasks, that's all."

"Well, whatever the reason, you have my thanks. For that and for listening to Clara and supporting her idea, and for getting me off the hook just now."

"I was trying to be a *goot* neighbor."

Sophie paused, but felt she had to speak. "Karl, you are the store owner and within your rights to hire a clerk. Clara has to understand that accepting help from someone else does not mean you think less of her."

"You're right. It's just that I have failed my children for so long I feel I must make up for my neglect. Clara is the way she is because someone needed to be in charge, and I wasn't up to the task."

His honesty was endearing. "You are now."

"I'm not sure that's true but tomorrow is another day. *Gott* willing, I'll have the chance to be the father my children need."

A yearning to help him achieve that worthy goal grew in her. He was an amazing man, but he wasn't meant for her no matter how much she cared about him.

Sophie managed a bright smile, but her heart was filled

with pain. "Joanna can help you if you let her. I'm sure you and Clara will be very happy working with her."

He gave her an odd look. "Let's hope she likes the job."

Sophie didn't want him to see how fond she had grown of him. She gazed at her cold fingers as she clasped them together tightly. "She will, I know it. You should get home. The children will be wanting their supper. Don't forget the casserole in the oven."

"Do I have you to thank for that as well?"

"You must thank Susanna. She sent some green beans along with the ham."

"Which you made into a casserole." He chuckled and shook his head as he walked out of the room.

Sophie heard the outside door close and covered her face with her hands. How long could she keep pretending she cared for him only as a neighbor and friend?

"What's wrong, sister?" Joanna asked.

Sophie drew a deep breath and sat up straight. "Nothing. I'm just tired, but happy you decided to accept Karl's job offer. You should know Clara isn't thrilled. I think she's afraid it means she isn't indispensable. I suggested you need to become more responsible and contribute to the household economy."

"Which is true. I'll make sure to seek her help and guidance whenever I can. Karl will understand. I'm starting to like the man." She stared intently at Sophie.

"He's nice enough," Sophie admitted and looked away.

"Just nice?"

Sophie met her sister's eyes without blinking. "We are blessed to have him as our landlord and neighbor."

Joanna nodded slowly. "I hope he is a *goot* boss, too." She left the room.

Sophie sank back against the sofa cushions. She would

keep pretending for as long as she needed. Karl's and her sister's future happiness was at stake.

On the off-Sunday, Sophie decided to visit her aunt Grace using the circle letter she had received from her father as the excuse. Rather than forwarding the collection of family letters in the mail, Sophie would deliver them in person. Joanna had chosen to visit some of her new friends for the day.

In the cozy living room of the inn with a cup of hot tea in her hands, Sophie listened to her aunt read the letters aloud to Rose and Susanna. The antics of Sophie's new stepbrother and stepsisters had all the widows chuckling.

Grace folded the last one and tucked it in the envelope. "I have a hard time seeing my brother as a new father after all this time, but it sure sounds like he is enjoying himself."

Rose and Susanna stood to collect the teacups and sandwich plates and carry them to the kitchen. Grace leaned back in her chair and smiled at Sophie. "How are you doing?"

Sophie flexed her fingers. "My shoulder is getting better."

"I don't mean your arm. How are you doing?"

Unexpected tears pricked the back of Sophie's eyes. "Maybe I should have stayed in Ohio, where everyone knew I was going to die instead of coming here to pretend nothing is wrong with me."

"You had breast cancer. I can name three women in this district who have had it, too. Folks here will be understanding and supportive. You don't have to keep it a secret from them. It's nothing to be ashamed of, and Joanna told me your cancer has been cured. Was she wrong?"

"I told her what she wanted to hear. I would do anything to protect her from worry and pain."

Grace pressed a hand to her heart. "You mean your cancer has spread?"

"It will."

Grace's sympathetic expression turned into a scowl. "*Gott* has granted you the gift of seeing the future, has He?"

"*Nee*, but I know what to expect. I was at my mother's side all those months as she was dying. Father and I kept Joanna away as much as we could."

"Does she resent that?"

Sophie was puzzled by her aunt's question. "What do you mean?"

"Don't you think Joanna wanted to be with her mother in those last days no matter how hard it was to bear?"

"I only wanted to protect her."

"By keeping her from the mother she loved? Would you have wanted to be kept away?"

"Of course not, but I'm the oldest. It was my responsibility." She had thought to spare Joanna the heartache of caring for her dying mother. Had she done her sister an injustice?

"Joanna is a grown woman and a strong one. She can make her own decisions. I'm sorry you aren't happy here, child. Will you go back to Ohio?"

"I'm not sure what to do." Sophie didn't want to leave. The thought of never seeing Karl again forced her to accept just how much he meant to her.

If she stayed, she'd have to continue pretending that she wasn't falling for him.

Karl stared at the tools he had rearranged on a display rack for the second time that afternoon. It was a slow Monday. The Black Friday sales at the larger stores in the city last week had drawn his customers away for the bargains and no one was out shopping today. Even Clara was bored. He knew because she had washed the inside of the bay window, a task she hated.

Rose stopped in again to visit briefly and ask about Sophie, but she didn't buy anything.

At four o'clock Clara locked the cash register. "We should close early and go with Sophie to see Bishop Wyse. I can explain things if he has questions."

"That's a good idea." Karl had been wondering how to bring up the subject for the past hour. Clara rarely wanted to close early. Judging from her worried expression, he guessed her vision of the school program meant a great deal to her. Sophie had been preoccupied when he and the girls accompanied her to the school that morning. He knew she was concerned, too.

Karl quickly put his supplies away, eager to see Sophie again. Was she feeling better? Was she concerned the bishop would oppose Clara's idea? She had his daughter's best interest at heart even though Clara wasn't one of her students. Her kindness went beyond the classroom, and he admired that.

Today marked the start of her second week at Harts Haven Amish School. To his mind that called for a small celebration, especially after her rough start. Perhaps he could convince her to come out to supper with him. And the girls, of course. He'd invite Joanna, too.

He didn't want it to seem like a date. He was too old for that sort of thing anyway.

Ten minutes later, he pulled up in the schoolyard. Rachel, Miriam and Thea were playing on the swing set. Rachel normally walked home with Sophie, so she must be working late. His daughter hopped off the swing and came running up to him. "What are you doing here?"

"We're going to see Bishop Wyse with Sophie," Clara said. "We need his okay for the living Nativity program."

"I hope he says yes. I want everyone to see how nice my lambs can behave."

Sophie certainly didn't need a repeat of the lamb calamity during the Christmas program. An idea occurred to Karl. "Rachel, if you put some alfalfa pellets in your pocket, you can teach the sheep to stay beside you."

"Will my shepherd's robe have pockets?" she asked.

Karl grinned. "I'm sure Joanna can add one."

"If the bishop approves our play," Clara cautioned.

"Will you be disappointed if he doesn't?" Karl asked.

Clara shrugged one shoulder. "Sure, but Sophie is right. We can come up with another idea."

"Sophie is *wunderbar*, don't you think so, *Daed*?" Rachel's wide-eyed expression made him wonder what she was getting at.

Sophie was interesting, attractive and charming, but how did he explain that to his children? "She's okay, I reckon."

Rachel looked disappointed. "Just okay?"

"She's a very nice woman." His comment seemed to satisfy her because she grinned.

Karl handed the driving lines to Clara. "I'm going to let Sophie know we're here."

He got out of the buggy and went inside the school. She was sitting at her desk reading a sheet of paper. She wrote something on it, turned it over and picked up another page from a small stack. She hadn't heard him come in.

He stood for a moment watching her. It wouldn't be right to seem too eager, even though he was feeling like a teenager about to ask his first girl to ride home with him after a singing.

Sophie wore a maroon dress with a black apron over it. The color suited her fair skin. Happily, he saw some color in her cheeks, too. He hoped that meant her arm was feeling better.

She finished reading and marking the small stack of papers. Gathering them up, she tapped the edges to straighten them and paper-clipped them together. Only then did she look up.

For a second, he saw delight transform her face, but it vanished so quickly he couldn't be sure. She looked down and slipped her papers into the top drawer of her desk.

When she glanced up again, her expression was bland. "What are you doing here?"

The abrupt change puzzled him. "Clara wants to accompany you to see Bishop Wyse. We weren't busy so I decided to offer you a ride."

"That isn't necessary."

"Considerate it the neighborly thing to do."

A half smile twisted her lips for a moment and then vanished. "I'll be ready to go in a few minutes."

Karl had the feeling he had somehow overstepped the bounds of their friendship. "I don't have to go along if you'd rather I didn't."

"Don't be silly. Your company is welcome."

So why didn't it feel like it was? "Okay, I'll be outside."

He turned and left the building wondering if he had been mistaken about her feelings. He was eager to spend time with her, but she didn't appear eager to be with him.

Fifteen

Sophie took a few minutes to compose herself before leaving the school. Looking up to see Karl smiling sweetly at her had caught her off guard. A thrill of happiness swept through her before she could gather her wits. Hopefully, he hadn't noticed.

She slipped into her wool coat in the cloakroom remembering their first meeting, when she had his puppies stuffed in the garment. The irritated, gloomy fellow she met that day was really a caring and considerate man. A perfect match for Joanna if her foolish sister could only see that.

The wind rattled the cardboard in the broken window. She would remind the bishop this afternoon that it still needed repairs. She tied her bonnet strings beneath her chin and walked out with the smile on her lips that she hoped looked friendly and nothing more.

Karl's faint puzzled expression vanished when he caught

sight of her. He turned to his daughters. "Get in the back, girls."

"Don't bother," Sophie said quickly. "I can ride in the back as easily as they can."

He frowned. "Are you sure?"

"I'm just grateful I don't have to walk. This is very kind of you. How was your day, Clara?" she asked as she got in behind the child. Karl turned the horse around and began driving. Sophie was glad she didn't have to try and maintain her composure while sitting beside him.

"It was a boring day," Clara said.

"You can look forward to visiting with Joanna when she starts tomorrow. I know she is excited about her new job."

"I hope she expects to do more than sit around and gossip with me all day."

Karl abruptly stopped the horse and turned to his daughter. "You will treat Joanna with the respect she deserves and make her welcome. Is that understood?"

"*Ja, Daed.*" Clara was clearly taken aback by his stern tone.

"The same goes for this visit with Bishop Wyse. No matter what he decides, you are to accept his ruling with humility and without comment."

"Okay."

"*Goot.*" He stared at her for a long second then urged the horse to start walking again.

When they arrived at Bishop Wyse's farm, he made them welcome and listened to Sophie explain her vision of the living Nativity based on Clara's sketches. He considered them carefully. Sophie waited anxiously for his decision.

He tapped the paper with one finger. "The artwork must be done by the children alone. I could not approve such a display done by a teacher. A baptized member of our faith must not seek recognition or praise but must be humble in all things."

Sophie nodded once. "I fully understand."

"If the painted scenes are not fancy, I believe I can approve this. The school board and I will want to see the final projects before the program."

"The children will work diligently to have everything ready," Sophie said. She shared a relieved smile with Clara.

The bishop pointed to the animals in the stable. "I have a friend who owns a donkey. She might be persuaded to let us borrow her for the play."

"Do you know anyone with a camel?" Rachel asked eagerly.

He chuckled. "I'm afraid I don't."

"Oh." Rachel's enthusiasm faded away. "I guess that's okay."

"The person you should speak to is Herbert Young," the bishop said. "He has acquaintances near and far. If anyone can find you a camel, it will be him."

"But he's not Amish," Rachel whispered.

Bishop Wyse grinned, hooked his thumbs under his suspenders and leaned back in his chair. "A serious oversight on his part, but a fine fellow, nonetheless. This is an ambitious program for your first year, Sophie. You don't have much time left."

She smiled but his words carried a painful reminder of her limited future. "About the broken window in the cloakroom."

"Joseph Troyer will be out tomorrow to take care of it."

"Danki."

They left the bishop's home not long afterward. Sophie climbed in the back of Karl's buggy and was surprised when Clara got in beside her.

Karl studied the pair of them briefly, then got in the driver's side with Rachel. He handed her the lines. "Why don't you drive us to the end of the bishop's lane."

"Really? Sure." She sat up straight and clicked her tongue to get the horse moving.

"Don't hold the lines so tight," Karl said. "Give them some slack."

Sophie turned to Clara. "All our worry was for nothing."

"*Mamm* used to say that to worry is to doubt *Gott*," Clara said softly.

"She was right, but sometimes I have trouble putting that belief into practice."

Clara gave her a wry smile. "Me, too. About what I said earlier. I didn't mean that I thought your sister was a gossip."

"I appreciate that. Joanna is very dear to me. Just as I'm sure Rachel is dear to you."

"Your horse is veering to the right, Rachel. Bring her back to the center of the lane. Gently," Karl coaxed.

"*Daed* never let her drive before," Clara said softly. "I was younger than she is when *Mamm* started to teach me. It's been hard on Rachel growing up without a mother."

"I don't imagine it is easy for you, either."

"At least I remember her. Well, I sort of remember her. I can't really see her face anymore and that makes me sad."

Sophie knew the feeling all too well. "My mother has been gone five years. When I miss her a lot, I close my eyes and I remember how it felt when she hugged me. With her arms around me, I was warm and safe and happy. She would give me a big squeeze, and I knew just how much she loved me."

Clara put her head back and closed her eyes. "Yeah, I remember how that felt."

"*Goot*. Hug your sister before you go to bed tonight so that she can share that memory with you."

Clara looked at Sophie. "I will."

Sophie blinked back tears. "And please be kind to Joanna. She lost her mother, too. She knows how we feel."

"I never thought of that." Clara glanced at her father, moved closer to Sophie and lowered her voice. "Does it make you angry that *Gott* took your mother too soon?"

"When it happened, yes. Now I have come to accept that He allowed it, and I don't question Him anymore."

"*Daed* says it's wrong to wish *Mamm* back here because she suffered so much, and she is at peace now."

"I think he's right."

"Granny Rose is always trying to match him up with another wife. I wish she wouldn't do that."

"Why? You don't think he deserves to find love and happiness again?"

"How can he love someone who isn't *Mamm*?"

"Clara, if your father falls in love with someone new, that doesn't mean he stops loving your mother. He won't stop loving you. He won't stop loving Rachel. Love goes on forever."

"How can you be so sure?"

"My father recently married again. His new wife is a widow with three small children. It does my heart *goot* to see how happy she makes him, but he still loves my mother. It's possible to love more than one person."

Up front, Karl said, "You're doing fine, Rachel. Get ready to stop her. You want to be well back from the highway, so a passing car doesn't startle her."

"Like this?" Rachel pulled back on the lines. Karl reached over to assist her.

"Are you sure he won't stop loving *Mamm*?" Clara whispered.

"I'm positive. Love is like butter on hot bread. It seeps in so you only see a trace of it, but inside the bread it is still rich and wonderful. Love stays inside us even when the person we love isn't with us."

Sophie watched Karl teach his youngest daughter how to turn the horse onto the highway before taking the lines from her. Sophie's affection for him was already seeping into her bones. She wanted him and his daughters to be happy. She prayed Joanna was the woman who could accomplish that.

The next morning, Karl and his daughters came outside to see Sophie and Joanna standing in front of the *daadi haus*. Joanna was wrapping the scarf around Sophie's neck. "You need a cover up today. It's cold out."

"Don't fuss," Sophie said.

Karl walked toward to them. "Usually, it is the older sister who makes sure the younger one is dressed warm enough."

"Most older sisters have more sense than mine does," Joanna said.

Sophie scowled at her.

Karl pushed his hands deep in the pockets of his coat wishing he had taken the time to put on his gloves. "It is chilly."

Sophie shivered and then nodded. "The wind goes right through me. It gets cold in Ohio, but I think you have more wind in Kansas."

"That's because there's nothing to slow it down. The old-timers will tell you there's nothing between here and the North Pole except a barbwire fence with a hole in it."

"Let's go before I turn into an icicle," Sophie said.

Karl shook his head. "Go back in the house. I'll bring the buggy around."

"That is not necessary," Sophie said. "It's only quarter of a mile to the school."

Joanna turned Sophie around and pushed her toward the front door. "But it's a mile to town and I won't say no to a ride. I'll be mighty glad when our horse and buggy get here."

The drive would only take a few minutes, which meant he wouldn't get to spend much time with Sophie, but her comfort and the comfort of his children had to come first.

With Rachel and Sophie deposited at the school, he drove into town. Clara opened the shop while he put the horse in the small stable behind his building.

When he walked in the back door, he saw Rose standing at the counter. She smiled brightly at him. "Joanna tells me that she is going to be working here now."

"That's right." Rose probably thought her matchmaking scheme was responsible. "Clara will be showing her where things are today."

Clara nodded toward the back of the building. "We'll start in the storeroom and work our way forward. You can help with any customers that come in if you want. Most of them know what they need and where to find it."

As Clara and Joanna walked away, Karl noticed Rose had something on her mind. *Please don't let it be another potential wife.*

"How is Sophie getting along?" she asked, surprising him.

"Well enough, I reckon. She's still wearing her sling. The bishop has approved her Christmas program."

"Has she talked about going back to Ohio?"

A sick feeling hit his stomach. "Not to me. Have you heard something?"

"It's just that Grace seems to think Sophie isn't happy here."

"How so?"

"Oh, never mind. It's probably nothing."

If Sophie was thinking of leaving, he wanted to know. "It would be a shame if she left. The *kinder* are becoming attached to her."

Rose looked at him over the top of her spectacles. "Only the children?"

He had grown fond of Sophie, too, but he wasn't about to admit that to Rose. "Did you suspect that she wouldn't stay with us? Is that why you said she was wrong for me?"

"I believe I said that you were wrong for her. You still are."

He raised his hands in surrender. "All right, Rose, I give up. What is wrong with me?"

"You don't have enough faith, Karl."

He frowned at her. "What is that supposed to mean? I attend our services. I read the Bible to my children. I will help anyone in need."

"Faith isn't simply about going to prayer meetings. It's about knowing *Gott* is merciful and kind. It's *believing* He will give you the strength to overcome any obstacles or sorrows you face. Sophie's faith is weak. She needs someone with a strong faith to strengthen hers and help her find *Gott*'s plan for her life."

Karl took a step back. Did he believe in God's kindness? Nora had endured terrible pain, but she never lost her faith. He was the one who had stumbled. If Sophie needed someone to help strengthen her faith, how could he do that if his faith had crumbled? "You were right then. I'm not that man."

"You were once. You could be again."

Rose sounded so certain, but Karl knew she was wrong. How did she know Sophie was facing a crisis of faith? Was that what caused the pain he had glimpsed in Sophie's eyes when she thought no one was looking? The last thing he wanted was to make things more difficult for her. Or for himself.

"Sophie needs friends now," Rose said. "People to show her we care about her and that we want her to stay no matter what. I know you care about her. Be her friend." Rose gave him a sad smile and left the store.

His children weren't the only ones who would be upset if Sophie left Harts Haven. He would miss her, too. For the first time since Nora's death, he'd found happiness in someone else's company. Now Sophie might leave. He and his children had endured enough pain. He wasn't willingly going to invite

more. If she was leaving, then the less they saw of Sophie from
now on the better it would be for them. And him.

When it was almost time for the children's first recess of
the day, Sophie walked to the front of her desk. "Before you
go out, I spoke with Bishop Wyse last evening. He has agreed
that we can go ahead with our living Nativity."

A cheer went up and she smiled at their enthusiasm. "We
will show Mary and Joseph's journey to Bethlehem using three
backgrounds. The hills where the shepherds were, the inn in
Bethlehem and the stable. Jason will be Joseph and Tamara
will be Mary. I am working on getting a donkey."

"My sister has a nice pony," Rachel said. "Can't we use
him?"

Sophie smiled at her. "If we can't get a donkey, I will consider that."

She turned to the other students. "Bartholomew, you will
be the innkeeper who sends them to the stable. The cow, donkey and some goats will be here. Does someone have a doll
we can use for a baby?"

Thea held up her hand. Sophie nodded. "*Goot*. Thea and
Miriam will be angels again. Rachel will be one of the shepherds. I need two more."

One boy and another girl held up their hands. "Okay. All
we need now are three wise men and the rest of you will be
part of the angel's choir. Betty and Edna, you girls are the oldest so I'm going to depend on you to help me get the younger
children into place. You will also be part of the angel group.
Phillip, will you be our narrator and song leader?"

He turned beet red. "If you think I can do it, teacher."

"I'm sure you can. This is going to take a lot of work and
practice. We have only three weeks to prepare. The bishop
wants to see our program before everyone else does. We have

to give ourselves enough time to make changes if he asks for them."

"What do we do first?" Betty asked.

"You *kinder* are going to draw and paint our backdrops."

Betty looked puzzled. "On what?"

Sophie smiled at her class. "I'm open to your suggestions."

Karl wasn't waiting to walk to school with Sophie the next morning. She had come to expect him and the children on her doorstep.

"I'll see what's keeping them." Joanna went to his door, opened it and called his name. There was no response.

She came down the steps and shrugged. "I guess they went on ahead of us. I hope I wasn't supposed to be at work early."

Sophie tried to ignore the stab of disappointment that struck her. She had taken his company for granted. Something special was missing from her morning.

Joanna would get to spend the whole day with him. Sophie's morning walk with Karl was the one time of day she had him to herself except for Clara and Rachel, who were usually running on ahead. She cherished those moments more than she realized until now. In the future, Joanna would be with them every day. It wouldn't be the same.

"At least it's not as cold this morning," Joanna said.

The two women started walking up the lane. Sophie tried to figure out why he would suddenly change his routine. There had to be a simple explanation. "Did Karl say anything about leaving early?"

"Not that I recall."

"Doesn't it seem odd to you? I hope everything is okay."

"Are you worried about him?" Joanna asked. Her tone hinted at a smile.

"I'm not worried. It's odd that he wouldn't have mentioned it."

"I'm sure he had a good reason. Although…"

Sophie waited for Joanna to elaborate. When she didn't, Sophie stopped walking. "Although what?"

"He didn't seem himself yesterday."

"What happened?"

"Nothing. Except Rose stopped in to visit."

"What did she say?"

"Clara was giving me a tour of the supply room. I didn't hear any of their conversation. I just noticed that Karl seemed preoccupied after she left. It's probably nothing."

Joanna walked on, and Sophie followed. At the school, Joanna waved and went toward town. Sophie saw Rachel playing on the swings with Sam.

She crossed to the children. "You got here before me, Rachel. I missed you."

"*Daed* wanted to get to the store early. He's expecting a shipment of new hardware today. I told him I could wait for you, but he said we shouldn't bother you so much. Am I a bother?"

Relief made her smile. There was a simple answer. He'd just forgot to mention it. "You are not a bother. I consider you my friend and a *wunderbar* neighbor."

Rachel gave Sophie an unexpected hug. "I love you."

The child's words pulled at Sophie's heartstrings as she returned the hug. "I love you, too."

Rachel drew back and cupped Sophie's cheeks in her hands. "I don't want you to ever go away. Understood?"

"Understood," Sophie said firmly although she knew it would an empty promise. "Now run and play while I get ready for school."

Sophie left the children and went in. Phillip had already

arrived. He was her most dependable student. He brought in a bucket of coal from the storage shed. Between them they soon had the stove burning brightly. When she went to ring the bell and call the children in, the room was warm enough that they didn't need their coats on.

They had all settled in their seats when the outside door opened, and Joseph Troyer came in with his toolbox. "I understand you need a window fixed."

"In the cloakroom," Sophie said.

"I'll figure out what I need and then I'll be back at noon while the children are at lunch. That way I don't disrupt your lessons."

True to his word, Joseph returned later while the children were outside. "The glass will be easy to replace, but fixing the busted frame is going to take some work. I'll have to take the whole thing out."

Sophie tried to concentrate on grading a few papers but the hammering from the cloakroom made that difficult.

"Teacher, would you like to look at our ideas for the backgrounds?"

Sophie glanced up to see Betty and Edna standing in front of her. She laid aside her pen and folded her hands together to give them her full attention. "Absolutely."

The hammering resumed.

"Betty, would you ask Joseph to take a break?"

"Sure." She headed into the cloakroom. There was silence shortly after she went in.

Edna laid three sheet of construction paper on the desk. "These are our sketches of the hills and sheep."

Betty and Joseph came up to the desk. Joseph motioned toward the cloakroom. "I'm finished if you'd like to take a look at my work."

"I will as soon as I hear what these girls have come up with. Go on." She nodded toward Edna.

She laid a second piece of construction paper on the desk. "This will be the inn on the streets of Bethlehem." She indicated an open archway in the building. "This is where the innkeeper steps out to tell them he has no room but sends them to the stable."

"You've done a fine job of creating the feel of a street. I see all the windows have lights in them."

"We wouldn't need real lights. We could just paint the building to look like there were lights in the windows."

"Of course. And your third set?"

"This is the inside of the stable. The cow will be here. We'll have a place for Jason to tie up the donkey. The manger will be at the front. My *daed* can build the manger for us."

Sophie contemplated the various drawings. The two girls had put a lot of thought into them. "What are we going to paint these on?"

The girls looked at each other. "We thought we could use white sheets and hang them from something like a clothesline."

"These are wonderful drawings," Sophie said. "But I'm afraid the sheets would flap in the wind and ruin the effect."

Joseph leaned over her shoulder to look at the sketches. "You could paint them on plywood panels. Two boards each would make a panel eight feet square."

It was far too ambitious for her twenty scholars. "I'm sure the children could do that if we had more time."

"I could build the panels for you," Joseph said, pushing his hat back on his head. "I'm sure my old construction boss will donate the lumber if we invite him to the program. He never misses a chance to stay at the inn and eat Grace's cooking."

"We must do the painting," Edna said.

Joseph stood up and crossed his arms. "Sure. I have several

partially empty paint cans from various projects that I could donate. That way you don't have to buy it all."

"That's very generous," Sophie said. "I'm not sure I could ask you to do so much. You don't even have a child in school."

"Yet," he replied with a grin. "Henry will be a student here one day. The Harts Haven community has been good to Abby and me. We'd like to give back."

"The panels would need to be stable in the wind." She didn't need one toppling over on a child.

"I'll make sure of it."

She bit the corner of her lip. "Can it be done in three weeks?"

"Two if Karl will help me."

Sophie nodded. "I'm sure he will. He knows how much this means to Clara and Rachel."

The rumble of thunder and the sound of rain hitting the roof dampened some of her enthusiasm. The children started coming in from outside. The forecast was calling for a wet week.

"My *kinder* will need to work on this during school hours. How can we paint outside panels in this damp weather?"

"Paint on sheets in here. Hang them on the panels when you're ready."

"That might work." By *Gott*'s grace, Clara's vision of the program was coming together. Sophie wanted to share the good news with her. And with Karl. But first she had to stop by the clinic for her appointment with Dr. Bertha. Since Rachel normally walked home with Sophie, she didn't feel right about sending the child home alone. Sophie and Rachel walked quickly to town after school let out and Sophie left Rachel at the store without going in.

At the clinic, she had to wait until two other women were seen. Dr. Bertha seemed pleased after she examined Sophie.

"The bruise is fading. Looks better. The lump is smaller, too. That's good. How does the shoulder feel?"

"Not as sore. It still hurts to move my arm."

"Keep using the sling for another two weeks. I heard back from the radiologist who read your ultrasound. He agreed the lump is a hematoma. He didn't see any sign of cancer in the tissues."

The relief made her dizzy. "None?"

"Were you expecting bad news?"

Sophie pressed a hand to her forehead. "I guess I was. I've always known my cancer could come back. I honestly thought you were mistaken."

"No doctor likes to hear a patient doesn't have confidence in their diagnosis, but I understand. When a person is resigned to dying, it can be difficult for them to accept that they aren't."

Sophie managed a shaky smile. "At least not yet."

"I haven't received your medical records, but when I get them, I want to sit down with you and go over them. Some types of breast cancer have a high rate of recurrence. Some are unlikely to recur. The genes for a few types can be passed on to your children. Once you know what you are dealing with, you can face it. Hopefully you will have many more years on this earth to do good."

"I don't expect many more, but I'd be happy with a few."

"Cancer treatments are improving all the time, Sophie. Come see me if you suspect something is wrong, and we'll face it together."

"Thank you, Doctor."

"My pleasure. Don't forget we are going bird-watching this Saturday. You have an open invitation to join us."

"I'll think about it."

After leaving the clinic, Sophie headed for the hardware store. She turned the corner at the post office and stopped.

Lance Switzer was inside at the large front window hanging his flying reindeer display. Underneath he had used a long, wide piece of white paper cut to look like hills of snow dotted with small Christmas trees.

Sophie was interested in the paper. The *kinder* could draw wonderful Nativity scenes on a sheet that big.

She tried the door, but it was locked so she tapped on the window to get his attention. He immediately opened the door for her. "Sorry, we close at four."

"I have a question about your window decoration. The paper you used on the bottom. Is that one piece?"

"Yup. I think it looks more realistic, don't you?"

She chuckled. "More realistic than the flying reindeer?"

Lance burst out laughing. "I do see the irony."

"How long and how wide does that paper come?" she asked.

"That's from a big roll, three feet wide and seventy-five feet long."

"If I ordered one, when would it arrive?"

He frowned slightly. "This time of year, about three weeks."

"Oh." She couldn't hide her disappointment. "That will be too late."

"Do you mind my asking what you need it for?"

"The school's Christmas program."

He rubbed his chin. "That's important. How much do you need?"

Sophie did a quick calculation in her head. "One hundred and ninety-two feet."

"In that case, I'll bring a roll over to the school. Free of charge."

She blinked in amazement. "Mr. Switzer, that's very kind of you."

"I like to be a good neighbor to the Amish. My dad broke his back when I was twelve. None of our wheat had been harvested. With dad's medical bills and no income, it looked like we would lose our farm. One morning a whole slew of local Amish families came with their horse-drawn harvesters and cut it for us. My folks were sure grateful. Those men never took a dime for their work. When I asked one why they did it, he said, 'To have good friends, you must be a good friend.' That stuck with me all these years." He wiped his eyes and sniffed and went inside.

Sophie shook her head in amazement. The town was full of caring people. With the promised paper, the children could paint inside the school. Then she'd simply staple the scenes on the wood panels at the last minute. She started toward the hardware store to share the news with Clara and Rachel. Pausing at the street corner, she waited for a buggy to pass. It was Mr. and Mrs. Imhoff. They waved and she waved back.

She had been in town for less than a month but the idea of leaving Harts Haven was quickly becoming unthinkable. Her students brightened her days and made her smile. She adored Clara and Rachel. And Karl. Sophie tried to imagine her life without them and found she couldn't.

What if Dr. Bertha was right, and she could have years to live?

Sixteen

Karl was at the back of the hardware store when the bell over the door jingled. He looked around the edge of the shelves he was stocking to see Sophie come in. His spirits lifted at the sight of her only to drop a moment later. He wasn't a man who could help strengthen her faith even if he knew what was troubling her. And she might be leaving soon. The less time they spent together, the better off they would all be.

Joanna, Clara and Rachel were at the front counter. Sophie went straight to them with a wide smile on her face. "I have the best news about our program. We won't have to ruin sheets."

Clara and Joanna exchanged puzzled glances.

"That is wonderful news." Joanna looked to Sophie for an explanation.

"The postmaster has generously offered huge rolls of paper we can use to paint our backgrounds onto. And Joseph Troyer has volunteered to make three eight-foot-by-eight-foot pan-els. We can attach the paper to them with staples just before the program so that the children's artwork isn't out in the weather."

"I never imagined the backgrounds would be so big." Clara's voice was filled with awe. "They will be amazing."

Joanna folded her arms over her chest. "What are you going to do if it rains or snows the night of the program? Is there somewhere we can hold the program inside?"

"Rose thought people wouldn't mind being out in the weather," Clara said.

"I know she did," Sophie agreed. "Joanna is pointing out that paper won't hold up in the rain."

"We must pray that it doesn't rain," Rachel stated. "*Gott* will listen."

It struck Karl that he might have an answer for them. He walked toward the front of the store. "I know someone with a large indoor space, and it isn't far from the school."

He watched Sophie's face closely. The sadness he had seen before flashed in her eyes and then was gone. She smiled at him, but it looked forced. "Any help you can give is welcome. I should warn you that Joseph Troyer is expecting you to help put the panels together."

"I can do that."

"Who has a big indoor space?" Clara asked.

"Our neighbor to the north," he said.

Clara wrinkled her brow. "Dwight McDonald?"

Sophie's eyes lit up and her smile turned genuine. "The farm with the indoor riding arena. Of course. That would be perfect."

Seeing her bright smile made him feel better in an instant. He had missed their time together that morning.

"*Daed*, Sophie says she missed us this morning and we're not a bother. We're her friends. Isn't that right, Sophie?"

Sophie blushed and lowered her eyes. "That's true."

Rachel wrapped her arms around Sophie and gazed at her. "I'm so glad you came here. I never want you to leave."

Karl saw the affection shinning in his daughter's eyes. What had Rose said? That Sophie needed friends now. People to show her support and make her feel wanted in Harts Haven. For Rachel's sake he could offer Sophie his friendship. Any other feelings would just have to be put aside.

Sophie looked at Karl. "Do you think Mr. McDonald would let us use his arena? How much would it cost to rent it for the evening?"

"He and his wife run the farm and ranch supply store at the edge of town. Why don't we go ask them?"

Her smiled faded and she looked down. "I don't want to take you away from your work."

"Clara, Rachel and my new clerk can manage the place for half an hour and then lock up. Can't you, girls?"

Joanna grinned. "Absolutely. I will do exactly what Clara tells me to do."

Karl laughed. "See, my daughter is training her well." He nodded toward the door. "Come on. I'll introduce you to the McDonalds. It's only short walk."

"Can I come, too?" Rachel asked.

"I need your help with something here," Joanna said quickly.

Rachel looked disappointed. "Oh, okay."

Karl ushered Sophie out the door. Now that they were alone together on the sidewalk, he was at a loss for something to say. The sun came out from behind the gray clouds. "Looks like the weather is going to warm up."

"It does." She didn't glance his way. She shifted her sling to a more comfortable position and flexed her fingers.

"How is your arm feeling?"

"Better."

"Is that the truth or are you trying to avoid talking to me?"

Her startled gaze shot to his face. "I'm not trying to avoid you."

"I'm glad. How's your arm?"

She relaxed. "The bruising has started to fade but it's still tender. It hurts when I move it."

"Are you using your pain pills or are you toughing it out?"

"They make me sleepy so I can't take them while I'm at school, but I do take some at night."

"I don't imagine the cold weather is helping. Are you warm enough now?"

She cast him a sidelong glance. "Will you produce a wool scarf from your pocket and wrap it around my neck the way Joanna likes to do?"

"I don't have a scarf, but I will give you my coat." He started to unbutton it.

She put her hand on his sleeve. "*Nee*, I'm fine, but the offer is gallant."

He stared at her hand, wishing he could take hold of it and lace his fingers through hers to see if their hands fit together. Nora's hand used to feel like it was made for him to hold. Would Sophie's feel the same?

She slowly pulled her fingers away. "How is Joanna getting along as your new clerk?"

That was a safe topic. "She catches on quick, has a good understanding of record keeping and she talks about customer flow."

"Getting a customer to move through the store to see more items. *Ja*, our father drilled into us how important it is. Good service is providing the customer with the things they don't even know they need." She did the reasonable imitation of her *daed*'s deep voice.

Karl laughed. "I did hear her tell Clara that today."

"I hope it works out for both of you," she said softly. He had the feeling she was talking about more than the job. He wanted to ask what she meant but they had arrived at Dwight McDonald's feed store.

Dwight was carrying a bag of horse chow over his shoulder, which he hefted into the back of a waiting pickup. A second man carried out another bag and tossed it in, too.

"Thank you, sir." Dwight touched the brim of his black cowboy hat and stepped aside as the customer got in the truck and drove away.

He grinned at Karl, showing a gap-toothed smile behind his grizzled mustache. "Howdy, Karl. What are you up to on this fine day?"

"I brought a friend of mine to meet you. This is Sophie Eicher."

Dwight pulled off his cowboy hat. "Pleased to meet you, ma'am. You're the new schoolteacher. I heard you were wounded in action on the first day. I'm sorry to see it's true. Mutton busting is a dangerous sport. That's why we let the little kids do it. They heal faster than us old folks."

Karl could see Sophie's confusion and decided to explain. "Mutton busting is a competition for the *kinder* at the rodeo during our county fair. Instead of riding bucking horses, the young ones try to stay on the back of a running sheep. The one who stays on the longest wins."

"My grandkids sure do enjoy it. Mikey won first place this year, and he's only six. What can I help you with today? I've got a sale on horse chow. Fifteen percent off."

"I'm here to ask about using your indoor riding arena," Sophie said.

"What date were you thinking? If my wife doesn't have something booked, I don't think it will be a problem. Come in and meet the missus, Sophie." He settled his hat on his head.

Sophie and Karl followed him inside the store, where his wife, Lucy, stood behind the counter. A display of ribbons, trophies and belt buckles from various rodeos filled the glass-fronted case. The walls and shelves were covered with everything a rancher would need from bridles to coiled ropes, saddles to post-hole diggers, bags of feed for chickens, dogs, cats and even goats. The place smelled of grains, leather and stale cigar smoke.

"Lucy, this is the new Amish schoolteacher, Sophie Eicher," Dwight said.

"Oh, the one that was knocked down by Rachel's lambs. How are you, my dear?"

Two spots of color bloomed in Sophie's cheeks. "Does everyone in town know about my accident?"

Lucy chuckled. "That's what small towns are like."

"They want to use our arena. I told them I had to check with the boss." Dwight winked at his wife.

"It would be for Christmas Eve but only if the weather is bad," Karl said. "We are looking for an alternate place to host the children's school Christmas program."

Dwight gave him a puzzled look. "What's wrong with the school?"

"We're planning an outdoor living Nativity," Sophie explained.

"We don't have anything planned for Christmas Eve," Lucy said.

"How much is your fee?" Sophie asked. "I will need to have any expenditure approved by the school board."

Dwight pushed his hat back with one finger. "I'm not going to charge you anything. Your school programs are something the whole community enjoys. Reminds me of when I was a kid and our little country school put on a show for family and friends. Mrs. Frick taught the fourth grade and music. She played the piano. We sang Christmas carols and did little skits. It was something pretty special to us and our folks."

Lucy smiled at him. "It certainly was. Dwight and I went to the same rural school. Remember the year you were a dancing snowman?"

He winched. "Don't remind me. When the program was over, old Mr. Heinz, the custodian, would come through the back door in a Santa suit with a beard made of cotton batting. He'd hand out fruit and bags of candy our mothers had made."

Lucy sighed. "To this day the smell of an orange reminds me of Christmas because that was the only time we got fruit that wasn't canned in the winter. Course you folks don't hold with the idea of Santa Claus, but your ways sure do remind us of the good old times. The place is yours free of charge if you need it on Christmas Eve."

Sophie smiled. "That's very generous. I hope you both will attend."

"We wouldn't miss it," Dwight declared. "A living Nativity, you say. How are you fixed for animals?"

"My daughter has her sheep," Karl said. "Bishop Wyse knows someone with a donkey."

"The Imhoff children are bringing three of their goats," Sophie added.

"What about a cow?" Dwight asked. "Our granddaughter Naomi has a grand champion Guernsey heifer, broke to halter, don't mind crowds. I know she'd be tickled to loan Molly to you for the night."

Karl looked at Sophie. She shrugged. "Molly sounds perfect for the part," she said. "We will have a final rehearsal on the Thursday evening before Christmas. If you could bring her then, that would be best. That way she and the children can get used to each other."

"Great idea. I'll see that she gets there. Anything else, folks?"

"I need a small bag of alfalfa pellets."

"Will half a pound be enough?" Lucy asked.

"*Ja.* I'll take two bags of your horse chow if I can pick them up later," Karl said.

"I'll put two aside for you. Can't wait to see your production, ma'am."

"It was sure nice to meet you," Lucy said. "We hope you like our town well enough to stay a long time."

Karl caught a glimpse of fleeting sadness in Sophie's eyes again. Was she planning to leave? The only way he would know for sure was to ask her. But did he want to know the answer?

Sophie tried to look cheerful as she left the farm and ranch supply store, but Lucy McDonald's comment was a reminder that her future was limited even if she were granted a few more years. It was something she wanted to forget when she was with Karl. When they were together the present was all that mattered.

He was silent as they walked back to the hardware store. He checked the doors and windows and then she fell into step beside him as they walked toward his farm. As they neared the inn, she saw Rose sitting on her front porch. She waved and got up. "Yoo-hoo!"

Karl groaned under his breath. Sophie tried not to laugh. They waited on the sidewalk as Rose hurried toward them.

"Tell me, how did your visit with the bishop go? Did he approve the program?"

"He had some reservations," Sophie said. "He and the school board want to see the play before Christmas Eve."

"Not surprising, I reckon," Rose said. "We are having a cookie exchange party here on the Saturday before Christmas. I wanted to make sure both of you were invited. Please pass on the invitation to Joanna and the girls."

"I will," Karl said. "We should get going. I have chores to do before supper."

"Wilma and Fannie Youtsey bought the building next door to yours, Karl. You will have new neighbors and our downtown will get a much-needed café. Wilma wanted me to be sure and tell you that Fannie is looking forward to the cookie exchange."

He inclined his head slightly. "Thank you for the information, Rose."

Sophie had to rush to catch up with him as he walked away. "Is Rose at it again?"

He glanced at her and the scowl on his face faded. "If you're referring to her matchmaking, I don't think she ever stops."

"I haven't met Wilma and Fannie Youtsey. I take it the daughter is the one she has in mind for you. What's she like?"

"You can decide for yourself when you meet them at the cookie exchange."

"I hope Clara and Rachel can help Joanna and I make cookies. A cookie exchange is something we do every year back home."

He stopped walking. "Do you intend to leave Harts Haven?"

She looked at him in surprise. "What makes you ask that?"

"Rose said you are thinking of returning to Ohio. If you are, I don't think you should be doing fun things with my daughters. It will only make them miss you more."

Sophie started walking again, not sure how to answer him. There was so much she wanted to say but she had no idea where to start.

"Does your silence mean you are leaving?"

"There are things that you don't understand."

"And I won't until you explain them."

She stopped walking and folded her good arm over her sling. "I did mention to Grace that I was considering returning to Ohio. I was homesick that day. I miss my father. He and I were very close. Letters can't fill that void."

"When are you going? Will you wait until after Christmas at least?"

"I have wrestled with this decision and come to the conclusion that I want to remain in Harts Haven for as long as the good Lord wishes me to stay."

"So, you're not leaving?" He sounded relieved. The scowl disappeared from his face.

"Not of my own free will."

He nodded and then smiled. "Okay then. The girls will be happy to hear that. Rachel is quite fond of you."

"I am very fond of her, too. Is it all right if I invite her over to make cookies now?"

"Sure. As long as I get a few."

"You will have to wait for the night of the exchange." She glanced at him and saw a guarded expression enter his eyes.

"I'm glad you aren't leaving us. I would hate to lose my newest friend before I've gotten to know her better." He started walking again, and Sophie followed.

For the first time since her diagnosis, Sophie prayed she would have years to live. For as long as God granted, she wanted to remain a friend to Karl and his family. Her common sense told her his friendship would be enough, but in her heart, she knew she wanted more.

★ ★ ★

The next day turned bitterly cold. Karl brought the buggy around for their trip to school and to town. Joanna and Sophie carried out flannel-wrapped hot bricks to warm everyone's feet and thick quilts to spread across their laps. When Sophie hurried back into the house to get her school papers, Joanna hopped out of the front seat and into the back with the two children. Buck saw his chance and scrambled in to sit between Rachel and Clara with a silly doggy grin of satisfaction on his face.

"Buck, get out," Clara said.

Joanna laughed. "Let him come with us. I know he's my dog, but he likes you girls better."

Karl turned to look at Joanna. "What are you doing?"

She gave him a wide grin. "You can thank me later. Sophie likes you. She just doesn't want to let on. Snuggle in, girls, I'm cold."

Rachel grinned. "*Daed* likes Sophie a lot, too. Don't you, *Daed*?"

"Sure." Did Joanna mean Sophie was interested in him? Karl's heart started hammering in his chest. Like as in she would want to see more of him? Spend time alone with him? His determination to simply be her friend started to waver.

Sophie came out of the house and frowned at her sister. Joanna waved her toward the front seat. "Hurry up and get in or the bricks will be cold. What do we have planned for today, Clara?"

"I was going to quiz Rachel about her spelling," Sophie said.

Rachel looked smug. "I know all my spelling words. Clara helped me last night."

Joanna chuckled. "That's what sisters do. They help each other."

Sophie pressed her lips into a hard line and Karl wondered if Joanna knew what she was talking about. If Sophie was this reluctant to sit by him, Joanna had to be mistaken about her feelings for him.

"Come on, get in," he snapped.

"Oh, very well." She climbed in the buggy and shut the door.

"Don't sit clear over there by the door," Joanna said. "Karl has plenty of blanket to share."

He lifted the edge of the blue-and-white quilt. "I don't bite."

Sophie's face grew beet red. "I remember when you almost bit my head off."

"Don't forget that I've seen your temper, too. Now is not the time to reminisce. It's cold."

She scooted over beside him. He laid the quilt across her lap and spoke to the horse to get him moving. It only took a few minutes to reach the school. Not nearly long enough for him to relax and enjoy having Sophie next to him.

He stopped the horse and pulled the quilt off her. "We spent more time quarreling that it took to drive here. Next time, just get in."

Her chin went up. He could tell she was miffed. "That was hardly a quarrel. I appreciate the ride. Our horse and buggy should arrive late this afternoon, so I won't be such a bother to you in the future."

Rachel leaned forward and put her arms around Sophie's neck. "You are not a bother. You are our friend. Right, Daed?"

Leave it to his daughter to remind him of his role in Sophie's life. "That's true. Write it on the blackboard fifty times, teacher, so you don't forget."

She didn't comment as she got out and walked into the

school with Rachel, but she did pause at the door and look back at him before going in. What was she thinking?

"Being friends is a good start," Joanna said. "Sophie needs friends. She doesn't make them easily."

"Why is that?"

"Because she keeps her feelings bottled up. Someday I pray she will learn that sharing her troubles makes them bearable."

"Does she have troubles?"

"We all do. That's why we lean on our faith and our friends."

Sophie's buggy and mare arrived on Thursday evening. When Nutmeg was unloaded, she immediately rubbed her face against Sophie's uninjured arm.

"Have you missed me?" Sophie whispered, scratching the horse behind her ears. Nutmeg gave a soft whicker as if saying she had.

"I'm glad you're here, but now I'll have no reason to ride with Karl again. I hope the weather stays nice enough to walk all winter and you can grow fat in your stall."

"What's her name?" Clara asked, coming up behind Sophie.

"Nutmeg, because of her red-brown color." Sophie patted her shiny neck.

"She's pretty. I imagine she is faster than Buster."

Sophie grinned at Clara. "Let's have a race and see."

Clara's eyes widened in shock, then she giggled. "You wouldn't. Teachers don't do those kinds of things."

Sighing loudly, Sophie rubbed her mare's white blaze. "Being a teacher can be so boring sometimes."

"You should try working in a hardware store. Nothing exciting ever happens."

"How are things going with Joanna? Is she a problem for you?"

Clara gave an indifferent shrug. "She's okay."

The grin tugging at Clara's lips was a giveaway. Sophie rolled her eyes. "Don't tell me you like working with her."

Smiling, Clara nodded. "I do. She has some *goot* ideas, and she's loads of fun to talk to."

"I can see it now. Clara and Joanna sitting around gossiping all day while your *daed* works his fingers to the bone."

"We aren't that bad. You should come by on Saturday to see the changes Joanna is making."

"I'll do that." It was wonderful to see Clara looking happy. Having Joanna take the job was exactly what Clara needed. Sophie knew her sister could win over the sullen child if anyone could.

Karl had an empty stall ready for Nutmeg in the barn, but Sophie wanted to turn her out into the corral first. As soon as Sophie unsnapped her lead, the horse took off running and bucking around the enclosure while Karl's horses looked on from an adjacent pen. Sophie leaned on the top board of the fence to watch her, too.

"She looks happy here." Karl stopped beside Sophie and leaned on the fence, too.

"Sometimes a change of scenery does a body *goot*." They weren't touching but Sophie's pulse raced as his nearness filled her stomach with flutters.

"Has it done you *goot*?" he asked softly.

"I think so. It's different than I expected but I like it here. How far away are those trees?" She pointed south to a distant line across the open fields.

"Two miles."

"It would be hard to hide out here."

"What do you have to hide?" he asked.

Flustered, Sophie looked at his face. His gray eyes drilled into hers. She took a step back from the fence. "You misunderstand my meaning. I was simply remarking that the country is flat. I'm used to hills."

"I don't think I made a mistake. This open county means people must be open, too. I should know. I did my level best to hide away with my grief. Fortunately for me, a busybody teacher found me out. I hope I have thanked her enough. Should you ever want to come out of hiding, I'm here."

He tipped his hat and walked away. Sophie wanted nothing more than to run into his arms and tell him everything. But she knew it would hurt him, and she couldn't bear to do that.

Saturday morning, Sophie drove to the hardware store as she had told Clara she would stop by. Pulling up at the hitching rail, she noticed three Amish couples standing in front of the hardware store window along with a pair of *Englisch* women.

What was going on inside that was drawing a crowd? She secured Nutmeg and went to investigate.

"What a cute puppy. Is it real?" one *Englisch* woman asked. "Let's go in and see."

The group entered the building before Sophie reached them. She stopped and stared at the window in amazement.

A charming display had been set up inside. A black woodburning stove was tucked against one side of the alcove. A beautiful pair of leather bellows were leaning against it as if the owner had just set them aside. Fireplace tools hung on a rack next to the stove. One set had shiny copper handles; the other set was plain black. A canvas firewood carrying bag sat behind the bellows with four cut pieces of firewood in it.

On top of the stove were tubes of stove polish and blacking holding up a sign that said Sale. A pretty hearthrug was centered in front of the open stove door, where a real fire flickered inside. Buck was curled up asleep on the rug. Overhead, a gas two-globe chandelier hung from the ceiling. In the center of the display sat a rocking chair, painted black, with a quilt hung over the back.

The other side of the window alcove held an assortment of small tables and crates painted in different bright colors with matching glass oil lamps displayed on top of them. Some of their shades were simple clear chimneys and some were beautifully etched glass. It certainly was an appealing display on a chilly winter day. Sophie pushed open the door and walked inside.

Arranged in baskets below the display window were items all marked On Sale. Two of the men she had seen looking in were picking up tubes of stove polish. Rachel stood on a box behind the counter helping Clara with the customers as they paid for their purchases. Everyone was smiling.

"What do you think?" Joanna asked as she hurried to Sophie's side.

"Was this all your idea?" Sophie asked in surprise.

"It was," Karl said as he joined them. There was a huge grin on his face. Sophie's heart turned over with joy at seeing him so happy. She had been right. Joanna was just the person to ease his sadness.

"You helped, Karl. Don't give me all the credit." Joanna grinned at him with a familiar ease. A bit of envy stole into Sophie's heart.

He turned to her. "I can't thank you enough for convincing your sister to take this job. She is doing wonders."

Sophie had hoped Joanna would prove useful, but she certainly hadn't expected her to blossom in the job.

"I just remember the way *Daed* had his store set up," Joanna said. "He had a beautiful seasonal display in the window to attract people's attention. Especially the *Englisch* tourists in town. He kept bins with sale items close to the counter to prompt impulse purchases and to remind people of things they might be running low on at home when they are checking out."

"The tables and lamps are beautiful, but an Amish woman isn't going to buy an emerald green table," Sophie said.

Karl chuckled. "True, but we have a lot of non-Amish in our community and Joanna has shown them what they can do with an old piece of furniture and a can of spray paint. I've sold more sandpaper, paint and stove polish these past two days than I did all last month. I've actually run out of the canvas firewood totes and had to order more. I didn't sell any of those last month."

Clara left the counter and came over. She gestured to the window display. "The quilt was donated by the fabric store so we can direct customers to them when they ask about it."

"That was Clara's idea. She's helping us and another local business," he said. "It was *goot* thinking."

Sophie smiled at Clara and Joanna. Despite her envy, she was genuinely glad her sister was happy. "It seems you've found the perfect job, Joanna."

And the perfect family.

"Do you want to stay and help us for a while?" Clara asked.

Sophie cast her mind about for a reason to decline. Watching them working together as a family shouldn't have left her feeling sad. This was what she had hoped for, but it was clear she didn't belong. "Dr. Bertha invited me to go bird-watching with her and Grace."

Rachel hopped off her box behind the counter and joined them. "If Mr. Young is there, ask about a camel. Clara, we have another customer. It's Rose. Oh, I have so much to tell her." The pair went back to the counter.

"Are you sure you won't stay?" Karl asked softly. "It could be fun."

"*Nee.* I've got to go." Sophie backed away and spun around before he could see how much she wanted to be with him.

Seventeen

Sophie discovered that bird-watching in winter was cold and uncomfortable. She didn't find the delight that her aunt and the others shared when some special bird was spotted and its song dutifully recorded by Herbert Young on his directional microphone. The one thing that would have made the morning bearable, other than the appearance of the much anticipated but elusive whooping cranes, would have been having Karl and the girls to share the adventure with her. Perhaps she had been foolish to pass up a day spent with them. This certainly wasn't more fun.

She couldn't stop thinking about the family. Karl had looked so happy with customers in the store because of Joanna's changes. Clara was coming out of her shell. Rachel was simply Rachel, always happy.

Joanna was making a difference in Karl's life. She was already friends with Clara and Rachel. She was doing everything Sophie had hoped she would do for the Graber family, so why wasn't she happier?

Because she wanted to bring joy to Karl's life, too. It was selfish, but true. Standing on the outside of the family looking in was more painful than she could have imagined.

The highlight of Sophie's afternoon came later when they stopped at the home of Joseph and Abby Troyer. While everyone enjoyed hot cocoa, Sophie held baby Henry and marveled at the beauty God had created in such a small package. It was a bittersweet moment.

She would never enjoy motherhood, never hold her own babe. For as long as she lived, she would be the dependable auntie, always available to help but never really a part of the family. It was a depressing thought. She kissed little Henry's cheek before handing him back to his mother.

On Monday the weather warmed up enough that Sophie was able to walk to school with Karl and the children, but she had been right when she thought it wouldn't be the same. Joanna's bright chatter and jovial nature along with Buck's antics made everyone laugh, but the closeness that had formed between Karl and herself was missing. Karl repeatedly tried to bring her into their conversations, but she resisted his efforts. By Wednesday, she began to feel like a spare wheel with no purpose in the group. She decided she would drive herself to school starting next week so she could get in early to put the final touches on the Christmas program.

At least at school things were better. Her scholars were delighted with the paper she provided. Edna and Betty soon had the first large sketches finished and assigned coloring tasks to the younger children. Overseeing their work left her feeling better about the upcoming Christmas season.

On Friday afternoon, Sophie had the children move their desks to one side of the room. She had Zack read the story of the Nativity while the other children acted out their parts and rehearsed the songs they would sing. Rachel was impatient to have her sheep at school, but Sophie encouraged her to practice with the animals at home until they had a formal rehearsal outside.

That evening Rachel came home from school with Sophie. After she finished her chores, she sat in Sophie's living room playing with a puzzle while Sophie swept the floors. Rachel looked up. "I wish I could stay with you forever, Sophie."

She smiled at the child. "That's a sweet thing to say, Rachel, but your father would miss you."

"Not if you stayed with us. If we all stayed together."

Sophie went back to sweeping. "I'm afraid that's not possible, but I'll live here, and you can some see me whenever you want."

"It's not the same."

Sophie carried her dustpan outside to empty it off the side of the porch. She almost dumped it on Buck, who lay sprawled in the grass watching Clara hang clothes on the line. She was surprised to see Clara home so early. The store didn't close until five and it was only a little after four.

She started toward Clara when the smell of something burning caught her attention. It wasn't woodsmoke. The front door of Karl's home stood open. A curtain of black smoke was rising from the top of the doorway. Sophie dropped her dustpan and broom and raced toward the house. "Clara! Something is burning!"

She entered the smoke-filled kitchen. Immediately she saw the source was the oven. She yanked open the door. Two loaves of charred bread were smoldering inside. She grabbed one of the pans with the corner of her apron, rushed outside and tossed it onto the grass.

Clara came running from the clothesline. "Oh no. I forgot my bread."

"Wait here." Sophie covered her nose with her apron and dashed back inside for the second loaf. She didn't want Clara to breathe the dense smoke. After tossing the second loaf onto the ground, she went back in and opened all the windows. The kitchen quickly began to clear.

Going back outside, Sophie saw Clara huddled on the front step with her head in her arms, sobbing.

"It's all right." Sophie sat down beside her. "There's no real harm done."

"*Daed* is going to be mad."

"Over a little burnt bread? I doubt it. These things happen. You should've seen the cookies Joanna once forgot in the oven for over an hour. They looked like charcoal briquettes and it took all night to get the smell of smoke out of the house."

"I try so hard to get everything done, but I'm a failure. My mother did it all so easily. Why can't I be more like her?"

Sophie put her arm around the child. "I can promise you that your mother did not do it easily. She might have made it look that way, but keeping a house and raising a family is hard work. I'm sure she had years of practice before you and Rachel came along."

"I'll never be as good as she was."

"Don't be so hard on yourself. Things will get easier. Dry your eyes. I will start another batch of bread while you finish hanging out the laundry."

"All right. *Danki.*"

"You will have to knead it. I only have one good arm." Sophie pointed to her sling. She was rewarded with the little smile from Clara before she went back to the clothesline.

Inside the kitchen that still smelled of burnt bread, Sophie laid out the ingredients for two loaves. Clara returned a few minutes later. "What do you need me to do?"

"Do you have a recipe book, or do you make your bread from memory?"

"*Mamm* wrote it down on a card." Clara got a wooden box off the shelf and opened it. She pulled out the card.

"How is Joanna getting along with your *daed*?" Sophie asked, a little ashamed of trying to pry information from the child.

"Fine."

"I'm glad to hear it. She will make a *goot* wife someday."

"I reckon."

"Has your father ever talked about getting married again?"

Clara shook her head. "Only when Granny Rose wants to introduce him to someone new. Then he says he's never getting married again."

Sophie couldn't blame Karl. "I'm afraid Rose isn't much of a matchmaker."

"*Daed* calls her an irritation."

Sophie chuckled. "Rose's heart is in the right place. Your father will change his mind when he meets someone he likes."

"Maybe."

"He likes Joanna, doesn't he?" Sophie prompted.

"I guess. He likes you, too."

Startled, Sophie gaped at Clara. "Me? What makes you say that?"

"He talks about you a lot. He asks Rachel about all the things you do at school. He even asks Joanna questions about you. When she told him that you liked him, but you didn't want to let on, he smiled big."

Why would her sister say such a thing?

Maybe because it was true but how could Joanna know

that? Sophie had never admitted it out loud. "When did Joanna say that?"

"When we took you to school in the buggy."

She shook her head. "We are just friends, that's all."

"Joanna said being friends was a *goot* start."

She was definitely going to speak to her sister and remind her that children had big ears. "What does it say to do first on your recipe card?"

"It says to mix the yeast and flour."

"Are you sure?"

"*Beweis* the yeast. That means add it to the flour."

"Let me see that." Sophie took the card and read the neatly printed words in a mixture of German and English. "*Beweis* is a German word. It means to proof the yeast. You put the yeast in about a quarter cup of very warm water, add a teaspoon of sugar and wait until it starts bubbling. The bubbles in the yeast are what makes the bread rise."

"Oh. Is that why my bread doesn't get tall in the pan the way it should?"

"Very likely. Read me the rest of the instruction."

As Clara continued, stumbling over some of the words, Sophie realized her lack of schooling was already affecting her. She should have been reading German much better by her age. All Amish children spoke Pennsylvania Dutch at home, but in school they learned to read and write both English and German. German because the Bible the Amish used was written in old High German. "Clara, what kind of schedule for homeschooling does your father keep?"

"I do my math at the store by adding up the cash register money."

But not subtraction, multiplication and division. "What about history and geography?"

"We went to see Lance Switzer's museum last summer. I

learned a lot about Harts Haven and the people who settled here."

The world was bigger than Harts Haven. Sophie couldn't stand by and let Clara fall further behind. Maybe she could help Karl with Clara's homeschooling.

"We'll finish this dough, clean up the kitchen a bit and I'll show you my American history book while we wait for our bread to rise. If you enjoyed Lance's museum, you might like to see how the Amish came to America and ended up here."

Clara grinned. "Okay."

Karl and Joanna stood in his front yard looking at two black lumps on his lawn. "I think that's bread," Joanna said. She glanced at him. "Clara's or Sophie's?"

"My guess would be Clara's." He looked from the ruined loaves to his home. "At least my house is still standing. I hope the kitchen isn't gutted."

Joanna pushed one black lump with the toe of her shoe. "She's going to feel awful about this. I know I would."

"I wonder if I can get bread from the widows at the inn?"

"I'm sure they'll have an extra loaf or two, but we have a half loaf we can spare for tonight."

"*Danki*. I'd better go in and see how she is." He rubbed his hands on his pant legs.

"Expect a few tears."

"Right." That was the one thing he feared about being the father of daughters. He was never sure how to handle a crying girl.

He quietly opened the door and stepped into his kitchen. The delicious smell of fresh baking bread didn't quite hide the lingered odor of smoke. Sophie sat at his table with Clara and Rachel. They were all leaning over a large book. Clara started laughing. "That isn't really the name of the town, is it? Pig, Kentucky?"

"Kentucky was the fifteenth state admitted to the Union, June first, seventeen ninety-two. It has many towns with unusual names including Pig, Hippo, Mud Lick and Chicken Bristle. There are over eight thousand Amish people in the state. One of the largest settlements is near Horse Cave."

Clara broke into guffaws. "I'm from Chicken Bristle. Where are you from?" she asked Rachel.

Rachel giggled. "I'm from Mud Lick but we're moving to Horse Cave. That is so funny."

"And when was Kentucky admitted to the Union?" Sophie's teacher voice calmed the giggling girls.

Clara settled and sat up straight. "June first, seventeen ninety-two as the fifteenth state."

"Very *goot*."

Sophie had found a way to teach Clara even though the child wasn't in school. He was fairly certain the baking bread was hers, as well. Clara hadn't got the hang of baking just yet, but neither had he. He had to admire Sophie's tenacity and creativity. She truly cared about his children. Every day he found more to like about her, but he had no idea how she felt about him.

"When was Kansas admitted to the Union?" he asked.

Sophie, Rachel and Clara turned to look at him in surprise. His eldest daughter sobered and stood up with her hands clasped in front of her. "I accidentally burned our bread today. I'm sorry."

"The house is still standing so no harm done." His gaze was fastened on Sophie. She kept her eyes downcast but there were bright circles of color in her cheeks. Was she happy to see him or embarrassed to be caught teaching his daughter?

"As for funny town names," he said, "Smileyberg and Buttermilk are both real towns in our state. When was Kansas admitted to the union, Clara?"

"I just learned that." Clara closed her eyes. "Kansas entered the Union as a free state, January twenty-ninth, eighteen sixty."

"Is that right, teacher?" he asked. The color in her cheeks deepened as he gazed at her. She wouldn't meet his eyes.

"Almost," she said slowly.

"It was eighteen sixty-one," he said smiling at Clara. "Rachel, what was the first state?"

"Um." She glanced at Clara, who mouthed the letter *D*. "Delaware!" Rachel shouted.

"I see you've all had a productive evening. I may work late more often. Who did my chores?" When no one spoke up, he sighed. "Guess I'd better get out there. Sophie, would you like me to take care of Nutmeg?"

She got up from the table and closed her book. "I don't want to be a bother. I'll take care of her myself."

"You aren't a bother," Rachel reminded her. "You're our friend."

"That is absolutely right," Karl said. He stood by the door waiting until Sophie got her cape and went out.

"I don't mind taking care of your horse. I'm out in the barn anyway," he said.

"As much as I appreciate the offer, Joanna and I need to take care of our own animals."

"Do you have more than one?"

"Joanna officially owns Buck, although I'm sure he eats more of what you put out for his mother."

"I don't mind. This way I don't have to separate him from his mother or from Clara. She's pretty attached to him."

"I've noticed he is attached to her as well." They stepped into the dim interior of the barn.

He studied her face. "Have you noticed how attached I've become to you?"

Sophie's eyes widened and she stopped walking to stare at him. "You don't mean that."

He sighed deeply and pushed his hands into his pockets. "Are you telling me the feelings only go one way? Please be honest."

At a loss for words, Sophie could only gaze into his beautiful eyes. How could she be honest with him? He was supposed to be a match for Joanna. Her sister was going to marry; she wasn't. How could she make him understand that without hurting his feelings?

He was still waiting for her answer.

She cupped her arm over her sling. "I care for you as a friend, Karl."

"Is that all? Because sometimes I see something different in your eyes."

She dropped her gaze to the straw-covered floor. "You must be mistaken."

He stepped close and used two fingers to lift her chin, forcing her to look at him. "I don't think I am, but I see you aren't ready to admit how you feel about me. I can wait, Sophie. I never expected to feel this way again about any woman, but you have managed to wiggle your way past my guard. Even if nothing comes of this between us, I must thank you for making me realize that my life didn't end with Nora's. Her daughters are here, and they need me. You have taken them under your wing and I'm grateful. Please don't let anything I've said keep you away from them. Because you are what they need as much as they need me."

"I don't know what to say."

"Say I can have hope."

"Rose thought you and my sister would make a match of it." She thought the same thing.

He smiled. "Rose is wrong. If I had a sister, I would want her to be exactly like Joanna."

Sophie dug her fingers into her arm to keep from laying her hand on his cheek. He wasn't wrong about her feelings, but she tried hard to keep them hidden. He had become dearer to her than she had imagined was possible.

Hope was the one thing she hadn't had until coming here. She wanted Dr. Bertha to be right. She wanted more years. With Karl, with his children, with her sister.

It was almost too painful to allow herself to think about a future. Yet *Gott* had brought Karl and his family into her life for a purpose. She wanted to understand what that purpose was.

"I can't promise you anything, Karl. There are things about me that you don't know. Things I don't wish to share. I hope you understand."

He looked disappointed. "I don't, but I will give you all the time you need. If there is anything I can do to help, I will. Can we agree to stay friends?"

"Absolutely." She wanted nothing more. It was as if a weight had been lifted from her shoulders. She wouldn't have to avoid him or feel the need to disappear when he was with Joanna. Perhaps she could even enjoy his company now.

"*Goot.* Then I have hope." The tender smile he gave her made her heart turn over with happiness.

"Now I have a proposition for you," he said. "I will feed and care for Nutmeg until your arm is out of your sling if you will continue to homeschool Clara."

"That's a *wunderbar* suggestion. I would be delighted to work with Clara one-on-one. I have found cleaning a horse's stall with only one arm is a challenge."

"Then I will officially take over your pitchfork."

"I happily relinquish it. I should go get supper ready. I'm sure Joanna hasn't started anything yet."

"Luckily, I have fresh bread to make sandwiches with for the girls. Thanks for that."

"She and I made them together. Kneading bread with one arm is as hard as wielding a pitchfork. I'm glad you weren't upset with Clara." He really was becoming a caring and compassionate father.

"I've made my share of mistakes. I haven't charred two loaves of bread, but there was a cake one time that came out as a brick. I used it as a paver in the garden."

Sophie laughed and he smiled at her. "That's a sound I hope to hear more often."

Maybe now that she didn't have to think of him as belonging to Joanna, she could relax in his company. "I'll work on it."

"Run along, I've got chores to do."

Sophie returned to her house and was surprised to find Joanna frying hamburgers for supper. "Do we have any sliced cheese?" Joanna asked.

"I'm sure we do." Sophie opened the refrigerator door and pulled out a package. She carried it to the stove and laid it on the counter.

Joanna opened two slices and laid them on the burgers. "What's going on with you and Karl?"

"I don't know what you mean."

Joanna rolled her eyes. "I saw you go into the barn together."

"I went to feed our horse."

"And?" Joanna arched one eyebrow.

"I won't be pushing you at Karl anymore. He thinks of you as a sister."

"Finally. I didn't think you would ever catch on. Now is it all right if I go with Jeff to the cookie exchange?"

"I guess it is."

"And will you be going out with Karl?"

Sophie shook her head. "We've agreed to remain friends."

"I wonder how long that will last." Joanna held up one hand. "Don't tell me that you will never marry or have children and it's not fair to him to let him think otherwise, because you have already decided what *Gott* has in store for you, and you don't want to hurt anyone. You don't need anyone to take care of you. Sophie Eicher can do it all and teach school with one hand in a sling."

"I'm not that bad."

"You put off everyone but the children. What if your life is short? Don't you want it to be a good life, surrounded by people who love you? Helping others instead of worrying about being a burden to them?"

Sophie recalled something Grace had said. "Joanna, did you resent that *Daed* and I sent you away when *Mamm* was dying?"

Joanna took the skillet off the burner and slammed the lid on it. "That's a stupid question. Of course I did. Was it because I was adopted and not her real daughter?"

Sophie's heart twisted with pain. "*Nee, liebchen.* We were only trying to protect you."

Joanna spun around to face her. "I didn't want protection. I wanted to be with my mother. It wasn't fair that you got to be with her, and I didn't. I resent it still. And I will resent it even more if something happens to you and I don't get to be with you. So don't think you can pass me off to a husband instead of our grandmother and fade away without me. I'm not going to let you." She burst into tears.

"I'm sorry. I'm so sorry." Sophie embraced her sobbing sister and cried with her for the grief and pain they had both endured silently for so long.

Eighteen

Karl lay in bed that night mulling over his feelings for Sophie. He wasn't sure where their relationship would go, but he was willing to take the chance on it. *Gott's* hand was visible in the way Sophie and Joanna had come into his life at a time when he really needed them.

Sophie had opened his eyes to his neglect of his children and to the way he had shut himself off from the world. Their relationship might not always be smooth, but something told him they would be good for each other.

Joanna was proving to be an excellent employee. Her ideas for running the store were different but effective. Clara was learning from her, too, about customer service and treating others with respect.

Rose had warned him that he was the wrong man for Sophie. She'd said his faith wasn't strong enough, but was that still true? With Nora's passing, Karl felt *Gott* had abandoned him, but now he realized *Gott* had simply been waiting for Karl to accept the comfort He offered. It was present all around him in the love he shared with his family and friends.

If Sophie needed a friend, Karl would be that. If Gott had other plans for them, Karl would accept His will.

Rose was wrong about them. She had tried to fix him up with Joanna. She had tried to fix Sophie up with Jeff. Rose wasn't right on either count, so why would she be right in saying that he was wrong for Sophie? She wasn't right. He needed Sophie in his life, and he prayed that she felt the same.

The next morning, he left the house with a lighthearted step. Joanna was waiting for him on her front porch. Her eyes looked puffy as if she had been crying.

His first instinct was to ignore the fact. Crying women made him uncomfortable, but Joanna was his friend. He couldn't ignore a friend in need.

He leaned down and looked her in the eyes. "Do you want to talk about it?"

"Do I look that bad?"

He shook his head. "Your eyes are a little puffy, that's all. What's wrong?"

She gave him a trembling smile. "Things are actually a lot better. Sophie and I had a long heart-to-heart. I aired some feeling that had been overdue for discussion. Things are better between us now."

He smiled at her. "I'm glad."

She stood up. "Are we going to go to work, or are you gonna stand there staring at me?"

"I'm ready to go to work. I'm just waiting on Clara and Rachel."

Joanna looked toward the house. "Where are they?"

"Clara said she couldn't leave until the kitchen was clean."

Joanna chuckled. "She sounds like she's been hanging out

with my sister too much. What's wrong with a few dirty plates in the sink?"

"My thoughts exactly."

A second later he heard the door of his house slam. Clara came running down the steps with Rachel behind her. "Okay, we're ready."

Karl looked toward the *daadi haus* and saw Sophie at the kitchen window. A surge of warmth swept over him when she smiled. He waved and she waved back. It made his day brighter.

He started walking toward the highway. Joanna and the girls hurried to keep up with him.

"What is your sister going to do today?" he asked Joanna.

"Joseph Troyer is coming at noon. He's going to build the panels she needs for the school play. She said she was going to supervise or help."

Karl wished he could help, too, but he had a business to run.

It was a busy Saturday morning. The Christmas season was drawing people into their little town looking for Amish-made gifts for friends and relatives. It was the time of year that many of the Amish craftsman saw their best profits.

Joanna was standing at the window arranging the quilt and lighting the gel alcohol in the wood stove to give the appearance of a merry fire. The alcohol gave off plenty of heat and flames but no smoke, which made it ideal for an indoors display.

"Next year we should think about adding some wooden toys to the window display. Maybe some simple games. What do you think?" She turned to him.

"I like the sound of the fact that you think you're going to be working here next year."

Joanna chuckled. "So far I haven't found a reason to leave.

Unless Clara decides to fire me," she said loudly enough for Clara to hear her across the room.

"Don't tempt me," Clara said without looking up from the glass case she was cleaning.

Several more customers came in. Karl stood back and watched Joanna, Clara and Rachel take care of them while he finished his reordering. Finally, he glanced at the clock on the wall. It was almost noon.

He walked up to the counter. "Clara, how would you feel about being in charge for the rest of the afternoon?"

"As long as Joanna is here, we'll be fine."

Karl struggled with his conscience. Should he take off work on a whim simply because he wanted to be with Sophie? He wrestled with the idea. The bell over the door jingled. He looked that way and saw Rose, Wilma and Fannie Youtsey come in. He turned to Clara. "I'm helping out at the school this afternoon. I will be back before closing."

He nodded to Rose and the two women as he walked out the door congratulating himself on a lucky escape.

When Karl reached the school, he saw Joseph had just arrived with a wagon. In the back were plywood panels and two-by-fours.

Joseph grinned at Karl. "I was afraid I was going to have to do this by myself. I think it's a two-man job."

Karl helped him unload the wood and they stood side by side studying the pieces for a moment.

Joseph pushed his hat back on his head "Joining them together will be easy enough. Making them stand up will be a little bit more difficult. I had considered using wheels so that they could be moved easily but I don't think that will leave them stable enough if the wind comes up."

"I don't want them blowing over on the children," Sophie said as she walked up with a large basket over her arm.

Karl hurried to take it from her. He gazed at her intently, looking for signs of distress but didn't see any. "How are you today?"

She smiled softly. "I'm better. For the first time in a while, I'm better."

"I'm glad. If I can do anything, just let me know."

"*Danki*. I brought some lunch for later."

She studied the wood and tapped her lips with her index finger. "Could you attach them to sleds or skids at the base? That would give them more stability."

"We could," Joseph said. "It would also make them easy enough to move especially if the ground is frozen."

Karl and Joseph looked at each other and shrugged. "Sounds good to me," Karl said. "Where's the saw?"

An hour later, there were three large upright panels arranged along the south side of the school. Sophie stood against the side of the building and looked toward them. "The benches will go here. The program will start at three o'clock in the afternoon so we should have plenty of light even if the day is overcast."

"We can leave them in the shed until they are needed," Joseph said. "I think a couple of boys should be able to slide them out into place without much trouble."

Karl studied the set up. "There will be men here who can help the day of the program."

Sophie stood beside Karl. "And if it rains? How do we get them to the McDonalds' indoor arena?"

"We cover them with tarps, load them into a wagon and take them over," Joseph said. "I'm actually surprised that the bishop is allowing this."

Sophie bit her lower lip. "He and the school board want to see the program before Christmas Eve. If they think this is too fancy, all your work will have been for nothing."

"We'll just have to keep a positive attitude," Karl said.

Sophie smiled at him. "You're right. I'm ready for lunch— how about you fellows?"

Joseph shook his head. "I have to get home to Abby."

Karl smiled at her. "I wouldn't mind some lunch, but let's eat inside. It's kind of chilly out here."

They waved goodbye to Joseph as he drove away. Karl took the basket and held open the door for Sophie.

Sophie couldn't suppress the anticipation that swept over her as she walked in the door with Karl close behind her. They were about to enjoy a meal alone. A thrill of delight made her giggle.

"What's so funny?" Karl asked.

She took off her cloak and rubbed her hands together. "I eat my lunch in here every day. I just never have the company of an adult."

"Shall I pretend I'm one of your misbehaving pupils and sit in the corner?"

She tipped her head to study him. "Did you spend a lot of time in the corner during your school years? I can see that."

"I might have been there a few times."

She laughed. "Then I shall remember there is hope that my unruly students can turn out to be good and productive members of our community."

He added coal to the stove from a bucket beside it, then stoked it to get the fire going. After that, he grabbed a folding chair from the back corner of the room and carried it up to her desk. She opened the hamper and spread a tablecloth, then laid out plastic containers of fried chicken, fresh-baked bread, potato salad, pickled beets and a thermos of coffee. "I hope this is enough."

"It looks like a feast to me. My lunch is usually a hard-boiled egg, or a sandwich gulped between customers." He sat down.

She sat, too. "That sounds like mine except I always have an apple or a pear and papers to grade." She adjusted the strap of her sling across the back of her neck. "I will be so glad to get rid of this thing. It chafes my skin."

"Let me have a look." He got up and moved to stand behind her. "I think I can help."

"Go ahead." She braced herself for the touch of his hands, but she wasn't prepared for the surge of excitement that shivered across her skin.

"It needs some extra padding. I have a handkerchief that might work."

Sophie was acutely aware of the man so close behind her. Even though he wasn't touching her, she could feel his warmth on her skin. When he leaned down to lift the strap, she felt his breath stir the hairs on her neck. She was glad she was sitting down because she wasn't sure her knees would've held her up.

He folded the cloth around the strap several times, let his hands linger on her shoulders for a moment and then stood back. "Try that."

She missed his gentle touch. She let the full weight of her arm settle in the sling again. The material was much more comfortable against her neck. "That is better."

He looked embarrassed as he sat down again. "*Goot.* When did the doctor say you can stop wearing it?"

"Next Wednesday. Then I will see her the following week and she will decide how I'm doing. I'm afraid if she wants me to put it back on, she will get an argument."

"You will do what the doctor says is best."

"Now you sound like Joanna."

"She said the two of you had a long-overdue talk."

Sophie nodded. "We did. When our mother was dying, I

convinced my father it was best to send Joanna to stay with his *mamm*, our *grossmammi*. I thought I was protecting her from the heartbreak of having to watch her mother die."

"She didn't want to be protected, did she? She wanted to be with her mother."

"Exactly. Joanna is adopted. She thought that was the reason we sent her away. I never knew how much she resented our decision."

"When Nora got so weak that she couldn't get out of bed anymore I thought about sending the girls away, but she wouldn't have it. She wanted every moment she could have with them. They were her comfort, but it broke my heart to see them together. Rachel was only three and she didn't really understand, but Clara was seven. She knew."

"Joanna was thirteen. I should've recognized that she needed to be with our mother, but I had always looked out for her. I should've trusted her enough to let her make that decision."

"I have learned that looking back on our mistakes is not a good way to move ahead. The past is the past and cannot be changed. All we can do is be better the next time."

"Words of wisdom that I shall try to live by." She bit into her piece of chicken.

It was pleasant sharing a meal with Karl. They didn't say much but there was a lot of unspoken communication between them. She didn't want their time together to end but when he laid down his fork, she knew the meal was over. There had to be a way to stall for more time together.

He patted his stomach. "That was *goot*. Fried chicken is one of my favorites."

She took a sip of coffee from the lid of the thermos and put it down slowly. "Do you have to return to the store?"

He leaned back in his chair and laced his fingers together

behind his head. "I told the girls I would be back before closing time. I'm sure they can manage without me for that long.
Did you have something in mind?"

"I never got to see the picnic area at the river." Would he
take the hint that she wanted to go for a ride with him?

He looked at the ceiling. "Yeah, that was a shame. It's a
nice spot."

"We could go see it today." Was that a strong enough suggestion? Was it too bold?

"But it's not snowing now. That was what made it special."

"Perhaps you're right." She tried to hide her disappointment.

He chuckled, got up and held out his hand. "You give up
too easily."

Her happiness came surging back. She tentatively placed
her hand in his. "In the future, I'll remember that you take
more persuasion than the ordinary fellow."

He helped her to her feet. "I do. One of my teachers said
I was a dense fellow. I like to think of myself as reflective."

"Is that another word for lazy?"

He chuckled. "You're the teacher, you tell me."

She loved the sound of his laughter. She reluctantly pulled
her hand from his, gathered up the remains of their lunch and
stowed it in the basket.

He checked on the stove and then waited for her by the
door as she got her cape. He took it from her and fastened it
around her neck. His fingers lingered for a moment on her
jaw. She looked into his eyes and knew that she wanted him
to kiss her.

It was a ridiculous notion. They were meant to be friends.
She wasn't going to marry or have children. She might not
have much of a future but for one intense moment, she wanted
the memory of his kiss to last until the end of her days.

Why was she drawn to him this way? An overwhelming desire to lay her hand upon his cheek and study him until the riddle was solved made her curl her fingers tight. What would his skin feel like? She could imagine the rough texture of his whiskers, the heat that would warm her palm.

His lips were slightly parted as he gazed at her. If he kissed, would they be soft and inviting or hard and demanding? Would she discover the answer if she took a step closer?

Where were these thoughts coming from? A rush of confusion stuck her. She was a level-headed person. She never flustered easily. So why was she flustered now?

He gave her a wry smile, as if he understood something she didn't. He stepped back and opened the door. "You could wait here while I go get the buggy."

The moment was gone. She sighed and shook her head. "If I did that, I would be compelled to finish grading papers, and I don't feel like doing work today. I'd rather walk."

"Sophie Eicher is putting off her work. Am I a bad influence on you?"

Because he made her crave a life that she would never have? "You absolutely are. I'm not even going to wash these dishes when we get to the house."

He threw back his head and laughed. "What is the world coming to?"

They walked together down his lane. About halfway home, he reached for her hand and curled his fingers between hers. She squeezed gently. It wasn't a gesture of friendship; she recognized that, but it felt right to hold hands with him. His smile said he felt the same way.

When they reached the barn, he slid open the door. "Shall we take my buggy or yours?"

"Let's take mine. Nutmeg needs to get in her harness again. She could use a workout."

Before he could get Nutmeg out of her stall, Sophie heard a buggy coming down the lane. Looking out, she saw it was Bishop Wyse. She shared a disappointed look with Karl. "Maybe another day."

"Next Sunday after church for sure."

A week away. It was a long time to wait, but she nodded and smiled. "It's a date."

They walked out of the barn as Bishop Wyse pulled to stop in front of Sophie's house. He seemed surprised to see Karl. "I thought you would be at the hardware store."

"I took the afternoon off to help Joseph Troyer over at the school."

Being certain that the bishop had come to see her, Sophie went up the porch steps and opened the front door. "Come in Bishop. Would you like some *kaffi*?"

"That sounds *wunderbar*."

"Karl, would you like some?" She smiled at him.

"I should be getting back to the store."

She understood but was disappointed anyway. "Then I will see you tomorrow. Come in, Bishop Wyse. What can I do for you?" She set her picnic basket on the table and pulled out the thermos that still held hot coffee.

When he was settled in the living room with a cup of coffee in front of him and a plate of cookies in the center of the low sofa table, Sophie took a seat and folded her hands.

The bishop sipped his coffee and put the cup down. "The woman I know with the donkey is Mrs. Carver. She has agreed to let us use her animal. However, the donkey is currently out in a pasture with a few hundred head of cattle. We will have to round her up ourselves. Dwight McDonald has agreed to transport her to the school."

"Is the donkey broken to ride?"

The bishop frowned. "I didn't ask that. She said the animal

is tame and halter broke so you shouldn't have any trouble catching her. The pasture is over by Hutchinson." He pulled out a slip of paper from his vest pocket. "Here are the directions."

Sophie took the paper and rubbed her chin. "That doesn't make it practical to bring the animal for our rehearsals and then take it home each time. Will she let us keep it for a week?"

He nodded. "She has agreed to that. She will meet you at the pasture gate Thursday at four thirty."

Sophie grinned. "That's great news."

The bishop took another sip of his coffee. For some reason he didn't look pleased, and she wondered what else he had to say. She folded her hands and waited.

He put his cup down. "In addition, I've been informed that four bishops from eastern Kansas and Missouri will be visiting us Christmas Eve. Several of our new families have come from Cedar Grove, Kansas, and another settlement in Missouri. I've been given to understand they are not pleased with what they have learned about our progressive Christmas programs. They feel that our school is not teaching the proper reverence for this holy day."

Sophie tried to work out which of the families might be unhappy, but she couldn't think of any among her current students. "Do they have children in our school?"

"None are school-age yet. Their concern is for the future."

Sophie could see that he was worried. "I'm sure they will be as delighted with the children's performances as the rest of the community has been."

"Because of their concern, they have invited their former ministers to give their opinion on the appropriateness of what we are doing. That is why it is important that the school board and I see your entire program before you present it on Christmas Eve. Divisions in Amish churches have started over things as simple as this in the past. I don't want conflict to arise among my flock."

Sophie understood. She, too, had seen a church group near Parker, Ohio, split in two over differences that resulted in life-long divisions between families and friends. "I will prepare the children for the possibility that our play may become much simpler. The songs we have planned are in common use. I have no worries about that."

The bishop took a cookie from the plate and stood up. "I have no concerns about your good judgment. Let us pray everyone else agrees. I will bid you good day and hope you have an easy time rounding up Jezebel."

Nineteen

It was the off-Sunday. Sophie and Joanna were discussing if they wanted to visit their aunt Grace at the inn that afternoon or not. Sophie had fixed a pot of coffee and was about to set the percolator on the stove when the front door opened.

Rachel came in. "*Guder mariye. Daed* wants you to come over for breakfast. And Rose said— I mean I want you to make macaroons for the cookie exchange. I'm telling you now so I don't forget. Bye." She turned around and shut the door behind her.

Sophie and Joanna looked at each other and started laughing. "Do you think he wants us to bring something to feed them?" Joanne asked.

"To be on the safe side we should take some cinnamon rolls. I'll grab them out of the freezer."

"Get a can of orange juice, too," Joanna said.

Sophie looked at the coffeepot in her hand and held it toward Joanna. "Do we take it?"

Joanna shook her head. "Karl always has coffee first thing in the morning."

"You're right." Sophie set the pot on the back of the stove and turned off the burner. Together, the women walked next door.

Sophie was pleasantly surprised by the smell of pancakes and coffee when she opened Karl's door. He stood at the stove with an apron tied around his waist and a tea towel over his shoulder. He pointed his spatula at them. "*Guder mariye.* Blueberry or chocolate chip?"

"Good morning to you as well." She tried not to laugh at him.

Clara was busy setting the table. "Would you like milk or just coffee?"

Joanna held up the can of frozen juice. "We brought orange juice if anyone wants some."

"I do," Rachel called out from the other room.

Karl put his fist on his hip. "Your order, please."

Sophie grinned. It wasn't the way she was used to seeing him. "Blueberries for me."

Joanna peeked over his shoulder. "I like mine plain."

"One blueberry, one plain coming up." He began stirring the mix in a bowl.

Sophie walked to his side. "We brought some cinnamon rolls. It will just take ten minutes to heat them up in the oven."

"Ah, the way to a man's heart is through a cinnamon roll." He turned the knob at the back of the stove and opened the oven door.

Sophie slid the pan in and closed it. "The bishop has arranged for Dwight McDonald to transport our donkey from its home to here. Do you have stable room for a burro?"

"That can be arranged." He poured the batter into the sizzling skillet. "When should I expect him or her?"

"It's a female, and we are to pick her up Thursday."

"We?"

"Dwight and I."

"What time?" He flipped the pancakes.

"Four thirty."

He turned to stare at her. "I could close early and ride along in case she proves to be stubborn as burros have been known to be."

"The bishop was assured that she is tame, and we won't have any trouble collecting her."

"Then I'll just go along for the ride and to supervise. Get your plate. Your pancake is almost ready. Joanna, get yours, too."

When everyone had their plates filled, they sat around the table, bowed their heads to say a silent grace and then started on Karl's excellent pancakes.

"These are *goot*," Sophie said. Her stack was bursting with fat blueberries. She covered it in a lake of maple syrup. It was a rare treat.

"It's the only thing that he makes well," Clara said. "You're lucky we're not having oatmeal. He always manages to burn it."

"Complaints from the girl who charred two whole loaves of bread?" Karl winked as he said it.

She grew red with embarrassment. "I'm never going to be allowed to forget that, am I?"

"Nope," Rachel said. "But he always burns the oatmeal."

"Remind you of anything?" Joanna asked.

"Breakfast when we were growing up?" Sophie shared an amused glance.

Joanna chuckled. "Exactly."

Later, after the dishes were done and the kitchen cleared, the family went into the living room, where Karl took a large

Bible off the mantel, sat in his chair and opened it. Everyone took a seat to listen as he read for half an hour. Sophie could've gone on listening to his voice all day.

He closed the Bible and handed it to Sophie. She chose a passage, read for fifteen minutes and then handed the book to Clara. Clara shook her head and handed the book to Joanna, who read the twenty-third psalm. When she was done, Karl replaced it on the mantel and turned to Sophie. "Would you like to lead us in song?"

"I'd be happy to. *'Das Loblied'*?"

Everyone nodded in agreement. The Hymn of Praise was the second hymn sung at every Amish prayer meeting. They all knew it by heart. Sophie started and the others joined in the slow and mournful song that had been sung by Amish people for over four hundred years.

After that, each of them took turn choosing a song. Joanna chose, *"Gott Is Die Liebe,"* "God Is Love." Sophie was curious what Karl would pick. When it was his turn, he said, "A Mighty Fortress Is Our God."

He had a lovely tenor voice that brought tears to her eyes and joy to her heart as she drew comfort from the words. It was a hymn she knew well and had sung many times, but Karl brought the meaning to life for her.

After they had all chosen a hymn, the children wanted to sing popular Christmas songs. Sophie spent another happy hour singing songs she recalled from her childhood, including her mother's favorite, "Silent Night," in the original German.

The morning when by quickly. Afterward, Karl fixed a lunch of egg-salad sandwiches on the bread Clara and Sophie had made the day of the burnt bread disaster.

Rachel took a bite and then stared at her sandwich. "This bread has a smoky taste." She glanced at Clara. "I wonder why?"

"No one is ever going to let me forget that!"

Sophie caught Rachel's eye and they dissolved into giggles. Karl smothered his laugh with his hand.

After lunch, Rachel brought out the checkerboard and Sophie spent the next hour laughing as one after the other, the girls fell to Karl's superior strategy. When Joanna groaned in defeat, she turned to Sophie. "It's up to you now. We can't let him win every game."

Sophie took her place opposite him at the checkerboard table and laid out her pieces. He rubbed his hands together gleefully. "Prepare to be bested."

Joanna snickered. "I wouldn't be too sure of that, Karl. Sophie knows a thing or two about the game."

Sophie had played against her father at least twice a week since she was seven years old. It was a neck-and-neck game until the very end, when she made her move and swooped in. Karl sank back with a look of astonishment on his face while the girls cheered.

"I demand a rematch," he said. His eyes sparkled with amusement.

She got up and stretched her stiff shoulders and arm. "Another time perhaps."

His daughters each sat on the arm of his chair. He put his arms around them. "Very well. It was a *goot* game. Are you leaving?"

She looked at Joanna. "Are we?"

Joanna looked at Karl and his daughters. "*Ja*, but I had a wonderful time."

Karl stared at Sophie. "So did I."

Back in their own house, Sophie and Joanna plopped down on the sofa. Sophie winced at the pain the movement caused. "It's too late to go visit Aunt Grace, isn't it?"

"Much too late. That was a really nice time. Just imagine Sophie, that could be your life every day."

Puzzled, Sophie frowned at her. "What you mean?"

"I have seen the way Karl looks at you. And the way you look at him. The two of you are halfway to being head over heels in love with each other."

Sophie looked away. "Don't be ridiculous."

"I'm not, but you are."

"I've told you that I'm not going to marry."

"Did you enjoy yourself today?" Joanna asked softly.

"You know I did."

"But you never want to spend another day like it, do you?"

"I would do it over in a heartbeat." It had been a long time since she had known such a joy-filled day.

"But not another three hundred days or six hundred days or *Gott* forbid twenty years' worth of days like today. You would turn your back on all those hours of happiness because it would come to an end. I have news for you, Sophie. Twenty years will come and go. The only difference is in how you choose to live for whatever time *Gott* gives you. Don't make the same mistake of trying to protect them that you made with me. They won't thank you for it."

Joanna got up, put on her coat and went outside. Sophie stayed on the couch.

All her days with Karl and the children or all her days alone?

Sophie knew her friendship with Karl could change into something more serious if she let it. She cared deeply for all the Graber family. If Karl should ask for her hand, what choice would she make?

Karl came in from doing his chores on Monday morning and found both his daughters sitting at the table with serious expressions on their faces. He went to the sink and began washing up. "It's starting to snow," he said, thinking it would cheer them up.

"We noticed," Clara said.

He turned around, drying his hands with a nearby towel. "Why the glum faces?"

"I think you're going to be upset with me," Clara said.

He sniffed the air. "I don't smell anything burning."

She rolled her eyes and he got serious. "I'm listening. Why do you think I'll be upset?"

"Because I want to go to school."

That was not what he was expecting. He leaned against the counter behind him. "This seems like a sudden change of heart."

"I know I said I wanted to keep working in the store, and that I didn't need schooling, and that you could homeschool me, but there are things I'm not learning."

He folded the towel and laid aside. "I'm not the least bit upset with you."

Rachel stuck her tongue out at her sister. "I told you."

Karl frowned at her. "That's impolite. Apologize."

Rachel put on a big fake smile. "I'm so sorry that I stuck my tongue out at you. Can you forgive me?"

"Sure."

Karl shook his head. "Clara, explain to me why you have changed your mind about school."

"I couldn't read from the Bible yesterday. I remember some of the German I learned in school, but I've forgotten a lot of it. I had trouble reading *Mamm*'s recipe cards, and Sophie saw that. I didn't know what some of the words meant, but I'm not stupid."

"*Nee*, you aren't stupid. Don't let anyone tell you that. It takes a smart person to realize their limitations."

"But what about the store?" She looked ready to cry. "Joanna is pretty good help, but she doesn't know everything."

He knew he had to tread carefully. "You're right. Joanna is still learning but she's a bright woman. I think she'll pick things up quickly. You are still going to have to work for me on Saturdays and after school sometimes. I can't do without you completely."

She sniffed. "You can't?"

"I certainly don't want to try. Maybe after Joanna has been there a couple of years but not before."

She sniffed and nodded. "Okay. I'll work Saturdays and after school."

He sighed with relief. "That will be a big help. I'm pretty sure Sophie's going to be happy with your decision."

"She's a good teacher. She made learning geography fun. Someday I want to go to Pig, Kentucky," Clara declared.

"Your *mamm* had some cousins in Kentucky. Not in Pig, but I'll bet if we went to visit them, they could take us there."

"Really?" Rachel asked. "Do they live near Horse Cave?"

"I'm not sure. I'll have to get out your *mamm*'s Christmas cards and see. We better get a move on or we're going to be late. Clara, do you have everything you need for your first day of school?"

Rachel slid out of her chair. "I told her anything she needed she could borrow from me. I have extra pencils and paper."

Karl smiled. "That's very generous."

He couldn't wait to see Sophie's reaction to Clara's news.

Outside, the snow was coming down heavily now. Buck raced around Rachel snapping at the flakes and pushing his nose through the snow on the ground. Sophie was standing in front of the barn with her head back and her tongue stuck out to catch snowflakes.

Did she even know how cute she was? Joanna came out of the barn leading Nutmeg harnessed to their small buggy.

Karl walked up to Sophie. "How do they taste?"

She looked embarrassed but quickly regained her composure. "Like winter. Joanna is going to take Rachel and me to school and stable Nutmeg there for the day. After school, I will walk her across the highway and Rachel can drive us the rest of the way down the lane."

"Sounds like a fine plan. Oh, Clara has something to tell you."

Sophie grinned at her. "What?"

Clara stared at her feet. "I've decided to go back to school if that's okay."

Sophie's grin turned to a fierce scowled. "That is not okay."

Shocked, Clara gaped at her. "It's not?"

"*Nee*. It's *wunderbar!*" she shouted. Grabbing Clara around the shoulders, she began jumping up and down while she squealed with delight. Joanna joined her and so did Rachel until they were all hopping and screaming.

Karl knew someday soon he was going to tell Sophie how adorable she was.

He cleared his throat loudly to break up the party then smiled at Sophie as she rubbed her sore arm. "Clara can drive you and Rachel to school and bring you home."

Sophie hugged Clara again with one arm this time and turned her happy smile on Karl. "This is amazing. Snow and a new student. I couldn't ask for more. *Danki*."

"I did not make it snow."

"I'm going to give you credit just the same. Don't argue with me."

He grinned, happy to share her joy. "Wouldn't think of it."

When they drove out of the yard, Karl turned to Joanna.

"You and I are going to be late opening the store if we don't get a move on."

"Right, but what about Buck?" she asked.

"What about him?"

"Is he going to go to school with Clara or is he going to come to work with me?"

Karl shook his head in disgust. "He should stay home and guard the farm with his mother."

Joanna nodded. "Got it. He's coming to work with me. Thanks. I'll go get the horse."

Karl gazed up at the snow swirling down from the sky as the fat, wet flakes landed on his cheeks and stuck to his lashes. "Women with minds of their own. Why have You surrounded me with women that don't listen to me?"

He didn't hear an answer, but he suspected God was laughing at him.

Over the next two days it snowed four inches. The unusually cold temperatures kept it from melting. The wind swirled it into deep drifts along the fences and trees and swept the ground bare in other places. Sophie spent recess everyday outside with the children making snowmen and snow forts and using Nutmeg to pull a makeshift sled loaded with children across the flat, snow-covered wheat field. She would have given almost anything for a sizable hill.

The only problem with her winter wonderland was that it kept her from her morning walks with Karl.

Finally able to take her sling off on Wednesday, she happily went to school without it. By noon, her shoulder was aching so badly she had to send Clara home to fetch it for her.

Thursday, at promptly four o'clock, Sophie dismissed school. Two minutes later a red pickup truck pulling a silver horse trailer drove into the schoolyard. It wasn't Dwight behind the wheel; it was Lucy.

Sophie opened the cab door and climbed in. "Thank you so much for doing this."

Lucy waved aside Sophie's thanks. "Glad to do it. Dwight has gone to a horse sale in Tulsa so I'm his backup."

"Karl wanted to ride along with us. Can you drive by his store?"

"Won't have to. That's him coming this way."

Sophie looked and saw him walking toward them on the highway. Her heart gave a funny little skip the way it always did when she caught sight of him unexpectedly. They hadn't had a chance to spend time alone together since their lunch in the school. She was missing his company, his smile, his amazing eyes. It was getting harder to hide how much she cared about him.

He opened the truck door and got in. "*Danki*, Lucy. Do you know where we're going?"

"I do. Shouldn't take us more than twenty minutes."

It took a little longer, but they couldn't reach the pasture gate. A waist-high snow drift blocked the entrance to the field.

"Looks like we're walking," Karl said. "Good thing I wore my snow boots."

Sophie had her sensible shoes on, but they weren't meant for deep snow.

Lucy looked over the hood of the truck. "No point in all of us going, but Sophie, I've got an extra pair of overshoes behind the seat if you want to use them."

"That would be great."

Five minutes later, with appropriate footwear on, Sophie got out of the truck. Karl took her hand to help her past the worst of the drift.

"I just noticed you aren't using your sling. That must feel good."

"I've had to put it back on a few times when my arm gets tired."

Once past the drift, Sophie shaded her eyes to stare across the vast snow-covered grassland. The landscape sparkled like glitter in the afternoon sunlight. Sophie trudged beside Karl to the pasture gate. The snow, having melted some the day before and refrozen that night, crunched loudly underfoot with every step as they broke through the crust.

"It's beautiful out here. I've never seen such open space." Her breath rose in puffs like white fog in the frosty air. She didn't see a gate, just a long expanse of barbed wire fence.

"It's cold, too. Where is the owner of this beast?"

"She said she would meet us here. Is that the animal on top of that hill?" Sophie squinted and pointed to the dark shape standing next to a thick cedar tree.

"It looks like a donkey to me. Does she have more than one?"

"I gathered that Jezebel is the only one currently in this pasture."

"The donkey's name is Jezebel?"

Sophia nodded. "Sad but true."

"And you're sure Jez is tame enough for the children to ride?" He fed out a loop of the rope he was holding.

"I don't know."

He looked around. "We don't have all afternoon to waste. I'll go catch her. You can deal with Mrs. Carver when she shows up. I'll get the gate."

"What gate?"

He pointed to a short section of fence between two larger posts. "Barbed wire gate."

He lifted a wire loop that held one gate post against the next section of fence and stepped inside. He put the post back in the hole but didn't attach the wire closure. "Hang on to this post so you can open it quickly if I need you to."

"Okay." Sophie watched him make his way up the hillside. She could tell it was hard going for him. Thankfully, the donkey stood perfectly still when he reached her and slipped a noose over her head. The sound of a vehicle approaching made Sophie turn around.

A battered red-and-white pickup stopped behind their horse trailer. An elderly woman wearing a well-worn cowboy hat got out of the driver's side. "Are you the teacher who wants to borrow my donkey?"

"I am. I can't thank you enough for allowing us to use Jezebel in our living Nativity. I do hope you will come to the school program in return."

Mrs. Carver waved to Lucy, then walked to the back of her truck and opened the tailgate. She lifted out a bucket and carried it toward the gate. "Only way to catch that rascal is to put out grain for her."

"Karl already has a rope on her." Sophie pointed up the hill. The donkey apparently spied the grain bucket at the same time.

Her ears went up, she brayed loudly and took it off at a dead run. Karl tried to hold her, but she yanked him off his feet. The burro made a mad dash across a hundred yards of snow-covered ground, dragging Karl behind her.

"Open the gate," Mrs. Carver shouted.

Sophie pulled the post out of the ground and staggered backward, dragging the barbed wire strands out of the animal's path.

The donkey skidded to a halt in front of her mistress and stuck her nose in the feed bucket. Karl came to a rolling stop behind her at Sophie's feet.

She bent to help him up and couldn't help laughing. "Oh,

Karl, you look like the snowman I helped the *kinder* make yesterday. Only not as plump."

He was covered in snow from head to foot. Clumps of snow hung from his hair. His hat was nowhere in sight. Even the tops of his boots were full, but he seemed to be in one piece.

"Are you hurt?"

"I can't tell. I've got snow packed inside my coat."

Sophie bit her lip to keep from laughing. "Why didn't you let go of the rope?"

"I thought if she got away, I'd never catch her again."

With Sophie's help, he managed to stand and began to brush off his clothes. "Tame. The bishop said she was tame, didn't he? I don't think we want Mary to ride this beast into Bethlehem."

Mrs. Carter patted the donkey's neck. "Jezebel hasn't been ridden in a year or more, but it shouldn't take much to get her used to it again. I do hope this Mary knows how to ride."

Karl looked at Sophie. "Maybe you should rethink this whole thing."

Hours later, when Karl was warm and dry and Jezebel had been unloaded into her stall on a bed of fresh hay, he had time to turn his attention to Sophie.

She stood beside him outside the stall watching Jezebel get settled for the night. The donkey turned around and around while sniffing the hay. Satisfied, she lay down and closed her eyes while Karl's other horses kept careful watch on the new intruder.

"The poor thing was so scared," Sophie said.

"She's gonna be fine. I got the worst end of our encounter."

"I want her to be calm. She was very agitated when she first arrived here."

"That's because she was surrounded by new horses. She'll get used to them quickly."

Sophie glanced at him. "Did you mean it when you said I should rethink this program?"

"At the time I did. Now that I don't have snow in my ears, I can think more clearly. If this animal can be ridden, you'll be fine."

What he was clearly thinking was how much he wanted to kiss Sophie. She looked so pretty in the lantern light. Would she return his affection, or would he ruin the cherished friendship they shared? There were more than his feelings at stake. He had to think about his daughters. Sophie was important to them, too.

"Maybe we should call it off. It was an ambitious plan. I wanted to make it happen for Clara. I thought it would encourage her to come back to school."

She was always thinking of ways to help the children. "You achieved that goal. She's back in school and loving it. I miss having her with me in the shop, but when she told me she couldn't read our Bible I knew I had made a mistake allowing her to stay with me."

"I'm glad she realized that she was missing something important."

"I'm amazed learning about Pig, Kentucky, got her interested in geography."

Sophie smiled and sighed heavily. "I should turn in. I have to teach school tomorrow and then I have to make six dozen cookies for the cookie exchange on Saturday."

He opened the barn door and stepped out into the darkness with Sophie at his side. He waited for his eyes to adjust. The wind had died down. The sky was clear, and the stars shone brightly above, surrounding a quarter moon. He could tell the temperature was climbing. The snow would be gone soon.

Sophie slowly came into focus. She was even more beautiful in the moonlight than in the lantern light. It suddenly became clear to him just how much he wanted her to be a part of his life.

He stepped closer until he could see the starlight reflected in her eyes. Her white *kapp* was a patch of brightness against the dark barn.

"How do you do it?" he asked.

She gave him a questioning look. "What?"

"How do you see what others need and then find a way to give it?"

She looked down. "I don't do anything special."

"But you do. You do something special for my children every day. You have earned Clara's respect, you teach her, you encourage her and you bring Rachel joy. You have a very special gift for making people happy."

She looked away. "Any gifts I possess are given by *Gott*."

Karl placed a finger beneath her chin and lifted her face until she was looking at him. "I give thanks to Him for what He has brought into my life. You."

He ached to kiss her. They were cocooned by the stillness of the night. The scent of fresh hay and cedars filled the cold night air. He leaned toward her slowly, waiting to see if she would reject him or welcome him.

Sophie raised her face and looked into Karl's eyes. They were filled with such tenderness it made her heart ache. He was going to kiss her. She should turn aside, but she didn't want to.

He leaned closer and she closed her eyes. The gentle touch of his lips on hers sent a thrill straight through her. The moment was everything she had dreamed it would be and more. Her heart soared with unbelievable joy.

He drew away slowly. "I have wanted to do that for a long time. Bless you, Sophie, you are a rare treasure."

She stepped back and reality brought her crashing to earth. As wonderful as his kiss had been, it didn't change anything except to make her want more of the same.

She had accepted her illness as God's will, but always wondered why she had to be the one without love in her life. She loved her students and they loved her, but it wasn't the same. That love couldn't hold her with tender arms or kiss away her fears in the darkness. She longed for the things marriage would bring, companionship, shared laughter, children, a sense of belonging to something important. Could she have all that with Karl for a hundred days, three hundred days, twenty years? Did she have enough faith in God's goodness to try?

But it was Karl's life, too.

Before this went any further, he would have to know the truth. But not tonight. The truth would spoil everything. She wanted this one glorious night to remember.

She cupped his cheek with her hand. "I have to go in. Good night, Karl."

He reached for her. "Sophie, wait."

She couldn't. If he kissed her again, she would shatter into a thousand pieces. Turning away, she ran into the house.

Karl let his hand drop to his side as he called himself every kind of fool. For a moment, with Sophie in his arms, he knew they belonged together. He'd been certain she felt the same.

Only now he wasn't sure. Was she running away from him or from something else?

Twenty

The next day, Karl went out to do his morning chores and was surprised to find Clara in the stall with the donkey. She was brushing the animal. The blanket and saddle she used for her pony were sitting on top of the stall gate. She was wearing a pair of pants under her dress.

"What are you doing, Clara?"

She looked up. "You said last night that Jesse needs to get familiar with being ridden again. I thought I would do that. Tamara doesn't like to ride."

"Jesse?"

"I decided to call her Jesse because I don't like her other name."

"She's likely to be frisky."

Clara leaned down to look into Jesse's eyes. "She just wants to have fun. We can have fun together."

"You won't think it's much fun if she bucks you off." He

took the riding gear and saddled the donkey. She laid her ears back but didn't kick or bite, which he found promising.

He led her out to the corral and stood by as Clara mounted. The donkey arched her back and did a few hops with her head down, but she didn't buck. Clara nudged her with her heels to get her trotting.

"Keep her head up and don't relax until you're sure of her."

"What's going on?" Sophie asked.

He turned to see her and Joanna come up beside him. Sophie avoided looking at him. Was she remembering the kiss they shared? He couldn't forget it.

He turned his attention to Clara. "She's riding some of the spunk out of Jesse. Clara renamed her."

"That is a much better name," Sophie said. "We're going to have our first rehearsal this evening after school with the animals. The school board will be there."

"Are the children ready?"

"They are. I'm not sure I am."

He could see she was nervous. "Have a little faith. Everything will be fine."

A shriek rent the air. He turned to see Clara sitting in the snow and Jesse bucking her way across the corral. He started to climb over the fence. Clara waved him back.

"I'm okay. I got careless." She stood with determination, dusted off her backside and went to catch Jesse.

Sophie hung her head.

Karl laid a hand on her shoulder and tried not to laugh. "Have faith. Everything's going to be fine. Just fine."

Somehow, Sophie got through the day. Between worrying about what she should tell Karl and the coming rehearsal, she was a bundle of nerves when four o'clock finally arrived.

She left the children inside putting on their robes and went to face the school board.

When she stepped outside, she saw more than the school board members gathered to watch the rehearsal. Rose, Grace and Susanna were there along with the mothers of most of the children and several men and women she didn't know. Were they the concerned parents the bishop had spoken about? The ones who had invited their former bishops to view the program? She prayed the rehearsal would show them they had nothing to be worried about.

Dwight McDonald arrived with his cow, a beautiful golden brown Guernsey with a white diamond on her forehead. Molly was as calm as he had promised. Jason and Debra Imhoff's father stood off to the side of the shed with three goats. Rachel and Clara ran home to get the sheep and Jesse. Sophie wasn't surprised to see Karl and Joseph moving the panels out of the shed. She knew Karl would want to see Clara's vision come to life.

Although the panels didn't have the artwork on them, the two men moved them into place. Sophie smiled her thanks and walked over to the school board members and the bishop.

"The panels will be covered with scenes the children have painted on paper. They're inside the school if you would like to look at them. They aren't finished, but you can see what they will be like. It'll take us a few minutes to get everyone dressed and ready."

There was a lot of chatter among the women off to one side. Sophie smiled at them but didn't join them. The children came out and she had them line up behind the school. The bishop came with her but stood back and watched.

Sophie gazed at her students' excited faces and her nerves disappeared. "It's important that you be as solemn and reverent as possible. You are retelling the story of Christ's birth.

Mary and Joseph made an incredible journey to Bethlehem. They were turned away at the inn and found shelter in a simple stable with the animals. Our Lord was born there. His mother wrapped him tenderly and laid him in a manger. I want you to keep these things in mind. Don't pay attention to who is watching or anything else that is going on. Can you do that for me?"

"Yes, teacher," they said in unison.

She then waited for Rachel and Clara to return. When she was about ready to send Karl to see what was taking them so long, the girls came hurrying up with their animals.

Rachel wore the robe Joanna had made her. She grinned as her lambs nuzzled her sides. When she walked past the goats, they strained at their ropes to follow her. She stopped in front of Sophie and patted the sides of her bulging robe. "I've got alfalfa pellets in my pockets. April, May and June will stay right beside me. We've been practicing at home."

"That's great. Now everyone take your places. Shepherds by panel one. Innkeeper and townspeople by panel two. Bartholomew, take the cow and goats to the stable and tie them up. Wise men wait behind the stable. Jason and Tamara, I will signal for you to start walking in front of the panels. All of you know the songs, so sing loud. This is just so everyone knows their places and how long it takes to move from one panel to the other as Phillip narrates. Any questions?"

They all shook their heads. Jesse brayed and Tamara stepped away from her. "She doesn't like me."

"You'll be fine. Remember, this is a rehearsal. It's okay if things go wrong. This is so everything will go right Christmas Eve. Okay? Phillip, go to the school steps and begin."

Sophie said another quick prayer and walked around to stand beside Karl and Rose. Karl leaned over and whispered, "Everything will be fine."

It didn't start out that way. Jesse balked at being led by Jason. Tamara looked terrified sitting on the animal's back. Jason dutifully stopped at the first panel, where Rachel's sheep were nibbling at her clothes. Jason had a tough time getting the donkey to move on. She kept trying to go to back to Rachel. When they reached the innkeeper, who pointed the way to the stable, the donkey refused to take another step. Bartholomew gave the reluctant beast a smack on the rump, and everything fell apart.

Jesse brayed, bucked and sent Tamara flying to the ground. She started crying. Rachel's sheep, impatient for their treats, began pushing her around. She tripped and fell. The goats straining at their ropes managed to get free. They rushed to mob Rachel, too. She started screaming. The cow calmly chewed her cud.

Joseph doubled over with laughter as Karl went to rescue Rachel. Mr. Imhoff and his sons began pulling the goats away.

Sophie rushed to Tamara, who was still sitting on the ground. "Are you hurt?"

Tamara shook her head. "I don't...think so," she managed between sobs. "But I don't want to be Mary anymore."

Her mother quickly helped the child up. "I'll take her home."

"I'm so sorry about this," Sophie said but they were already walking away.

She glanced toward the bishop. He shook his head sadly and her heart sank. What an utter disaster. There was no way she would be allowed to present the program on Christmas Eve. He and the school board walked into the building. Grace followed them. One by one the onlookers left.

The remaining students gathered around her. Bartholomew looked ready to cry. "I'm sorry, teacher. I didn't mean to make her buck."

She slipped her arm around his shoulder. "It wasn't your fault."

"What do we do now?" Jason asked.

"I know you are all disappointed. I'm sorry it didn't go well. Class is dismissed for the day. Go home. We'll talk about it on Monday." They walked away with long faces to where their mothers were waiting for them.

Karl came up with Rachel in his arms. He had emptied the alfalfa pellets from her pockets onto the ground. The sheep and Jesse were busy munching on them. "Clara will bring Jesse home. Joseph and the other men are putting the panels away." He set Rachel on her feet. "The sheep will likely follow us when they're done eating."

"I'm so sorry, Karl. Rachel, are you okay?"

"Stupid goats. They tore the robe Joanna made for me." She held out her ruined pockets.

Sophie managed a smile. "Joanna can mend it for you."

Clara came up leading Jesse. "It was a *goot* idea."

Sophie stroked her cheek. "It was a beautiful idea, but I fear we will need a new one."

"Are you okay?" Karl asked gently.

Sophie struggled to hold back her tears at the sympathy in his voice. "Not really. I don't think it could have been worse."

Rose cackled as she walked up and patted Sophie's shoulder. "That was the most entertaining Christmas program I have ever seen in my life."

Sophie covered her face with her hands and began sobbing.

Both Clara and Rachel wrapped their arms around her. "Don't cry," Rachel said.

"I'll think of something new," Clara added. "Don't be sad."

Sophie cherished their attempt to console her. *"Danki."*

Karl slipped his arm around her shoulders, and she leaned

into his comfort. "Come on. I'll walk you home. Rose, make sure the place gets cleaned up."

"I will. Everything happens for a reason, Sophie. Don't despair. Something *goot* will come of this. See all of you at the cookie exchange tomorrow," she added brightly.

A public outing was the last thing Sophie wanted to attend. At the moment, she never intended to show her face again.

Karl scrambled a half-dozen eggs and put four pieces of toast on the rack in the oven. A quick glance at the clock told him he had plenty of time to go check on Sophie before he had to leave for the shop. The Christmas program meant a lot to her. She would be worried about the bishop's decision, but he didn't want her sitting at home alone brooding about it. He'd give Joanna the day off to stay with her. The plan was to close early and attend the cookie exchange with the girls. All he had to do was convince Joanna to make sure Sophie came, too.

He chuckled. A month ago, he would rather have walked across broken glass than attend a social event. A lot had changed since Sophie Eicher arrived in town. Much of it for the better even if her rehearsal hadn't gone well. She was dear to him. Her company cheered him and gave him a reason to look forward to each new day. Just knowing she might come to the cookie exchange made him eager to go. Maybe they could work in that buggy ride in the snow after the party.

The coffee was perking so he pulled it off the heat, took the basket out and poured himself a cup. When the toast was brown enough, he juggled the hot pieces onto a plate and carried them with the eggs to the kitchen table, where Rachel and Clara were waiting.

He sat down and folded his hands for silent prayer. When he was finished, he looked up. Both his girls had their heads bowed and their hands folded. They looked so young and innocent. His heart swelled with love for them. For the first time in a long time, he felt truly blessed. Nora was missing from his table, but she had left behind the best parts of herself.

He picked up his coffee cup to signal the prayer was done and took a sip to wash down the lump that had formed in his throat.

The girls helped themselves. Rachel was talking about all the things she thought could be done to improve the Christmas program. He didn't have the heart to tell her the bishop might not allow it. Her chattering normally annoyed Clara enough for her to demand silence during the meal but his oldest daughter was strangely silent this morning.

"Clara, is something wrong?" he asked.

She spread a dab of butter across her toast. "Did you know that love is like butter on hot bread?"

"I did not," he said slowly. Where was this going? He wished Sophie would appear so he could hand off this conversation if it got complicated.

"You can't see much of the butter now, but it isn't really gone. It's just melted inside."

"There's more butter if you want some. Rachel, hand your sister the butter."

Clara smiled at him. "I don't need more. It's all still there. Love stays inside us even when the person isn't here anymore."

"Is this about your mother?"

Clara nodded. "I know Rose is trying to find you a new wife. Sophie says you won't stop loving *Mamm* if you do marry again, so it's okay."

It seemed Sophie was already a part of this conversation. He wasn't sure if he was annoyed or grateful that she'd had this discussion with his daughter.

He put his coffee cup down and rubbed his damp palms

on his thighs. "Sophie is right. I won't ever stop loving your mother."

"But it's okay to love someone else," Clara said, slanting a look in his direction.

"Does this mean we will have a new *mamm* like Granny Rose promised me?" Rachel asked. "I hope it's going to be Sophie."

He wasn't ready to have this conversation with his daughters. How could he when he wasn't sure how Sophie felt about him. Clara and Rachel were talking about a having a new mother. That was a much bigger step than a simple kiss. Was he ready to propose to Sophie?

Suddenly, Karl could barely breathe. "I don't want to discuss this at the breakfast table. Finish eating, put your plates in the sink and get ready to go." He took his coffee and went out the front door.

On the porch, he took several deep breaths of the biting cold air. Love for Nora still filled his heart. There wasn't room for anyone else. Pacing across the porch and back, he held on to that thought. He'd told himself and others that same thing a thousand times, so why didn't it ring true this morning?

He stopped and looked toward the *daadi haus*. Because his old coat of grief no longer fit. He wasn't just attracted to Sophie. He was falling in love with her. The thought made his knees weak. Looking back, he saw how easily and quickly Sophie had become an important part of his family. The truth was, he wanted her in life. But did she feel the same?

The bishop's buggy pulled up and stopped in front of the *daadi haus*. Sophie came out on the porch to greet him. It seemed she was about to learn the fate of her Christmas play. Karl pushed his personal thoughts aside and walked toward them.

★ ★ ★

Sophie saw Karl coming her way and breathed a silent prayer of thanks. She needed all the moral support she could get. "Come in, Bishop. We have fresh coffee on."

He removed his hat and hung it on a peg beside the door. "That would be most welcome." He took a seat at the kitchen table.

Karl came through the door, looked around and nodded to her. "Morning, Sophie."

She smiled at him. "Have a seat, Karl. Joanna will be ready in a minute. I see you brought your own cup. Can I warm it up?"

"Please." He moved to sit beside the bishop.

After serving both men, she sat down and folded her hands to wait.

The bishop cleared his throat. "The rehearsal was quite a spectacle yesterday."

Sophie looked down at her tightly clasped hands. "It did not go as planned."

"You can hardly blame Sophie for the antics of the half-wild donkey you suggested she use," Karl said.

Bishop Wyse's lips pressed into a thin line. "Grace made the same point yesterday."

"Please, Karl. It's all right." Sophie looked at the bishop. "I assume you and the school board have reached a decision."

"Not a unanimous one, and Karl, I do accept some responsibility for what went wrong. We will allow the Nativity play to go ahead but with a few changes. We suggest fewer animals and perhaps you should forgo the donkey. The artwork the *kinder* have done is acceptable."

Sophie couldn't hide her relief. "The children will be so glad. They have worked very hard on the drawings."

Bishop Wyse stood. "I should be going then." He put on his hat and opened the door. Sophie and Karl followed him.

He stopped and held out his hand. "It's snowing again."

Sophie saw he was right. She also saw Clara galloping toward them on Jezebel. She was riding bareback. At the porch, she pulled the donkey to a stop, made her back up and then turn in tight circles.

Clara grinned at Sophie. "Jesse doesn't like the saddle, but she minds perfectly when I ride without it. Tamara said she won't get on her again, so can I play Mary?"

"I don't see why not." Sophie looked at Bishop Wyse. "Can she?"

The bishop gave a weary sigh. "I guess it will be okay. *If* you show you can control her."

Clara grinned. "I will. I'll practice with her every day so she isn't scared around people."

The bishop looked at Sophie. "I'll be praying for you."

Sophie and Joanna arrived at the inn on Saturday afternoon just as the cookie exchange was getting underway. Sophie remained in the buggy after Joanna got out. Even the snow couldn't cheer her. "How am I going to face everyone?"

"Don't be ridiculous. Children and animals. Things were bound to go wrong. At least the bishop said you could go ahead with a few changes. Come on. People who weren't there will want a firsthand account."

"Great. I'll get to relive my nightmare again and again." Sophie got out while Joanna secured Nutmeg.

Joanna carried an empty pail while Sophie held the ones full of the snickerdoodles and macaroons they had made that morning.

Grace met them at the door. "I'm so glad you made it. I was afraid the weather would keep people away, but it seems to have put everyone in the holiday spirit. There is hot cider, eggnog, tea and coffee in the dining room. Just put your cookies on any table. What have you made?"

"Snickerdoodles," Joanne said.

Grace chuckled. "I happen to know that they are someone's favorite cookie, and he is in the dining room already."

Joanna gave her aunt a coy smile. "Are you going to make me guess who 'he' is?"

"I think you'll find out soon enough."

Joanna handed her empty pail to Sophie and took the full one into the dining room.

"Sophie, my dear, how are you?" Grace asked, her voice full of sympathy. "After yesterday?"

"I'm fine. We had a few setbacks with our program. However, I'm confident we will be ready for our big night."

"Everyone is looking forward to it."

Sophie rolled her eyes. "They are all hoping for a repeat of the disaster, I'm sure."

"Nonsense. We just have to pray the weather cooperates."

"We do have an indoor site. Dwight McDonald has offered the use of his indoor riding arena. Your *Englisch* neighbors are generous people."

"Indeed, they are. That is wonderful. We'll spread the word."

The inn's main dining room was filled with people standing in small groups chatting while the children went from table to table to check out what was being offered.

She saw Karl in one corner with Joseph and Abby. She started toward them. They began laughing about something. Most likely her disaster. Joanna had made a beeline for Jeff Hostetter and a group of young people their age. Sophie changed course and headed toward Rose.

The elderly woman was smiling from ear to ear as she nodded toward Joanna. "They look happy, don't they? I knew they would."

Sophie followed her line of sight. "You said Joanna and Karl were meant for each other."

"I said Joanna would never go out with someone her sister disliked. You took it to mean you should mend fences with Karl so she would go out with him."

"But I thought you wanted to fix me up with Jeff."

"I just wanted the two of you to be friends. It worked out. How are things with you and Karl?"

Sophie had no idea how to answer that. "Fine."

"Oh, well, don't give up. He can be a bit slow to catch on sometimes."

"He told me you said we were wrong for each other."

"You were at the start, but I knew you could both change. For the better. Faith shared is faith doubled. Now, what did the bishop say about the play?"

"He liked the concept but said fewer animals. Karl has promised Rachel will not stuff two pints of alfalfa pellets in her pockets."

"Is that what the beasts were after? How funny."

"*Nee*, it wasn't. Tamara has refused to be Mary, so Clara is taking her place. She likes Jesse. She was out riding her in the snow this morning."

Rose chuckled. "It has worked out then. Take a plate of the macaroons you made over to Karl."

"How did you know I made macaroons?"

"They're his favorite." She smiled and walked away.

Shaking her head, Sophie put several of her cookies on a paper plate and went over to Karl. He snagged one from her. "Yum, I love these." He ate it without taking his eyes off her.

Sophie frowned slightly. "Did you ask Rachel to have me make these?"

He shook his head. "*Nee*, she doesn't like them. Why?"

"Never mind." She smiled at Abby. "How's the baby?"

"Growing. Eight weeks old now." She smiled lovingly at the child she held.

"That was quite the show you put on yesterday," Joseph said.

Sophie shuddered. "Don't remind me."

"It will all be fine on Christmas Eve," Karl assured her. "I have faith."

She wished she had as much as he did.

Karl stayed by her side for much of the afternoon. It was fun to meet the people he knew and had grown up with. After she repeated the rehearsal story numerous times, the pain of her failure began to fade, and she saw the humor in it. When she was finally ready to leave, Joanna wasn't. She made a sour face when Sophie suggested it and nodded toward Jeff.

Rose came up to Sophie. "Karl will take you home. I sent him to get your buggy."

"But what about the girls?"

"They are staying over with us. You two *kinder* have a nice evening."

It was snowing lightly when Sophie walked out onto the inn's porch. Karl drove her buggy up and stopped at the steps.

She had been tired, but a new energy swept through her at the sight of his smiling face. They were going to alone together for the evening. She hurried down the steps.

He got out and opened the door for her. "I believe I promised you another drive along the river. Are you up for that or would you rather I take you home?"

"I'd rather go home."

That surprised and disappointed him. "Oh."

A slow smile curved her lips. "After you show me the river. We'll need hot chocolate to warm up with later, won't we?"

He grinned. "Sound like a perfect evening."

They didn't talk much as he drove along. Once they reached the river, he slowed to an ambling pace. It was pretty following a track that wound in and out of the groves of trees. They stopped to watch the snow fall on the water.

"Everywhere is touched by the beauty of *Gott*'s handiwork," Karl said softly.

She couldn't agree more. No matter how many days she had left on earth, she wanted to spend them near this amazing man if he would allow it. She shivered at the thought of what she must tell him.

He glanced at her. "You're getting cold. Let's go home."

They were both quiet on the drive back. When they reached the farm, he unhitched Nutmeg and led her in the barn. Sophie walked over to the corral fence. Rachel's sheep were frolicking in the snow while the horses and the donkey munched peacefully on their bale of hay. Such a simple, peaceful backdrop for the most difficult thing she had ever done.

When he came out, she gathered her courage.

He stopped beside her and leaned on the fence. "Sophie, you are an amazing woman." His eyes were filled with tenderness as he gazed at her. "You turned my world upside down."

She smiled, remembering her first time on his farm. "I would've put the hammer back if you had given me a chance."

He chuckled. "You used it to beat down a wall I had built around my heart. I'm not sure how to say this but I want to court you, Sophie, if you will allow me."

Stepping closer, he took her hand. The light in his eyes set her heart thumping madly.

"We have something special, and we should give ourselves a chance to find out if it's the real thing. I can't imagine a future without you." He cupped her chin and turned her face toward him. His eyes searched hers. "Tell me you feel the same."

She wanted to believe in a future with him more than

her next breath, but she couldn't. Not yet. Pulling away, she clasped her hands on the top of the fence. "I have something I must tell you first."

"I hope you're going to say you care for me, too."

"I do, but there is something else."

"Whatever it is it doesn't matter."

"It does matter. Please hear me out. This isn't easy for me."

She glanced at his face and saw concern fill his eyes. "All right. I'm listening." Fear had crept into the edge of his voice.

"Seven years ago, my mother died of breast cancer. Three years before that, her mother passed away. She had breast cancer, too."

"Sophie, I'm sorry. To lose two important people in your life so close together had to be difficult."

"It was." She swallowed hard and closed her eyes. "Then last year I was diagnosed with breast cancer. I had a mastectomy. They removed my left breast. Chemotherapy treatments followed for six months."

When he didn't say anything, she turned to study his face. His sympathy was heartbreaking. "I'm so sorry."

"It may have spread already, Karl. I need you to understand that."

He stared at her in stunned silence as what she'd said sank in.

"I can't know for sure how long I have, but my mother only lived three years after her diagnosis. I know this is hard to hear. I do care deeply for you, Karl."

She saw the disbelief on his face. She held out her hand, praying he could understand and want to be by her side no matter what. To share however many days she was given.

He backed away. Her hope died as anguish filled his eyes.

"Nee." Karl held up his hand as if he could block out Sophie's words. *"Gott* wouldn't do that to me again. I can't.

Nora's life was sucked away, and I could do nothing. The fervent prayers, the endless visits to the doctor, the long and terrible days watching the woman I loved robbed of strength and beauty by a killer I couldn't see. I can't do that again."

He turned on his heels and staggered to his buggy. *Not again, Lord. Why open my heart only to tear it out of my chest?*

He glanced back. Sophie was still standing by the fence with one of the lambs nibbling at her hem. She had her arms crossed as if holding on to herself. He didn't want to see the pain in her eyes. He was a coward. He made it as far as the buggy, but he didn't have the strength to climb in. He clung to the door frame praying it was all some horrible dream.

He looked at her again. Tears streamed down her face, then she walked toward her house.

Climbing in the buggy, Karl drove toward the inn. Anger and pain boiled inside him as he neared the town. He fought to calm down.

Rose saw him coming and walked onto the porch when he got out of the buggy. "Karl, are you all right? Where is Sophie?"

"You knew." Anger made his hands shake.

She seemed to shrink in front of him as sadness filled her eyes. "I'm so sorry."

"I should have listened. You said I was all wrong for her. You are right. I should've listened."

"Sophie needs a very special person in her life. You are that person."

"She needs someone who doesn't know what it is to lose a spouse to cancer!"

"*Nee*, she needs someone with faith strong enough to fight for her, because she doesn't want to fight for herself."

"I'm not that man. I can't do this to my children."

"Do what? Give them a mother they love and who loves them in return."

"For how long, Rose?"

"Karl, that is up to *Gott*. Sophie's love has lifted you from despair and brightened the lives of your daughters in just a few weeks. Do you know what a gift that is? She needs you now. She needs to believe in a future with someone who loves her."

He shook his head in disbelief. "I pray to *Gott* she finds it, but it won't be with me."

Twenty-One

Sophie had stopped crying by the time Joanna came home later that night. She had no tears left. Her soul was as dry as a desert, but there was no disguising her distress from her sharp-eyed sister.

Joanna sank to her knees by Sophie's chair and gripped her hand. "What's wrong? Tell me."

Sophie had no emotion left to put into her voice. The pain had numbed everything. "Karl asked to court me."

"That's wonderful. Oh, how I have prayed for this."

"I had to tell him I'm not a whole woman. Just a mutilated shell pretending to be a woman who is going to die. He walked away."

Joanna gripped Sophie by both shoulders and shook her. "Don't ever say that about yourself again. A woman is not defined by her breasts. She's defined by her brain, by her heart and her soul. You have an amazing brain, a loving heart and the kindest soul of anyone I know. If he can't see that, then you deserve someone much, much better."

Sophie knew there would never be anyone better. "It doesn't matter. I won't marry. I won't date. I will teach and I will love the children in my classes, but we can't stay here. I can't stay here."

Joanna sank to her heels. "You want to leave Harts Haven?"

Sophie laid a hand against her sister's cheek. "I know you want to stay here. I hope Jeff is the one for you. I meant we need to find a different house. I can't live next to Karl." Even saying his name sent a stab of pain into the depths of her soul.

She drew a shuddering breath. "I can't see him every day. I'm in love with him, and I will never have him." She started sobbing again and covered her face with her hands.

Joanna wrapped her arms around Sophie. "You should stay with Aunt Grace until we find something new. Oh, my sweetheart, I wish there was something I could do."

There was nothing to be done. There was only life to be endured. Sophie dried her face with her hands. "Take me to the inn tonight."

In the depths of a sleepless night, Karl realized with gut-wrenching honesty that he had been brutal to someone he cared for deeply. His knee-jerk reaction to avoid reliving the paralyzing pain created by Nora's death had resulted in cruelty to Sophie. With a little distance he could see that now. He knew it had taken a great deal of courage for her to share the story of her illness with him.

She had suffered and was still suffering unbearably, and he had heaped more pain on her. The thought of losing Sophie the way he had lost his wife was terrifying. He wasn't strong enough to endure that, but he had to tell her that he was sorry for the way he reacted. She deserved better.

He left the bedroom and stood looking out the window where he had last held his wife and waited for dawn to brighten the sky. When the sun slipped over the horizon, he went to the *daadi haus* and knocked.

Joanna opened the door. "She isn't here."

He needed to see her. "Where is she?"

"She is staying at the inn until we find a new place to live. Don't go see her, Karl. You don't know how hard it was for her to believe *Gott* had some happiness planned for her. She finally began to have hope when she met you. You destroyed that. I'm not sure my sister will ever recover."

"I know what it is to lose all hope, Joanna. I can't watch someone I care about die. I can't."

"Did she tell you she was dying?"

"She said your mother only lived three years after the same diagnosis."

Joanna sighed. "Sophie wouldn't talk to the doctors taking care of her, so I did. She had it in her mind that her cancer was the same as *Mamm*'s, and even if she lived long enough to have daughters, she was dooming them to the same fate. But Sophie's cancer was different. Her last scan was negative. She should have been praising *Gott*, but my sister was afraid to believe she could have a future. Until she fell in love with you."

Sophie loved him? Karl stared at the floor. "Did she say that?"

"She did not, but I know her well. I'd like to tell you that she is fine, but the truth is I can't promise her cancer won't return. That is up to *Gott*."

"Joanna, I'm sorry for the way I reacted when she told me. I want her to know that."

"My heart breaks for both of you, but she is my sister, and I must do what I can to protect her. Leave her be, Karl. Give her some time."

He nodded and went home.

Later that morning he went through the motions of attending the prayer service the way he had in the months after he lost Nora. Sophie and Joanna did not come. He took his daughters straight home afterward. They didn't understand, and he couldn't find the words to explain.

Monday morning, he drove Rachel and Clara to school. He tried to think of a way to tell his daughters that Sophie wasn't going to be living next to them, but the words wouldn't come.

He kissed them both. "Be kind to Sophie today. She hasn't been well. Don't mention anything to her, just be kind."

Rachel patted his hand. "I always am. She's my friend and I love her."

Sophie didn't know how she got through the next two days. When it was time to dismiss the students that afternoon, she couldn't remember a single thing she had taught them. At least the Nativity backgrounds were finished, and the children had practiced their songs until they were perfect. Their excitement was growing while hers was nonexistent.

She walked out the door and saw Rachel push Phoebe Kemp to the ground. "That's not true," Rachel shouted. "Take it back."

Sophie hurried down the steps to the children. "What's going on here?"

Rachel glared at Phoebe. "She said you are going to live on her farm. It's not true. You live with us. You're always going to live with us."

Phoebe got to her feet. "Joanna talked to my *daed* last night about renting rooms in our house and he agreed. Tell her I am not a liar."

Sophie dropped to her knees beside Rachel. "My sister and I are looking for a new place to live. I didn't know that Joanna had found one already or I would have told you. Phoebe is not making this up. You must say you're sorry."

Rachel pushed Sophie away. "You're always going to live with us. Rose said so." She took off running toward town.

Clara had tears in her eyes. "I'm sorry you're leaving. Is it something I did?"

Sophie gathered her into a tight hug. "Of course not. I can't explain right now but your father and I have had our differences. It's best that I don't live there anymore."

"Is that why he's so sad?"

Was he? It couldn't be easy learning the woman he cared about was going to die. Sophie had been so wound up in her own hurt that she hadn't thought about what Karl was going through.

She led Clara over to the school steps and sat down. "You must tell your *daed* not to feel bad. Things didn't work out the way we wanted them to, but I still care about him. And I still love you and your sister. That love is never going away."

Clara wrapped her arms around Sophie. "It's going to sink in like melted butter and always be with me."

"That's right," Sophie said sadly.

Clara stood up. "I need to find my sister. I think we'll have jam on our toast from now on. You can see jam."

For the first time in ages Karl was happy to see Rose come in his shop. He hurried to meet her when she came through the door. Sophie was staying at the inn. Rose knew how Sophie was doing and he needed to know, too. Buck had taken to staying by Karl's side the last two days. If he didn't know better, he would have said the dog was moping with him.

"Afternoon, Rose."

"Sophie isn't eating much but Grace did get her to eat one of her pastries this morning. At least she isn't crying herself to sleep anymore. I'm sorry I was wrong about you. I thought you would find the faith and courage to stand beside her."

The outside door burst open, and Rachel ran in. Her face was wet from crying and she was out of breath from running. "It's not true, is it, *Daed*? Sophie says she's moving away."

He knelt beside her. "Honey, she is still going to be your teacher. She's just going to live in a different house."

She turned on Rose. "You said if I helped, she would be my mother. You said she would love me always. You lied to me." She turned and ran for the door with Buck right behind her.

The squeal of brakes, a scream and a thud turned Karl's blood to ice. He dashed out to the street. Rachel was lying in a heap on the sidewalk. A car had plowed into the hitching post out front. Karl couldn't breathe as he ran to his daughter. "Please *Gott*, no."

Rachel's started to sit up as he reached her. Buck was licking her face. Karl was afraid to touch her. "Where does it hurt, darling?"

She pointed to her scraped knees. "Buck knocked me down and tore my dress."

A man got out of the damaged car. "Is she all right? That was a close thing."

Karl lifted his daughter in his arms. "Are you sure you're okay?"

She pushed on his chest. "I'm mad at you."

He hugged her tightly. "That's okay. I deserve it."

Clara came running up. "What happened?"

The man raked a hand through his hair. "This little girl came out of nowhere. I hit my brakes and swerved. The dog grabbed her dress and pulled her down. I must've missed her by inches." He sat down the sidewalk. "I've never been so scared in my life."

Karl carried Rachel into the store and put her on the counter to examine her knees.

"How is she?" Rose asked.

"Just scrapes, thank *Gott*."

Rachel hopped off the counter. "Buck and I are going home."

Karl didn't want her out of his sight. "*Nee*, you are not. You are going to help Clara clean the stockroom. We'll go home later."

Rachel frowned at him. "I hate cleaning the stockroom. I want to go home."

Clara took Rachel's hand and led her toward the back. "Come on. If we do it together, we'll be done in no time."

Karl leaned against the counter and pressed a hand to his heart. "It could have been so much worse."

"At least you would have had six years with her. Do you wish you'd never met Nora? Never married her?"

Karl scowled at Rose. How could she ask that? "Of course not."

Rose nodded. "If you had known how few years you would have together, would that have made a difference? If you had known what you would watch her endure, what you yourself endured, would you have married her anyway?"

"There is no way to see the future, Rose. Every day with Nora was a blessing. Every day. If I could have died instead, I would have done that gladly."

"I'm not talking about dying, Karl. I'm talking about living. Sophie is a woman with a heart made for loving a man, a home, children. She deserves to have that happiness."

"I know she does."

"You are the only person who can give that to her, Karl. You and your children."

"You're asking too much, Rose."

"Am I? What if you were the one who might not live to old age? What decision would Sophie make?"

He thought of the woman who stood up to him, fixed his drapes, cared for his children, made him smile and led him to be the father he needed to be. "Sophie wouldn't bat an eye. She devotes herself to caring for others. Somehow, she sees what they need."

"She does. Sophie is the only one Sophie can't take care of."

Tears gathered in his eyes. "I love her, but what if I don't have the strength?"

"None of us have the strength we need to face what life brings. That's why we rely on *Gott*. He brought Sophie to you for a reason, Karl. If you do nothing you will live every day without her. How many days you have on this earth is up to Him. How many days you have with Sophie is up to you."

Rose was right. Days, weeks, years without Sophie? Without her smile, without her loving his children, without kissing her again, how could he choose that? How could he not be there when she would need him the most?

"Do you think she can forgive me, Rose?"

"Karl, all you can do is try."

Clara met with Dr. Bertha on Wednesday. The sharp-eyed elderly doctor knew something was wrong as soon as Sophie entered the exam room.

"What's going on?"

Sophie took a seat on the exam table. "Nothing. My arm is better."

"I've seldom seen someone who is better look so miserable."

She examined Sophie, then sighed heavily as she opened her chart. "My diagnosis is heart trouble. Want to talk about him?"

"I don't know what you mean. And no."

"All right. I received your medical records and I've reviewed them."

"I don't want to know what you found."

Bertha adjusted her glasses. "Are you sure?"

"I'm sure. My life is in *Gott*'s hands. I accept that. How short or how long it may be only He knows."

"I will say your life is unlikely to be short, but you are right. Now is all we are promised. Love with your whole heart today and that will be enough."

Sophie nodded. She loved Karl despite everything and that would never change. Their one kiss would be enough for a lifetime, a memory to be treasured as the pain of his rejection faded. She had hoped for too much from him.

Christmas Eve finally arrived. The program was tonight. Karl would be there. Sophie braced herself to face him.

"Our ride is here." Rose came into the living room where Joanna and Sophie were waiting. "Go on out. I'll be there in a minute."

The day had turned chilly, but the skies were clear. Sophie nervously put on her coat and bonnet.

Please let the animals behave. Please let the children remember all the songs. Please don't let me break down in front of him.

She walked outside and stopped short. Karl and his daughters were in a sleigh in front of the inn.

Joanna ran down the steps. "Clara, Rachel, I've missed you." She got in the back and hugged both girls, then settled under their quilt and tickled them.

Rachel laughed. "Hi, Sophie. *Frehlicher Grischtdaag*, Merry Christmas!"

"Scoot over, Rachel, and give me some room," Clara said.

Rachel tugged on the quilt. "I'm cold and you have more of the blanket."

"I do not."

"Enough," Karl said, putting an end to the rising squabble.

Karl smiled at Sophie. "It's good to see you. Merry Christmas. Clara insisted we take the sleigh. She said it feels more Christmas-like, and I remembered you liked sleigh rides in the snow."

He lifted the edge of the quilt over his lap. "Don't stand there freezing. Get in."

She didn't dare sit next to him. Her carefully maintained composure would fall apart in an instant. "I'll wait for Rose."

Karl looked in the back seat. "Clara, go see what's keeping Rose."

Clara dashed up the steps, stopped beside Sophie and hugged her. "I'm so excited, aren't you?" She went into the inn.

Sophie's feet were growing cold. The horse snorted and stamped impatiently. Clara came back out and got in the back seat. "She's not coming. She has a headache."

Karl lifted the corner of the quilt again. "They can't start the program without you."

Sophie reluctantly got in the seat beside him. He gently smoothed the quilt over her lap. "Do you remember when I said a teacher once called me dense. Sometimes I take more persuasion than the ordinary fellow, but when I've made a mistake, I'll admit it. I'm sorry, Sophie. You deserved to be treated better."

"You're forgiven," she muttered, afraid she was going to burst into tears.

"Ready, everyone?" Karl asked. Three confirmations rang out. He slapped the driving lines, and the horse took off down the snow-covered lane. Sleigh bells jingled merrily in time to the horse's footfalls. The runners hissed along over the snow.

As long as he didn't touch her, she could keep it together for the children.

★ ★ ★

Karl lifted his arm and laid it along the back of the seat to give Sophie more room. As much as he wanted to slip his arm around her shoulder, he knew that was a bad idea. He had hurt her badly. This time he had to make sure and get it right. He leaned close to her. "Are you warm enough?"

She nodded, but her cheeks looked rosy, and her nose was red. Karl took off his blue woolen scarf and handed it to her. "You can cover your mouth and nose. It will help."

"*Danki,*" she murmured. "Won't you be cold?"

"Nope. It's a perfect Christmas Eve afternoon."

The surrounding fields lay hidden beneath a thick blanket of white. Cedar tree branches drooped beneath their icy loads. A hushed stillness filled the air broken only by the jingle of the harness bells. It was a picture-perfect moment in time and Karl knew it. Sophie liked snow and sleigh rides. Maybe it would help his cause.

They reached their destination much too quickly. As they drew closer, they saw a dozen buggies and sleighs parked along the north side of the school building while the parking lot was full of cars and trucks. Benches and chair were set up along the south side of the building.

As the kids scrambled out of the sleigh, Karl offered Sophie his hand to help her out, but she stepped down without touching him. His heart dropped but he couldn't give up.

Inside the building, the place was already crowded with people. Tables along the wall bore trays of cookies and candies. An atmosphere of joy, goodwill and anticipation permeated the air. Outside, Karl took a position ready to intercept any wayward animals.

At a sign from Sophie, Phillip Kauffman began to read the second chapter of Luke in a loud clear voice.

"And it came to pass in those days, that there went out a decree from Caesar Augustus that all the world should be taxed. (And this taxing was first made when Cyrenius was governor of Syria.) And all went to be taxed, every one into his own city. And Joseph also went up from Galilee, out of the city of Nazareth, into Judaea, unto the city of David, which is called Bethlehem; (because he was of the house and lineage of David:)"

Joseph led Mary into view. They stopped by the drawing of the hills, where Rachel and several other children dressed as shepherds were sitting with two of Rachel's lambs.

Phillip began to sing, "O come, O come, Emanuel," and all the children joined it.

At the end of the song, Phillip continued reading. Jesse didn't hesitate as Mary urged her forward. At the next panel, the two weary travelers looked disappointed as the innkeeper came out, shook his head and pointed the way to the stable.

Suddenly there was a small commotion as one of the angels hurried over to Sophie. She turned to look at the crowd, walked over to Abby and whispered something. Abby handed over baby Henry, who the little angel then carried to Mary, who laid him tenderly in the manger and the children sang "O Little Town of Bethlehem."

Phillip resumed reading when the song finished.

"And there were in the same country shepherds abiding in the field, keeping watch over their flock by night. And, lo, the angel of the Lord came upon them, and the glory of the Lord shone round about them: and they were sore afraid. And the angel said unto them, Fear not: for, behold, I bring you good tidings of great joy, which shall be to all people. For unto you is born this day in the city of David a Saviour, which is Christ the Lord. And this shall be a sign unto you; Ye shall find the babe wrapped in swaddling clothes, lying in a manger. And suddenly there was with the angel a multitude of the heavenly host praising God, and saying, Glory to God in the highest, and on earth peace, good will toward men."

Then the angel from the stable hurried to the shepherds. Other angels stepped from behind the panels and began the carol, "Hark! The Herald Angels Sing." After the song ended, the angels stepped behind the panels and the shepherds went to the stable as Phillip continued reading. When he finished, all the children gathered around the baby and began to sing "Silent Night." Their young voices raised in song could have passed for angels in Karl's book. Baby Henry slept through the whole thing.

Phillip began the song "We Thee Kings" and the wise men in the foil crowns and their fathers' robes came forth to lay gifts at the foot of the manger.

As the last song notes died away, Sophie took center stage. He could see the relief on her face. "Thank you all for coming. *Frehlicher Grischtdaag*, everyone. Merry Christmas! Please thank our wonderful scholars for their fine program."

She was immediately surrounded by people congratulating her on a wonderful program. Mrs. Kauffman wiped her eyes. "It was almost like being there with them. It was beautiful."

"The children deserve all the credit," Sophie said.

Clara led Jesse over to Karl. "She did *goot*."

He hugged his daughter. "Your idea was *wunderbar*. I'm proud of all your hard work."

Abby walked down to get her baby. The manger tipped over as she picked up Henry and the hay spilled. Jesse brayed and took off toward the food. Sophie got between the new mother and the charging burro. Karl hung on to the halter as the donkey dragged him across the frozen ground. Jesse stopped suddenly and Karl fell at Sophie's feet.

She pressed her hands over her mouth to stifle her laughter. He smiled up at her as his heart overflowed with love for this amazing, beautiful, brave woman.

Karl looked at the crowd, then at Sophie again. As much as he wanted to tell her how he felt, now wasn't the time. He got to his feet. "The program was *wunderbar*. I'll take you home when you're ready." He led Jesse away.

Rose made her way through the crowd to his side. "Harts Haven is never going to forget this Christmas Eve program. I can't wait to see what the new teacher does next year."

Karl frowned. "What new teacher? Is Sophie leaving after all?"

Rose patted his cheek. "Married women can't teach. I don't know who we'll get to replace her. I'm proud of you. You are exactly who she needs."

He wished he had Rose's confidence. "Do you think she'll have me after the way I acted?"

Rose cackled and walked off into the crowd.

It was full dark by the time the festivities wound down and families began leaving. Karl tied Jesse and the sheep on behind the sleigh, then lit the lanterns on the sides. The horse stood quietly, one hip cocked and a dusting of snow across his back. Karl stepped inside to tell Sophie they were ready.

Scanning the room, he saw her with Henry in her arms. She tenderly stroked the baby's cheek. As she did, her gaze met Karl's across the room.

In that moment, he knew exactly what he wanted. He wanted Sophie to have the life she was meant to live, and he wanted to be a part of it. He wanted to spend every Christmas with her for the rest of their lives no matter how long that was.

"Is it time to go home? I'm tired." Rachel, sitting at her desk, could barely keep her eyes open.

"Yes, it's time to go home." He picked her up and she draped herself over his shoulder. Sophie joined them a minute later. At the sleigh, Karl let Clara take the reins. Joanna got in beside her while he settled in back with Rachel across his lap and Sophie seated beside him. She drew the quilt over Rachel, and he gave her a grateful smile. A bright three-quarter moon slipped in and out of the clouds as they made their way home.

At his place, he got out of the sleigh with Rachel in his arms and turned to face Sophie. "I'd like you to come in and help me get the girls to bed. If you'd rather not, you can take the sleigh to the inn. I'll pick it up another day."

He held his breath as he waited for her reply.

Sophie couldn't mistake the pleading she saw in his eyes. "I should go back."

"Nonsense," Joanna said. "I'm putting the animals away. We're staying here tonight. Stop being such a coward. Give Karl a hand with his daughter. At least open the door for him. Clara, come help me." The two of them walked away toward the barn.

Karl waited without speaking. Sophie could hardly leave him standing in the cold. She hurried past him and opened the door. Inside, she went ahead of him to the bedroom the girls shared. She pulled down the quilts and he laid Rachel on her bed. Sophie unlaced the girl's shoes and pulled them off.

Karl removed Rachel's *kapp* and laid it on her bedside stand, then he pulled up the quilts and tenderly tucked her in. He placed a kiss on her head and headed for the door, where he waited. Sophie put down the shoes and followed him. He closed the door and turned to her. "Sophie, I'm sorry for the way I reacted when you confided in me. You deserved better."

Her heart started hammering so hard she thought he must hear it. She wanted to run out of the house but the look in his eyes made her stay. She gripped her hands together. "It was understandable."

"*Nee*, it wasn't. I never should have turned my back on you. I never will again. Can you forgive me?"

"There's nothing to forgive."

He smiled softly and her heart started to melt.

Stepping closer, he cupped her face in his hands. "You have endured so much. I made it worse by my actions. I know that. I'll spend the rest of my life trying to make up for it."

"You have lived through great tragedy and unbearable grief, Karl. I can't ask you to do that again."

"When Nora was taken from me, I lost my faith, but I have found it thanks to you. *Gott* brought you here to mend me. I believe that. I love you, Sophie. Will you marry me?"

She covered his hands with her own and knew she was breaking his heart as well as her own. "I can't do that to you."

"Do what? Love me? Love my daughters? Stand beside me during my trials and joys?"

"I will only bring you more sorrow." Why couldn't he understand that?

He sighed and pulled her into his arms. "I wish you could see how much I need you. You lift up my heart and soul. Your amazing spirit will teach my daughters how to grow into strong women. If you leave us, the sorrow you don't want to burden us with starts today. Not in a few months or years— it begins right now. *Gott* decides how many days we have on this earth. But He has left it up to us to choose what we do with those days. I want to spend my time loving you. What will you do with your days, Sophie?"

She buried her face against his neck. She didn't deserve this man. Nor did she understand why *Gott* placed him in her life, but she knew what she wanted. The warmth of his embrace allowed courage and faith to flood her heart.

"I love you, Karl. I choose to spend what time I'm given with you."

He held her away so he could look into her eyes. "Does this mean you'll marry me?"

"I will."

A slow smile spread across his face. "His mercy and goodness knows no bounds."

He leaned in to kiss her and Sophie smiled all the way down through her heart. No matter what came, he would face it with her, and she could endure anything with him at her side.

They stepped apart at the sound of the kitchen door opening. Clara came through the room. "We put the animals away. Joanna has gone to bed. Good night." She went into the bedroom she shared with Rachel and closed the door.

"That is my cue to leave." Sophie started for the door, but her heart was singing with joy.

Outside on the porch, Karl pulled her close and tucked her head beneath his chin. "Sophie, I know what we are facing, and it doesn't matter."

"Are you sure?"

"Do I have to write it on the blackboard for you to believe me?"

"*Ja*, a hundred times."

He chuckled. "I love you. Good night, teacher."

"Good night, darling." Her voice was a soft whisper. The glorious moonlight sparkled on the snow, turning the night into a beautiful Christmas card scene. Slowly, he lowered his lips to hers and kissed her and her heart soared with joy.

When she pulled away to catch her breath, she cupped his face with her hands. "When should we tell the children?"

"In the morning. Come over for breakfast."

On Christmas morning, Karl hurried to finish his chores before the girls got up. It was a special day. He was nervous about what their reaction would be. He knew Rachel would be happy, but he wasn't sure about Clara.

He opened the kitchen door and stopped to drink in the sight of Sophie at his stove, humming a Christmas carol as she turned slices of French toast on the griddle. His heart filled with joy he knew he didn't deserve. He might have turned his back on *Gott*, but the Lord had not turned his back on Karl Graber. To prove His love and mercy were boundless, He had given a doubter the most wonderful gift of all. A woman to love him, to complete his family and to make his house the home it should be.

"Close the door. You're letting all the cold air in."

He crossed the room and slipped his arms around her waist as he rested his cheek against the top of her head. "Is it cold out? I hadn't noticed. My heart is burning with love for you."

She turned in his arms and gave him a quick kiss. "Go take off your coat and sit at the table or your breakfast will be burning."

"I'm not the least bit hungry." He kissed her again.

"Stop that," she said, turning her face aside. "The children will be up any minute." She bit the corner of her lip. "They will be happy, won't they?"

"They will be overjoyed."

"But what if they are not?"

"Then we will give them time to get used to the idea and to love you as I do." He kissed her nose and went to take off his coat and hat.

Rachel came running into the kitchen. "Merry Christmas, *daed*. Sophie, what are you doing here?"

"Making a special Christmas breakfast as my gift to you. I hope you like French toast."

Rachel looked at her father. "Do I?"

"I reckon we will find out. It sure smells *goot*," he said.

Rachel climbed on her chair and stared at the gift wrapped in plain brown paper sitting on her plate. "Is this for me? May I open it?"

"Let's wait for your sister to join us," Karl said.

Rachel scrambled down. "I'll go see what's keeping her."

She dashed out of the room before Karl could remind her not to run in the house. He shared an amused glance with Sophie. "You will have your work cut out turning that child into a modest *maydel*. Do you want to change your mind?"

"Not a chance. I learned how to herd sheep, didn't I? How difficult can one six-year-old child be?"

Rachel returned a moment later pulling Clara by the hand. "Hurry up. It's Christmas morning."

Clara tried to look bored. "I know what day it is. Good morning, Sophie. Merry Christmas."

"Merry Christmas to you. Have a seat. Breakfast is ready." She carried over a plate heaped with golden slices of French toast and a small glass pitcher filled with syrup. Then she took her place at the foot of the table.

Rachel scrambled onto her chair again, her gaze pinned to the package on her plate. Karl bowed his head to say a silent grace and to thank God for the many blessings he had received. When he looked up, Rachel was still staring at her package. He took pity on her. "You may open your gifts now."

Instead of ripping off the paper as she had last year, Rachel carefully untied the bow, and removed the string, laying it aside. Then she unfolded the paper to reveal a packet of colored pencils and a tablet of paper.

"*Ack*, these are *wunderbar*. Thank you, *Daed*."

Karl looked at his oldest daughter. "Aren't you going to open your present?"

Like Rachel, Clara unwrapped hers carefully. Inside were two new bread pans and a new white *kapp*. Clara lifted the *kapp* gently and fingered the delicate pleats and stitching. "This is lovely. *Danki*, Sophie."

"How do you know I didn't sew it?" Karl's mock outrage caused all of them to start giggling. After that they were too busy devouring Sophie's delicious French toast to say anything.

When the girls were finished eating, Karl sat back in his chair and gazed at Sophie. The moment was at hand. He prayed his daughters would be as happy about the turn of events as he was. "I have one more Christmas gift for you."

"It's from both of us," Sophie said, smiling at him.

He cleared his throat. "You know that Rose Yoder is determined to find a new wife for me. I discovered the only solution to her nagging is to find a wife myself. With that in mind, I have asked Sophie to marry me."

Rachel began clapping. "Yes! Sophie is exactly who Granny Rose picked for you. And I helped her." Rachel got down from her chair, raced to Sophie's side and threw her arms around her.

Clara had been silent the whole time. Karl turned his gaze to her. "What do you think of the idea, Clara?"

A slow smile spread across Clara's face. "I reckon my toast can hold more butter."

Sophie reached across the table and took Clara's hand in hers. "*Danki*, you all are exactly the family I have always wanted."

Rachel smiled at her dad. "A *mamm* for Christmas is the perfect gift."

★ ★ ★

Rose, Grace, Bertha, Herbert and Susanna were gathered around the kitchen table at the inn enjoying coffee and Grace's famous cinnamon rolls two days after Christmas.

"That went well," Rose said smugly. "Rachel spilled the beans when I stopped in at the hardware store yesterday."

"It was almost a disaster," Susanna said. "When Sophie moved in here, I thought it was over."

Rose waved her hand. "Nonsense. A match made at Christmas was what I planned all along."

"Humph." Susanna rolled her eyes.

Grace stirred a spoon of sugar into her coffee. "Sophie is going to be all right, isn't she, Bertha?"

"God decides, and you know I can't share my patient's medical information. When Sophie is an old woman with her daughters and granddaughters gathered at her side, let it be remembered that I maintained her patient confidentiality."

"You are to be commended," Herbert said proudly, and then glanced around as the women chuckled. "What?"

Rose rubbed her hands together and looked around the table. "So, who is in need of my matchmaking skills next?"

★ ★ ★ ★ ★